BLOOD AND IRON RULES

A BIRDIE KELLEY MYSTERY, BOOK TWO

ROBERT L. JOSWICK

Black Rose Writing | Texas

ISBN: 978-1-68513-511-9
LIBRARY OF CONGRESS CONTROL NUMBER: 2024945682
PUBLISHED BY BLACK ROSE WRITING
www.blackrosewriting.com

Printed in the United States of America
Suggested Retail Price (SRP) $24.95

Blood and Iron Rules is printed in Chaparral Pro

*As a planet-friendly publisher, Black Rose Writing does its best to eliminate unnecessary waste to reduce paper usage and energy costs, while never compromising the reading experience. As a result, the final word count vs. page count may not meet common expectations.

A special thanks to: Kirsten Schuder of Apex Literary Management, for her coaching and encouragement. Steve Amos of Crossroads Writers (my writer's group leader), for his and the writer's group timely suggestions and editing help. Of course, my very deepest thanks go to my wife Janie and our daughter, Katie who jointly inspired my valiant Birdie Kelley.

BLOOD AND IRON RULES

CHAPTER ONE

Early December 1957

The Rolls Royce engine hummed, following sweeping curves, turning with ease along the Pacific Coast Highway. Hamilton Jaminson leaned back into the leather seat of his two-toned gray Phantom, leaving behind fields of wildflowers and blooming oleanders. Not a sightseeing trip, but he yielded, allowing himself to enjoy the scenic road. His long-expected mission promised a prize more significant than the fortune he'd amassed.

Since pulling from the busy Beverly Hilton Hotel, a pair of cars had trailed. Hamilton brushed away the idea of being followed. The excursion, known only by his trustworthy security team, remained confidential. He'd curb his imagination, blamed on nerves and anticipation of closing the arrangement made while visiting Argentina.

San Clemente's white sand and tall palms became a blur. He'd scarcely noticed Dana Point's rocky cliffs sloping to pristine beaches and calm blue water, imagining his rendezvous. A long-anticipated dream bridging today's medicine to the future waited.

Steel mills and coal placed him among the world's elite. Hamilton gave thanks for the grit and ambition his father carried to America as a youthful Scottish miner. Within decades, the Jaminson family dominated worldwide coal and steel production. His steel shaped the skeletons of New York's skyscrapers and stood as tributes to his accomplishments. War and the following booming expansion brought unprecedented growth to a wounded world. With no slowdown in sight, the rebuilding needed steel. With more to accomplish, he intended to keep living and enjoying beyond a conventional lifetime.

Sweet honeysuckle scent swirled past, carried by the morning's cool, balmy coastal breeze. On his return to Hollywood, he'd concede to a slight detour and venture into the wilderness of Cleveland National Forest and its rolling hills, motoring the fabled Ortega Highway.

Hamilton considered a Harley-Davidson motorcycle to snake through the coasts scenic twisting and turning canyon roads. The diversion, an adolescent fantasy, allowed time to ponder his new, renewed future. He'd left New York without warning, relishing long-sought independence. Wealth bore responsibility, bringing demands, stripping him of joys.

The open road allowed pleasure, not measured by a man's financial means, granting expansive views of the glorious Pacific to all who allowed time to seize the moment. This memory, he wanted to be embedded into his deep consciousness when the time came for his rebirth.

Hamilton reached overhead, adjusting his rearview mirror, noticing two cars in the jammed Southern California traffic. They were no longer imagined, sharing fresh ocean air, crowded together along the popular beach highway. The black Ford and blue Chevy remained at a distance since entering the coastal road.

Pangs of guilt pestered. Holiday travel plans with his ex-wife, Lenora, had been delayed and likely deferred. Their arrangement allowed distant closeness with pleasant companionship as needed—more so than during the fifteen-year marriage.

This junket ventured light years beyond conventional. Lenora wouldn't understand—nor would anyone. He had kept her in the dark, along with his bankers and lawyers. This secret remained his, with few exceptions. No one outside Shelley and Falk would appreciate the unconventional arrangement. The concept appeared futuristic, resembling a Hollywood low-budget sci-fi film.

Not that he cared.

The acquisition of a lifetime waited for his signature. Close to a million dollars, bundled hundred-dollar bills packed in suitcases, rode in the rear next to the spare tire. Money well spent, an investment in the future. In a few hours, Hamilton would change his fate. Cash came from a private reserve. The deal would remain invisible, maintained by a Swiss corporation endowing the ongoing operation, independent of him or his estate.

Later, an overnight stay at the Hotel Del Coronado, and dining in its famed Crown Room, would celebrate his secretive victory, beating Father Time.

South of San Diego, a bullet-riddled, black-and-white highway sign marked his destination, signaling his exit to Chula Vista, a quiet town with San Diego to its north and a short seven miles to Mexico.

Expansion and crowding came with the war's end. Bulldozers cleared the remnants of dead orange and lemon trees, giving way to orange tile-roofed home sites in planned golf communities and industrial development.

Watching road signs, passing cookie-cutter, wood-frame homes, Hamilton worried he had taken a wrong turn. Chula Vista, meaning beautiful views, was not what he'd expected.

Pulling to the side of a freshly oiled, tar and rock chip rural road, Hamilton checked the hand-drawn map, spotting Otay Road leading to his future property and facility.

The rambling industrial park's brick and cinder block structures formed a sea of dull gray, single-story warehouses. Alongside tall cranes, resembling long-necked, feeding dinosaurs, hoisted massive concrete panels. According to the scribbled map, his investment sat near the bay, viewing the nearby Pacific. The scene lacked what he envisioned—vistas of lanky, swaying palms dividing vast orchards of sweet-smelling orange and lemon trees. Under the eccentric circumstances, it didn't matter—nor did near-ideal weather twelve months a year.

Zero hour approached.

His heavy Rolls bumped over twin sets of railroad tracks and slowed. Hamilton made an abrupt left near the entrance of a bulk concrete plant. As he made the turn, a cement hauler pulled from between walls guarding tall stacks of gravel, forcing Hamilton to skid to a stop. Dust billowed, surrounding the car in a thick white haze.

Before Hamilton grabbed the gearshift, intending to jam it into reverse, racing from the near-collision, two cars suspected of following him skidded to a stop, tapping his rear bumper. A heavyset man in baggy overhauls, his face distorted by women's silk stockings, stepped from behind a wide row of oleanders aiming a handgun. Hamilton raised his arms, resting them on the steering wheel. As he did, another masked member of the ambush team appeared. Unarmed, the new arrival opened the passenger door and slid next to him.

"You're here with the cash? Give it to me."

"I don't know you," Hamilton answered.

"Do you have the money?"

A gun came through the open window, pressing against Hamilton's temple.

"Last chance, Mr. Jaminson."

Hamilton nodded. "I have it."

"That's better," the passenger said.

"In the trunk. Take it." Jaminson said.

The movement came without warning. Pain pierced his arm, stinging as if they had shot him. If a bullet, he didn't know where it had lodged. No sudden bleeding, only a sharp tingle in the back of his arm. So far, he remained alive.

Hamilton Jaminson, dazed and overcome with nausea, slumped against his door. An empty hypodermic needle dangled from the upper sleeve of his silk jacket. He realized he was about to lose the battle to stay conscious. Numb heaviness overtook his legs and arms, making them useless. He forced his heavy eyes open, seeing hazy shades of light. The warm breath of a faint voice spoke in his ear.

"Bye, bye hound dog complements of Elvis."

The calm tone didn't belong to the person who'd entered his car. The voice faded as someone grabbed and yanked his jacket's lapel, dragging him from the car, dropping him to a gravel and dust-covered road.

Hamilton slurred the familiar words, "Bye, bye hound dog," as he slipped into blackness, then soundless slumber.

CHAPTER TWO

January 4, 1958

On the day Sputnik died, Birdie Kelly stepped over and around packing boxes scattered about an apartment the realtor generously described as a fashionable Manhattan Midtown. The city's Hudson rail yards separated her from gritty Hell's Kitchen, home to poor, immigrant working-class Irish. She thanked and blamed Gaelic roots for her brazen tenacity. Passionate as Joyce's mundane Leopold Bloom for Dublin, she'd obsessed with New York City as her aphrodisiac.

Her infatuation went unrewarded in the town that delivered overnight celebrity and fortune. An anemic bank account would not cover the upcoming rent. Lingering at a young forty, she wasn't bad looking, with a passable figure in the right light. Summer—she'd turn heads strolling Coney Island's boardwalk, providing onlookers stood at a distance. Birdie had dodged severe injury while serving as a Pinkerton and starved on her own as an independent private investigator.

From habit, she rubbed her damaged hip as she bent to unplug a table lamp. The painful wound worsened on chilly, damp winter days. A crooked scar along her back troubled some lovers.

She recalled her charred hair. The accident would never leave her. Hot, scorching lighting burned her scalp and face. Dazed, she had laid trapped under massive stage rigging. Massaging her shoulder, blood oozed between her fingers. Craving air, she twisted, straining to expand her chest and draw in enough to avoid passing out and eventual death. Her life depended on remaining conscious. With another push, aided by an adrenaline rush, she moved the metal framework, letting her shift a few inches, allowing her lungs to take in oxygen. Her next thought—would she make the curtain call or lose her part? Seconds later, the scalding lights and steel lifted away, leaving the bearded face of a transit cop staring down at her.

Birdie finished unwrapping newspapers from the thrift store lamp. She couldn't escape the moment her fledgling acting career died and wondered if she imagined visions of the transits officer would haunt her to her grave. From the day of her rehearsal injuries, there were occasional suspicions in her mind it hadn't been an accident.

Across a murky Hudson River, on a day too cold to snow, her picture window overlooked dreary brick smokestacks of a slumping Hoboken. Todd Ship Yards, once the pride of American shipbuilding, laid decaying before her eyes. On the waterfront, less than three hundred feet below, the new heliport, catering to the rich and famous, reminded her of how life might have turned out.

Her first case as a private eye hit big, landing a well-heeled Broadway producer with a murdered daughter. She'd found the murderer, a deranged city transit officer. Before the arrest, the murderer vanished along with his home and evidence. To make matters worse, her client became a victim of the same killer. The promised fee and bonus were forever lost in her dead client's probate. The estate's crafty lawyers, led by Breen's former wife, voided the verbal contract, leaving her broke.

A change would do her good. Around the room of half-filled boxes, stuffed with crumpled newspaper-protected knickknacks which needed unpacking. Single with no known relatives, she'd ditched her boyfriend, Jark, and his Park Avenue home.

Aside from work, her world turned into a protective cocoon shared with no one, shutting off hope of love and family. The city became a constant reminder of her disastrous life. She required a change of attitude and latitude, somewhere to forget and restart.

Birdie's hands shook, unwrapping a towel covering a chipped ceramic angel. A fitting image for her recent failure. Her mind ventured to Mount Hebron Cemetery.

Had she remained with her client, Sid Breen, his sizeable billing fees and promised bonus would have paid her outstanding medical bills. Instead, Birdie had permitted herself to be outflanked, allowing the killer to make his way to the gravesite. She'd left her mourning client defenseless and dead. In the brief span of one day, she neglected to prevent two needless deaths.

Uncontrolled impulses she blamed on her Irish roots manipulated her emotions into reacting without consideration, triggering her lowest times. Some compulsively ate and drank, others ran, circling Central Park like carousel ponies. She caused others pain and death. Birdie desired to stuff those habits into cardboard cartons to store away and never unpack. Like most over-compulsive people, she'd hidden her real self, showing the world the character they expected.

Steady rumbling approached her building and faded. It came again, this time louder, growing more deafening, vibrating the picture window she sat near. Annoyed, Birdie pushed the packing box aside, stepping closer to the fogged glass. She looked to the morning sky, half expecting, according to rumors, to see the feared Russian Sputnik plummet into the Hudson River. The doomed satellite threatened America, and she couldn't recall when it wasn't a front-page story.

A burning stench stopped Birdie. Had the Russian spacecraft smashed into the roof, sending red-hot, roaring flames through the floors above? New York papers speculated the city to be a target for a surprise Communist attack. Joe McCarthy's endless rantings promised escalation of the Cold War and Red Commies invading America.

Black smoke rose, in a spiral, from the toaster near the kitchen sink, ruining breakfast and the last slices of marble rye. The day's frigid air prevented opening windows, permitting the harsh, burned smell to linger, filling the cramped apartment. The odor would continue to remind her of how foolish she'd been—fearing an unlikely attack from a country she scarcely knew.

Birdie tossed the charred bread and toaster into the trash. Her next residence, she promised, would be close to a white sandy beach with drinking and eating establishments, preferring patrons in sandals, not wingtips.

The clear sky was unusual for Manhattan in early January. Patches of crusty Christmas snow remained in the shadows. Freezing water dripped from a roof gutter, shaping long, thin spikes threatening to spear a passerby. Birdie's annoyance faded as soon as the pestering sound vanished—likely one of many sightseeing helicopters plaguing the city, disturbing her rest, morning, and night.

Wiping a gauzy layer of frost from the glass, Birdie shuttered, feeling a damp, icy chill. Spots of bright sunshine hinted the day would allow her to enjoy what she most loved—a quiet walk in Central Park. Maybe a well-deserved treat—a Broadway play, *The Music Man,* had opened at the Majestic—if she got lucky finding cut-rate tickets. A break from the stuffy two-room apartment was long overdue. The escape excused her to ignore three weeks of accumulated, unopened mail stacked on the kitchen counter.

Birdie squeezed between a wicker hamper and room divider, retreating to her bedroom looking forward to strolling and window-shopping Manhattan's over-priced shops and boutiques. She marveled at the mixed population walking the streets, inches apart— rich, poor; all nationalities crossed paths. She heard it often—should anyone stay long enough in Penn Station, America's crossroads, they'd pass someone they knew.

As she slipped on a woolen NYU sweatshirt, the beating noise returned, noisier this time, growing larger, cruising head-on at her apartment, not appearing too slow. The sound disrupted the quiet morning once again. It approached less than a hundred feet away. The noise elevated, vibrating her thin walls. With a sudden turn, the invader pulled up, rearing back, like a halting stallion, rocked, and descended in an abrupt dive to the heliport's large asphalt tarmac jutting directly below her into the choppy Hudson River.

A plume of light snow dusted up around the slowly rotating blades as the black and silver intruder wound to a stop. An attendant sporting an orange vest raced from a shed, placing chocks under a pair of wheels. A figure in a tan raincoat ducked from the copter's door and walked, showing a slight limp, entering the terminal.

Birdie's interest died out after losing sight of what she presumed was the pilot. She guessed the VIP passenger preferred to stay inside the copter, snug and cozy—waiting on a late-arriving limousine. Although Saturday, Manhattan's ongoing construction tied up traffic on the island. She'd kept her dead father's binoculars near the window, hoping to spot celebrities. On New Year's Day, she'd watched Ed Sullivan scratch his groin as he departed to wherever wealthy personalities go in private helicopters.

With the excitement over, she returned to selecting her day's wardrobe. She glanced in the mirror, pulling on a beret, flashing the practiced stage smile of Audrey Hepburn. Next to her tarnished and cracked reflection hung a souvenir of her crashed existence. The black-framed photograph captured happier days, her class photo, graduating, becoming a Pinkerton detective, and earning a badge and handgun. The group picture would go into a box—forgotten. Before that happened, Birdie required a challenge, unlike the trinkets life had tossed at her. She wanted more from her journey—an exclamation mark, not a question mark.

After a final twist of her scarf, she headed to the door considering her planned Roman holiday, not as a traveling princess but as one hoping to score show tickets. Over time, she'd worn many hats. Fame and glory were not among them—the two she cherished. That dream, like others, didn't pan out. Her obituary would read, a jack of all trades, master of none. Birdie wanted challenging cases—not a spurned wife tracking a roving spouse. Well-paying clients favored male PIs, believing women frail, and much less lame ones.

After a final makeup check, Birdie was about to step out of her apartment. Her telephone rang. That—a rarity.

Leaving the door wide open, she wove through a path of boxes and newspapers, hoping bill collectors didn't work Saturdays.

"You're getting company," the voice said from the phone.

CHAPTER THREE

"Can't talk," Birdie shouted over the scratchy phone line. "I'll make a payment next week."

"I won't take no," the caller said. "I need your help."

"Write me a letter."

"I sent two telegrams."

Birdie glanced at the collection letters scattered across the kitchen counter. Two Western Union envelopes rested against a sugar bowl. In a lifetime, she had not received a single, cheerful telegram. The pale yellow envelopes carried bad news, as did long-distance phone calls.

"Haven't read them. I've been busy."

"So? Here I am."

"You wasted time coming," Birdie said.

"We need to talk. I'm in a rush."

"Where are you?"

"At the heliport, across the street."

Tearing open the telegrams marked urgent, Birdie cradled the phone between her shoulder and ear, reading both. She didn't recognize the sender's name and, despite not caring for the caller's boldness, paused and reread the messages.

She dropped the telegrams and straightened the phone to her ear. "Why didn't you say this involved a case?"

The phone line hummed, clicked, and became silent.

Birdie stared from her window, realizing she'd let a client getaway.

The puzzling silver helicopter remained unmoving—no dull whooping of blades beating the air. Its long rotors sagged as the attendant anchored the copter to the tarmac. The terminal's phone booth's door stood folded open and vacant.

She'd retreated but not surrendered and endured a long way from giving up her hard-earned PI license. The slip-up came without thinking. Late karma of the holiday season attempted to bring work. Unlike Kris Kringle, her surprise caller arrived by helicopter, bearing the gift of a well-paying client and, in irony, caught undeserved insults.

"Who are you?" Birdie shouted toward the helipad.

The unlocked apartment door banged open. "I'm Lenora Jaminson."

A lady stood with one hand leaning against the doorjamb. Long white braids laid against an angular, tanned face. The surprise visitor dipped under sagging garland and mistletoe, entering.

Birdie eyed the woman she guessed looked twenty years younger than her age. Makeup hid flaws, but the lady's striking features were not the result of hours spent with a cosmetic artist or surgeon. She remained fit and tight, most likely through exercise and healthy living. Anyone wearing form-fitting riding pants earned Birdie's admiration and a touch of envy.

"May I help?" Birdie asked.

Lenora Jaminson pushed away empty boxes with the toe of her boot, not bothering to give a polite knock, and limped across the small room. In the kitchen, she pointed to a beat-up, compact Sears refrigerator.

"Got a beer?"

"Beer and flying don't mix," Birdie said.

"This foot's killing me. It'll help."

"I looked at the telegrams," Birdie said, pulling a chair close to her guest and popping open a tall, cold Schlitz.

"You're moving," Lenora said, pressing the frosty bottle against her foot and then lifting her beer. "Bottoms up."

Birdie watched Lenora glance around the kitchen and den. Stacks of boxes and newspapers covered the living area. For Birdie, this was not a time to tell the whole truth. She couldn't admit to taking three months to move into a new apartment to a promising client—a sure sign of inefficiency, and not a desirable trait for a professional investigator. Well-heeled clients expected to deal with someone well-balanced, although they were far from that. She'd keep her story simple, offering no details, as liars tended to.

"I'm remodeling, giving the place a new look."

"Those boxes must have memories," Lenora said.

Birdie joined her guest, opening the second and last cold beer. She needed it and hoped to find something stronger during her planned stroll.

She knew nothing of the stylish-looking lady seated in her kitchen. The manner she arrived and the white gold Cartier bracelet and watch shouted this chick had access to big money.

Far too many recent clients had been gratis—helping so-called bar friends build divorce cases against cheating spouses did little to pay her mounting bills.

Her guest nodded and smiled, not asking added questions. After another guzzle, Lenora Jaminson slumped back, appearing relaxed for the first time. She stretched both palms on the table, taking in a deep breath. What did she expect? Should Birdie have taken her offered hands as if they'd been long-time friends greeting one another at a country club cocktail hour? Birdie remained patient, waiting for her surprise visitor to reach the point. Something told her a job offer was near. The first impression Birdie had told her—people with big money had bigger problems.

"I haven't heard from my former husband, Hamilton Jaminson, since Thanksgiving."

"That Jaminson!" Birdie said.

The name jolted Birdie. The prominent Jaminson mansion on Fifth th. Avenue was one of Manhattan's unique estates. The few art dealers she occasionally worked for claimed its art collection rivaled the city's finest museums.

Birdie remained constrained, forcing herself to remain professional, not allowing herself to become impressed by affluence, something New York City overflowed with. She'd stay calm, sticking to facts like Dragnet's methodical Joe Friday.

Birdie waved her beer bottle. "You're no longer married to him."

A smile crept onto Lenora's face. "Hamilton and I divorced fifteen years ago. We remain good friends and traveling partners, despite our preferences for younger companions."

"You came in a helicopter, so I could help you find him?"

"I flew Hamilton's Bell Ranger. It's the only way to find parking in Manhattan, wouldn't you say," Lenora answered. "Do you mind the sudden intrusion? Besides, it's the fastest way to the airport."

It had surfaced again, a tinge of briskness. Birdie let it pass.

Most likely, her surprise guest existed in a circle of the rich and haughty, accustomed to their prominent names opening doors. Lenora had qualities Birdie could learn to enjoy.

"What makes you think he's missing?"

"He never fails to spend the holidays with me."

"You said he likes younger women and...."

"We always travel to a tropical and warm place."

"Did you make plans?"

"He shows up and surprises me."

"Did you hint where you'd like to go?"

"He has a secluded place on Catalina Island."

"Where?"

"Near LA."

"Maybe he's there?"

Lenora shook her head. "Neighbors didn't hear him arrive. He's hard to miss."

"The police?"

"Yes, and I've hired private detectives." She took another long swallow. "Nothing has shown up. I'm worried."

"You checked the Manhattan home?"

"First place."

Birdie pushed herself to calm down with a deep breath and exhaled. Combat breathing allowed relaxation and buying time. The solution appeared clear-cut, confident the flamboyant coal and steel baron found a new toy and wanted privacy. Birdie preferred not to be the one to break the news, nor did she need to. Lenora knew how her ex-husband lived. Denial would give way to accepting—she'd lost out to someone younger—possibly for good.

The silence lasted until Lenora placed her empty bottle on the wooden table.

"Can you help?"

"Is there proof Hamilton is in trouble?"

"Just my feelings," Lenora said.

Birdie left the kitchen and walked to the window. She looked up and down rows of bleak red brick apartments. Tired women leaned from windows hanging tattered clothes and linens on lines strung between buildings. She came to think of the billowing white bedding as guardian angels and hoped for guidance. She prepared to turn down a wealthy client by telling Lenora Jaminson the truth.

"I'd trust the police and your detectives," Birdie answered, continuing to watch neighbors hang laundry.

"I do. My guys are looking. I must do something or go crazy waiting. It wouldn't hurt if we visited LA to look around?"

"That the last place he was seen?" Birdie asked.

"The concierge of the Beverly Hills Hotel saw him leave for a drive."

"Nothing else?"

"I'm not giving up."

"There a ransom demand?"

"No."

"No?" Birdie repeated.

"They could be waiting," Lenora said.

"It's been over a month. There's a chance he wanted time alone traveling," Birdie said. "Likely a—."

Before Birdie finished, Lenora held up her hand, stopping her.

"You don't know me. I didn't come from wealth. You're looking at a West Virginia coal miner's daughter. I'm tough."

Birdie tried to interrupt, but her guest continued.

"I know reality. You think Hamilton Jaminson brushed me off, and he could have," Lenora paused, "I don't believe so."

"Why's that?"

"I understand his little tarts. It's not unusual," Lenora added. "I've accepted that part of him."

"Men are men, I guess, even the wealthy," Birdie said.

There was more than met the eye. Lenora's brusqueness attempted to hide a deeper worry. A measured second look checked Birdie's judgment. She no longer saw Lenora as the social butterfly she'd pegged her as. Lenora's desperate strength of conviction to find her former husband shifted her opinion.

"You with me?"

"How did you find me?"

"It wasn't easy, but—."

"I don't mean here. Why me?"

"Sid Breen's son, Jark. The family's a friend."

"You know how Sid died?"

"Enough to be aware to know you found the killer, but crazy things happened, and he vanished."

"That all?" Birdie asked.

"You're brash and unconventional."

"… and you don't need me," Birdie said.

Lenora stood and limped to the window. "I almost landed in the river. Let's say five hundred a day plus ten grand when we find him."

"I'm sure he's safe. I can't take your money."

In her years as a Pinkerton, knowing the lack of a ransom could indicate several possibilities. Revenge killings topped the list, and this was not the case suiting her. In her experience dealing with the super-wealthy, many often went AWOL for months. Money and means gave freedoms and not always responsibility.

At the door, Lenora stopped and turned. "Judas Priest, I need you. That copter will take us to the airport." Lenora pointed towards it. "What's it gonna take?"

Birdie stared across the tiny apartment and the half-filled boxes. She craved change. No playing safe. She wanted her life back as a gamer, not a spectator. The past year she laid low. What did it get her? She lived in a high-rise tenement, hanging laundry on a rope above a rodent-infested alley. To run with the big dogs meant getting off the porch.

An opportunity dropped from the blue, requiring a decision for honesty to herself and the troubled lady standing in her home.

To hide in regret over past failures served no one. What would be her next step? Runoff, retreat deep into the Application Mountains, living in a log cabin at the end of a rutted path. This case could become her unsought specialty, preferred above pursuing murderers.

Did turning down Lenora represent indecision? Had she woven such a tight cocoon, she'd bound herself with fear? There had been no doubt she'd relish a break from frigid New York to enjoy the warm California sun. The lady in her living room offered that. Lenora was vulnerable. Something Birdie couldn't use to her benefit.

Lenora flashed a smile. "It's written all over your face—say it."

Birdie hesitated a moment. "To be honest, I think he dumped you. You're wasting time."

"... and you don't want to take advantage of a scorned woman."

"My experience tells me that."

"At last, we got it on the table," Lenora said. "If that's the case, I can handle it. I trust Hamilton. You can go with a clear conscious. I'm not giving up."

Birdie watched Lenora's eyes, seeing her determination grow as she spoke. As a woman, she understood Lenora's unspoken love for her former husband. As a PI, she sensed she was about to walk into something much more significant than hunting a missing person.

Well-mannered rich were good at keeping dirty secrets.

What did her new client keep from her?

CHAPTER FOUR

Birdie sat next to her new client, watching the ground drop away as the Bell Ranger lifted, hovering over a choppy Hudson River. She adjusted her headphones and squeezed the ear pads snug, dampening the thunderous beating surrounding them.

Lenora gave a smile, a quick thumbs-up, and flipped an overhead toggle. "We can hear each other now."

Birdie watched her home drift away. The wilted Christmas wreath looked less pathetic, hanging in her window as they escaped the city. An hour ago, she lamented the dullness entering her life. Five minutes ago, she'd tossed her suitcase in the back seat of a helicopter owned by the world's wealthiest coal and steel producer and piloted by a woman she met thirty minutes ago.

Leaving New York had been simpler than expected. A short note including a rent check slipped under the manager's door, thanks to Lenora's advance. Regrets, she had a few, but not enough to keep her from picking up an easy paycheck and enjoying the warm West Coast sunshine. The possibility of seeing Clark Gable, The King of Hollywood, sent a girlish shudder up her spine.

Over the Hudson River, the helicopter's blades beat furiously, buffering murky water into a foam, throwing mist against the cockpit's glass. Birdie braced, gripping an overhead handle. The other hand squeezed the underside of her leather seat. The copter tilted forward with a jerk and gained speed, climbing into a cloudless Manhattan sky.

Jolts, turns, and shakes gave the sensation of a New Year's hangover. Birdie convinced herself the experience would be her last.

Lenora clicked on her mike as she flew north, following the river. "At least it's Saturday."

"Meaning what?" Birdie asked.

"Light ferry traffic gives us more open water should we go down," Lenora answered.

Birdie grinned. It had been the first time her client joked.

She second-guessed her decision. With no experience in Los Angeles, she'd work cold, void of contacts inside the police. Her new client refused to accept no. Rejection existed as a temporary condition. It had been easy to judge Lenora Jaminson as a gambler with political clout, and money, knowing only one way—her way, presented problems.

Birdie vowed to safeguard Lenora, regardless of the situation. There had been no point remaining home, not enjoying the warmth of Southern California. The adventure could persuade her to abandon the city she loved and learn to exist with a year-round tan, sporting beach sandals full time.

"Where to?" Birdie asked, taking a last look at Hell's Kitchen. Her apartment building, by this time, blended into the maze of tenements lining waterfront docks.

"Teterboro. Hamilton keeps a plane there. About ten minutes, if I don't get lost," Lenora said over the whine of the throbbing 260-horsepower engine.

Time passed fast without conversation. The flight carried them to New Jersey and north, crossing the Hackensack River. A short while later, the copter brought them over snow-covered, abandoned homes and began to descend.

The copter lowered and hovered. Lenora aimed at a large H centered inside a yellow-painted circle. The flying egg-beater dropped from the New Jersey sky much too fast for Birdie's taste. Clusters of leafless trees bent and twisted as the Bell Ranger touched with a bounce, setting down near the edge of the concrete helipad.

For the first time, Birdie felt confident enough to loosen her death grip. The arrival couldn't come soon enough. A red and white hanger's wide double doors rolled open. Inside, gray-uniformed attendant's added fuel to a silver twin-engine plane, while another balanced on a ladder wiping the windshield.

The copter's door slid open, letting in a frigid blast of air and icy rain. A gloved hand reached inside, assisting Lenora to a wooden ramp.

Stepping from the copter on her own, Birdie pulled the collar of her down coat snug to her face. Jersey's icy drizzle and Lenora's flying had aggravated her flight queasiness. She fought off heaving, knowing it wouldn't install confidence.

Inside a Quonset hut office, Birdie found Lenora settled on a leather couch, removing a long brown riding boot and white sock. Her client appeared unconcerned, unwrapping layers of cloth, exposing a wooden foot attached to her ankle. With a quick twist, she removed her foot from a notched metal and wood socket. At a nearby desk, a gum-chomping secretary continued typing, not fazed by the sight of a footless Lenora Jaminson.

Birdie held her questions, knowing the look on her face asked plenty.

Lenora eyed her. "So, ask me what we're doing," she said, massaging the stump at the end of her ankle.

"Hamilton's vanished before," Birdie stated.

"A few times," Lenora answered, not looking away from her exposed leg.

"Where did he go?"

"He always showed up on his own...."

"But not this time," Birdie finished.

Lenora stretched her footless leg across stacks of newspapers and magazines covering the coffee table. "We'll start with the hotel."

"In Beverly Hills?" Birdie asked.

"Their presidential suite."

"Not exactly low-key."

"Hamilton liked the security."

"There a reason?"

"He didn't trust LA people. He always said that."

"He say why?"

Birdie suspected Lenora withheld information. Most clients, in the beginning, followed the pattern until trust developed.

"Thought they drove too fast."

Seconds later, Lenora pushed her head back on a scuffed and stained leather sofa, stuffed a pillow under her foot, yawned, and dropped off asleep.

Her client's nap came as a welcome break, giving Birdie time to gather her thoughts. There had been no slowdown from the time the persuasive woman strolled into her home. Control of a case belonged in Birdie's hands. She operated alone and would not permit a client's interference. Keeping the paying customer informed ordinarily worked. She'd allow a small amount of involvement, but at a distance.

Beginning at the last known location was the logical step. It had been too much to hope the suite remained untouched. Birdie expected the hotel staff and the local PI Lenora hired had examined and cleaned it, spoiling clues. She was not Sherlock Holmes, but she'd developed a knack for seeing the unseen.

"Want to know the story?" Lenora nodded toward her leg, peeking at Birdie from half-shut eyes.

"If you feel like it," Birdie said.

"My horse threw me, and my foot stuck in the stirrup. Next, the horse ran off, and my foot stayed with the horse. The good news, I fell away safe except for my foot."

"Still ride or like to dress like one?" Birdie wanted to pull the words back. Before she rushed an apology, Lenora chuckled.

"Took me a while to ride a showjumper, and I did it on that same horse. I got thrown not because of the horse, but because I was not a good enough rider for the horse." Lenora smiled.

"Never blame someone for our failures," Birdie said as she stood.

"A long as you don't have too many while working for me," Lenora added.

Birdie had misjudged her daring client, forming the wrong image, and becoming jealous. She hadn't been the woman papers and magazines portrayed. Lenora lived boldly, flying a helicopter. Birdie crossed her fingers, hoping Lenora didn't fly planes.

The two had something in common—the grit to recover and move on.

"One more thing," Lenora said while they were alone. "We've kept Hamilton's situation quiet. It would cause problems in the stock market."

Regardless of Birdie's sympathies toward Lenora, her coal and steel tycoon former husband had homes scattered throughout the world. The search they embarked on was likened to hunting a needle in Jaminson's coal mines. Birdie intended to give her fullest effort. Every man she'd known had the same fires burning at one point, wealthy or poor. They were boys at heart.

Birdie guessed Hamilton stabilized Lenora's life, and that pointed to a potential snag. Her client may not accept reality. Hamilton perhaps wanted to get away, and his disappearance—his way of letting Lenora go.

The mission Lenora planned had been her counter to keep the fires burning. Being alone can bring about withdrawal and hiding from reality. Most learned to—just as she had of Jark.

The sleek Bell Ranger, pushed by men in long, furry Eskimo coats, rolled by, entering the DC 3's hangar. She didn't have long to wonder about the pilots. They materialized before her eyes. Once inside, the men pulled off their thick coats. A pair of wings adorned identical white starched shirts. Birdie guessed Marines, reminding her of a former client, Jark. They walked in cadence, with straight, rigid backs. Both sported matching flat tops, and she half expected a snappy salute.

Their presence reassured her they'd arrive safe in California.

Entering the hangar, Birdie noticed a yellow and black Ford cruising an access road toward the airport's only gate. The car slowed and turned through the unguarded entrance of a tall chain-link fence. As it passed a departing Texaco fuel truck, Birdie noticed the vehicle's faded Western Union emblem. It turned on a narrow, unpaved road, speeding toward them. As the Ford closed in, Birdie didn't like the looks of the vehicle or its occupants.

CHAPTER FIVE

Hamilton Jaminson opened his eyes, disbelieving. Could he blame cheap tequila on the horrid dream, or was it brought on by lunch in a Mexican border town? Bright glaring light, perhaps sunlight, he couldn't be sure, surrounded him. Coarse rope and gray tape, wrapping him to a metal chair, prevented shielding teary eyes. Perfect 20-20 vision refused to focus, only permitting a blurred view of cluttered tables and sofas. No clues about the location. What did he expect, sandy beaches? Tapping his fingers against the chair's arms, reassured. He kept the ability to move.

How long had he been unconscious? Pockets hung pulled inside out, a gold watch and diamond ring remained. Jaminson leaned forward, pressing against the body-hugging tape and rope. No visible injuries, except pride, suffered for allowing himself to drive into an ambush on what stood to be his greatest triumph.

A roll of cash and a Diners Club card rested next to a calf leather billfold at his argyle-socked feet. No doubt, the captors had found the suitcases of money during the well-planned and executed attack. It was clear they sought more than cash. If not, his body would lie in a ditch, dead.

If he expected a rescue, his shoes needed to be located.

Born a stubborn Irishman, Hamilton rejected close personal protection. In its place, he relied on new technology.

Years ago, he disregarded his security chief's advice and announced to the world that his company or family would pay no ransom. A trust controlled all assets, preventing extortion payments. Unknown to anyone, an offshore Barbados account allowed Hamilton sole access, forcing kidnappers to negotiate with their captives.

Accompanying it came an aggressive recovery scheme, exposing Hamilton to risk. Seeking a secure hiding place out of the line of fire during rescue became crucial. Nothing in the barren room promised to shield him from the expected onslaught of gunfire and explosions.

No clues in the near-empty room hinted at the date. White clouds floating in a blue sky, unobstructed by rooftops, gave no hint of a location. Occasional blasts of car horns and sightings of gray, orange-beaked seagulls broke his monotony. For a good part of the day, a bad-mannered, sporadic jackhammer interrupted chemical-induced sleep. Musty, damp air told the location had been unused for an extended time.

An image of his ancestral homeland flashed in his drug-dulled mind. Ulster, a land of rolling lush green hills, lakes and rivers, defended by towering stone castles, became a living portrait.

His shoes—where were his shoes?

Before lapsing out, a hand shook his shoulder. A pair of bifocal glasses fit inside a black frame, and the sparkle of silver pushed close. A wiry-framed man smiled, showing off a silver front tooth, shoved a paper cup at him.

Hamilton kept his senses, recognizing it as a ploy to develop a link between them.

Trust became a rare commodity, and he wouldn't buy the gesture. How many years had it been since a bogus nun entered his Manhattan estate, intending to kill him? He'd lived a low-profile life, a near recluse. Few knew his plans and schedule. How in blazes did this person in front of him enter his life?

"Drink this," the man said. "It will help."

Hamilton's mouth remained dry, refusing, shaking his head.

"Been a while. Take a drink," the voice said.

Again, he shook his head.

"Suit yourself. Last chance."

This time Hamilton took it.

The man rested the paper cup against Hamilton's lip. "Go slow."

His first reaction to spit out the warm, fizzing liquid kicked in. Luckily, his reflexes, slowed by drugs, lagged.

The sip tasted like Alka-Seltzer entering his parched mouth.

He had lived through capture—the most dangerous time. For now, he'd stay composed, enduring captivity and anguish, waiting for rescue. Concern for the first attack became his biggest fear— explosives, followed by adrenaline-filled men tearing down walls, crashing windows, firing automatic weapons—being killed by his own people.

Hamilton didn't intend to be set free in a police body bag.

Survival required playing along, and dignity be damned. No attempt to manipulate, challenge, or befriend his abductors would occur until he learned their state of mind. Whatever their motives, he'd force himself to remain unruffled. His life depended on it. Kidnapping victims, more often than not, survived... statistically.

An immediate priority—locate a safe place for cover. Hamilton guessed his captors were well prepared and armed and planned to avoid being caught.

For a moment, he saw a blurred face. Lenora smiled. Why did he let her get away?

The answer never changed—independence. Absolute freedom and money were cornerstones of his life. He answered to no one, indulging in pleasures granted by wealth. His concern, growing in age, a severe ailment, and the finality of the grim reaper's visit.

He'd found death's loophole in South America.

Hamilton's head slumped to the side. Heavy eyelids dropped, nearly closing. Before dozing off, he stared into a pair of familiar hazel eyes.

"You back to soften me up?" Hamilton asked.

"Not a chance," the soft-spoken voice answered.

Hamilton detected the scent of sweet bourbon as the visitor spoke in a German-accented voice. His face refused to come together, distorted and twisted as if inside a child's kaleidoscope. Hamilton needed to shake off the drugs inside him. In time, he'd be called to identify the kidnappers in court. The silver tooth sitting next to him was all he saw.

Silver tooth pulled a waxed paper pouch from his shirt pocket, removing a meat patty. Hamilton accepted all nourishment offered. He remained breathing because the abductors wanted something beyond suitcases of cash.

The offer resembled a plug of tobacco spit to a street gutter. He wouldn't take the chance of refusing, grateful for nourishment.

The visitor held the food in his palm, near Hamilton's nose and mouth. "Our guest is hungry? Yes?"

Hamilton pulled against the constraints to gain slack, loosening his arms and legs. The show of resistance, no matter how subtle, could be dangerous. He took the risk.

Silver tooth made no move, keeping the meat in place, inches away. Hamilton relaxed, reminding himself to stay calm and survive.

A door opened and closed. From behind, footsteps shuffled on the wood floor and approached. Would the new arrival be the interrogator?

Nausea returned the moment Hamilton twisted his head. Silver tooth shoved the hamburger nearer, allowing him to take the offered meal.

Footsteps moved closer, pausing at the back of Hamilton's chair.

"He appears hungry. Does he not?"

Silver tooth folded the wax paper. "In a few days, our friend will tame."

"Don't bet on it," Hamilton said, regretting the words. How long had they held him captive? His mind failed. Had rational thought diminished? More humiliation was to come; he was sure of it.

"That is disappointing," the voice behind him answered.

He gained nothing from an exchange. The captors had plans. Why allow him to regain consciousness and feed him?

"No one will rescue you," silver tooth said.

Hamilton felt a hand on his shoulder, gripping him.

"What were you doing in San Diego?"

"Vacation," Hamilton answered. "What about my car?"

"Sorry, I can't help," the man behind said.

"Don't be," Hamilton said. "Keep it all."

"None of this is necessary," silver tooth said, holding water to Hamilton's mouth.

"What do you want?"

"Who knew about the San Diego trip?"

The sound of a police siren approached and faded.

Hazy sunshine surrounded the space but did not surrender clues of a location. Hamilton heard enough to recognize being in an urban area. Perhaps his captors filled the room with puzzling sounds like the British used to confuse German captives. What prevented him from throwing himself, the chair, and ropes against the glass, freeing himself?

"What were you doing in San Diego?" the voice asked again.

"Reliving old memories," Jaminson answered.

"Some good, some bad," the man inches from his face said.

"Good," Jaminson said. "Why did you stop me?"

"Who knows what you were doing?"

Jaminson's head dropped to his chest.

"Drink?" the silver-toothed man held another cup.

Jaminson nodded, allowing the paper cup to his dry, creased lips, swallowing, feeling the water's coolness spill, running down his shirt, and vest soaking his skin.

"Cooperate, and the sooner we release you."

Outside, the unmistakable whap-whap of helicopter blades arrived and weakened, not appearing in the windows, but the sound gave hope.

"Mr. Jaminson, you are wearing on our patience."

Dull numbness replaced the ache in Hamilton's feet and arms, forcing him to question reaching safety on his own.

How many captors? If more, they'd be close by. Once alone, he'd stand, allowing his weighty physique to fall back onto the metal chair, jarring its frame, loosening the rope bindings. With one hand free, he'd break loose his legs, and reach one of the many windows, and risk the fall.

Unlike the abductors, those interrogating him did not hide their faces—they didn't intend to let him live. The information wanted kept him alive. Would they continue to drug him?

A lone blackbird appeared, spreading its wings, landing on the window's ledge, and tapping its long pointed beak on the glass. In a moment, more arrived resembling cheerless choir members awaiting Sunday devotions—silent, at perfect attention, watching Hamilton.

Had the vigilant crows interpreted his morose thoughts, waiting to escort his tumble through the glass, circling his sprawled body, fulfilling duties as pallbearers? Or an omen of luck, as the prodigal Raven arrived, announcing Noah's sea captivity ended.

Cruel irony slapped Hamilton, jarring him alert. He faced death. Planned emancipation from man's greatest fear almost attained— minutes from defining a new future.

His senses regained, Hamilton chose the raven's later revelation. The private army of Israeli mercenaries would arrive, crashing through every window in the building.

Hamilton jerked as a hypodermic needle pinched his skin.

The sharp stab jolted him, forcing a fall. Prone on the hard floor, he spotted his shoes, reassuring him.

CHAPTER SIX

"Why use two men to deliver a telegram?" Lenora asked Birdie.

Birdie never heard the question, guiding her client, pulling her behind a mechanic's tool cabinet.

"Stay down. Don't say a word," Birdie whispered while she positioned her leather shoulder bag. A .38 pistol rested in a separate pocket—lacking a spur hammer allowed little chance of jamming while fired inside her shoulder bag.

Birdie crouched next to Lenora, watching the Ford approach. If there were more passengers, they hid behind tinted windows. Her hand remained in the purse, gripping the revolver, wishing she'd spent more time at the range during her self-imposed seclusion.

"What's the matter?" Lenora asked.

"I don't like the looks of this. Stay put."

Birdie kept the tactical advantage, at least she'd hoped so. She and Lenora hid in shadow behind a bulky, steel box of tools. Behind them, the hangar's back door offered an escape. Her client was safe, and Birdie intended it to stay that way. Unlike her last, who she left alone to be trapped and murdered.

She wanted this to be an overreaction. Perhaps the local Western Union office trained a new delivery man, explaining the two. The messaging company, well known for its "boy on a bicycle" image, carried regret letters to families of killed soldiers. She hoped this messenger didn't bring death. Lenora or her former husband could have run afoul with a Jersey crime family. She may have jumped into something bigger than a kidnapping. Today had been full of surprises, rekindling fears from a past case. The day remained young—besides, she didn't want to appear timid, afraid to take action.

"What's going on?" Lenora asked.

"If there's trouble, run out the back to the next building."

Birdie felt foolish, reacting as she had. There had been no reason to frighten her client. She blamed her paranoia and crossed her fingers, never forgetting the trap that backfired in the Brooklyn cemetery.

The Ford rolled to a stop on the tarmac, blocking the open hangar's doors. Birdie approached the two with her coat collar pulled, covering her face. It came from instinct, a sixth sense owed to years as a Pinkerton, shielding wealthy female clients, acting as a decoy from an invasive New York City press.

Birdie's mind fashioned a terrified picture of Lenora attempting to run from their attackers. A hatchet-wielding man emerged. Her blood-coated client stumbled, bouncing off blackened, moss-covered tombstones and falling into a freshly dug grave.

Tripping on the tracks of the hangar door, Birdie realized her mind had not deserted her earlier case hunting a deranged transit cop.

The late morning became colder. Graying Jersey skies threatened more snow for the new christened year. If the Russian satellite fell on New York today, she didn't have time to fret—in front of her stood potential trouble.

Buttoning his overcoat, a heavyset driver climbed from the idling car. The uniformed Western Union man waved a yellow envelope over his head. His other hand remained in sight. He'd blocked her view of the car's occupant. She countered and stepped to one side. The passenger rolled down the window and smiled. Neither fit the description of young bike-riding Western Union delivery boys she'd experienced on Manhattan's congested streets. Birdie heard the repeated sound of a camera shutter.

What were the chances a gun rested in his lap?

"Telegram for Lenora Jaminson."

"That's me," Birdie answered, surprising herself. Her right hand inside her purse, gripping the chrome .38 aimed inches above the delivery man's heart. Her hand trembled, she'd be lucky to hit her target. Slow inhaling and exhaling eliminated tension, lowering her pounding blood pressure and relaxing her mind. She had a job to do protecting her client.

She'd allowed herself to become a sitting duck. What had she been thinking? In the short time, knowing Lenora, she stood a good chance of being killed. For what? Lenora's ex-husband, who maybe wanted a simple getaway.

"How did you find me?" Birdie asked.

Several yards away, the man stopped. Birdie saw his eyes roam the hangar and nearby office. What did he search for? She refused to look back at the hanger, fearing she might give away Lenora's position.

"I'm the lucky one, I guess," he said, flashing a weak smile.

"How's that?" she asked. Birdie continued to grip the gun nestled in her leather handbag.

"You Lenora Jaminson?"

"I am." Birdie stepped forward.

The man nodded.

"Then give it to me."

He slipped a hand inside his overcoat.

Birdie held her breath. Her trigger finger tensed.

He pulled out a long, narrow receipt book. "Sign here."

She scribbled her client's name and noticed the tablet was new and unused. The suspicious Western Union man didn't bother to glance at her signature before returning it to his coat pocket. Birdie took the envelope while keeping a hand inside the purse.

"Is that all?" Birdie asked.

He pointed to the DC 3. "Glad I caught you. Going somewhere?"

"Seeing a friend off."

The man slowed and turned to face Birdie as he walked away. "Don't go anywhere before you read the telegram."

The Ford's door slammed.

Birdie squeezed the grip of her small revolver and shouted, "Who are you?" as the car drove away.

CHAPTER SEVEN

Washington, DC

CIA director Allen Dulles slammed the stack of files on the conference table. "We can't afford another slip-up."

Doctor Hubert Strughold studied the man he despised. The arrogant, pipe-smoking Dulles walked a fine line. The CIA boss covertly aided in ending World War Two and soon after headed Project Paperclip—bringing sixteen hundred highly trained German scientists to the United States.

Following The Third Reich's surrender, Strughold and his family found safety in America. He'd became embedded in America's space race. Not a scientist like von Braun and his V-2 rocket, but just as necessary. Strughold knew how to keep a man alive in space. As a German military doctor, he studied war prisoners' ability to withstand extreme pressures and stress. Russia's Sputnik lit a fire under the Americans, opening the rivalry. The basketball-sized satellite circling the globe kept him from facing war crimes. Dulles took pleasure and advantage of protecting many Nazis from a Jewish hanging rope.

High-ranking SS Nazi officers, like Strughold, escaped a crumbling Germany. Dulles and The United States benefited, recruiting

Germany's best minds—many as spies against hated Russia, and hidden from the American public.

Americans no longer feared the defeated Germans and turned their paranoia against their former ally, Russia—the sleeping bear of Europe.

Dulles stood over the six men in the hazy room. A few cigarettes were lit, and a cigar puffed, coming from a corner of the room near a row of coffee pots.

Gustain Hilger held a lit cigar and hadn't mixed with the others. He remained quiet, to no surprise of Strughold.

Hubert Strughold opened a metal tin in his jacket pocket, slipping four Tums antacid tablets into his hand. As lights faded and the projector brightened the screen, he popped the large white pills into his mouth. This meeting was about him and his colleague, Doctor Falk.

"First slide," Dulles commanded. "These arrived by radio fax minutes ago."

An image snapped in place, filling the curtain.

To Strughold, the slide triggered the sound of a bolt-action rifle opening and closing, encasing a cartridge in its deadly chamber, launching a personal battle he feared not surviving.

"This is Hamilton Jaminson," Dulles announced to the quiet room. "We had a security breach in a location near San Diego and are at risk of losing top-secret work."

They looked at a black-and-white photograph of a short, plumpish, balding man walking near a Rolls Royce.

The projector went blank, followed by a second image.

The same person appeared slumped in a chair arms, and legs tied. "This man owns US Steel and gave Eisenhower's campaign millions. We lost him after we took this.

Dulles broke the silence, slamming his fist on the table, rattling coffee cups and ashtrays.

Doctor Strughold waited for his name to be shouted. In the darkness and smoke haze, he felt the CIA boss staring at him.

Instead, the next slide popped on the screen.

Strughold waited, eventually, the spotlight would shine bright on him. Dulles and his Princeton smirk would get around to pointing his; prized briarwood pipe in his direction. He possibly had a slide chosen to queue for the moment. The experimental lab, his brainchild, but represented Falk's significant discoveries, had been kept from Dulles, hidden in a Brea, CA orange grove.

With a few more years and added subjects, the process would advance medicine and leapfrog death. So much so, he worried they disturbed God's plan. Hubert Strughold held his breath, hoping the recent upheaval would not expose his chance to rebuild his mother country.

The bogus photograph on display simulated Dulles's Chula Vista laboratory. Stainless steel tables and a resuscitator centered the screen. Against a cinder block wall were tall storage vats. Wires and hoses ran like intertwined snakes over a white tile floor. The following slide was grainy. However, the close-up revealed a white lab-coated Hubert Strughold alongside Horst Falk and his glaring silver tooth, standing over a dissected cadaver.

Strughold realized Dulles planned to sweep this failed operation under the big CIA carpet as he often did. The ranking agents attending were tied to Dulles and his cloak-and-dagger world. What they heard and saw would be held private—what went on inside the room never left under penalty of an extended vacation in Fort Leavenworth.

Hiding failures from Eisenhower had been one of the CIA director's areas of expertise, and how he kept his job.

Hubert Strughold protected what he and Falk had in their grasp. The project had come too far. For now, all he could do was sit and learn what Dulles planned. After seeing Gustain Hilger in the room, he got a strong hunch, one he disliked.

Another slide flashed overhead.

Strughold knew the hunt was on, and innocent civilians were about to be hurt.

"We took these a few moments ago in New Jersey," Dulles declared as if he had snapped the photograph.

Strughold looked at the scene in surprise. Agents slid their chairs close to the table and took notes. They stared at the back seam of a man's overcoat as he stood facing a tall woman wrapped in a long coat. Her face appeared, shrouded by a shawl and a large fur collar. In the blurred background, a plane sat in an open hangar.

"The female posed as the subject we're looking for," Dulles said.

There wouldn't be interrupting questions. The chief wanted full control until he asked. He handled meetings as classroom seminars. Tardiness and disruptions not tolerated. Rumors had it that those daring to interrupt the CIA's leader found abrupt transfers to undesirable and frigid locations.

"Two agents in Patterson, New Jersey, posed as Western Union people attempted to deliver a telegram to Lenora Jaminson, Hamilton Jamison's ex-wife. We sent one to every known location, including the Pittsburgh Zoo, where she works as a veterinarian." Dulles relit his pipe and went on.

"This was the closest we came." Dulles snapped shut his Zippo lighter. "The agents believe our subject was there and left by plane. Our men called in backup to keep the airport under surveillance while they tracked the plane's destination to Los Angeles. The CIA would prefer Jaminson's ex-wife stay out of the matter. However, she may lead us to Hamilton Jaminson and Doctor Falk, the source of our problem."

The projector flashed to the next slide.

Grainy and out of focus, the photo showed a tight close-up of the coated lady's face. "We're working to identify this person and her role."

Strughold leaned back, expecting his introduction into the tale. Dulles's flair for the dramatic wore thin. Since the day he negotiated an early end to the war with Germany, he'd held center stage spotlight granting him privileges. Dulles and his CIA operated under a cloak of top secrecy shielded from his boss, Dwight Eisenhower. The slip-up in

California would stay classified with blame laid at the feet of Hubert Strughold, one of Dulles's prized German trophies. Today Dulles would show off the former Nazi doctor while dressing him down in front of select CIA officers.

After a moment, the lights returned. Doctor Strughold watched all heads turn to him. Sweat beaded his forehead. He was accustomed to the role of interrogator, not answering pointed questions from Dulles.

Dulles walked in front of the screen, casting a shadow. "Questions?"

"What do you want done to Lenora Jaminson?" an agent asked.

Dulles rested both palms on the table and leaned forward. "Nothing. The CIA does not take action against United States citizens. We intend to observe her for her safety."

Hubert Strughold watched the CIA director scan the room, knowing the chief invented a search for his other prize Nazi recruit, Falk. Dulles enjoyed theater drama, building the moment until he displayed his rapid and cunning ability to plan covert operations.

"Doctor Strughold, your project is in the center of all this. Tell us something helpful."

Hubert Strughold fixed his narrow bowtie and straightened his smudged white lab coat as he stood.

"They took the picture you saw of me inside the Noah Institute."

A hand shot up from across the room. Dulles waved off the disturbance and went on.

"A former German doctor and SS officer, Horst Falk, runs the lab. He is a refugee living in San Diego."

"Falk reports to you, does he not, Doctor Strughold?" Dulles asked.

"He does," Strughold answered. "We worked on a project that showed promise."

"You told me the work showed <u>great</u> promise," Dulles said.

"Poor choice of words," Strughold answered. "Great potential is what I meant."

"You knew Falk during the war?"

"We worked together. That was all."

"You weren't friends?"

"I never saw him outside of our work."

"Go on," Dulles said, puffing his pipe.

Hubert Strughold pointed to a blank screen and paused until a photograph of a red brick, two-story building appeared. White block letters across the roofline read, Noah Institute.

"We worked together, here, on a cryonics process for the United States space program. Sometime back, we made a significant advancement. After many years, we discovered a deep-freezing process for whole-body preservation."

"For deep space travel," Dulles said.

Strughold nodded and went on. "That was until Doctor Falk and I found other applications."

Dulles jabbed his pipe toward Strughold. "Get to the point."

"It's a simple principle—life retention. Medicine and research are improving every day. If someone dies or becomes ill with something medicine cannot cure, we, in a few years, will preserve them in a deep freeze until a cure is discovered."

"For example, doctor?"

Strughold's expression remained unchanged as he spoke. "If you contracted polio and died a few years ago, we would have kept your blood circulating and protected your cells from dying. Today, with Salk's new vaccine, we'd bring you back to life and cure the polio. We can bridge the gap between today and future medical discoveries...."

Dulles cut the doctor off. "The good doctor Falk bit the hand that fed and went rogue. He saw money and planned to sell our discovery to Jaminson. We now are swimming in a mess Falk and Doctor Strughold created."

A slide picture appeared of Dr. Falk alongside a black-haired young woman.

Dulles pointed his shadowed finger to the screen. "That's our vanishing Doctor Horst Falk. The woman, Shelley, no last name, is from Argentina. We believe she works with Falk. We tapped her telephone, but all we got was small talk. If she's communicating with him, we have intercepted nothing."

Dulles shouted, "Gus."

From the corner of the room, Gustain Hilger stood, at least a head taller than the other men.

The projector flashed two side-by-side photographs.

Dulles stood next to the large screen, puffing his pipe. A thin stream of tobacco smoke drifted through the bright glare.

"These are the two Gustain Hilger will look for. Hamilton Jaminson is being held in a location unknown to our Doctor Strughold. The lady, seen earlier and his former wife, Lenora, may be involved. She's suspected of being in New Jersey or headed to California. Hilger will keep her from butting in and possibly exposing our work."

The conference room's lights flashed on. No one budged. Dulles's dismissal waited.

Dulles brushed pipe tobacco from his coat's lapel then cleared his throat. "Gustain is not officially working for the CIA and is seeking information on the matter which we'll code name Jacob's Ladder. This agency wants to establish what the two Jaminson's know. No action is to be taken against them."

No expected dressing down came. For the moment, Hubert Strughold relaxed. His part in the kidnapping passed over. By no means did he believe the CIA chief intended to overlook his involvement. Strughold observed Gus during the briefing. The man appointed leader of Jacob's Ladder showed no expression. He looked at no one in the room and glanced at the photographs projected on the giant screen. Gustain kept his eyes cast on the floor. Strughold was sure the often used unofficial agent had looked at these same pictures many times and committed the images to memory, along with dossiers detailing the two Jaminson's lives. Gustain's role was to clean up the mess in California.

He killed for Dulles.

Strughold awaited a harsh dressing down in the privacy of Dulles's office. A wrist slap compared to Falk's expected punishment. His research colleague was not alone in grabbing Jaminson's million-dollar payment for the Noah Institute. Horst Falk would retreat to Buenos Aires, followed by Strughold, joining hundreds of German officers taking refuge In South America.

As the father of America's space medicine, he counted on notoriety and reputation within the higher reaches of the American space program to make him untouchable to the CIA chief.

Gustain's command to clean up the disaster in California risked their undisclosed venture hidden deep in the hills of California's Carbon Canyon, not Chula Vista, an elaborate smokescreen, withholding Strughold's and Falk's real discovery from Dulles.

Strughold glanced across the room at Gustain, knowing he'd been commissioned for a killing job, a task the former German soldier would carry out with no remorse and containing the skilled executioner needed to be done, regardless of consequences including the loss of his own life. A visit with Gustain in their usual location, hidden from CIA spies, became necessary before their years of work were destroyed.

CHAPTER EIGHT

Birdie gripped the message, watching the suspicious Western Union car back into the frozen grass, turn and drive off. She remained outside the hangar, intending to wait until the vehicle exited the airport's gate.

"What did they want?" Lenora called from inside the hangar.

"You. Here's your telegram."

Birdie held out the small envelope as Lenora limped from the shadow, joining Birdie.

"Who knows, you came here?"

"I'm stunned. I didn't tell anyone."

Birdie pulled her hand off the pistol hidden in her purse. "They took me by surprise."

"If they're from Western Union, I'm Peter Pan," Lenora said, tearing open the yellow envelope.

Birdie fought off reading the message over her client's shoulder and waited.

Lenora lowered the telegram and raised it for a second look.

Birdie had no luck reading her client's expression. It could be the bitter temperature and chilling Canadian wind freezing Lenora's features—or this lady had more grit than a gunslinger. Her reaction revealed nothing, and Birdie gave her credit.

Throughout the surprise drop-in visit, Birdie had observed the car's passenger. Judging by the sudden movements and camera clicks, they had taken photographs.

What had she jumped into? This morning, her life remained uneventful, on course to nowhere. Hours ago, she'd contemplated a tranquil Central Park walk followed by a Broadway play, topped off with a sloppy pizza, hand-spun in a quiet bar. It figured rich people led complicated lives, and with that came substantial problems. Scratch that—gigantic ones.

They paid her to do things the wealthy wanted to do but were unwilling to do themselves. If she continued, she required more convincing—not more money; she'd make that clear. Lenora proved generous and perhaps too free with her cash. Pieces of the jigsaw puzzle didn't fit. More accurately, some weren't in the box. Like it or not, she'd placed herself between danger and another well-to-do client.

Her concern, she hadn't formed a connection to the case. She sympathized with her one-footed client. However, Birdie expected more. The entire day, since Lenora arrived, gave her the sense of a bad joke with her its punch line, leaving her weighted down in disaster. Something more went on besides the folly of a scorned woman pursuing a running man.

Lenora laughed and held the message to her side.

"Who's it from?" Birdie asked.

"It sure as hell's not from my Hamilton."

Birdie waited a moment, watching her client's face.

Lenora handed the telegram to Birdie. "He signs his name Ham on personal notes, at least to me."

**Request you stay home. Enjoying an extended vacation.
See you upon return. Hamilton.**

"Maybe a signal?" Birdie said.

"He didn't send this. I'm a zoo veterinarian. I know bull crap when I smell it."

Birdie reread the message, looking for a clue.

"You won't see anything," Lenora said.

"No?"

"Ham never uses telegrams. His staff, yes, not him. Doesn't trust them."

Birdie waited for an explanation—none came. She'd wait, not press her client. Not now, later—if she remained on the case. She'd decide during the long flight.

One at a time, the plane's Rolls-Royce engines fired up, throwing an abrupt rumble through the fuselage. Both roared and coughed, sputtering a moment until the fine-tuned motors spun twin propellers.

The uniformed captain walked to Lenora, touching her arm. "Ready when you are, ma'am."

Birdie eased into a deep white leather seat, across from Lenora as the DC-3 rolled toward a nearby runway. Indecision bothered Birdie. Remaining with Lenora gave her finances a hefty boost, allowing her freedom from annoying bill collectors.

How much risk came with the sudden appearance of bogus Western Union men? It wasn't an everyday missing person case. No ransom demands with proof of life photos, only a suspicious telegram asking her client to stay out of whatever went on.

The whirlwind experience left Birdie skeptical and at odds with herself. A Manhattan socialite walks into her apartment, and hours later, she's facing off with men she's prepared to kill.

How much could Birdie accept as truth from Lenora? How deep would they wade into danger? She'd placed herself in a vulnerable spot for a person she didn't know or checked out. Sympathy for Lenora's refusal to accept being jilted was not enough to place her life on the line. The coast-to-coast flight gave her time to judge her client, and in the worst case, she'd have a one-way trip to warm sunshine and beaches courtesy of Lenora Jaminson.

Birdie pushed open a curtained window, looking forward to saying goodbye to the snow and dreariness of New York and Jersey. The Western Union car was nowhere in sight. The modest victory lifted her confidence enough to lessen her white-knuckled grip on her leather armrest. While her maiden flight, she'd appear relaxed, although the plane's wheels remained grounded.

She didn't have time for a farewell to dear Mother Earth as the airplane sped down the long runway, passing waiting planes and aviation offices. Birdie kept an eye on the DC-3's wings as they lifted and became airborne. Off the tip of the wing, she spotted the men standing beside the Western Union car. One waved while the other aimed a camera at the plane. Birdie guessed the pair's next stop to be the control tower for the aircraft's flight plan.

It took a moment for Birdie to correct her thoughts—the two likely were not connected to organized crime and doubted law enforcement—a badge would have been flashed the moment the over-coated man stepped from the car. She knew plenty of Jersey cops, each relished flaunting police muscle. As far as organized crime, the two men's suits came off a bargain-basement rack.

Businessmen like Hamilton Jaminson matched wits daily with the world's elite. If ordinary cops bent laws, she would not presume the Hamilton played anywhere near fair and square. Nothing today conformed to what she knew was conventional. She'd soon engage kingmakers and mingle among those accustomed to making the rules.

"A Bloody Mary to relax?" Lenora asked, breaking Birdie's thoughts.

If her client signaled the pilot, Birdie missed it. Moments later, the co-pilot appeared, balancing a tray of tall glasses, garnished with leafy celery stalks, peeled shrimp, and wedges of lime.

Birdie took the beverage, not a stranger to potent morning libations, and returned Lenora's toast.

"Hamilton's safety and our success."

Clinking glasses carried sharp chimes of leaded crystal as both inclined their seats.

Birdie deliberated probing her client about the circumstances of the curious telegram and instead relaxed. Plenty of time awaited during the long flight and refueling stop. Broad reclining seats and stout beverages made thoughts of sleep attractive—not that she could. Scenarios shot into her mind. Someone attempted to discourage Lenora from her search, signaling Birdie that Jaminson remained alive—maybe not well, but at least breathing.

What waited in Los Angeles?

The same thought kept reoccurring. If a kidnapping occurred, why was there no ransom demand? Or Lenora chose not to reveal it. Her client had a starting point—although the trail a month old would be difficult to follow. In their favor, Hamilton Jaminson was a recognizable face from newspaper and magazine exposure. Also, people remember celebrities. Their recollection would be intact after spotting one of the world's wealthiest men.

Aspirations of a film career had never materialized. A crushed shoulder, hip and visible scars collapsed, calling to the Broadway stage. Heading to Hollywood, she'd see what she'd missed.

The second drink did its trick. Tension in her back and shoulders lessened. Across from her, Lenora relaxed with her legs curled on her chair. Fresh-made cocktails rested on a table between the glasses. A flesh-toned wooden foot laid on a cloth napkin. Lenora massaged the swollen stump at the end of her leg.

"I can only take that thing so long," Lenora said.

Birdie realized she'd found a kindred soul. It might have been brought on by altitude mixed with generously poured drinks. To her, it didn't matter. She looked at a woman with a fighting spirit, unwilling to take her place among the upper class. Manhattan's high society, super-wealthy banished ex-wives of business tycoons, were supposed to host charitable benefits, spending thousands of dollars getting even with former spouses. Birdie looked at a one-footed lady who flew helicopters and possessed a passion for bringing home her missing ex-husband.

Before she questioned her client on Hamilton's habits and to satisfy her curiosity why Hamilton Jaminson snubbed Western Union, Lenora's head slumped against a pillow, napping. Somewhere in the sky over Middle America, Birdie formed a fondness for the woman.

The plane rumbled and shuttered, cruising at twenty thousand feet, rattling cubes of ice in her empty cocktail glass. Lenora remained asleep throughout the turbulence. Birdie hoped to survive the flight and what faced them if they touched ground in California. A strong hunch told her, the one-footed lady had moxie.

Did they both have enough to withstand what waited?

CHAPTER NINE

Gustain Hilger remained in the conference room watching CIA brass exit past Allen Dulles—each of them his pawn. He disliked the man, but not for the harsh methods used running the American spy organization.

Dulles, his boss, persisted in calling him Gus, something he detested. His mother died giving birth, naming her only child Gustain. As he saw it, Dulles dishonored her last request.

The slim odds of finding himself in America swung his way in a Frankfurt beer garden after an introduction to Allen Dulles. Dulles served as a field officer and rose to power, fostering an unholy alliance between the United States and the Nazis during and after the war. Dulles searched out Nazis fleeing Germany, secretly bringing war criminals to America as useful spies and scientists.

Unlike them, he hadn't committed brutal crimes. The CIA chief had no hold over Gustain, but knowing the agency, they often altered German war records. Gustain Hilger, a loyal ground soldier, fought on the front lines. Distinction and honor came from killing English, Russians, and Americans on both fronts as a sniper. Skills ranged from firearms to building bombs and stalking. Handling a crossbow or throwing a dagger occurred naturally as using a fork and knife.

Tossing a grenade into a target's home or placing a blade into a neck failed to keep him awake at night.

Something deep in him craved to resist taking innocent lives. Had maturity uncovered morality hidden within? A quiet voice from an unworldly youth spoke of homeland and promised prosperity.

Gustain gathered the confidential envelope and documents into his expanding folder. The upper corner of the black file read Jacob's Ladder. He shook his head, recognizing the code name's irony and symbolic reference to Hebrew myth suggesting man's connection between earth and heaven—one he'd never enjoy. Did the German doctors unearth a physical link? The CIA director flaunted his moral Puritan superiority, compelling Gustain to question how Dulles allowed Strughold's and Falk's experiments.

After tying the folder's strings, he made a crease using the table's edge and folded photos of Lenora and Hamilton Jaminson, sliding them into the metal trash can next to his chair—their faces and vitals imprinted in his brain. He'd developed a reserved desire for the soon to be met private investigator, slipping her five by seven into his jacket's breast pocket, near his dependable .45 Luger. In the upcoming days, he'd get to know her. The attraction, unexplained, was nothing more than professional respect.

Tracking wild game or people, each similar, following predictable patterns. Both satisfied him and before long, Birdie Kelley would join his trophies.

The time to pursue came.

* * * *

In his Arlington home, across the Potomac River, Gustain leaned over the small sink, pulling back long curls, twisting them into an elastic band. His Aryan blond hair no longer hung on his broad shoulders, instead, nice and neat behind him, unseen under a black watch cap. A few clothes went into a worn leather shoulder bag he'd carried to European and South American cleanup jobs. The razor knife and short barrel Luger rested, cushioned next to pairs of socks, and rode concealed in the false bottom. The assignment appeared less than challenging, far from CIA routine, yet puzzling. Dulles planned to assassinate civilians. His prey—harmless women, traveling alone, and two aged men. With no promise of a challenge.

No official report would reach Dulles. The cleanup remained off record. No one in or out of the agency would question him. Following his return, five thousand dollars, unreported to the IRS, would appear in a Swiss bank. The money accumulated reached levels far more than he needed. Despite slight wealth, breaking away seemed hopeless— killing overtook him as alcohol and tobacco. Pulling the trigger intimately near his prey proved addictive. Each kill, unlike a sharpshooter, became personal, watching fright and surprise register on the shocked face of a dying victim made his job difficult to walk away from.

The envelope he'd torn open provided a starting point.

Santa Monica Airport, California, Clover Field.

The words brought a smile. A photograph showed the plane's tail number from a takeoff in Patterson, New Jersey. He'd arrive unnoticed. If the female targets assumed anyone followed, they'd suspect the agents encountered in Patterson. He'd stay a ghost.

Gustain kept several options, knowing the two lady's destination. Choosing the kill and disposal locations allowed control, decreasing the chances of detection. Following them, Jaminson and Doctor Falk would be eliminated. In a few days, he'd expect another assignment. The agency had plenty.

Gustain finished rolling socks and shirts, stuffing them into the satchel. In the street below rain fell, steady and hard, filling ruts and potholes. About to shut the curtain, a yellow cab stopped near his house, too early for his late flight. If the car carried a passenger, he failed to spot anyone in the rear seat. The driver raised an umbrella and stepped from the running car—wipers continued to beat against a cracked windshield. In a moment, heavy footsteps pounded on the wood-planked front porch. Not wanting to be disturbed, Gustain waited. He guessed the driver lost and searched for an address among poorly marked neighborhood streets.

From the upstairs bedroom, a gabled overhang blocked his view of the front door. The first knock came, then a second and a third— seconds passed—more knocks led to heavy pounds.

To Gustain, they sounded panicked.

He had no alternative. The knocking didn't appear as if it would end.

With a practiced move, the Luger slid from the packed satchel and rested next to the small of his back. He couldn't afford to take chances.

At the door, unseen, Gustain took another look at the surprise visitor. The guest in front of him appeared frail and balding. He wouldn't allow outward appearances to override caution and judgment that had kept him alive. Were the loose-fitting pants and a baggy flannel shirt and coat hiding weapons?

Gustain watched the taxi driver knock again. He made no move, nor did he unconsciously or from reflex check, ensuring his weapon remained in place.

"Can I help?" Gustain shouted.

"Gustain Hilger live here?"

"Who's asking?"

"I have an envelope for him."

"Leave it inside the storm door."

The aluminum door opened and banged shut. Gustain waited until the cab splashed away.

The flat, brown, ordinary envelope bore no address or markings identifying the sender, appearing inexpensive—dime store-bought.

Doctor Hubert Strughold had sent a message in code.

CHAPTER TEN

The silver DC-3 descended over crisscrossing freeways and palm trees, bordering vast fields of fruit and vegetables. Birdie jumped awake, gripping her seat's armrests. Sleep during the cross-country journey scarcely qualified as a catnap. Manhattan cab rides and Coney Island roller coasters took distant seconds to the turbulent flight.

The prospect of re-boarding Lenora's plane following refueling in Kansas City had been in doubt. Anticipation of California and escaping New York's numbing cold won out.

Dropping altitude, the plane glided through scattered thin cloud cover, allowing Birdie views of swarming farmworkers tossing crates onto carts pulled by weathered and worn tractors—not how she visualized the allure of Southern California.

As if Lenora knew her thoughts, she'd pointed west toward the Pacific Ocean. "That's Santa Catalina Island. Hamilton thinks it paradise."

Across from them, the co-pilot arrived and ripped a piece of paper from a steno pad, handing it to Lenora.

Birdie waited a moment and asked, "News on Jaminson?"

"Radio message from my previous investigator."

"Hamilton showed up?"

Lenora shook her head.

"I warned Hamilton. He hired them on his own."

Birdie slid the note from her client's hand and sat next to her.

"He has a private army hunting for him?" Birdie asked.

"Former Israeli commandos."

"We dropping the search?"

"No!" Lenora said. "We need to find him before they do. He swore he wouldn't. It's suicidal. Hamilton's mercenaries, when he's found, will make a military assault on his captors. His life is secondary to the rescue. Hamilton reasoned it would discourage abductors."

"Better to know what we're dealing with." Birdie passed the handwritten note back and returned to her seat.

"Then, you believe me?" Lenora said. "It's not another woman."

Birdie absorbed the deserved I told you so. Her client's subdued pleasure showed in a sudden smile. The search became more urgent. No longer alone looking for a missing person, they competed against a small army. If not money, what did Jaminson's captors want? Regardless, she and Lenora risked becoming trapped in a crossfire.

"We have no time to waste," Birdie said, slipping on her shoes.

"Don't be shocked by what we find," Lenora said. "Hamilton leads a fascinating and shocking life. He's no stranger to a bar stool and a pretty face."

Dull thumps below Birdie's feet startled her. "Hear that?"

Lenora touched her arm, surprising her. "Landing gear. Nothing to worry about."

Birdie eased back into the seat, pulling snug her lap belt. "I never imagined this."

"Orange County began with farming and cattle. Tract houses and highways are taking over," Lenora said.

The plane shuttered veering north, hugging a thin coastline, over white cresting waves.

"Looks peaceful," Birdie said.

"From here." Lenora smiled. "Down there, sharks will suck you down and pull you into deep trouble."

"I don't plan on swimming."

"I'm not talking about the water," Lenora said.

"Somewhere in that jungle, we'll find Hamilton," Birdie said.

"We'll start with his hotel."

The plane rocked and banked eastward, slowing, descending, and gliding toward a narrow black-topped landing strip.

"Where are we?" Birdie asked, drawing herself deeper into the leather armchair.

"Santa Monica. Clover Field," Lenora answered as wheels touched and rolled between the runway's yellow lines.

The DC-3 taxied by rows of tied-down Piper Cubs, Quonset huts and machine shops. A Texaco fuel truck sped past in the opposite direction. Minutes later, they turned at the control tower, heading toward Jaminson Hanger 79. Its double doors open, expecting their arrival.

Birdie waited, tapping her shoulder bag, looking forward to escaping the cabin's stale air and confined area. Being rid of Lenora for a few hours would feel enjoyable. Not that her client annoyed her, Birdie cherished private time and personal space—far from a loner or recluse, preferring to think of herself as contemplative, liberating her mind from distractions.

"Enjoy. Its twelve degrees in Manhattan," Lenora said and pointed to the open door near the rear of the parked plane.

Her reward waited—a first whiff of salty Pacific sea air blowing through her hair. Thinking of their sudden New Jersey visitors, she hoped the pair didn't follow.

Light breezes refreshed Birdie as she trailed Lenora, stepping from the plane. Although a city dweller, she recognized a hint of fresh-plowed soil and sweetness in the air.

Lenora inhaled and turned back. "I love the orange groves."

A hand reached up, assisting Birdie on the short stairs. She noticed the man's well-tanned face, aware of her paleness, blaming New York's winter and Irish blood. She'd not blend in, looking like an out-of-place Minnesota tourist.

"That's our car," Lenora said as the pilot placed the luggage in the trunk.

A red MG convertible's engine ran.

Welcoming balmy sunshine soothed chronic aches in her hip and shoulder as Birdie tossed her leather purse inside the narrow back seat. Why had she hesitated to take the job? Living in paradise, basking in Southern California's tropical warmth while New Yorkers suffered through a frigid, damp January, could be the answer to the doldrums she fell into.

Her case had changed for the worst. An unexpected tactical army hunted Jaminson, and two New Jersey men attempted to keep Lenora home.

For the moment, they were free of worry. The MG sped along a smooth, long stretch of fresh, paved road, kicking up pebbles of asphalt and dust. Santa Monica's Clover Airport disappeared behind them. Broad and scenic Sepulveda Boulevard took them north, passing beneath lanky palms lining traffic-clogged streets. At every corner, tropical flowers and ferns grew wild. Ripe oranges and lemons drooped over brick and stone walls guarding red-roofed stucco homes.

In backed-up traffic, Birdie resisted an impulse to poach handfuls of fruit hanging inches from her grasp. She thought better of the idea. The reality of Hamilton Jaminson being in danger from both captors and rescuers left no room for adolescent pleasure. Hamilton's death, and theirs, became an obvious possibility. Birdie carried the responsibility to free him and protect Lenora. Something she hadn't done for her well-heeled client a year ago.

Lenora steered east onto Wilshire, past lavish storefront windows displaying minks and diamonds, flaunting affluence.

"Welcome to Hollywood," Lenora said as they approached the gold signage of the Beverly Hills Hilton.

They bumped up a slight grade, parking next to lush potted palms.

"We're home," Lenora said, nodding to the hotel.

The lavish shops, homes and mountain views delivered what Birdie had expected. The job would not differ much from working in

New York. People told lies, and witnesses seldom recalled what they had seen. It was time for her to tackle the task and bury her past missteps.

"I'll check in and get the key to Hamilton's old room," Lenora said as a doorman opened a heavy glass door.

"Give me some time in the hotel bar," Birdie answered.

Lenora stopped. "Where?"

"Checking a theory."

"There will be a bar stool with his name on it," Lenora said.

It was late afternoon, and Birdie played a hunch, knowing it wouldn't be her last. She carried her purse in front of her as a shield and walked into the dimly lit lounge, inhaling liquor and stale cigarette fumes.

A small rabbit-eared television greeted her from a shelf above the bar. Few heads turned; most remained hunched over highball glasses, preferring to stir cocktails and stare at a muted TV while nibbling bar peanuts.

Drinking dens such as this drew well-dressed vultures no different from the high-class bars of New York City's theater district. Birdie guessed the hefty man, with his bow tie pulled open, delivered a well-practiced fairy tale of show business connections to a girl, looking no more than eighteen, vowing movie parts. A beat-up suitcase sat at her feet. The so-called talent scout had most likely met her at a Greyhound bus station. Another mark arrived, from who knows where, full of ambition, willing to believe a promise of sudden fame and glamor. Like New York, Hollywood attracted plenty of con men with "guaranteed" contacts. Hopeful actors flocked these Meccas, chasing dreams—only to wind up waiting tables and parking cars, if lucky.

Birdie understood how stylish watering holes operated. The jackals, in Brookes Brothers' suits, waited to pounce defenseless prey.

The hotel bar's heavy smell of whiskey returned her to her teens. She arrived in Manhattan from Queens, not royalty, she sometimes joked. Her stepfather peddled hot dogs from a rolling food cart in Times Square. On game days, he hiked up and down the aisles of

Ebbets Field, tossing ten-cent bags of peanuts to drunken Dodger fans.

Her stepfather's late-night stopovers—the dark, stumbling figure, and whiskey stench slid past a curtained doorway of her basement bedroom. Soft footsteps and the cry of a worn-out mattress came as a callused hand pressed her mouth.

The following day a subway token delivered her to a new life, a derelict hotel in the Bowery, making her a starving actress desperate and vulnerable, looking for work—singing and dancing like the thousands flocking New York, running from unhappiness to misery.

Birdie guessed it early for the regular crowd, but she'd scout around. After spending the entire day with Lenora, she wanted time alone. The long flight dulled her senses, and the smell of cigarettes and booze didn't help. She needed sleep, something which she expected to become a luxury.

It took a while for her weary eyes to adjust to the lounge's flickering red candles. At the rear, she spotted a gold-vested bartender leaning over a polished mahogany horseshoe bar. He spoke to a patron, pointing to a cluster of tables near an idle grand piano and microphone.

Birdie heard a few of his fast-spoken words. "See Oleta tonight; she'll take care of you." The barman straightened and palmed a roll of cash.

In a lounge like this, high-priced working girls noticed big spenders like Hamilton Jaminson. She'd return with the regulars and toss Lenora's money around. Cash spoke volumes and attracted plenty of talkers.

Birdie intended to work alone, keeping her client safe, out of the way, not disrupting her investigation. Crossing her mind came the possibility of personal indulgence, tempted by the forbidden fruits of The City of Angels. She couldn't pass up a little pleasure, releasing pent-up female energy.

CHAPTER ELEVEN

"Anybody here?"

Hamilton Jaminson's weak, scratchy voice struggled to carry from his parched throat.

Turned-up shirt sleeves exposed red needle marks covering bruised forearms.

A frail echo answered in the vacant room. Boisterous birds squawked against a backdrop of sporadic blasting horns during his time as a captive.

Grueling hours bound to a chair left Hamilton Jaminson fighting to keep a small amount of personal dignity. He did not recall when he'd last relieved himself. In his semi-conscious state, discomfort arrived in agonizing phases—each moment more punishing and made worse by knowing there appeared no end. Uncertainty became his enemy. Body and mind verged on collapse. His only hope relied on his band of mercenaries.

Would they make it in time? His lone prospect of being located rested on the tracking device hidden in the heel of his shoe.

"What do you want?" he shouted to an empty room. The last of his energy drained away.

Time eluded him. Minutes became hours, vanishing in his solitary world.

Blackout curtains wrapped the circular room's windows. A sliver of light peeked under a visible door. Hands and feet long ago advanced past dulling numbness, useless as petrified stumps. Opportunity to crawl, inch his way to a window gone. The earlier unexplainable hesitation, resisting escape, may have cost him his life. Known as a cunning business predator, he relished pouncing on and outflanking helpless rival companies, enlarging his coal and steel fortune.

How much humiliation could he endure? Surviving to enjoy his empire drove him.

With difficulty, Jaminson turned his head side to side, hoping to spot the missing shoes. Behind his back remained unsearched—it might as well have been the dark side of the moon.

The specially equipped shoes emitted low-level vibrations produced by a tiny diaphragm and tuning post hidden in a hollow heel, placing him under constant surveillance.

Thanks to Great Britain's security service, MI5 discovered the efficient Soviet eavesdropping bug hidden in a British embassy. The self-powered diaphragm created a resonant frequency from sound pressure passing through small holes in his shoes. Hamilton's private army used a sophisticated, high-powered transmitter, hunting the minute vibrations.

He wouldn't give up.

The slightest twist of the heavy chair would yield a glimpse behind him, hopefully discovering the missing shoes, enforcing hopes of rescue. His legs refused to respond, no reflexes, only deadness. He'd push his captor—forcing a reaction if he had not been abandoned and left to die.

Nausea and muscle cramps gripped his weakened body. Jaminson's head drooped, leaving his thick chin resting on his chest. About to make a plea to his unseen captors, he again saw the light under the door, convincing him someone watched, ignoring his shouts. He'd detected movement—a shadow blocked the thin light for an instant. Could it be the guard who delivered him water and food? Should he shout and plead for help? Would he provoke added retaliation and isolation? Nothing remained other than to survive a moment at a time.

Had fatigue turned him into a coward?

Water slapped against his face, jolting him. Jaminson twisted while his visitor stood over him, spilling clear liquid on his lap, drenching urine-saturated slacks. His eyes stung from the vinegar soaking his clothes.

"You're sinking," a familiar face said.

"What do you want?"

"To release you. We are not enemies."

"I'll forget this happened."

"We know the reason you were in San Diego. Who else knows your plans?"

"No one," Hamilton answered.

"This is not a game."

Hamilton's chair and head yanked back, pulled by a pair of black, rubber-gloved hands. "You may get your wish sooner than planned."

"Let me go," Hamilton forced out.

"Mister Jaminson, your safety rests with me. I can give you a long and perhaps healthy life if you cooperate."

"I'll tell you whatever you want."

"Did you visit Argentina recently?"

"Yes."

He'd endured isolation, and endless needles poked into his bruised arms. Nothing asked offered a clue of their demands. He'd hand over keys to his vault, and any amount demanded in exchange for his life.

"Tell me about the Noah Institute?"

The question surprised Jaminson, allowing him to piece together connections between the men with thick German accents, his capture and Argentina.

The probing came from an interrogator with mud on his shoes. Hamilton thought of him as Mudge—maybe their leader. Why was his recent trip to South America significant?

Hamilton's strong suit remained—an ability to think and plot in adverse conditions. He'd battled labor unions and Congress, keeping his dominant family coal and steel empire under his control, preserving his monopoly. This battle differed, not waged against a committee or a room full of picketers, but a small group of men who, he expected, had no qualms killing him, needing little provocation. The slight hope he held—his private army looked for him, and he'd endure.

Despite spreading numbness, he found the energy to shift, hoping not to be noticed. Feeling hot, burning pricks of what seemed like massive needles probed deep into his hips and thighs. His interrogator leaned close, exposing the edges of a toupee along his forehead. Before a word came from his lips, Hamilton struck with the only weapon he had. Drawing on fast-disappearing strength, he lunged forward, head-butting Mudge, landing a blow to his mouth and nose, bringing a gush of blood and screams.

A third person in the room stepped close, smashing a thick phone book against Hamilton's jaw, knocking him and his chair to the ground. Twisting and turning his head, he bounced on the wood floor. Seconds before passing out, Hamilton spotted his scuffed brown loafers near his face.

Charlotte Brontë's words flickered in his waning mind, "There's little joy in life and little terror in the grave."

He'd beaten his captors.

CHAPTER TWELVE

Gustain watched the taxi pull into traffic, disappearing among cars and yellow cabs splashing up and down Highland Avenue. A few miles east, the historic Potomac River separated Arlington, Virginia, from the District of Columbia. Its low, sprawling skyline, abundant with shrines and memorials, did little for Gustain's bitterness. Mighty American authority suppressed his weakened homeland following the war, failing to relieve Germany of prolonged stagnation.

The recent message from Doctor Strughold brought concern and clear signs of trouble, forcing a delay in his California trip. Hubert Strughold had something important that he could not say within the walls of the CIA office or their homes. Very few times had the prominent doctor summoned him.

Gustain Hilger slipped on a thick raincoat, and fedora kept on a hat rack near the entry. The torrential downpour slowed to a bone-chilling drizzle while afternoon daylight faded, leaving a foggy, grayish sky. Barren oaks and maples lined Highland Avenue, overhanging the cracked and potholed street. Neighboring German Shepherds jumped against a sagging wire pen, barking at passing cars. Cold, damp air relieved him of a headache that started during Dulles's meeting.

Neglected homes and dirt-patched yards could be mistaken for a war-devastated Berlin. He survived at the cost of what he became. No longer an innocent fatality of a Nazi fighting machine, but a cog in its brutality.

American and British bombs had rendered his home unrecognizable, and the desire to return left him. He'd become a man without a country. Cherished memories of family and youth remained embedded in his mind.

His destination, meeting Strughold, reinforced the consequences of warfare. Gustain crossed at a flashing yellow light, dodging splashing cars, hurrying to get somewhere they'd been before. Washington, DC, housed the world's most influential individuals. The very dominant derived power from creating and planning wars. His boss, Allen Dulles, no exception. For that reason, he and his friend, Hubert Strughold, met.

Arlington National Cemetery appeared in the shifting haze. Gustain gripped the wide brim of his hat and picked up the pace as the rain increased. Well-developed muscle memory rose from youth training, resurrecting one or two strides of the German ceremonial goose step. Entering from the north yielded a panoramic view of the thousands of white headstones filling 624 acres.

Rushing along a wide stone pathway, Gustain questioned how many soldiers he placed there. A knack for disguises and accents allowed him to penetrate the allies' fortified areas. His bombs, planted in enemy military quarters, kept fighting men from entering battles fought on his homeland's western front.

Unlike low-flying bombers, his work is silent and strategic. He fought as a soldier, in contrast to the many Nazis who waged war against unarmed captives. Eight years sped by, and he found himself as a mercenary for an enemy.

In quiet moments and sleep, images flashed in his mind—unknown men standing over him, placing probes against his shaved skull, others injecting fluids into both arms.

At the top of a small knoll, his destination appeared—the tall mast of a salvaged American battleship, *The Maine*. Gustain continued at a steady pace, not wishing to call attention to himself, expecting to see his ally, Doctor Strughold, pacing. Despite their friendship, Gustain disliked delaying his California mission.

The doctor understood the urgency requiring the quiet termination of four Americans. Strughold held responsibility, yet avoided Dulles's wrath. His attempt to interrupt and delay the "off-the-book assignment" brought concern.

The Tomb of the Unknown Soldier appeared deserted as the drizzle turned into a relentless downpour, nothing like the days-long rainstorms encountered fighting along the western front. The Tomb's hilltop area offered no cover from the storm as the Army guard maintained his precise twenty-one-step march behind the Tomb rain or shine, day and night. Doctor Strughold would expect him at their designated meeting spot—any variance signaled the plan compromised.

To the north, dirty low clouds shrouded Washington's monuments and dozens of what he dismissed as unneeded government buildings. Power brokers lurked behind cement and brick walls, waging wars, defining lives and countries. DC and New York's United Nations stood on shaky ground, as a front for the dominant forces of the United States. Real control stopped and started at Pennsylvania Avenue—the White House. Eisenhower and Congress credited the CIA for penetrating the German high command and inducing peaceful defection of their top scientists. Gustain knew differently. Following the war, Allen Dulles used the CIA to wield strong-arm control over Germany and communist Russia. Dulles's spy network and assassins moved silently throughout the world, manipulating world leaders. World War II ended a bloody shooting war, and soon after, the Cold War erupted with its high stakes, further elevating Dulles.

Former allies shifted roles. New combatants played the game of espionage—a chess match of strategic moves. To many, the end came, leaving governments collapsed. Battlefields of Western Europe remained free of bombs and dead soldiers. In this war, men wearing coats and ties lost their lives.

Gustain reflected on his futile years at Oxford interpreting Yeats. "I know I shall meet my fate, somewhere among the clouds above. Those that I fight I do not hate. Those that I guard I do not love."

As a student, those words held modest meanings. Should he be fortunate enough to have a headstone, Yeats's prophetic verses would speak his epithet, chiseled in granite marking his resting spot. He was in too deep to retreat. Dulles would not allow it. Another agent, like himself, would see to it.

Something big loomed and required hiding. Inside fortresses like the Pentagon or CIA, nothing remained confidential. He'd learned zero specifics from those within the walls living their lives in top-secret meetings. Instead, his instinct read faces and unsaid words. As an outsider, a contractor, he had no visible or official part of the spy organization. No identification card or record connected him to the CIA. No bailout if captured—only denial. Dulles's men shunned him. If closeness among agents existed in the cold and sterile agency, it lay buried under layers of practiced indifference. Superficial courtesy smiles and nods passed if eyes met. Most ate breakfast, lunch and dinner hunched over reams of paper or grainy photographs searching for tail-tail signs of Russian plans against America and its allies. Gustain would stay an outcast, resisting conformity. Paisley, no-iron shirts hid a Beretta 9 millimeter but clashed with the CIA's Ivy League basic button-down white oxfords.

Water dripped from the brim of Gustain's hat. Chilled and wet, he could not fault his only friend. Strughold kept him waiting—there had to be a reasonable explanation. His ally could be injured or detained. His flight to Los Angeles missed. The warm weather could wait one more day.

Down the slope, a hundred yards, he estimated, three black umbrellas popped from a red idling cab and traveled as one in a straight line through thin ground fog to a group of gravestones. In a moment, thick, wet evergreens blocked Gustain's view of the mourners. They appeared to be searching for an interned family member. Gustain glanced again, finding only two umbrellas bobbing above lush green shrubs. The other lay open on the soggy grass.

"Enjoying the day?" a voice asked from behind.

Gustain didn't turn, answering the expected voice. "I should be in California."

"It'll be there tomorrow."

Gustain tipped the brim of his rain-soaked hat. "Why are we standing outside like naughty children?"

Doctor Strughold pointed to the expressionless soldier marching in perfectly measured steps guarding The Tomb. "Like him, we must also believe in our mission."

Gustain nodded, turned, and stepped close to his friend. "I served my homeland with honor."

"As I hope you continue to do, unlike Dulles, who has killed so many with a nod of his head, from the safety of a conference room."

"Where I stand, I have no choice," Gustain said, glancing over his shoulder at the three umbrellas.

"The vital work for our new Germany is elsewhere, not known to Dulles. The lab near San Diego is a diversion."

He heard Strughold admit to treason.

Gustain had little knowledge of the CIA's covert operation but enough to carry out his job—cleaning up, whitewashing failures. Who did Dulles have on standby to take care of him when he failed? Someone outside the agency, he suspected. The FBI? Hoover couldn't be trusted. DC worked that way. The powerful insulated themselves with layers of subordinates. What would his friend ask that would endanger his life? There would be no nameless star on the CIA wall for him. More likely an unmarked grave in a frigid sea.

"Doctor Falk is one of the people you're looking for," Strughold said.

"Orders from Dulles. You were there this morning. You brought this on."

"Dulles does not know what's going on with Jacob's Ladder."

"Nor do I," Gustain said. "I have a job to do."

Gustain sensed what came next. Doctor Strughold, his thinning white hair plastered to his scalp, stood there in somber dignity, knowing what he had asked sentenced Gustain to death. He'd ask regardless. The man lived a life of moral failures; he evaded his Nazi past and the countless tortures performed in the name of science.

"Falk is part of a larger plan that will return our leaders and Germany to us," Strughold said.

Despite professional friendship, Gustain knew the doctor kept secrets well beyond what he'd learned in this morning's meeting of a program called Jacob's Ladder, extending lives of the dying. There was something more, much more, than they had told him. Killing innocent women was not a part of his job, especially Lenora's companion. He'd taken an interest in the attractive and athletic-looking lady identified as Birdie Kelley in the intelligence photographs.

"It would help if I knew more," Gustain said, knowing an answer would not come.

"I must keep that secret."

"When I locate your Doctor Falk, what do I do?"

"Do not find him," Strughold said. "He will soon have a new name and passport in Argentina. Dulles will believe you took care of him."

Gustain knew of the thousands of Argentine passports Juan Peron sold through the Red Cross and the reigning Catholic Pope to escaping Nazis, allowing them to flee Germany with plundered riches before the war's end.

He had almost forgotten the gravesite visitors. They retreated and neared the idling cab, one of the trio yanked wires from an umbrella; another slid a narrow black box under a raincoat.

Strughold's back remained to the three. Gustain saw no reason to call this to his attention. He hadn't seen their faces. Whoever they were, they were not mourners.

The cab pulled away. If Gustain were not on foot, he'd have followed the men interested in their conversation.

Had it been a test? Strughold asked for an order to be disobeyed—allow Faulk to escape while he eliminated innocent people. Were the eavesdroppers there because his friend gave them the location?

Nonstop rain fell harder, striking marble pavement with a dull plopping. The honor guard remained at his post, striding in perfect rhythm, each step unchanged, reminding Gustain of unquestioned duty.

Without a handshake or goodbye, Strughold strode off.

Gustain stood alone, speculating. Had his friend conspired with the grave visitors, or had Dulles discovered their secret rendezvous?

Although not committed to Strughold's scheme, Dulles would suppose the worst and have him shot as a traitor or deported.

He'd know soon enough. Survival in the bloody war zones of Europe and Germany had served him well. His nose suspected something. Battlefield instinct would keep him alive.

Long-dormant oak leaves dropped in a flurry. In a storm, a single leaf never fell by itself; it brought down others.

Nor would he fall alone—once he learned Strughold's secret.

CHAPTER THIRTEEN

Birdie slipped away, leaving Lenora to explore Hamilton Jaminson's hotel suite. She doubted her client would conduct an effective search, but the distraction allowed an opportunity to return to the lounge and begin her investigation.

Speculation is all she had. Hotel bars, like watering holes, drew hunter and game. Less than twenty-four hours into the hunt and without a single clue, her mind remained open to the chance Jaminson contacted someone in the bar.

The crowded elevator opened, allowing Birdie to escape the Stetson-wearing cigar smoker who pressed against her since shoving his way in. As expected, the watering hole came to life with a white-tuxedoed piano player bouncing a jazz tune, Birdie, to her surprise, did not recognize. For a short time, she lost touch with the world, except music, she'd prided herself on remaining current with new and old. This perplexing melody carrying a smooth, swaying rhythm escaped her. Should a Sinatra song happen, she'd join in, forcing between those gathered at the oversized grand piano.

Birdie had swapped her leather over-the-shoulder work purse for a tan handbag, with enough room for walking around money, a photo of her client's ex-husband, and a trusty .38. Self-conscious, she couldn't remember the last occasion she'd worn a dress. The simple blue sheath fit snug, falling at mid-calf. It had been too many years since Saint Lucy's narrow-minded nuns shook disapproving heads at her short, pleated skirt. Catching a glimpse of herself in the bar's mirror, she pulled in her tummy.

She belonged—an LA girl looking for a good time.

If Hamilton spent so much as a minute in the expensive watering hole, she'd learn who he spent it with. If needed, she'd toss around her client's cash, buying information—reminding herself she raced against Jaminson's captors and a private army she wished not to meet.

She'd bet her two-year-old PI license Hamilton's liberal drinking habits led him to the upscale cocktail lounge. A good deal of his personal background came from Lenora during the long flight, but Birdie suspected he'd kept secrets, like any man. Pressure and stress needed releasing and what better place to blow off steam than The City of Angels? New York tabloids exposed the steel and coal tycoon's many affairs. Starving starlets walking the streets seeking sugar daddies tilted the tables in Hamilton's favor despite his aging, round, puffy face.

The saloon business, sinning, boozing, and, she guessed, a hidden gambling parlor picked up since earlier. The joint, already crowded, continued to grow with the Hollywood set and shady talent agents and pretenders lingering in the background, snatching at leftovers.

Glances came her way. The room was target-rich for either sex. Birdie let herself take notice, returning smiles of the handsome, hard not to notice, piano player.

She still had it; confidence pumped like adrenalin. Pushing forty, she fit in aided by softened lights and tables glowing with flickering red glassed candles. After her trembling hands smoothed the lines of her dress and a quick dampening of her deep scarlet lips, Birdie entered the minefield humming, feeling like a burlesque queen, teasing the gathered hunters.

Everybody Loves Somebody played as she adorned herself in her best show smile, parading toward the scrutinizing singer, returning his look without staring. She hoped the piano player a fan of Ol' Blue Eyes. On her new stage, she had a convincing role to play if Hamilton Jaminson were to survive.

Using theater skills, immersing in the local crowd came easy. Deep in the corner of her affection-starved libido, she let herself admit she'd welcome the right opportunity. Love the one you're with unseated reason on long, lonely, cold New York nights. Mixing business with pleasure required keeping a level and sober head, with an occasional slip from time to time. She'd take no risks, and drink less while hoping Irish luck of the Kelly clan would be with her.

Birdie strolled, circling, sizing up the crowded, noisy horseshoe bar, deciding to venture away from mister white tux and perfect teeth, sending a signal—she was not easy but worth it.

The woman named Oleta sat at a corner table, a few years past fifty and stunning. Earlier, the bartender mentioned she could be helpful. Before approaching the madam, Birdie intended to continue eyeing the crowd, avoiding Oleta for the moment. Birdie guessed hotel security took its share in hard cash or trade from the elegant lady.

Booths and tables crowded a small, empty dance floor. Gold-vested waiters glided from table to table, keeping cocktail glasses full, cash registers ringing, and drinking patrons satisfied. Despite liquor and smoke, Birdie detected heavy perfumes mixed with powdered war paint and clusters of diamonds attempting to conceal age-revealing necklines.

She had to laugh, knowing no woman to be content with their stage of life.

From the corner of her eye, she spotted the friendly cigar smoker she'd endured on the elevator, stumbling toward her, carrying a drinking glass. Needing a fast escape, Birdie looked to the stretch grand piano—every stool taken and elbow room nonexistent.

A tiny edge of the bench opened once the singer shifted. She continued his direction with a broad smile, trusting the pianist recognized her dilemma. Birdie slipped next to the pianist joining, in a Perry Como tune, *Catch a Falling Star*. To her surprise, the drink carrier followed, placing a wine glass on the piano. He tipped his Stetson and returned to a table of three giggling ladies.

Birdie thanked him with an okay sign. She sat next to what fantasies were made of.

The song finished with a round of applause.

"Time for a break. Did you enjoy?" the piano player asked.

Birdie sipped her white wine and nodded.

"You're not bad. Am I being replaced?" the singer asked.

Birdie felt him slide close and smelled spicy cologne.

Patrons sitting at the piano remained, watching the pianist roll a felt cover over the keys and give it a tap.

"Its the only seat," she answered as she and others watched him, with a dramatic flair, lower the fallboard.

"I'm delighted. And you're not a regular."

She held up her wine glass. "Birdie Kelly. Buy you a drink?"

From behind, she heard a high screech. "Buy a drink? Buy a drink?"

"Friends call me Pello."

"I've interrupted."

"No. Stay!" The pianist commanded.

Birdie turned and spotted the large blue and gold parrot flap its wings.

"Gigi's part of the act," the piano player said. "She'll stay put."

The parrot quieted, raising its colorful wings several more times, and resettled on its wood perch.

"They're social and dislike being alone," Birdie said.

"Same go for you?"

"Depends. Will you join me?" Birdie asked.

"The pleasure is mine. Is there a catch?"

She forced her mind to return to why she was here. It would be easy to play a game of cat and mouse with the gorgeous man she enjoyed sitting next to.

"Could you answer a few small questions?" She made herself say the words, breaking the mood that could have carried over to later tonight. Lenora would soon arrive, cutting off any romantic plans Birdie conjured.

Neither slid apart, and he waved to a waiter. Birdie deliberated if the two had an agreed signal bringing him swooping in, rescuing the charming piano player from admirers he wished to rid himself of.

In a moment, a server balancing a brandy snifter and wine glass on a small oval tray appeared.

Pello took both glasses into his hands, directing her to a sofa. "Its quieter."

How could she let this opportunity pass? He was athletic, trim, and prettier; she hated to admit—hers for the taking, at least tonight. He'd led her to a private, intimate spot, removed from the crowded and noisy bar.

A voice in her head shouted to end the fantasy she'd created. Birdie inched away from her prized catch.

She dropped her handbag to the side. Doing so, the concealed .38 clunked, rattling the glass and chrome table. Pello looked at her with a smile. Birdie slid a photo of Hamilton Jaminson from the offending purse, careful not to expose the pistol. If she hadn't killed the spark between them, the sight of the handgun would force a mood-killing conversation. She didn't give up and remained a lady priding herself on keeping a man's attention. She slid forward on the couch, letting the tapestry fabric draw her dress up her thigh.

"Do you remember seeing this man?

A brief career as a Pinkerton taught her saloon entertainers observed the room they worked. While hands ran up and down the black and whites, their eyes scanned, often recognizing approaching trouble and rushing to a soothing melody, calming hot tempers as Sam often did in Humphrey Bogart's Casablanca bar.

"You a cop? He have a problem?" Pello asked.

"PI from New York and no."

"Why look for him?"

"A friend wants to make sure he's okay."

Pello palmed the snifter, taking a small sip. "He spent time here."

"He mingles with anyone?"

"You referring to Oleta?"

Birdie questioned if her new friend turned coy or looked for money. She reminded herself this was LA; no one was who they appeared in tinsel town.

Pello's ego may have challenged him to force her to earn the information. She didn't wish to push her witness and planned to go easy extracting evidence in small amounts.

She held up the photo again. "This man, did he come here often?"

"Couple times…" Pello sipped from his glass. "Acted like he owned the place,"

"How's that?"

"Nothing particular. He talked to everyone like he was a regular."

"Talk to you?"

"He thought he could sing." Pello nodded to the oversized glass bowl on the piano. "Tipped big." The piano player glanced at his watch a second time. Birdie countered, allowing her skirt to slide higher.

A rush of excitement hit Birdie. Her charms did the job. Pello crossed his legs, sitting back, resting an arm on her thigh.

"Did he spend time with anyone?"

Birdie watched Pello's eyes drift from the photo to his glass but didn't drink. Instead, he shifted the long fingers of his free hand to caress his chin. She had his tell; he looked across the room to the oval bar. A stunning young lady in a sequined dress took a seat alone, stirring a cocktail. The new arrival seized his attention without uttering a word.

Jealousy and resentment prevented Birdie from backing away. She enjoyed the gentleman's company while his soft voice and deep-set blue eyes soothed her. She'd been lonely too long. In Manhattan, she'd preferred drummers, but here she sat with a piano player who sipped brandy without slurping. Who did she kid? She'd lost work focus on a starched white shirt and tuxedo. She'd sit here all evening.

"What's her name?"

"Who?"

"The smart-looking number at the bar."

"She's not a regular."

"You know her. That's obvious."

After a sip, he answered, "She's a singer, Shelley. That's all I know."

"Shelley and the man I'm looking for spent time together?"

"Can't say I noticed."

"You'd tell me if you knew?"

"I play the piano. I'm not a chaperone."

The suddenness of Pello's terse remark deserved a witty retort. Before one came, a surprise arrived.

From the gloom and smoky haze, the parrot entered, wings spread, and claws extended, landing on Pello's shoulder. The bird remained quiet, bowing and bobbing side to side, staring at Birdie.

She got the message, knowing she'd interfered long enough. Pello and the bird gave clear signals they were ready to free themselves of her.

"Excuse me." Birdie slid forward, eased from the couch, and walked to the piano tip jar, dropping two crisp twenty's inside the crystal bowl. She smiled over her shoulder.

"There was a song when I arrived. I never heard it before."

"It's from Brazil, a Bossa Nova, *Menina*."

The parrot screeched, "Play piano. Play piano." Pello appeared prompted by the parrot's command and rose.

Birdie headed toward the night spot's entry and turned, circling, returning to the crowded bar. She'd avoid being seen by her new objective—Shelley sitting at the far end of the bar. As she closed in, she guessed by the way, Shelley's eyes trained on Pello; there might be a link between the two and her client's former husband.

Chances were slim but improving. Shelley connected to Pello and Jaminson. Not solid proof in a court of law, but a lead. Despite the three-deep mob at the bar, Birdie planned to get next to the girl in the sequined gown.

Taking a last look at Pello, she spotted the parrot cuddling the piano player's neck. Across the room, Shelley smiled, watching the two.

CHAPTER FOURTEEN

Conrad puffed, lighting his pipe as he looked down on traffic-clogged San Pedro and Long Beach. He rode in the lead plane, a modified Beechcraft Twin Bonanza, and directed the search. A former British intelligence officer, he understood sophisticated sound equipment. Today the device went into action. His client's life depended on it.

"We must be within five miles of Jaminson's transmitter," Conrad said into his headset.

"That covers a lot of real estate," the white-shirted pilot answered.

"He's down there. We will work until we find him," Conrad shouted to his colleague, operating multiple radio receivers.

Specially outfitted private planes flew above Southern California, widening search radiuses with each pass. Both carried identical equipment and technicians. Conrad referred to the Russian directional antenna and listening device as "The Thing" from the time of its accidental discovery inside Britain's Moscow embassy. For years Nikita Khrushchev and Kremlin spies eavesdropped, learning Great Britain's secrets.

As director of security, its finding brought disgrace, forcing him to step down as an MI agent.

The signal he and his team listened for would come from a miniature device requiring no batteries or electrical circuits, yet created modulations generated by a diaphragm and tuning post transmitting a radio frequency. The source of its power and simplicity came from sound pressure against a sensitive metal diaphragm producing energy from sound waves.

Sound vibrations captured by nearly invisible holes within the hollow heels of Jaminson's shoes struck a miniature diaphragm and tuning post, making modulations. From high in the LA sky, Conrad's crew broadcast a powerful radio frequency searching for the faint shoe modulations. Once detected, the stronger frequency would carry them to the search team.

The Beechcraft cruised at 200 miles per hour while expanding its coverage. Airports presented problems, restricting air travel. Cars, carrying the same scanning equipment, covered Southern California's no-fly zones.

Conrad peeked out the square window. In the distance, over the hazy Pacific, the second Beechcraft banked to join the non-stop dragnet.

Once the planes triangulated Jaminson's signal, the ground team, former Israeli commandos, planned to deploy from two vans equipped to fight a small war. C3 explosives, Uzi submachine guns, shotguns and sniper rifles filled their shelves.

Conrad examined his road and aviation maps pinned to a makeshift desk. Red and blue circles marked flying and ground routes to be checked off when completed. To avoid suspicion, each Beechcraft towed a long, trailing copper mesh receiving antenna, disguised as a banner imploring Angelinos to, "DRIVE SAFE."

With no time to spare, Conrad, against better judgment, planned risky low-altitude night flying. In the back of his mind, he considered the possibility of Jaminson testing his army's effectiveness.

Conrad tolerated his client's quirky habits and occasional aloofness. He worked behind the backs of Jaminson's hierarchy of bankers and lawyers—an arrangement he liked. A little-known private bank in Western Pennsylvania honored Conrad's inflated invoices and expenses.

After a visual check of ground coordinates, the convoy of Beechcraft completed several tight loops of Long Beach and the San Pedro Peninsula. Conrad detected occasional errant signals from cargo ships and fishing boats in the vast port and sardine canning area. Thick steel-hulled ships provided excellent locations to conceal their client, one he had no answer for.

A few hours into the search, Conrad rechecked his amplifier and pressed the headphones tight to his ears. He hated small planes, hoping the sudden turbulence didn't bring air sickness or worse, a county sheriff's helicopter.

When they picked up Jaminson's signal, he preferred a daytime attack in isolated locations, as in the rugged mountains surrounding the Southern California basin. A night mission places the client at greater risk and is used as a last resort. Jaminson had rehearsed his job, securing himself against the all-out assault for thirty seconds. The initial attack called for automatic weapons and explosives.

The mission belonged to Conrad. No one would override or debate procedures. This operation remained his call. Negotiations—out of the question. This military rescue, with luck, brought a live escape of Jaminson and allowed no witnesses.

Collateral damages be damned.

The pilot turned back to Conrad. "Your man in the hotel bar spotted someone looking for Jaminson—a woman PI and his ex-wife."

Conrad re-lit his pipe. "Have Tex break into their room. Scare them off but, do not harm them. Not a hair."

The pilot clicked off and hung the mike in the slot while he turned back to Conrad. "What makes you think he'll follow orders this time?"

"What makes you think I care?"

"Our last job, the woman and kid, were defenseless," the pilot answered.

"Coup de Grace," Conrad said. "A blow of mercy. We gave them a fast death."

"Killing two women for this rescue is crazy," the pilot said.

CHAPTER FIFTEEN

Birdie weaved, excusing and forcing her way through the bar crowd, hoping Shelley and her blue sequined dress stayed put at the busy bar. Irish luck showed promise in Los Angeles, an improvement from New York. Could it be she lived on the wrong coast?

The group thickened between her and her target. A single-stemmed glass of champagne sat at the waiter's pickup station. If she needed a drink, it was now. She grabbed it, taking several swallows. Carrying the glass above her head, she continued to squirm through the boisterous mob of men in well-cut suits.

Shelley remained alone, stirring a tall cocktail. Birdie persisted, confident she'd not attracted Shelley's attention. Birdie faced a cluster of Roman columns, wrapped in mirrors, obstructing her view. Multiple reflections came at her, disturbing her balance. It may have been the bubbly wine. Slight panic set in, activating Birdie's hunter instincts. The last few steps she found blocked and pushed her shoulder between two men's chests.

A half-full cocktail glass, resting on a folded paper napkin, was all that remained of Shelley. A conspicuous red lipstick kiss branded it, while a used book of matches balanced on the edge of an ashtray.

Shelley had vanished.

Birdie glanced at the piano bar. Pello sang and played a tune; she again failed to place. Should she call it a night? She lost her musical ear, not recognizing two songs, and misplaced Shelley in a room full of men. Three for three, a strikeout in any league.

Pello had been watching her. There was no question a connection existed between the handsome musician and the mystery woman in the sequined outfit. Something else about the piano player troubled her—the abrupt shift in his tone and attitude with Shelley's appearance.

"Help you?" a voice asked.

Birdie jumped at the intrusion.

"No... yes." She turned to the bartender. "A lady wearing a blue dress sat here. See where she went?"

"Sorry, we're busy."

"That song playing," Birdie asked, "know it?"

"*Gone*, he likes it. The Drifters were just starting."

Birdie looked at the piano player. He smiled and continued to sing—taunting her failure? It worked. Despite the snug-fitting dress, she swung herself up to the tall stool and sat looking over the filled nightspot.

She'd held the glass of bubbly, raising it, and grinned, offering a toast not knowing why, flinching at the notion she'd felt jilted coming in third, losing to whatever had gone on with the curious parrot and the attractive girl at the bar.

Birdie found herself in an awkward spot—scrutinized by a jealous parrot and Pello. Exhaustion and trials of a long day hit, and no energy remained to give chase. She'd traveled three thousand miles, and it felt as if she'd walked every inch.

Missing person cases presented challenges brought by client emotions. She'd weathered many during years as a Pinkerton. Nothing came easy dealing with a smart criminal. Judging by what occurred within the past twenty-four hours, this search smelled like trouble. A strong hunch told her someone in the room took an interest in her. Birdie looked for the heavyset, Stetson-wearing, cigar smoker. If he remained, she'd misplaced him, making her four for four.

The sip of pilfered campaign tasted bitter. Birdie guessed the adrenaline flowing in her smothered the flavor. Sitting alone is all she desires. The man in the Stetson had forgotten, and she convinced herself he posed no threat. She'd sit at the bar, hibernate, and wrap a cocoon around herself. Adjacent stools were full, and their occupants engaged in movie talk and auditions.

Pello looked her way with the start and finish of each tune. Did he watch her, or had he sent a signal? Either way, she didn't plan on coming between him and the aggressive, protective parrot.

A big spender like Jaminson attracts good and bad attention, commanding presence in a room feeds their ego. Birdie counted her mission a minor success. She'd uncovered two people at the watering hole Jaminson had known.

An everyday working man boasted of near success after a few drinks. Powerful men like Jaminson accomplished what others failed at—and their unchecked egos bragged. In both cases, men told secrets to beautiful ladies. In the movie capital, plenty of that went around. Birdie reminded herself that no one in Hollywood is real. Their world relies on image and make-believe.

About to seek out the bar's madam, Birdie pictured the stylishly dressed lady as a scornful Madame Bovary who escaped from reality, living an empty life selling her flesh. Birdie looked at herself, how satisfied had she been, no family or likelihood of romance, sitting alone. Would it be too much to imagine somebody taking an interest in her?

A tap on her shoulder came without warning. Lenora smiled, wedging between Birdie and the occupied stool next to her. Her client, still in form-flattering jodhpurs from early this morning, appeared refreshed and energized.

Pangs of guilt smacked Birdie. She'd left her client alone, searching Hamilton's suite. If Lenora harbored hurt feelings, she covered them.

"I went through the room three times," Lenora said.

"Anything?" Birdie asked.

"He left his best clothes."

"Probably planned to return."

Lenora grabbed Birdie's glass and took a long drink.

Pello and Gigi watched. Birdie caught them and didn't know which of the two she should be more concerned with. She accepted parrots and their social nature—she wasn't sure how hazardous handsome piano players in tuxedos were.

Lenora waved a twenty-dollar bill, catching the busy barman's attention, and moments later, two bottles of champagne appeared.

After a sip, Lenora nudged Birdie. "That gorgeous singer noticed you."

"He's already taken."

"Honey, he keeps looking at you."

Birdie laughed. "Tell you later."

The dark-suited man next to them stood and offered Lenora his stool, which she accepted after she'd poked his ribs and pressed her thigh against him.

"This is Hamilton's kind of place. I smell old money chasing new starlets and top-shelf booze," Lenora said, gazing at the piano player.

"Sure is," Birdie said and drained her glass.

"Besides Mister Lovely, any luck?"

"Hamilton spent some time with a young lady."

"What else is new?" Lenora said, refilling her drink.

"She sat here. I fought my way to this spot and missed her—she vanished in this mob."

"She may be a regular," Lenora said. "We'll come back tomorrow."

After pushing from the bar and about to leave, Birdie stopped. She returned to her stool and gripped her bottle of Champaign. Taking a second look, she grabbed the pack of matches resting near the cocktail napkin.

Raised red letters, imprinted over twin crossed palm trees, covered the front flap—The Congo Club

"We got her," Birdie said.

* * * *

From the Beverly Hilton's lobby, they heard the soothing tones of the piano. Birdie pictured the red and green parrot flapping its long wings, weaving side to side, like a prizefighter at the start of a match, defining its territory. She feared the images would return to haunt her dreams if she found time for sleep. She'd discovered nothing substantial, only a strong suspicion and questions, the rocky beginning of a trail.

The husky desk attendant identified The Congo Club to be a favorite nightspot for an older crowd, preferring top-end drinks, light jazz and friendly cocktail waitresses. The clerk turned the matchbook over, pointing out the address on Sunset Boulevard.

Lenore looked at Birdie. "You had your fun. Now it's my turn. Want to go?"

The Yellow Cab pulled near the hotel's well-lit entry. Before the valet swung open the rear door, Birdie jumped into the front seat, giving the driver the address, 9009 Sunset Boulevard. After a tip to the doorman, Lenora took a seat in the rear.

"Ladies looking for a good time?" the cabbie asked.

"Will we find it at The Congo Club?" Birdie asked.

"Tame, but first-rate Brazilian jazz," he answered as they pulled from the hotel.

"Then we'll make our own," Lenora answered the driver.

Traffic moved slowly along clogged Santa Monica Boulevard until they'd reached Sierra, heading north to Sunset. It approached ten o'clock, and Birdie hoped the lounge remained lively, and the vanishing girl in the glitter dress made an appearance.

She played a long shot. Anyone could have left the book of matches. Pello said Shelley was a singer, and why else wear a sequined gown? If she was talented enough to vanish and avoid Birdie, she couldn't be that careless, leaving behind her work address. If what the hotel desk clerk said were true, they looked forward to great jazz, excellent booze, and a slower environment. It wasn't a warm bed, but a sexy, smooth saxophone came close.

The moment they entered Sunset, Birdie spotted a long line of clubs, jitterbug to ballroom, all going strong, judging by partygoers lining both sidewalks. Traffic crawled, taking in Hollywood sights, eager to spot a movie star. Birdie hoped to see her idol, Tony Curtis.

In the next block, the cab pulled to the curb near a bail bond office. Its orange fluttering neon sign lit a queue of parked taxis.

The jazz club's marquee resembled the book of matches. A pair of crossed palm trees rose from behind a flashing red sign—The Congo Club.

"What do we have to lose?" Lenora said, paying the driver.

"Long as there are no parrots," Birdie answered.

With no waiting line, the two entered.

CHAPTER SIXTEEN

Gustain Hilger placed his luggage and fedora above his seat and settled in as the plane's twin engines rumbled to life. Take off only a few minutes away; he pushed a pillow into place, hoping to sleep. Twenty-five thousand pounds would lift and climb into a clean sky, escaping the filth below, freeing him from what life trapped him in.

Did he, a German farm boy, evolve as a product of his country's war machine? Over and over, conflicting memories surfaced as momentary flashes pushed away the chaos of the life he led. He didn't fit with what his mind told him. Blind to killing and misery, he found no gratification. Pleasure came from executing a well-planned hunt—a significant distinction. Death was man's fate. He took the mystery out of the eternal question—when.

The Allies and the British inflicted heavy casualties on helpless German women and children left to manage farms, longing for their husbands' and fathers' return. They had forced him into war after watching his mother and sister burn to death, following a bombing raid.

A foot soldier at eighteen, he craved the front line. Death waited to claim him; he had nothing to lose. Fighting not for Hitler or fondness of motherland, but to hunt and murder. As an officer, he'd advanced to the elite Waffen-SS combat unit assigned to the bloody eastern front. Fighting despised Russians. Gustain preferred death to capture.

His unique abilities to kill in silence bailed Dulles from many difficult situations and had become leverage. An end to what newspapers termed the Cold War would make him obsolete.

Hubert Strughold, his friend, kept secrets, but rarely from him. The doctor's request to spare Falk's life, disobeying Dulles's command, disturbed him. Their pasts buried in the CIA's classified "paper clip project" bonded them, hiding them in America, protecting them—their secret files locked in a vault accessible only by Dulles.

Since their meeting at Arlington, Gustain recognized this cleanup, altered his relationship with Strughold. What his friend requested risked their lives, pitting them against one another.

The CIA provided reliable intelligence on Lenora Jaminson and Birdie Kelly, putting the two women in his sights—sitting ducks waiting for disposal. Falk and his captive Hamilton Jamison posed a challenge. Falk had deceived Dulles, exposing secret government programs, and lived on the run in Los Angeles until he could escape to South America. Fugitives slip up or tire of the chase, yielding capture or death by their hand. In this circumstance, Gustain remained positive Strughold continued to inform Falk of the agency's discoveries and ongoing search.

Strughold and Falk, jointly complicit, betrayed Dulles and had panicked, kidnapping Jaminson. The CIA spared Strughold from fault, protecting him as vital to the American space race against the Russians. Dulles concealed Strughold's involvement and offered Falk as a blood sacrifice, not to American justice, but to a hired gun.

Medicine and human hibernation consumed the two researchers. As far as Gustain knew, neither fired a gun during the war. The two lacked tactical and field experience, making both trouble-free targets. Cleaning up the two's mess would not be compromised by wartime friendship.

Dulles laid the assignment out, unlike in the past, pinpointing the Southern California targets. The job appeared to be an easy mission, perhaps too clear-cut. He hunted a pampered capitalist, a helpless doctor, and two unsuspecting women. Falk, a war criminal, protected by the CIA, double-crossed Dulles selling top-secret research to Jaminson. Gustain was in the middle, unsure of who he trusted.

Gustain considered taking his targets quietly, with no guns. He'd become rusty, relying on explosives and long-range rifles. Close-up kills allowed encountering death, holding life in his hands, determining its finish, experience life exiting victims, deciding finality. Each furnished a unique rush of energy, clutching their bodies, feeling momentary resistance, and then none.

The wheels of the DC-3 bounced, touching the ground in Los Angeles. Outside his window, a rainstorm pounded the runway. No one greeted him at the gate. He worked alone. Gustain intended to blend in. The sudden squall spoiled his scheduled tour of Marilyn Monroe's Hollywood home.

He'd track Birdie and Lenora, hoping with a day's head-start, they'd lead him to the others. He planned to dispose of the victims within a week, along with the mysterious lab Strughold wanted spared.

There would be no schedule to rush him into forced errors. Time remained on his side. Besides, he was curious to learn the secret work Strughold kept from Dulles.

Gustain directed the taxi to the Beverly Hilton and slid into the rear seat. The sour smell and cigar smoke reminded him of a South American flophouse. Gustain opened the back windows, enjoying the blowing air and mist against his face.

He preferred traveling without reservations and used a bogus government ID. Any room would suffice. Dulles's men did their jobs, tracking the two ladies, making his job simpler. Completing the assignment became his to execute with his full control. The CIA kept its hands clean, remaining out of illegal actions against American citizens.

Doctor Strughold's interference continued to puzzle him. The unexpected meeting at the tomb in Arlington, along with the three suspicious umbrellas visiting a section of graves, reeked of sloppy agency surveillance. The sharp, gabled headstones the iffy visitors huddled over housed bodies of unknown Confederate soldiers.

Had he walked into a setup? Had Dulles no longer needed or trusted him?

CHAPTER SEVENTEEN

Hamilton Jaminson's face pressed against the wood floor, inches from his last remaining chance to survive. Tiny holes molded into his shoe's heels accessed the small chamber gathering and sending audio signals to his covert search team of mercenaries. His circular prison grew to become his chief tormentor, allowing glimpses of freedom, although his legs were no longer capable of escape.

Unconsciousness arrived and departed, seemingly at its pleasure. Time in captivity became indiscernible. Fast, dulling senses told him they had kept him in a tall building—not conventional apartments and offices. No sounds passed through adjacent walls or ceilings. In rare, diminishing lucid moments, he speculated being perched in a tower. Other times, he'd heard an elevator operating nearby.

A tip of a well-polished shoe nudged his ribs.

"Mister Jaminson, who knew your plans?"

Twisting his head, the familiar winged-tipped shoe stepped near his prone face. His throat and mouth parched. How long had it been? It remained vital he spoke, generating sound. Vocal cords had grown faint and feeble. Gasps escaped cracked lips, he hoped enough to register movement on the diaphragm buried within his shoes. Forcing his oppressors into an interrogation, bringing stronger sound waves, involved his resistance, yielding painful blows and kicks while shouted questions came. Hamilton Jaminson gathered remaining energy and, with a quick snap, head-butted the leg belonging to the shiny wingtips.

"That's the way it's gonna be?" a voice asked.

The next moment, he and the chair lifted upright. A thick telephone book banged the side of his face, snapping his head back. Hamilton caught a view of his shoes, hoping they transmitted.

Another shouted, repeating the question. "Who knew your plans?"

Hamilton forced garbled words between his teeth. His jaw was possibly dislocated from the fall or the recent bashing.

Water. How long had it been? Despite severe ringing in his ears, Hamilton detected the roar of a plane circling. From reflex and nothing else, he swung his head in another show of resistance, contrary to what a captive is to do, provoking and antagonizing his tormentor. The phone book remained on the table, and more shouted threats followed. He'd stretched their patience, achieving the small victory necessary to keep his sanity and will to live.

If he'd attracted his rescuers, he won.

"We do not wish to harm you," a voice said.

Hamilton guessed it to be Mudge, the interrogator.

"Your pain is unnecessary," Mudge said. "Who else is involved in your plans?"

"No...body." Jaminson forced out.

"The truth, and we will let you go," Mudge whispered, "We won't be found." We will not kill you. It is that simple."

"I saw it," Hamilton mouthed.

Mudge smiled. "Saw what?"

"Strughold showed me."

"Noah?"

Hamilton gave a painful smile.

"We are not criminals, Mister Jaminson," Mudge said.

This time Hamilton forced a nod.

"We wish to make the world better."

CHAPTER EIGHTEEN

"Dark and cozy," Leonora said, whispering as she limped, entering the jazz club.

Birdie guided her client past small cocktail tables cluttered with overflowing ashtrays and empty glasses. Soft lights, hidden behind shell wall sconces, bordered the room with a warm glow. Near a rear door and an out-of-order cigarette machine, a booth showed itself, and the two slipped in.

"Looks like they're on break," Birdie said.

Lenora pushed a red candle holder next to a scarred and chipped brick wall. "Quiet night, I guess."

A black-shirted server appeared and leaned over the table.

He smiled, pointing toward the bar. "Two gentlemen wish to buy."

"Welcome to Hollywood," Lenora said while waving both arms. "No, thank you." Her voice carried across the room.

"Good call," the waiter said. "Couple of second-rate actors."

"Your best white wine," Lenora ordered.

Birdie preferred a double shot of strong Irish whiskey after the strain of the rushed day but went along with Lenora. Breakfast in Manhattan and late dinner drinks in Hollywood. This is not how she'd planned to sulk her day away in self-pity, as an out-of-work PI with little prospects. Her challenge had been to dress for a cold walk in Central Park.

Opportunity sauntered through her door—bonanza gold, a wealthy socialite, searching for her ex-husband. A change of fortune had brought her to a Hollywood jazz club, steered by a book of matches discovered in a hotel bar. She'd followed the trail, like breadcrumbs, desperate for any lead. Locating Shelley and her hard-to-miss glitter dress perhaps led to Jaminson. Birdie wagered to herself; he would not be far behind.

House lights dimmed below what Birdie considered dark, exposing miniature rows of stage lights rimming the returning musicians. A few hands applauded as a saxophone's sweet notes crooned, filling the nightspot, blocking out Birdie's concerns. She permitted herself to be lulled by the soothing melody—at least pretending to be.

The distant freight train's rich, comforting horn bellowed as she relived a cherished childhood memory. She laid on the cooling blanket of green grass—her grandmother's New Jersey farm, a fortress safeguarding her from her stepfather. The solitary howl of a locomotive's whistle lingered, serenading. Birdie's dream had come true, she'd traveled west to palm trees, movie stars and sidewalks lined with rows of oranges and lemon trees.

The saxophone played. Jolting Birdie to reality.

Behind the drummer, a gold curtain separated. Stepping into the spotlight, a young woman appeared and dabbed a cigarette into a whiskey glass. She stepped to a stage microphone.

The vanishing lady in the sequined dress resurfaced.

"That's our girl!"

"You're sure?" Lenora asked.

"Hamilton spent time with her, according to our hotel piano player," Birdie answered.

Lenora sipped her wine, gazing at the singer, and said, "I don't believe my own eyes."

"She may know something," Birdie said.

"What now?"

"Wait. Next break—we talk to her."

"What did you say her name is?"

"Shelley."

"South America... maybe Argentine," Lenora said. "But, I'm guessing."

"She's beautiful."

"They all are, believe me. Good Spanish and Italian blood," Lenora said.

"You were there?"

"Hamilton and I. He met investors planning to make steel in Buenos Aires," Lenora said. "Told me he met former German military officers."

"Like who?"

"Wouldn't say, but Shelley...no never mind."

"What?" Birdie asked. "What were you about to say?"

"I'm tired. It's my imagination."

Birdie gripped Lenora's arm. "Say it. It may help."

"I may have heard Shelley sing before."

"Where?"

"Some swanky jazz bar in Buenos Aires."

"You're sure?"

Lenora took a long sip of wine and pointed the empty glass to the singer. "The song caused me to remember."

"*Fly Me to the Moon*," Birdie asked.

"A year ago," Lenora said, "I sat at the bar alone while Hamilton met with three men. Shelley joined them."

"That's when you saw her?"

"That's all Hamilton talked about, her voice and the Germans he'd met."

"And she shows up at his hotel in Hollywood."

"Some luck," Lenora said, filling her glass.

Birdie recalled the steady eye contact between the beautiful singer and Pello at their hotel bar earlier that evening. There was a connection between the two, perhaps not romance—he'd stiffened, becoming noticeably less cordial after noticing her arrive at the bar. Did Shelley summon the parrot's sudden arrival on the pianist's shoulder, stifling Birdie's questioning? She glanced down at the table. Next to an oval ashtray laid a new book of Congo Club matches—identical to the one found left behind at the Beverly Hills Hilton hotel bar. The colorful matchbook appeared after they arrived at the jazz club booth. Birdie guessed it had been delivered by their waiter.

Coincidence? She considered it for a moment, refusing to accept the long odds. Instead, the realization slammed home, someone had lured them.

Birdie excused herself for the lady's room. Before pushing open the tall door resembling a piano keyboard, she paused and turned back to the club floor. Her eyes adjusted to the dimness but didn't pick up anyone watching. The smoke, whiskey, and mellow music may have dulled her sharp senses. Nothing appeared out of the ordinary, and that bothered her.

Couples sat snug next to one another while solitary drinkers stooped over their night's companions, nursing mind-numbing whiskeys. The two gentlemen she and Lenora encountered found ladies and sat laughing in a far corner, unaware of the singer. Upturned champagne bottles rested inside a pair of silver top hats near an over-sized booth. Its sole occupant slept—face plastered on the tabletop. If they had been followed, she'd missed the tail—no apparent signs of a trap. The question remained, what did Shelley intend—bringing her and Lenora here?

From Birdie's position, she observed the entire room. What motive had there been for deception? Could someone have confused her with someone else? Did she and Lenora walk into something beyond a search for a missing person? Did Pello and Shelley expect her and Lenora? How did they know the two would show up? Unanswered questions flew at her despite jet lag and far too much wine. Had the men posing as Western Union messengers wielded badges or used typical New Jersey muscle to learn the flight plan of Lenora's plane? It had been a hunch added to a growing list of uncertainties.

Birdie favored working solo, at her own pace, and sought to question the tall, gorgeous singer alone. Her client's emotional attachment would affect the dynamics of her interrogation. Above all, Birdie's nagging personal doubt traveled with her to California. Could she safeguard this client? She'd failed to keep Sid Breen, a former client, alive.

Shelley completed her set and stepped from the stage, lighting a cigarette, and took a seat at the bar.

The saxophone began another deep, husky tune.

Birdie pondered her next move, believing she'd chased a white rabbit. Instead of sporting an English waistcoat, she wore a sequined cocktail dress.

What did Shelley plan in the dark hole of the jazz club?

CHAPTER NINETEEN

With a gold pen, Gustain scribbled, signing the Beverly Hilton's registration book. He had no reason, only habit, to conceal the Christian name given at baptism. His background clean. No recorded fingerprints existed outside those locked in a vault alongside the CIA's deepest secrets.

"Enjoy your stay, Mr. Hilger," the desk clerk said, handing the key across the polished granite counter.

Gustain failed to spot security cameras but noticed an obvious, overweight hotel detective near the gift shop. The simple assignment had been the least ambitious since Dulles removed him from a British prisoner-of-war camp.

Well, past six feet, youthful looks worked to his advantage, blending into a crowd, ignored by witnesses. With few exceptions, his assassinations occurred as he preferred, at a safe distance, unnoticed. On this job, he intended to make the kill up close and intimate, feeling the victim's pulse slow, fading to a life-ending stop, muscles slackened, surrendering.

His first victims were effortless to track, thanks to Dulles. The ladies were sitting ducks, waiting to be picked off at his pleasure.

Gustain pulled Lenora's and Birdie Kelly's photos from his coat pocket, giving them one last look. Birdie Kelly held particular interest. Separating the two may be a challenge. He'd follow and take the first opportunity—a back alley for one, the other, privacy and comfort.

With his two primary objectives, conflicts remained. Doubts lingered over his friend Strughold, pleading for Falk's escape to South America, a blatant attempt to counter Dulles's orders. Since their private Arlington meeting and the three umbrella-carrying observers, he questioned if the CIA tested his reliability. Failure ensured his sudden accidental death.

Gustain stepped close to the hotel clerk. "This is for your guest, Lenora Jaminson."

He pulled a small box from inside his coat pocket. "She's expecting it."

The young clerk took it, turned, and slid it into a vacant slot behind him, giving it a final tap as the silver box slid into place.

Gustain had the room number, guessing it a suite on the ninth floor—room 902.

CHAPTER TWENTY

Birdie waited near the battered cigarette machine, watching Shelley. The jazz soloist stepped from the stage and strolled to a barstool. In queue, the barkeeper delivered and poured a glass of wine, resting it on a paper napkin. Tapping a cigarette from a new pack, she glanced at her sequined dress's shoulder, brushing the offending item away with a casual flick, allowing it to drift to the floor.

The sultry black-haired singer remained alone, not attracting fans or well-wishers. She appeared content and relaxed, sipping wine, taking short, quick draws of a cigarette resting at the tips of her slender fingers. From close range, Birdie judged the entertainer in her early twenties. With her looks and talent, she'd go far.

Why did she play cat and mouse?

Birdie stopped; there was no time for second-guessing. She'd operate, presuming Jaminson's disappearance connected to Shelley's presence in Los Angeles. The likelihood of a link with German Nazi officers concerned her. Possibly Jaminson's South American business dealings involved more than steel making. As a former Pinkerton, she'd learned men, rich, poor, and famous, shared the same weaknesses.

Hamilton Jaminson controlled the world's coal and steel supplies while his ego and lust for young ladies ran out of control, according to his ex-wife. Cardinal indulgences may have provided bait for his attackers. Something more significant loomed behind his disappearance.

Birdie returned to their corner booth as chilled Dom Perignon popped open. Lenora's prosthetic foot rested on a red cushioned seat between them, nested in gauze wrapping.

"Pour and bring another," Lenora said. "We're thirsty."

The youthful server bowed in a deep, sweeping motion and filled two tall flutes.

Birdie was sure she looked at an unemployed actor working Lenora for a sizeable tip.

Lenora smacked her lips, took a long sip, and fell back against the leather booth.

It had been easy to see her client made an uncomfortable connection between the beautiful young singer and her former husband. Birdie guessed the pricey champagne aided in swallowing her pride. Lenora took care of herself, maintaining a youthful, trim figure and elegant appearance. With all that, she still sat on the wrong side of fifty.

They had known one another for a day, yet Birdie identified with her wealthy client. A protective fondness developed, and she hoped it mutual. Lenora made it clear Hamilton had flings. What was different now? What changed?

Birdie went through the motions of sipping from her glass, not enjoying the champagne's sweet taste and aroma. Bitterness in her mouth came when expecting danger. A trait that kept her alive.

Lenora appeared fatigued, and the day's travel, mixed with generous amounts of alcohol, didn't help. She was in no condition to contend with the planned show-down with Shelley.

"My guess, all this involves the piano player at our hotel," Birdie said.

"Pity. What can I do?" Thankful for the opening to rid herself gently of Lenora and potential risk. Birdie intended to send her client off to a low-risk job.

"Go back to the Hilton. Watch Pello and his bird from a distance."

"And you?"

"I'll do the same here."

Lenora slid to the edge of the booth and jammed her shoes, prosthetic foot and wrappings into her large purse.

"I'll take a cab," Lenora said.

Birdie backed away, withholding comment on her client's exposed blood-stained stump, knowing Lenora despised sympathy.

"Keep an eye on him," Birdie said. "Behind his gorgeous smile, he knows more than what he told me."

Lenora pointed to the bar and Shelley. "What about her?"

"I'll handle that."

The club's burly doorman signaled a cab with a sharp whistle. Lenora hopped, while one arm gripped Birdie's shoulder. After stopping several times to regain her balance and breath, she reached the front door and fell into the arms of the muscular bouncer.

Birdie couldn't help but roll her eyes toward her client as she snuggled against his red Hawaiian shirt which hinted as covering his muscled chest. With the yellow cab's rear door held open, the driver extended his hand. Instead, Lenora clung to the bouncer's shoulder and ducked into the idling taxi.

Visible in the bouncer's hand, a hundred-dollar bill.

"Rewards of chivalry," Birdie said to no one, giving herself an idea.

"Don't take any chances. Be careful," Birdie said to Lenora.

"I'll treat him with kid gloves," Lenora answered as the cab door closed.

Birdie had expected Lenora to resist and stay at the jazz club, working as a team. She didn't have the heart to tell her fun-loving client she wanted her out of harm's way. If time permitted, she would have preferred to escort Lenora to the Beverly Hilton, locking her inebriated client into their suite. Birdie attempted to hide anxiety.

Acting as a fearless PI, risking her safety, she had no plan other than to wait for Shelley to make the first approach, and she was tired of dragging around a shadow.

Jaminson's disappearance favored Shelley's involvement. Soon they would come face to face. If a winter and spring romance existed between the two, Birdie didn't care. Gaining the release of her client's ex-husband was the sole aim. The revelation of Jaminson's South American business trip and earlier ties to the beautiful singer, along with a liaison to Nazis, came as a surprise.

Birdie doubted the Germans divulged their real identities. Lenora stated she believed them to be Nazis, according to Jaminson's admissions, which led Birdie to consider Lenora's former husband knew the company he kept.

If so, why associate with war criminals? Questions spun. How deep would she dig to learn what went on? The beautiful Brazilian singer may hold more answers than Birdie wanted to resolve.

Being honest with herself, along with a high level of street smarts and caution, told her the case had been more than she prepared for.

Could she remain on the job with such doubts? Abandoning a client risked harming what modest reputation she owned in New York City. Something she could not afford to lose. Birdie preferred not to return to the sleazy part of private investigation, clicking off rolls of black and white film, peeking into windows, and watching people in personal moments. She'd failed at acting; now another botched career looked her in the face. She reminded herself, the best form of judgment came before a fall. What happened after, the adage promised, was useless second-guessing. Would she regret her decision?

In the short time together, she'd grown close to her client and perhaps imagined non-existent dangers. Lenora hired her to discover the truth, not conjure up narratives of cloak-and-dagger Cold War fears.

Sticking with facts, no hospitals had reported admitting or treating Jaminson. No ransom request surfaced, and he may not wish to be found.

With Lenora safe, Birdie would return to business. She unfolded a hundred-dollar bill and approached the next waiting cab.

"Busy tonight?" Birdie asked.

"Slow as hell," the cabbie said, poking his head from behind a crumpled newspaper.

Birdie held a crisp hundred-dollar bill near the driver's face, tearing it in two, handing the driver half.

"That's no good to me, lady."

"Wait for me," Birdie said. "You'll get the other one."

After a shrug and undiscernible mumble, the driver pushed the torn bill into his shirt pocket. Seconds later, the cab pulled into a narrow alley near the jazz club. Its lights flashed off, followed by a flared match and red amber glow of a cigarette.

Pleased that she'd dispatched her client while tailing Shelley following the showdown. Doubts swirled for Birdie, and with luck, the face-off inside The Congo Club would answer questions.

Inside, nothing changed. Cigar smoke hung like a river fog in the darkened room. No eyes lifted from nursed drinks. Despite not catching a watching eye, she had a hunch someone observed.

Under a blue-tinted, muted light, Shelley, caressing a microphone, performed. Birdie delighted in the mellow tango beat and gentle swaying movement of the glamorous entertainer.

Birdie reminded herself to stay calm and not break laws. The young singer had not committed a crime to Birdie's knowledge and was not guilty of anything besides sitting in a bar and leaving behind a pack of matches.

She had no cop friends here, and her New York PI license carried no weight. There was no point stepping on the toes of LA cops. Lenora wanted no police, and Birdie would do her best to keep it that way.

Slipping between tables, she returned to her booth; she hoped, without distracting Shelley's attention. The singer, Birdie was confident, had watched every move made by her and Lenora. For the moment, her immediate worry had been a newly arrived, single male night hunter. With closing time near, they'd pursue an unattached female remaining in the nightspot. Watered-down ginger ale would have to keep her alert.

If the singer had lured her here, Shelley would approach if she intended to talk. Birdie would oblige. Then again, she misread many subtleties in past cases, costing lives.

After allowing her client to persuade her into a precarious helicopter ride followed by a cross-country flight, she counted herself fortunate to stay alive. The pursuit of finding Jaminson led her here, and she'd toss the dice confronting the Brazilian. She'd aim the revolver in her purse at anyone across from her.

For the moment, Birdie remained content, sipping weak bar ginger ale and enjoying light jazz. Lenora had been taken care of and was safe, as long as she stayed away from the pugilistic parrot in their hotel bar. Pello was pleasant to watch and listen to. Her client most likely would tire soon and retire once the hotel bar closed. She expected a full night's work stalking the singer once she'd stepped from the jazz club.

Shelley continued on stage the rest of the night. Waiting and watching is what streetwise PIs did. Gun battles and car chases existed in the minds of movie and television writers. Had she given the cabbie enough to keep him waiting? This was LA, not New York. What do cabbies earn? She should have offered more of Lenora's money.

Relaxed by soft jazz, Birdie remained alone. Not a single male bar patron approached, and no offer came her way. Did she appear unapproachable?

The combo wrapped up the evening with a peppy jazz rendition of *Good Night Lady* while the ceiling and wall lights flashed on. Sleepy-eyed men and women rose and stumbled toward the club's double door. Musicians packed instruments into cases pulled from beneath the stage. The pair of "B" movie moguls she and Lenora had rebuffed strode like banty roosters, arm and arm with two heavily jeweled ladies. Birdie found Shelley looking her way as she stepped near the bar to retrieve her matching glitter purse and sensed the vocalist looked for someone.

Birdie remained seated and reached for her purse, sliding the handbag closer to her, touching the revolver for assurance. Her next move depended on the singer. The black-painted concrete floor and drab cinder block walls became exposed. Low indirect lights, rosy candles, and soft-toned jazz had camouflaged the featureless room. The Congo Club proved to be little more than a filthy alleyway with broken and splintered tables and chairs. She reflected on jazz's deep roots in the work songs of southern cotton field workers.

Birdie smiled at what she'd forgotten. Harsh lighting unveiled what Shelley plucked from the shoulder of her dress earlier. She recognized it at once, bird plumage. A single green feather lay near a bar stool.

From the corner of her eye, she caught a figure step from behind the bar, perhaps who Shelley expected, and pushed into the booth against her. She'd allowed herself a moment of carelessness, letting her guard drop. A hand grabbed her arm as she reached for her purse, tipping the bag to the floor, useless at her feet. She would have enjoyed ramming her pistol into the brute's ribs, hoping to break a few. Birdie heard the heavy clunk of her revolver as her bag tipped over and hoped it went unnoticed. The intruder said nothing as they sat together.

Should she flee or stay?

CHAPTER TWENTY-ONE

Gustain opened the door while he slid the lock picks into the pocket inside his sports coat. He hadn't expected to find Lenora or Birdie but knocked entering their suite. Credits to his sainted mother and Oxford for his good manners.

He didn't know what he was searching for. Nosing around personal items offered a sense of his target's habits and, in rare cases, cash and jewels contributed to retirement. Nothing out of the ordinary caught his attention besides expensive luggage stored under a bed. Few clothes hung in a walk-in closet and less occupied a white gilded dresser. Gustain guessed, by their overnight suitcases, that they had not expected a lengthy stay or favored mobility.

Unlike his room, the spacious penthouse furnished more than a sink, bed and chair. An array of domestic and imported, high-priced whiskeys: Glenfiddich, Cutty Sark and Seagram's 7 stood at attention on glass shelves fronting a full-length mirror waiting his inspection. A view of downtown Beverly Hills, backlit by a full moon shining on snow-covered peaks of the San Gabriel Mountains, warmed the dim suite.

Gustain abandoned his hunt, opting to pour a half tumbler of Seagram's, mixing it with warm Coke. He made himself at home, dropping his long frame into a low, deep sofa facing the suite's marble foyer. While rummaging through their belongings, out of habit, he'd unplugged each lamp, keeping himself hidden in shadows.

Hollywood, California surpassed the usual spots traveled. Previous jobs took him to crumbling, war-ravaged towns and cities. Sitting back, relaxing, and sipping whiskey brought a question—why the sudden cushy assignment?

Yesterday's meeting with Doctor Strughold and his appeal to allow Falk's escape to Argentina raised uncertainties. It was viable that Dulles contrived the proposal as another so-called loyalty assessment. The American spy agency tested Germans for dedication and subjected them to trials. He'd executed twenty CIA targets during seven years of service. Had this not proved him reliable or at least committed?

The operation, his first in country, involved three American civilians besides Doctor Falk, a former German chemist working alongside Strughold. Their offenses, according to the CIA, included theft of a classified CIA program. If Doctor Strughold risked the cemetery meeting, requesting Falk be spared, created a strong hunch the Nazi physicians shared a secret kept from Dulles. Knowledge of buried skeletons remained cherished currency in Washington, DC, and Gustain craved to enhance his standing. The two doctors harbored resentment against the American government while taking its money to develop mind control and truth drugs. Gustain suspected there had been a great deal more, and Nazi Germany's new revival at the core.

Gustain poured more of the smooth blended whiskey and swirled the old with the new, not bothering with ice. The mirrored image behind the bar looked back. What happened to the young, ambitious college student with ideas for entering Germany's political arena? He lived with the results of the decision. There was no need to look for an answer. The dream vanished the day he said yes to Dulles.

After downing several tall glasses of whiskey and Coke, the job of killing two women, he hoped, would come soon. The pair would enter the darkroom, and with the aid of hallway lighting, he'd verify his targets. He'd slip behind Lenora, letting his blade do the work, clean and smooth, slicing her throat, leaving her dead in minutes. Birdie would panic, allowing time to control her.

Growing memory flashes grew more frequent and realistic, invading silent moments. Falk and Strughold hovered over him, jabbing dozens of tiny needles into his exposed brain. Disturbing visions ran as a continuous loop, and only heavy doses of whiskey provided an antidote.

Dulles's graphic pictures of Falk's lab darted into his head. Why did he feel a detached awareness of the laboratory's sterile steel tables and rows of tall cylinders bordering the room? Gustain couldn't shake the uneasiness experienced after viewing the grainy photos. Curiously, he sensed their presence in California through expanding memory flashes.

Rolling up a trouser leg, he snapped free a six-inch knife, setting it on the table. He had nothing to do but wait, enjoying the hospitality found in the suite's lavish bar. In the still of darkness, he attempted to reconcile the murder of two American women.

Gustain took in a quiet, deep breath as footsteps approached in the hallway.

CHAPTER TWENTY-TWO

Birdie's purse rested near her feet on the concrete floor, out of reach. Her sudden, unexpected visitor squeezed close, pushing against her. How did she allow herself to be so careless? Instincts deserted her; she had no time to react to being caught off guard. Could she blame old-fashioned nostalgia brought on by the serene spell of the quaint jazz club?

Remembrances of past years in New York City rushed at her. The camaraderie, celebrating alongside fellow actors following a performance, shaped her warmest memories. As friends grew, they squeezed together in the dingy basement of the Village Vanguard, enjoying fine libations, and mellow tones from Miles Davis's trumpet, recorded or live.

The intruder slid closer, bumping her hip, shoving his warm thigh against hers, forcing her to push to the center of the booth.

"You also play at this club too, Pello?" Birdie asked, withholding surprise.

"Shelley wants to talk."

"I'm choosy who I speak to."

"Fine with me. She'll be right over."

Birdie looked at the man sitting shoulder-to-shoulder with her. His long, slender hands rested, folded on the table. What had she missed? Could there be something wrong with her? A short time ago, they shared a drink and chatted. She had been close to developing a hotel crush, flirting with the handsome pianist. Were LA males like that—aloof? She'd been around the block once or twice—no bar hustler is picky at closing. They all fell for an alluring smile, a low-cut dress, and a peek of a girl's well-toned thigh—at least New York men.

Pello stumped her. He behaved as if they'd never met. No longer in his smart tuxedo, but a simple blue collared shirt and tan slacks. He remained the same gorgeous man she'd admired at the Beverly Hilton a few hours ago. Her pride took a shot broadside, not sinking her, but doing damage.

"Pardon me," Birdie said, looking him straight in the eye. "You play the piano at The Beverly Hilton?"

"None of your business," he answered.

"Got a name? You're not Pello, are you?"

After a pause, he answered, "Fabian."

"Fabian," Birdie repeated, taking a long second look at the handsome man beside her. He did not merely bear a resemblance to the piano player, Pello; he was the exact copy. The facial features, down to the slight blemish of a thin scar near his cleft chin, matched. If he had not been Pello, he was more than an identical twin—a mirror image. As a precaution, she examined the room for a red and green parrot.

Birdie positioned her purse, dragging it, using both feet to locate it to a spot she could reach. The handle straps remained out of reach; she'd need to lower an arm and blindly grab her small revolver. Once the gun was in her hand, she considered, if needed, firing it into the floor to attract attention. A few employees and patrons lingered at the bar and stage. She had no way of knowing if they played a part in the sudden ambush. She couldn't risk an errant bullet endangering bystanders. Something more cautious was required. Did she overreact? The only physical contact had been Fabian grabbing her elbow and a slight bump, which she didn't mind. No violence followed. Could it be paranoia from an emotional-year-old case hunting an ax murderer that laid in wait in her kitchen, trapping her?

Shelley stepped from behind a beaded curtain and approached their booth. No longer in the blue glitter gown, but a simple knitted outfit. If the second member of the snatch team carried a weapon, Birdie didn't spot it in the singer's form-hugging dress.

"You get around," Birdie said.

"I could say the same."

Birdie expected Shelley to slide next to her, pinning her in. Instead, she stood in front of the oval table.

"Enjoy the show?" the singer asked.

"Which one?"

"Both."

"Let's not play games," Birdie said and pushed Fabian, gaining space she may need later. "My name's Birdie Kelly. I'm a New York private investigator looking for Hamilton Jaminson. I don't want trouble."

Their reaction would decide Birdie's next move. She was not allowing Shelley and Fabian to intimidate her. Once the pair removed her from the public place, into a controlled area, she became their prisoner, at their mercy.

Remaining calm provided an advantage. Shelley and Fabian would not expect what she planned. She slipped off her shoes, wedging her toes around the purse's heavy clasp, and opened the snap closure after several tries. The revolver rested in a side pocket, loaded, ready to go to work. With her slim and once-agile frame, she'd fall, slide to the floor, grab her concealed handgun, and heave the free-standing table upward with enough ramming force to harm or distract the two. Improvising her next action, she'd dash to the door as the last option.

"Did Fabian cause trouble?" Shelley asked.

The singer's question and warm voice came as genuine. Birdie relaxed, surprised by the young woman's caring tone.

"Nothing but a gentleman," Birdie answered.

Three coffee mugs appeared, landing with a thud. The barkeeper smiled at Birdie and poured from a tall carafe, filling each with steaming black coffee.

"My family grows the finest beans in the Andes," Shelley said, as she took a mug.

Birdie remained silent, waiting for what came next. Her experience, as a former Pinkerton, taught her to be wary of pleasant gestures coming from suspects; they hid cruel intentions.

She pushed her steaming cup to the side, but near her. They'd placed a hot, dangerous liquid in her hands. It had been careless. If they meant to do her harm, the barkeeper gave her a weapon. She'd stay on guard, although she felt the nerves relax along her spine. The question remained, what did the two want and why the look-alike? A hunch told her to stay calm and play their game. She'd discovered a connection to Hamilton Jaminson. The unexpected eccentric parrot, twins and a controlling, beautiful South American jazz singer complicated the hunt.

If the cab driver kept his bargain, she intended to use Fabian and Shelley to track down her client's former husband.

That part of her strategy was a long way off. Her captors did not appear ready to release her.

The red and green parrot flapped its wings, appeared from the darkness and flew from behind the bar, landing on Shelley's shoulder.

"Don't shoot. Don't shoot," the bird screamed in a clear voice.

CHAPTER TWENTY-THREE

The twin-engine Beechcraft banked over Southern California's coast near Seal Beach, six hours since the start of the mission.

Conrad tracked their slow, deliberate progress, red-marking his flight chart after spotting the pair of landmark inland waterways and a fishing pier stretching into the dark Pacific. The pilot dropped altitude, heading toward Santa Ana and Anaheim, completing another search loop. Below, Disney's new sprawling amusement park appeared, glowing bright, centered among citrus groves and neighborhoods. The radio signal searching for Jaminson faded and vanished, one of many false readings he'd collected.

His eccentric client offered a day's notice of his intent to travel. Conrad accepted the sketchy California itinerary against better judgment and scuttled the advance security detail. Precautions dropped by the wayside, and his protection team let Jaminson slip out of sight. There was plenty to fault. But, ultimate responsibility fell on his shoulders. He'd allowed the world's steel and coal king to vanish.

For all he knew, Jaminson rested comfortably, enjoying a pleasant drink while he remained trapped inside a small plane, listening for a tiny echo, a needle in a haystack buried deep within densely populated Southern California.

On the ground, a heavy-duty step van holding similar equipment moved at a snail's pace, attempting to catch the same weak but distinct signal sent by a device in Jaminson's shoes. The rest of the search team burned shoe leather. Two cars, identical black Cadillacs, carried teams of private detectives. With nothing more to go on than pictures of the client, eight men canvassed bars, gas stations, and eating places.

Cramped legs ached and needed stretching and a message. On the next lap of the sprawling metro area, they'd refuel in Long Beach. Conrad was looking forward to a hot meal with a pint of ale and fresh air that had not been recycled thousands of times through a cockpit. Although the odds were slim, their client may have returned and slumbered in his room. At each refueling, he'd phone the Beverly Hilton.

* * * *

Conrad's man in the hotel's lobby heard the page for a fictitious Randy Knock. He took the expected call at a house phone in the far corner of the entrance, isolated from the front desk and busy elevators.

His assignment—sit and wait for the return of their client. After a few glances around the room, he picked up the cream-colored phone from a table near a cluster of empty sofas and wingback chairs.

"Please tell me Jaminson's sitting in the bar with a blond," Conrad said.

"Negative."

"How about his ex and the PI she hired?"

"They showed."

"They may be helpful. What did they do?"

"Went to the bar separately, then joined up and grabbed a cab somewhere."

"That's it?" Conrad asked.

"The PI is a looker. She talked to the piano player chummy-like. After that, Lenora showed, and the two women took off."

"Hotel security getting nosey?"

"I can handle 'em. What do you want me to do?"

"Let me think."

"There's something else," Conrad's man said.

"Tell me."

"We're not alone."

"How's that?"

"Somebody besides us is looking for Jaminson and the ladies."

"You sure?"

"Positive. He tricked the desk clerk and got the room number for Jaminson's ex."

"Lay low and watch yourself," Conrad said.

"Don't I always?"

"Look at their rooms."

"They have a penthouse."

"While you're at it, search Jaminson's again. We could have missed something."

"I have the maid's key. The suites are attached."

Conrad hung up, slamming the receiver into the hook, and remained inside the phone booth watching the refueling of the Beechcraft. He faced a non-stop search with no relief and the complication Lenora added. He expected Jaminson's daring ex-wife to join the chase. On top of it all, a much greater worry appeared. A third party materialized.

Who were they, and what motives did they have?

After a few moments, Conrad reconciled his dilemma. Should there be a conflict, he held a tactical advantage only the military could outdo.

In a nearby hangar, two Sikorsky H-34 attack helicopters waited for deployment. Each carried an array of missiles along with a squad of former Israeli soldiers of fortune that would lead the land, sea, or air rescue.

Jaminson's status remained quiet from the world. This pleasure trip, like all private and business travel, stayed secret and known only by his security team. Jaminson, according to protection protocol, showed up at events unannounced.

* * * *

Conrad's man avoided being noticed and climbed nine flights of a fire escape stairwell to the penthouse level. Grabbing the passkey from the maid's cart had been an unexpected break after he'd checked in. They would terminate the careless housekeeper for the offense. Her loss became his gain.

Stepping to the penthouse floor, he bypassed a stairway marked ROOF AND HELIPORT. He smiled, knowing the Beverly Hills location catered to reclusive clients. H Howard Hughes once set up shop at the lavish Hollywood hotel, living on chocolate bars, chicken, and milk.

Jaminson kept a copter in the Long Beach Airport. Knowledge of the quick flyaway escape route became valuable intelligence and could come in handy.

Outside Jaminson's suite, Conrad's man eased the master key into the slot and waited. He could not afford to be spotted. His ear pressed against the door—no sound. The possibility of a maid cleaning the vacant suite was remote, but the chance of a late visit by management tending to high-end guest rooms remained.

His stolen key turned, needing a slight jiggle to trip the stubborn tumblers, and the double doors swung open. Open drapes admitted the soft glow of a giant, full moon hanging over the Hollywood hills. Shadows of unlit lamps reflected against a pair of tall paintings covering two walls.

The suite was neat and in order to the inexperienced eye. It didn't take long to notice items had been shifted. A clumsy intruder left tale-tale signs of a search. Drawers had not been closed. A large framed mirror hung off square. He assumed Jaminson's ex and her PI tossed the room, looking for what he too hunted for—clues of Jaminson's whereabouts.

The rescue teams were engaged in the hunt until completion. He had time on his hands—babysitting the hotel lobby, waiting for the client to show.

According to his bosses' written procedure, once the clock started twenty-four hours ago, the mission would continue non-stop. His job, modest and safe, by comparison to the assault commandos, was to sit and wait. He'd conduct another search. First, he'd help himself to the stocked bar, compliments of their client.

The connecting door pushed open unnoticed as he poured Scotch over cubes of clear ice.

CHAPTER TWENTY-FOUR

Birdie continued to watch Shelley. The young, attractive singer could be a dead end, or luck had led Birdie to the jazz club, and gave her a clue to finding Hamilton Jaminson. From fear or admiration, she wasn't sure. Her pale blue eyes and charismatic nature captured Birdie, so much so, she took an uncomfortable pleasure at the moment.

Shelley's subtle power of persuasion triggered Pello's altered temperament, cutting off the conversation at the Beverly Hilton bar. What role would she play alongside the good-looking Fabian at the steamy jazz club? Birdie conceded being manipulated and outflanked by a younger and confident adversary. She'd avoid making the situation worse.

The tight spot she found herself in was not beyond salvaging. No threats came from the two she sat with, and Birdie guessed she was free to leave, but uncertain. No one pointed a gun at her. Anyone, seeing the trio, would assume friends shared good times over coffee. If accused of threatening the peace, a quick search would find her loaded firearm lying at her feet.

She'd looked after her client, guarding her against harm, putting Lenora in a cab, and sending her to the hotel. Birdie's worry—would her assertive client stay a safe distance from the hotel bar's piano player? There would be no time to return to the Beverly Hilton. An image of Lenora sitting alone with Pello stuck in her mind.

All but a few of the mid-week crowd cleared out, emptying the club. Shelley nodded to Fabian. Birdie guessed it was a private signal. Few lingered, finishing drinks, chatting with weary musicians packing instruments, cradling them in worn red, felt-lined cases. Birdie deliberated—should she read this as a subtle warning?

Circumstances were not under her control, yet confidence to manage the situation grew, at least, while bystanders remained. With them gone, the environment changed.

"You led me here. Why?" Birdie asked.

"I was curious."

"I'm looking for Jaminson, and you know him."

"Suppose I do?"

"Tell me about Jaminson," Birdie said.

"He is generous," Shelley said. "We met at the bar. The same place you saw me."

"That's the first you met?"

"Yes, the first."

"And you hit it off?"

"We had a few drinks and laughs," Shelley answered.

Birdie clenched her fists and resisted disputing Shelley, recalling Lenora knew the singer from a stay in Buenos Aires. Shelley lied, and Birdie caught her, choosing to let it pass. Added queries weren't necessary. It was clear Shelley hid more than Jaminson's whereabouts. Birdie's safe bet was to walk away, accept her story, and escape—no point aggravating her hosts. Birdie realized she'd stumbled into an intriguing situation light years past a routine missing person case. The South America meeting linked Jaminson to Shelley and the Germans Lenora saw. She was worried about what she'd find when she uncovered her client's ex-husband.

"You see him again?" Birdie asked.

"We're adults. We had a few good times."

"Do you know where Jaminson is?"

"Now?"

"Right now," Birdie said.

"No. There was nothing between us."

"Where did you last see him?"

"Here, having a drink. Then he left."

"When was that?"

"A few weeks ago."

The Congo Club emptied. Dim lights remained over the bar and exit doors. Suddenly quiet, Birdie caught an echo of a distant, dripping faucet matching pace with her racing heart. Another deep breath followed. Each lungful released slowly and relaxed her. She would not let them see her lose composure.

Had she become too confident pushing Shelley, interrogating her as if she were a criminal?

Once the musicians and the last of the small crowd departed, as if on cue, the heavyset barkeeper appeared, positioning himself near the exit.

"Where's your friend?" Shelley asked, lighting a cigarette.

"Shopping," Birdie answered.

Birdie considered making a retreat. She'd like nothing more than to shove past Shelley, making a dash to the door, taking her chances with the overweight barman. The impulse vanished as quickly as it arrived. Appearing nonchalant gained information, and she sensed Shelley respected self-confidence.

What came next? Would she follow the two, leading her to Jaminson? Had the cabby deserted her?

"Did Jaminson say what his plans were in LA?" Birdie asked.

"He didn't tell me anything."

Fabian slipped from the booth, almost unheard, taking a position near Shelley. If another silent signal passed between the two, Birdie missed it. Remaining seated, she lifted her purse to the cushion next to her. From this location, she could fire in seconds. With adrenalin flowing, maybe less.

Shelley knocked on the Formica tabletop. "Don't follow me, sister."

"Wouldn't dream of it," Birdie answered.

"Wait ten minutes," Shelley said, with a glance over her shoulder. "Before you leave."

Fabian exited, followed by Shelley, through the same double doors she and Lenora used to enter, which seemed ages ago.

Birdie considered Pello's and Fabian's roles. It could have been her overactive imagination—did Fabian react in the same way as his twin, Pello? She couldn't pin it down. What did the singer hold over the two men? It could be as simple as love or affection. Intuition told her something more complex. Regardless, she noticed an offbeat and uneasy chemistry between Shelley and the two look-a-likes. Fabian first appeared relaxed and casual. As the evening passed, he seemed less at ease, growing rigid and stern, keeping his oversized arms crossed against his thick chest. Birdie would have enjoyed alone time with the handsome man. Playful talking and a tender touch never failed to break a man's resolve to keep secrets. Males shared similar goals with women in bars—impress and conquer. Los Angeles men were no different.

She had fallen into something. Shelley knew much more. Birdie would bet her two-year-old PI license Hamilton's disappearance connected to South America and the Germans he and Lenora met.

Birdie had little time and hoped the cabby kept his word. She needed to warn Lenora of her concerns with the piano player and his twin. Payphones sat near the bathrooms between two cigarette machines.

She had company and scratched the idea, hoping the cab driver trustworthy.

Escorted by the barman, who reappeared from the darkness, Birdie stepped from The Congo Club's door. Thankful to be free of the room and stale cigarettes and whiskey. The night air turned chilly, and she regretted not carrying a light coat.

At the street, she spotted Shelley and Fabian, walking at a rapid pace, single file following a sidewalk leading to a crushed gravel parking lot surrounded by low-slung chains hung from metal posts.

Birdie's yellow cab was not in sight.

Although late, traffic remained heavy along the well-lighted four-lane road. Many cabs passed carrying passengers. Her hopes faded in locating the cabby holding the torn half of her hundred-dollar bill.

Street noise quieted for a moment, thanks to a stoplight, allowing Birdie to pick up Shelley's conversation.

"You'll return to Brea. Jacob's Ladder may be at risk," Shelley said, opening the taxi's door.

Brea hung in Birdie's mind as she slipped around the corner to avoid being seen. Was Brea a place or a person? Would she find Hamilton Jaminson there?

From a side street, a car pulled to the curb of a darkened roadway. The cabby waved the torn hundred-dollar bill out the window.

Sliding into the cab, Birdie stifled her surprise, although sure it showed as a smile on her face. The taxi driver had not failed her.

The cab driver turned, throwing his arm over the back of his seat. "Thought I could make a few extra fares."

"I had faith," Birdie answered.

His open palm stretched in her direction.

Birdie stuffed the matching half into his hand. In her brief time with Lenora, since her rushed departure from New York, she'd learned hard cash opened doors, trumping her persistence. Had she developed a mistrust of humanity?

"Where to?" the cabby asked.

Birdie again felt a pang of guilt. She needed to speak to her client, warning Lenora of Pello.

"Where to lady?" The driver rested his hand on the cab's meter.

"Pull ahead a little."

Birdie watched the two enter a red and white Corvette. Shelley was behind the wheel, with Fabian beside her.

Birdie pointed to their sports car, pulling into traffic. "Follow them."

The cabby turned to her. "I don't do that, lady."

CHAPTER TWENTY-FIVE

Footsteps on the marble floor slowed, stopping near the door of Hamilton Jaminson's penthouse.

In the nearby suite, Gustain waited for Lenora and Birdie's return. He'd broken his rule of drinking on the job. For a moment, he disconnected from the reality of his occupation, enjoying the pleasure of a superior whiskey while pondering the future... if he had one.

Jaminson, the wealthy American, triggered the CIA dilemma, which rested in Gustain's hands. He guessed Jaminson's connection to Falk and Strughold had drawn Dulles's ire, prompting a death warrant for Falk and three Americans while pardoning Strughold. In a surprise, Strughold requested he spare Falk, allowing his escape from the United States.

Assassinating American citizens overstepped CIA authority. Had Director Dulles become reckless in issuing the orders? The DC gossip grapevine never slept. Secrets leaked, exposing skeletons, gaining influence or payback in the power-hungry town. Gustain craved to wash his hands of the CIA and Dulles. With cash and passports, he intended to get away.

The adjacent suite's double doors opened.

He had company. A visitor entered Jaminson's unoccupied suite.

Gustain rose from the sofa and stepped along the suite's carpeted floor to the adjoining doors connecting the suites. He placed one hand on the center of the door while twisting the lock, easing the deadbolt open, not permitting the latch to click as it released, exposing the neighboring door. Confident he had not alerted the visitor, he pressed his ear against the wood door. Heavy footsteps moved about the room. No clatter came from keys or a wallet tossed to a table. No television or radio blared. The occupant made little noise besides the opening and closing of drawers and closets.

After several minutes, the unmistakable sound of ice clinking into a glass tumbler came.

Gustain presumed it an intruder, not hotel staff, paused for refreshment. The search conducted appeared hasty and performed from curiosity, perhaps boredom. Curious, Gustain intended to eyeball the invader. The interloper, Gustain guessed, possessed a key, but they didn't belong.

Had Dulles sent someone behind him? The CIA's trademark sign of no confidence. Would the prowler next enter Lenora's suite, the one he waited in?

The visitor's footsteps continued, circling each room, not appearing to rush. Gustain's curiosity grew. Fighting back impulses to storm through the door, he resolved to stay quiet and wait, keeping his advantage. Success came from patience, allowing the intended victim to come to him.

Hearing the cling of ice cubes and a second drink being mixed, Gustain lifted a chair, placed it near the connecting doors, and took a seat.

The visitor remained still, worrying Gustain he had been detected. Did his unknown companion suspect being listened to—go silent, plotting countermeasures?

Gustain readied himself, quieting his mind, erasing time from his conscious state, intending to stay near the door, a sentry. The beating of his heart calmed.

The interruption came.

A drinking glass slapped on the bar countertop. Footsteps moved to the suite's entry lobby. Would the individual next door enter his suite? Gustain stepped from the connecting door, closing it without a sound. He preferred to avoid a blood trail. Inside his coat pocket, he checked the thin wire cord he intended to use. The six-inch blade, no longer needed, returned to the leather sheath strapped to his calf.

Gustain inhaled, paused, and released his breath, slowing, envisioning a quick killing strike. Steel nerves and remoteness were vital. The instant the door opened, Gustain would attack.

His ear pressed tight against the wall, hearing a metal latch and deadbolt click from the adjacent entrance door. He dashed into position. The moment the neighboring suite's door swung open, Gustain shouldered it with an overpowering force, driving the intruder back, knocking a cigar from his fingers. His target froze a moment, allowing Gustain to dive the palm of his hand upward, striking the victim square under the jaw, stopping his exit, forcing both into the suite. Grabbing the stunned man's shoulder and with a snap kick to his knee, the man fell, grasping Gustain. As both collapsed to the marble floor, taking wild swings at each other, a hand yanked at Gustain's tie and slipped away. A gold tie bar slipped free and bounced on the foyer's Persian rug.

Gustain watched the unexpected visitor for weapons.

His opponent weakened and suffered a smashed knee. No gun came from inside his coat or shoulder holster. His hands pushed against the floor, attempting to stand, struggling to bring his uninjured leg under him. His face showed surprise as his stare bored into Gustain.

"Wait," he shouted.

Gustain stepped behind his victim, pulled the garrote from his coat pocket, and gripped one of its wood handles. His other hand looped the piano cord over the victim's head, wrapping it around his exposed neck. A thin wire dug into muscles and bone as Gustain yanked the opposite handle tight, finishing the slow, quiet kill, watching his unlucky prey suffer, battling for air until falling unconscious, with death following.

The victim carried no identification and was not recognized as an outsider, although the possibility existed someone separate from the CIA looked for Jaminson, not to assassinate but as a rescuer. If so, there would be more.

Was Strughold involved?

It was a useless murder. Gustain laid the blame at his own feet. He detested interference and could have escaped the suite unnoticed and returned to wait for Lenora and Birdie. Had he been restless and impatient, killing for pleasure, out of madness, without reason or motive? Did he kill to satisfy embedded commands? His friend, Doctor Strughold, took a personal interest in him. Was he a part of Strughold's studies of espionage and mind control?

The dead man sprawled at his feet presented a problem—disposal? Gustain could not leave the body behind, nor signs of their presence. Repeating his steps, Gustain removed traces of his fingerprints. Although no record existed, he took no chance. He had all night, and the housemaid had turned down the king-size bed, leaving a mint on the oversized pillows.

* * * *

Lenora waved off an approaching bellman as she dropped her purse, then collapsed on the lobby sofa. She'd arrived at her hotel worn from the long journey from New York and one too many bottles of overpriced bar wine. Tonight's outing proved productive, encouraging her to believe Hamilton remained alive. Birdie Kelly's instincts steered them to the jazz club and a link to her former husband. She'd no longer attempted to deceive herself. Hamilton Jaminson had been addicted to young, beautiful ladies and them to his well-publicized fortune. His incurable obsession led him to search the world for a magical remedy to slow aging and chronic illness. The fountain of youth, according to his claims, was no mystical dream and existed through a German medical breakthrough. He'd hinted at progress to gain the discovery since their Argentine trip.

What was she to Hamilton, a convenient travel companion? Nothing else?

The appearance of Shelley at Hamilton's hotel and what she learned at the LA jazz club tied together events with his so-called chance encounter in Argentina. Whatever the conspiracy, it now included her and Birdie.

Lenora half sat and lay in the busy hotel lobby, recalling who she once was, beautiful and young, turning heads, grabbing men's attention. Her prosthetic foot delivered tortuous jolts of pain to an inflamed and bloody ankle. The thought of the gorgeous, smooth-voiced piano player in the nearby lounge should not have entered her mind, but perhaps it was the antidote needed. He wasn't her future, but he existed permanently in her present.

In certain ways, Pello struck a nostalgic chord. An image of Casablanca's Rick Blaine, a cynical club owner, assisting a former lover to escape the Germans at the onset of World War II. Matching the motion picture, her family fled Poland using forged Italian passports. In much the same way, she faced a date with her destiny and future relationship with Hamilton Jaminson.

Nothing made sense at the moment, and she'd not decided, fearful of his well-being. Thoughts faded and returned to the present. She needed to discover more of Hamilton's connection to Shelley and the Germans. Further down her list, but moving up rapidly, was a hot, soaking bath.

Her inflamed ankle would not carry her to the elevator and suite. Exiting the lobby became a test of determination. She won the first round, standing, holding herself upright, leaning against a tall wingback chair. Nearby, a blazing fireplace warmed and enticed her to drop into the chair and enjoy the mood of the moment and the seductive spell of the lounge's piano. As that temptation tantalized her, she forced herself to walk—no time for self-pity.

Awkward steps came first—more of a stiff-legged shuffle resembling a Cracker Jack toy pulled by a string and weight. After a few stumbles, she'd regained her sea legs and crossed the marble floor toward the front desk and elevator—one of the rare victories she celebrated.

"Hello," someone called.

Lenora paused and turned, finding the piano player, Pello, doing a slow jog toward her. He carried a purse waving it. Arriving next to her, he flashed a broad smile.

"Thanks, I need that," Lenora said. Pleased, she avoided slurring, but wished she had come up with something witty.

Pello introduced himself, touching her shoulder, and handing her the purse. "I noticed it on my way to dinner."

Despite her shaky condition, she felt a slight stirring from his light contact.

"Lenora," she responded, withholding her full name, looking up at the attractive entertainer, watching his face. She'd gotten the feeling he'd already known her and the meeting, not a coincidence.

"I noticed you earlier," Pello said.

"Same here."

"I am having a late dinner."

"Very late, I'd say," Lenore answered.

"Care to join?"

Lenora hid the agonizing pain and would not let the invitation pass. She recognized a second offer would not come.

"I'm game," Lenora said.

"Hotel restaurant never closes," Pello said, placing his hand on her waist.

She couldn't help questioning his motive. Earlier, she and Birdie caught his frequent glances knowing they were watched.

Despite suspicions, the meeting sobered Lenora. Her mind stirred with the prospect of spending time with a charming companion who may provide a lead to locate her ex.

As they strolled arm and arm into the Beverly Hilton's dining room, a red-jacketed waiter appeared and slid a chair from a table. As Lenora sat, he placed a white starched napkin in her lap.

"Nice to see you, Mrs. Jaminson," the waiter said, handing her a menu.

"You get around," Pello said, flashing a smile.

"Will your bird join us?" Lenora asked, changing the subject after failing to spot a change in Pello's demeanor. She was certain the charming entertainer knew who she was.

"Gigi is a parrot but thinks of herself as human," Pello said. "She's home for the night."

Lenora recalled Birdie's comments on the bird's aggressive nature.

"Just one?" She asked.

Pello held up two fingers. "Matching pair and very social. They keep each other company."

As they chatted, Lenora became distracted, noticing the distant lobby elevator door slide open and close. Inside the car, a well-dressed man stood next to a white canvas laundry cart.

* * * *

The elevator stopped at a musty sub-basement. Gustain pushed the wheeled cart into the dimly lit garage and storage space. The area remained empty, and with the late hour, the hotel operated with minimum staff. His car waited near a caged wire room, storing tables and chairs. Removing sheets and towels from the laundry cart revealed a lifeless body folded into a fetal position. The unplanned kill produced a problem of disposal. His next targets, Lenora Jaminson, and her PI, would pose none, he promised.

The anonymous visitor would kill them, leaving no trace, and then follow it up with his rapid departure. The anonymous visitor forced him to operate outside his routine—something detested. Improvising brought slip-ups and came with the cost of being discovered. His night and much of the following day were lost. Resolving what he'd do with a body robbed him of his plans for Lenora and Birdie. Eliminating the women would wait. Leaving the unknown corpse in their suite tempted him; however, he risked frightening off the two.

As Gustain opened the car trunk, he recognized he was no longer alone. A faint echo of a door latch opened and closed in the distance. Slow-paced footsteps approached from a metal staircase behind his back.

He pulled a handgun from inside his jacket. There would be two unwanted corpses to dispose of. Each brought risk and threatened his original mission.

"Perhaps you are correct?" the intruder asked.

"About what?" Gustain said.

"With the job you are doing, of course."

"I can use a hand," Gustain said. His back remained to the visitor.

CHAPTER TWENTY-SIX

Birdie waited in the idling cab, watching her only lead to Jaminson drive away. She risked not seeing Shelly again and folded two crisp hundred-dollar bills, handing them over the seat.

"I'll make an exception," the driver said.

"Go! They're leaving," Birdie shouted.

"What about the meter?"

Birdie drew another hundred from her purse, courtesy of her generous client, dropping it near the driver.

"That'll cover it. Drive!" She pointed to Shelley and Fabian exiting the distant parking lot, speeding away in the white Corvette.

Birdie took a last look at The Congo Club's flashing neon palm trees. She headed into the unfamiliar territory of The City of Angels, and it might as well be a jungle, one she may not survive. Soon, she'd toss herself into whatever jumbled web of deceit Shelley concealed. If she sought a way out, choosing to play safe, now was the moment— her hotel was a mere fifteen minutes away.

She intended to link Jaminson's disappearance with Shelley. Connections to Nazis and South America belonged to Washington. The two men in New Jersey, posing as Western Union messengers, troubled her. She'd missed something—could there be another player, a third angle she'd overlooked? One thing she had learned serving as a Pinkerton—affluent people were poles apart from the working class. This case proved that.

Had it been more than a winter and spring flirtation between Jaminson and the youthful Shelley scheming to separate him from his money? It was too much to hope her pursuit brought no added complications, and it was nothing more than Jaminson sowing the remains of his wild oats. Birdie dismissed the idea. It had been more, much more. Hamilton Jaminson's trek to Buenos Aires, Argentina, and Shelley's arrival in Los Angeles was no coincidence; instead, a cog in a well-coordinated plan resting at the core of Jaminson's vanishing.

No solid motives came to mind, nor did her client disclose anything beyond steelmaking. Birdie forced herself to stay confident she was not far behind the answer.

Birdie reminded herself she trod on dangerous turf. According to Lenora, Jaminson contacted former German Nazi officers hiding in Argentina. Linking Jaminson to the hated Nazis during present cold war tensions invited attacks of communist subversion from the notorious Senator Joe McCarthy, damaging Jaminson's empire.

She had no intention of harming her well-paying client's former husband. Investigation of Jaminson's business with Nazis didn't fall within the job Lenora hired her for.

That stood as her official position.

Birdie coupled Shelley to the German military officers and would not rule out Hamilton Jamison's connections to both. Her task was to find Jaminson—nothing more.

Speeding away from the jazz club, Birdie lost her sense of direction in the maze of cross streets and fast-moving cars. At the late hour, traffic remained congested. Her cab continued un-phased, weaving, climbing along twisting narrow roads flanked by flat-roofed apartments and rows of lifeless shops safeguarded by metal security gates.

"This is Sunset Boulevard. Heard of it?" the cabbie asked.

"Keep your eye on the white Corvette," Birdie said.

"Dead ahead, lady, heading into the hills."

Birdie caught a glimpse of the stoplight as the cab slid to a halt, avoiding a crowd of white-robed, long-haired men and women chanting bible verses, slowing traffic in the crowded crossroads.

A member waved a knobby cane while the group shouted a flurry of words at the cab. Birdie didn't understand but recognized it as well-practiced. The obvious leader limped through the intersection, crossing the street, approaching the taxi, and shaking his walking stick as if the cab threatened an attack against his flock.

"The New World Children will die and return. You cannot do us harm." The long-haired young man bowed and stepped away, aiming his cane toward the red stoplight.

"Satan's symbol," he screamed.

"What was that?" Birdie asked.

"LA draws cults like bees to flowers."

"Must be the water."

"Sunshine and money. Hollywood likes wacko causes."

"They seem harmless."

"New World Children make lots of noise and cash," the cabby said, pointing to a distant illuminated structure atop an abandoned nine-story water tower at the far end of Sunset. "Their founders, a sign painter from Long Beach, got faith and claims to use cosmic wisdom to heal and return the dead to earth. I call it UFO religion."

"Don't let the Pope hear you say that." Birdie let herself laugh.

Birdie detected a connection between the cabby and the long-haired man. She chose not to comment, avoiding quizzing her driver, needing his efforts on the pursuit.

Before the light changed, the taxi backed away, speeding in the opposite direction, bumping over a curbed sidewalk blaring its horn. The cabby sped through a vacant bank parking lot and exited onto Beverly Boulevard. Ahead of them, at the next stoplight, sat Shelley and Fabian.

After several blocks of stop-and-go and sluggish traffic signals, the bright glow of Hollywood faded and died out. The road calmed, narrowing to a tight, single lane. Massive leafy oak trees shielded homes tucked deep into canyons and hillsides.

"Where are we?"

"Close to Stone Canyon Reservoir."

"Still have the Corvette?"

"Next turn, you'll see its lights."

Birdie doubted her resolve and will to keep up the pursuit. She recalled Shelley's warning to stay away. To do an about-face and return to the safety of the hotel for a hot shower and a well-deserved Irish coffee would not be in the cards. She'd started this and intended to see it to the finish. A small .38 rested in her purse. Tonight may be the first time she fired it in over a year.

The yellow cab slowed, pulling from the street to a patch of hard-packed dirt, rocks, and sparse wild grasses that found life along the desolate road. As the car coasted to a stop near a dry creek bed, the driver turned off headlights while yanking the emergency brake, allowing the low rumble of an idling motor to meld with crickets and buzzing cicada. Few lights shone from homes populating Stone Canyon Road.

"That's them," the driver said. "You're paid up. This is as far as I go."

Birdie studied the white Corvette parked in the driveway fronting four closed garage doors. The passengers remained in the car.

Had the taxi been spotted?

The chaotic day began in her New York apartment with Lenora's unannounced helicopter arrival and a well-paying job offer. Since then, she'd taken a wild ride and most recently experienced the freakishness of two look-a-likes and their pugilistic bird. What revelations waited within the remote home?

"Could you wait?" Birdie asked.

"I don't like it, lady. Something's not right. Maybe you shouldn't stay?"

"Got no choice."

"Some say devil winds haunt this canyon."

Bright dome lights flashed inside the Corvette as doors swung open. Shelley and Fabian stepped from the low, road-hugging sports car and, the instant Fabian reached her, Shelley turned and slapped his face. Displaying no reaction, he walked under a dark carport and vanished. Seconds later, a solitary light came from inside the large rock home.

Tempted to make the ride back to her hotel, Birdie forced her hand to lift the handle and exit. From here on, she'd take pains to avoid sudden noises. The stillness grew disturbing, tiny sounds amplified in the deep canyon.

The overcast sky turned clear while late-night air became balmy and desert-dry. High on the canyon ridge, trees rustled and bent. Once gloomy stars sparkled like new lanterns, reminding Birdie of Frost's hugger-mugger farmer desiring to improve his view into the heavens and foolishly destroyed his home to buy a telescope. Not unlike the misguided farmer, she came to be curious about Shelley and the men she controlled. What would be her cost?

The cab rolled forward, inching onto the street, turning across the single lane in a U-turn, and sped off. Once its red tail lights faded and disappeared on the winding road, she regretted the choice. The wise decision would have been a retreat and return in daylight. Who knew, besides the cabby, where she'd gone?

Would her screams be heard?

Birdie swore this to be the last time she took ill-advised risks. What did she think would take place? Hamilton Jaminson sitting, stretched out, slippers at his feet, enjoying a blazing fireplace?

Looking at the surrounding canyon ridges—tree tops tipped, bowing, and flaying, beaten by rising winds, while low guttural roars grew as if the salty Pacific tide crashed into the ravine. The distraction had been appreciated. The howling provided cover. Birdie intended to look at the house up close.

Taking careful and slow steps, she walked at the edge of the gravel road along stubby, grassy patches rooted in soft sandy soil. Breezes worked through the rough canyon walls, at first refreshing and pleasant. Nearing her target, the air continued to warm. It may have been her confidence allowing her to relax, losing the stress that gripped her since arriving in California.

Ground-level windows appeared accessible. Guard dogs were a concern and a risk she'd take. The Corvette sat in the wide driveway. A high-priced sports car in Brooklyn would have been stripped in fewer than twenty minutes by amateurs—less by professionals.

The sky brightened, glowing stars and a moon free of cloud cover returned soft light once claimed by January's early nightfall. Hot desert air swept like a flowing river down steep ravine walls. Sweat covered her bare arms and forehead. Tree branches scraped against the home's red-tiled roof and leaded windows, shielding Birdie's footsteps.

Birdie glanced through a window and found no evidence of life. At the rear of the house, she discovered a spacious glass veranda overlooking an expansive lake. Birdie stopped in the heavily forested and steep yard, catching a view of the large, silvery moon reflecting on the nearby reservoir's choppy water. Not a swimmer, she intended to stay far from the danger.

Inside, another light flashed on. Shelley walked into a sparse, almost empty room. A soiled gray unmade mattress laid on a narrow metal bed frame. Next to it, a low table covered by a towel. The stark scene reminded Birdie of a school nurse's office. Fabian followed behind, clad in white boxer shorts. Sweat wrapped his smooth, muscled, well-proportioned, and flawless body. At first, Birdie believed she snooped on a pagan ritual emphasizing female dominance.

What she saw next took a curious twist.

CHAPTER TWENTY-SEVEN

Gustain recognized the high-pitched voice. Before turning to the unexpected caller, he bent low and lifted the limp body from the laundry cart and let it slide into the car's trunk.

"Are you here to help?" Gustain asked. "Should a corpse shock you?"

"Perhaps not," his visitor answered.

"Killing is not new to Germans like us."

"Often experiments fail," Dr. Hubert Strughold answered.

Slow and steady, Gustain closed the car's trunk and turned, intent not to alarm his caller, watching his friend manage the concrete stairs one at a time. Gustain, from reflex, pictured a target point centered at the base of the throat, near the top of Strughold's chest. At a close distance, the shot would be quick and silent, a comfortable solution— one he excelled in. Here, his new adversary befriended him, the sole individual he'd once trusted.

Had he misjudged? Mistakes would get him killed.

Gustain rested his arms and hands in full view, displaying no intent to grab his firearm. His well-practiced draw, if needed, occurred within the wink of an eye. The snub-nosed revolver would, practically by itself, slip from the speed holster under his left arm.

Strughold guided a trembling hand along the unpainted block wall. The other, in his jacket pocket, held Gustain's full attention. Given the slightest movement, he intended to draw and fire his silenced weapon—no warning, a credo instilled in the German secret army.

Misplaced trust would cost him his life. In the faint light, the former Nazi scientist looked worn down, more than he had during their not-so-private meeting in the Arlington cemetery.

Gustain recalled Strughold's admiration of the disciplined Unknown Soldier's honor guard's inflexible commitment. Virtues he lacked.

He questioned, could he assassinate a friend?

Gustain watched each step, resisting inching his hand forward, retrieving his weapon.

Age eroded the abilities of the man he faced, but the former Nazi doctor could recognize the slightest aggressive action and would defend himself.

Gustan delayed, relying on agility and rapid reflexes, which enhanced over the years.

Gustain surveyed the garage with a glance.

No backup appeared.

They were alone, at least for a short time, apart from a flock of scavenging pigeons entering through an open door, hovering over crammed trash bins. Trust didn't come easy, and their boss, Dulles, knew it. It could be why he'd sent what seemed to be a harmless friend.

On second thought, the cold and cunning Dulles would not have risked Strughold on a killing mission. His value to the American space program a top priority, racing the disliked Russians to the moon. Dulles enjoyed an enviable closeness to President Eisenhower thanks to his contacts within Germany and the country's rocket experts.

The surprise arrival showed Strughold operated on his own, hiding the visit from Dulles.

Gustain grasped Strughold, embracing, patting him down. Gustain pulled away, accepting his friend came unarmed. If he'd carried at his ankle, it would have been slow to retrieve.

"Please, tell me that body is not my colleague Falk," Strughold said, resting his hand on the car's trunk.

"A mistake. Falk is yet to be located.

"Collateral damage?"

"Possible."

"Then, who?"

"An intruder in Jaminson's suite."

"Few know you are here."

"It's likely someone besides his former wife is looking for Jaminson."

"Then we have another snag."

"What brings you to Hollywood?" Gustain asked.

"You and the situation with Falk we spoke of."

"In the cemetery?"

Strughold nodded. "I will get to the point, my friend. Falk can restore our true homeland. The one we fought for."

"Our cause was futile. We committed cruelties."

"That is past. The future of New Germany lays in Falk's hands."

"Dulles gave me a job."

"Jacob's Ladder is far more important than a man's words."

"What do you want from me?"

"Grant me a day to convince you?"

CHAPTER TWENTY-EIGHT

Pushing aside overgrown bougainvillea branches, Birdie cleared a narrow path closer to the large lake house. If the canyon was haunted, according to her cab driver, its ghostly missiles took the form of long prickly thorns grabbing clothes, scratching, and clawing her bare arms.

Reservations and doubt lingered. Shelley steered her to the jazz club and the isolated house. What gave? Her active imagination failed her for a motive.

Were Shelley and the look-alike's, Pello and Fabian delighting in a contest of cat and mouse? She'd play, risking capture, willing to gamble the three would be the unfortunate victims ensnared.

At the rock home, she poked her head near the open casement window. From a narrow gap in the curtains, she viewed Shelley strike Fabian, and, as before, he displayed no response besides extreme reddening of lips and cheeks.

Grasping his wrist, Shelley guided Fabian to the metal-framed bed. As he bent to lie down, the bedroom door swung open. A bulky man entered, appearing roused from a deep sleep. Thinning gray hair pasted to his scalp, and a silver front tooth flashed a sparkle. For a moment, he looked around the room while he struggled, pulling on white surgical gloves. Birdie stepped back, pressing against the rough cobblestones of the house, fearing the unexpected arrival had spotted her.

"Our Fabian misbehaved?" he asked. His heavy German-accented voice carried from the room despite growing winds.

"Acting sluggish, like his battery ran down," Shelley answered.

"Perhaps you are correct."

"About?"

"You believed the two were not yet ready."

"They need more time," she said.

"I wish to avoid our Brea lab."

"It's over, Doctor Falk, until we return to Argentina with the money."

Falk nodded, pushing a metal cart toward Fabian's bed.

"More testosterone?" Shelley asked.

Falk remained quiet. His hands trembled to lift a glass hypodermic syringe. He filled the fist-sized barrel and inspected the thick needle. After injecting the mixture into Fabian's exposed thigh, he did the same to the other.

Fabian stayed unmoving.

"That's more than usual," Falk said, removing his gloves.

"What else did you give him?" Shelley asked.

"Something from Strughold's research. No need to worry."

"We have come far. Your work must continue," Shelley said.

"We are done here unless Strughold can convince Dulles to go on."

"Should the Americans be told everything?"

"They will see it as morally wrong."

"What about Fabian?" Shelley asked.

"With what I gave him, there's a risk of aggression, possibly violence. Watch them both."

"... and the birds?"

"The parrots are unstable. Eliminate them."

"Pello adores Gigi, and the birds need each other."

"Then they will be companions for Jaminson."

Birdie heard Falk's rushed words despite increasing winds. Hamilton Jaminson was alive. Her suspicions proved correct. The two, inside the house, held answers she sought. No hint of Jaminson's role or location came. The off-beat case continued a puzzle, and Birdie became determined to search the mysterious home.

Her mind wandered back to the cabbie's unexpected stop and confrontation with the cult leader. Birdie dropped to her knees as Shelley approached the window. The singer yanked the drapes aside while rolling the window shut. Birdie waited, hoping she remained hidden. Pushing herself deeper into the delicate blooms of the leggy bougainvillea. Sharp thorns grabbed her clothes, poked and scraped, jabbing bleeding arms and shoulders. Unwrapping from the endless assault of clawing vines worried Birdie, she'd invite attention.

Her position was no longer secure, she needed to move and think through what she'd seen. Catching her breath and craving an escape from the violent, exhausting winds, she found a spot in tall, sparse grass tucked between clusters of oaks.

Birdie admitted, for a moment, being drawn to him physically and imagined spending alone time with Fabian—information she'd keep from Lenora. Although identical to Pello, she detected something genuine in Fabian's behavior.

Lenora had been alone too long. Her client lacked patience, requiring an update—her former husband lived. An honest appraisal of Jaminson's involvement in events she'd seen would wait. Birdie, beyond doubt, no longer viewed the case as Jaminson being AWOL on his own. Privately, she wasn't sure what went on. Had laws been broken? Fabian appeared to take the macabre procedure voluntarily, although she sensed it connected Jaminson to Shelley and not romantically.

Nothing came to mind, shedding light on the scene inside. Did she see a crime or a doctor assisting an ill patient? Fabian showed no resistance, cooperating. She had no actual evidence to give the Los Angeles Police.

Options were few. Tonight she'd return to the Beverly Hilton, check on Lenora's safety, and get a night's rest.

Birdie became confident, for the moment, she went undetected. In her spot among the tall oaks, she'd nest in a patch of sedge grasses, keeping the devil winds at bay. Raising to her knees, she watched the stone house for anyone who exited.

Her mind drifted, brought by fatigue and lack of food. A welcome soft mattress waited at the hotel. Instead, she bedded down in scratchy grass and likely hunted by feeding coyotes while rodents burrowed alongside her.

Had Shelley lured her, with the enticement of discovering Jaminson, into a dead-end canyon, trapping her in the wilderness of the Los Angeles foothills? The desolate street wouldn't see a cruising cab, and a bus stop would not be handy. With plenty of Lenora's cash, she could have bought off the cabby, keeping the car at a distance while the meter ran the entire night.

Relentless winds intensified, and no sign of easing made the long hike out of the canyon less appealing—trapping her. Before she had time to consider another plan, a clatter came from within the house. Curiosity forced her from the sheltered spot, and Birdie pulled free from the sedge grass and oaks, inching back to the home, challenging the aggressive thorn bush minding Fabian's window. Inside, Fabian thrashed and tugged against the bed frame's rigid posts.

Torture chamber straps nor heavy chains restrained him. His muscled body was not of a well-defined bodybuilder, but instead, lean and powerful, borne from manual labor. Fabian forced the top of his head against the metal headboard, pulling his flexed, spread-eagled arms downward, bending the pair of heavy bed posts.

Fabian appeared drained, needing rest. What had Falk given him besides testosterone? The sturdy gray metal frame looked like the hospital bed she'd spent several months in. Anyone normal needed a pry bar's leverage to do what she witnessed.

Was he a conventional man? Her feelings were mixed, and common sense advised she should be afraid. Lenora hired her to locate

Jaminson and nothing more. She wanted to turn and run. Everything seen shouted she'd stepped in over her head. The handsome Fabian and Shelley represented more than she had been willing to take on.

Fabian's sudden aggression appeared not to disturb Shelley and the silver-toothed Doctor Falk. A mix of fear mingled with curiosity held Birdie at the window. Alerting police exposed Lenora's mission to shield Jaminson from unwelcome publicity. No apparent harm came to the patient. Both doctor and singer would claim to administer needed medication, nothing else. What seemed ghoulish could be explained as standard treatment if Falk proved to be an actual doctor.

Birdie dropped below the window. Fabian, wavering side to side, walked in her direction.

Would he crash through the unprotected window, attacking her?

He stopped and, with a quick jab, flattened his palm against the windowpane, sending a spider web of cracking lines through the heavy glass, inches from where she crouched. His face reflected an erratic, distorted image in the glare of shattered glass. Could the misshapen visage exist as the handiwork of a labored imagination earned by lack of sleep and fatigue? Had the window been open, she'd touch Fabian confirming or refuting the illusion.

Did sympathy attract her? She wished to believe him a victim. Of what, she couldn't speculate. His eyes fixed straight ahead. Chest muscles flexed as he stood rigid, faultlessly proportioned. Beads of sweat covered his clean-shaven scalp. Birdie guessed the drugs given Fabian controlled him. Their purpose evaded her. If he was a captive, escaping the house presented no challenge.

Fabian exhibited no great rage, startling her after dismantling the massive steel bed. He remained calm, standing quietly in his shorts, gazing through the tall casement window. The vast reservoir, less than fifty yards from where he rested, offered his only view. What did he mull over, behind his deep-set dark eyes, in the mysterious moonlit night?

How would she explain tonight to Lenora?

Dry, parched desert air of the Santa Anna's intensified, slipping lower into the canyon. Live Oak and pines whipped against the house's steep gabled roof and the incessant northeastern gale, mocking as a sorrowful wail of a wounded beast, overtook the darkness as it danced in the canyon's treetops.

"Devil wind!" Fabian screamed, repeating the words over and over.

Within seconds, the room's door opened, bringing Falk and Shelley. Falk entered, armed with a syringe shielded at the side of his white lab coat. Shelley snapped her fingers, pointing to Fabian.

His shouting stopped.

Fabian turned toward the two, affording Birdie a view of dark, bold letters branded into his well-muscled calf—5.

CHAPTER TWENTY-NINE

"A hotel basement is not the place for debate," Strughold answered.

"What can be achieved?" asked Gustain.

Strughold raised his voice. "We stand at a crossroads. A new homeland!"

Gustain, for the first time, saw his friend angered. Composure vanished from the normally calm doctor, worrying Gustain. He'd, without difficulty, handle the older man in front of him. Could the parked cars conceal Strughold's backup? He didn't check, and the error may cost him his life.

"What can change?" Gustain asked.

"Give me today."

"Our Fuhrer abandoned us."

"All is not lost. Many remain devoted to the Nazi party."

Gustain placed a hand on Strughold's shoulder. "Empty words."

"No," Strughold said. "We have made genuine discoveries. Real, not empty."

"You know where Falk is hiding."

"I do," Strughold answered.

Gustain gambled and raised his handgun, forcing the barrel against Strughold's forehead.

"I work for Dulles. Nothing you told me changes my orders. I have no option, my friend. Where is the traitor?"

Strughold stepped closer to Gustain; the blunt tip of the gun pressed tighter against his pale skin.

"Since Arlington, I realized you would force me to make a choice."

"I'm an old man with only my work," Strughold said. "Doctor Falk and I have accomplished significant advancements. I must protect him."

"Theories brought from Germany?"

"Americans know nothing of this."

"You've betrayed two countries," Gustain said. "How can I believe you?"

"Those that die today will be cured tomorrow," Strughold said. "We have proven cases in our lab."

"You're playing God?"

"What are you afraid of?"

"That's why you came?"

Strughold shuffled back to the basement stairs and lowered himself to sit. Gustain slipped his handgun into his jacket and faced his friend. He guessed the aged Nazi doctor planned his argument to spare Falk's life. Gustain knew the doctor's past, and the recognition gained with Americans and Nazis. The buttoned-up, bow-tied doctor had been a prized catch and valued as highly as von Braun. Wernher von Braun put American rockets in the air while Strughold kept high-altitude pilots alive. Few in Washington recognized him for killing scores of human guinea pigs drawn from German prisoner camps.

Years of friendship would not be thrown aside. Not knowing what to expect, Gustain looked down at the hunched-over man. Had the doctor reverted to his earlier cold-blooded ways to protect Falk?

Strughold spoke. "You of little faith, the author of life promised the dead shall live, and their bodies will rise."

Gustain stepped close and sat next to his friend. "You believe that?"

"We can do more with Falk alive."

"Have you come to convince me or kill me?"

"Cryopreservation."

"That from your bible?"

"The procedure will return the Germany we fought for."

"You have proof I can see with my eyes?" Gustain asked.

"You are free to decide."

"Jaminson, and the two women?"

"They are not my concern."

"What happens to Falk?"

"He will vanish as if you had killed him. This will satisfy Dulles."

"I never lost hope," Gustain said, "Show me."

Southern California traffic cruised along Highway 101 at the posted speed. Gustain took precautions and remained in the slower lanes. His friend, Hubert Strughold, stretched out in the back seat.

Heading south, they approached the small city of LaHabra. Strughold sat up and leaned over the driver's seat, pointing east toward the cluster of valleys and rolling green hills.

"We are going to Brea."

"Not to San Diego?" Gustain asked.

"Dulles and his spies do not know this place."

"I don't like surprises," Gustain said.

"Our Noah Institute near San Diego was for Dulles's eyes, a decoy."

Gustain slowed and exited the highway, pulling the car into a parking spot along a narrow surface street. Shutting off the engine, he turned back to his passenger.

"You understand, I intend to destroy your Noah Institute," Gustain said. "You were in the room with Dulles."

Gustain drew his gun, setting it in his lap.

"Continue to Brea." Strughold pointed ahead. "This is where Falk and I made our discoveries."

"You lied about everything to Dulles?"

"No. What Dulles wanted, we achieved."

"That was?"

"Mind control and interrogation drugs. CIA weapons to win the Cold War."

"You built a second lab," Gustain said. "This is what you intend to show me?"

"Dulles gave us an open checkbook and not once asked where the money went. I suspect he did not want to know," Strughold said. "That is how America works." Strughold slapped Gustain on the shoulder and laughed in a high pitch.

"Who knows?"

"Only three and our patients."

Gustain craved to trust his only friend but feared driving into a setup. He realized the German doctor was passionate, and he'd stop at nothing to keep Falk alive. Strughold's remark on mind control captured his attention. Could those same medications account for the unrest he'd experienced? Did his ally, who brought him to the CIA, have underlying motives? Could he have been one of Strughold's guinea pigs?

Gustain stared at Strughold.

"Show me your burning bush."

Valencia Avenue carried the two through a small business district lined with flashing yellow lights and stop signs. Escaping Brea, they passed abandoned oil derricks followed by endless lush groves of navel oranges and lemons. Hidden between clusters of towering, lanky palms, a single-lane road appeared in the car's high beams. Gustain slowed as instructed. A signpost nailed to a rail fence read Carbon Canyon Road.

"Look for the first turnoff," Strughold said.

Once on the winding canyon road, Gustain pulled onto an unpaved shoulder and stopped, jolting Strughold forward from his seat.

"I smell a trap... and only one of us is going home."

"Have faith, my countryman. You are about to see our future."

Gustain nodded. "I am curious."

Strughold hinted at a smile, something Gustain rarely saw.

The German doctor poked Gustain's arm. "You have the destiny of our homeland in your hands. I trust you will make the correct choice. Nothing can be of greater importance."

"Our dead friend in the trunk?" Gustain asked.

"He will like the accommodations."

Humor, of any kind, was out of character for his German friend. Gustain presumed nervousness, letting it pass. Aided by a large, lustrous moon that emerged from low clouds and smog, his eyes became alert for the slightest movement near the road's shoulder. In an attack, he'd escape into the orchards, distance himself, and circle back, hiding in the rows of trees to pick off his assailants. He judged there would be three, maybe five. They most likely did not intend to capture him, instead trapping him in the car for speedy execution. Gustain expected they came equipped with automatic weapons and jet fuel to incinerate his remains—the CIA's preferred practice left no traces.

Not far into the canyon, an asphalt road forked off, leading to wooden sheds and dozens of canvas-covered transport trucks parked in straight rows. The street emptied into a parking lot of newly sprouted weeds popping between crushed gravel.

Gustain stopped, sending fine dust around them, and yanked the emergency brake.

"Is this a joke?" Gustain asked, stepping from the car, holding his revolver at his side.

Strughold faced his friend, "It's a packing house."

"I didn't come to pick oranges," Gustain said.

"In a few months, harvest begins."

"Show me something I can believe."

Gustain scanned the buildings and sheds, finding no signs of a trap. He wouldn't drop his guard. They were in an ideal spot, removed from civilization. Yelps of hunting coyotes broke the late-night calm.

"This way." Strughold pointed to a two-story wood and brick building identified by a painted white sign, Brea Fruit Co., attached to the rusted tin roof.

"Stay close," Gustain warned.

"Our lab is underground, two floors beneath our feet. Private and safe."

"Show me what you have that's worth your life."

Inside the musty room, wooden sorting tables linked by idle rubber belt conveyors dominated the massive space. Walking on a hard-packed dirt floor and in darkness, Strughold led them past aisles of flimsy packing crates and pallets stacked at the base of each conveyor. At the far end, Strughold slapped his palm on a tall, steel gate.

"This way. Mind a few stairs?" he asked.

"No secret passages?"

"Nothing to attract suspicion," Strughold said, flipping a light switch after the door closed.

Arriving at the lower basement, two floors below, Strughold stopped and forced a second door open, lunging his bulky shoulder into its sturdy frame.

"This once guarded a cold storage room."

"And now where you and Falk made your discoveries?"

Strughold used two sets of keys to unlock the thick wooden doors and disarmed multiple alarms using three individual keypads. Wobbling on large suspended rollers, the last door slid open,

"This is the only entry?" Gustain asked.

"The site is secure. Better equipped than Hitler's bunker."

"Do I need protection?" Gustain asked before entering.

"There is no danger. Our patients are safe."

Gustain cherished his home and dreamed of a reborn Nazi authority as his Fuhrer promised. He shared the same love as his friend for Germany's return. His motherland, following surrender, suffered at the hands of punishing Allied forces. The country remained isolated from the world, shunned, and starving, while the Nazi military lived polite lives hiding in South America. He knew of false passports and identities used before and after Germany's surrender. The Catholic Pope had not been above aiding fleeing Nazis for a share of looted treasures.

What was he about to view—an extraordinary discovery promising a new Germany?

Or a trap?

Gustain's speculation halted. The door opened with an icy blast of air, refreshing him. Its interior resembled photographs shown him by Dulles.

No larger than a basketball court, the laboratory represented what his friend had risked his life for and demanded the same from him. Brown tiled floors and white walls housed ceramic and steel autopsy tables. Huge cylindrical vessels circled the room.

"This equipment is nothing but a tool," Strughold said. "The results are why we are here."

The exhaust fans in the tall ceiling kicked in and ran silently, causing stringy cobwebs to jar loose, float free, and be vacuumed away. More fans followed, adding a soft humming to the underground room, enough to hide footsteps.

At first, the lab appeared routine, like many pharmaceutical laboratories dotting California—test tubes and beakers sat scattered on laminated tabletops.

He wasted precious time, allowing himself to visit nothing more than a dreary high school chemistry lab in the middle of an orange grove.

Strughold pointed to tall stainless steel cylinders near where both stood. "We have come a long way."

Gustain and Strughold climbed narrow metal stairs to the top of a well-braced platform.

"You are about to see man's greatest discovery," Strughold said.

The aged doctor slid open a metallic shield, exposing a curved glass window built into a large cylinder.

"I am showing you what only three people in the world know."

CHAPTER THIRTY

Birdie pushed her throbbing shoulders against the brick and stone home, hoping to stay hidden. She deliberated whom she feared more: Shelley or Falk.

The scene may have been a clip from a late-night Frankenstein horror movie. Fabian followed Shelley's command and shuffled to the damaged steel bed. Falk jammed the long needle into Fabian's biceps, and within minutes, the two eased him into a laying position. The silver-toothed doctor waved Shelley off after she pulled a set of handcuffs from a drawer.

Involving the Los Angeles police risked Jaminson. Until a better choice surfaced, her primary concern was to use Shelley and Falk as a path to Hamilton Jaminson.

Questions came faster than those answered. Finding Jaminson led to a greater puzzle, one she suspected but unprepared for. Unveiling the mystery of Fabian and the canyon home raised the possibility of exposing Hamilton Jaminson—for what, she didn't know and doubted Lenora wished to open her former husband to scandal and, judging by tonight, a field day for the media.

Birdie had sent Lenora away to the safety of their hotel bar and Pello at the piano. Unhindered by her client, allowed Birdie to work, not looking over her shoulder, concerned for her client's wellbeing.

Her plan had backfired. Pello represented danger.

How long would she stay unnoticed? Would capture lead to handcuffing to a bed or arrest as a peeping Tom?

Thankful for flat shoes, retreating against gale-force squalls wouldn't be as agonizing. The exercise allowed time to sort out events since arrival in Los Angeles. The absurdity of a parrot's envy and threatened attack ranked far behind what she'd viewed in the house, yet she remained shaken by the bird's aggressive behavior.

Building furious winds continued, carrying tree branches, pine cones and fragments of broken roofing shingles as menacing and lethal projectiles. Trapped, something blunt jarred her back, knocking her to the ground. Moments later, an errant boat cushion blew free, bouncing, rolling upright, snared in brush and tumbleweed, piled against a rocky hillside.

A cluster of swaying lights, trimming the home's boathouse, appeared, and Birdie intended to make it her refuge. Not a swimmer and fearing water, she battled the wind and salvaged the boat cushion from a thorny scrub bush.

Birdie retreated toward the boathouse, gripping the cushion, shielding her face. As she ran, she heard the rumble of Shelley's Corvette race into the street and speed off. Whether she carried a passenger, Birdie could only guess.

Did Shelley return to the Hilton lounge to retrieve Fabian's look-alike? Birdie was in no position to follow. She'd placed herself in a trap. The windstorm intensified, forcing her to grasp tree limbs to remain upright. The Devil Winds, the hurricane-force storms her cab driver had described, would put her survival skills to the test in the dark canyon.

She thought the exaggeration intended to frighten her, gaining the taxi a return fare to the jazz club.

Birdie stumbled, approaching the boathouse ramp, noticing Fabian's bedroom. He rose to his feet. To her disbelief, he staggered to the metal door, attempted to open it, pounding with both fists.

She became irritated at Shelley and Falk. Had they left him alone? Did he see her and intend to hunt for her, knowing she couldn't travel far in the storm?

Curiosity needled her—what went on inside? It was the last thing she should want. Birdie craved survival, not to return to the home. She had no answer. Arguing against her Irish stubbornness proved foolish. This time, it would not stop at the window. She'd break in.

Birdie stepped from the tree she'd gripped, slipping, falling to the dry grass. From her knees, she reached and grabbed the trunk of a broad Oak tree—fingers of one hand dug into deep ridges of rough bark. The other hand clung to her purse and cushion. A gust pushed her, breaking her free of the Oak. She gathered her feet under her, attempting to gain balance, intending to use the massive trunk as a shield.

In an instant, before she celebrated victory, she skidded and slipped. The boat cushion tumbled from her, remaining on dry land. She grabbed at the sparse grass growing among loose rocks. Nothing promised a rescue, Birdie slid down the bank's abrupt drop-off toward deep, choppy waves. Had invisible hands of the Devil Winds seized her, carrying Birdie in a free fall? The sensation of a momentary escape, seeing her life flash in front of her before a disaster.

Her purse and handgun dragged her down as her arms flailed, pounding cold water, shouting, struggling to keep her head above breaking whitecaps.

The boathouse, she sought as protection, looked beyond reach. Surging wind and waves beat against her, pushing her further into the vast lake. How much strength did she have to resist? She shouted for help, expecting none.

From the bank, a hand reached, grabbing her wrist.

CHAPTER THIRTY-ONE

Gustain gripped the handrail and leaned to stare into the tall steel cylinder. Soles of four wrinkled feet, kept by metal clamps, hung in cloudy, bubbly liquid. Wispy long hair floated, drifting past dull, hollow faces.

Fighting Russians on the bloody German eastern front had hardened him to broken, dead bodies bulldozed into massive graves. Gustain stepped from the platform. The disturbing image desecrated nature.

What troubled him? He killed for a paycheck.

The flaccid corpses produced images of Strughold's experimentations, exposing imprisoned Poles and Jews to extreme cold till their death.

Strughold slid an aluminum door over the round viewing window.

"Cadavers?" Gustain asked.

"Much more. Patients waiting for a remedy."

"What did I just see?"

"The future," Strughold said. "Once the patient dies, Falk and I restart blood circulation and inject medications to protect cells from dying. Later, Falk and I replace the fluids with medical-grade antifreeze.

"That is the result?" Gustain pointed at the group of tanks.

"A preserved human, yes."

"Dulles does not know."

Strughold shook his head, stepping close to the tank's gauges. "He would not understand. As you do not appreciate Falk's value."

"To hang bodies in steel caskets?"

"Our patients are comfortable in a warm solution of preservatives. In two weeks, they go into freezers." Strughold pointed to rows of slender, horizontal tubes connected to braided stainless hoses suspended from the ceiling.

"For what?" Gustain asked.

"A cure for their cause of death."

"It's not natural."

"Since the 1700s, they have brought people back to life," Strughold answered.

"Like this abomination?"

"Cardio-Pulmonary Resuscitation," Strughold said slowly. "CPR. Our German army used it."

"No. There is a difference."

"Cryonics is comparable to pounding on someone's chest and breathing into their lungs." Strughold tapped on a tall cylinder and went on. "We allow the dead to wait for advanced technology."

"This helps Germany?"

"Military leaders are aging and dying in South America. This will give them back to our Homeland."

"You plan to accomplish this here?"

"In Brea, no." Strughold's footsteps echoed, walking past stainless steel cylinders, running his hand along each. "Our work is at an end here. Falk conspired with ailing generals to finance and hasten our effort by stealing from a wealthy American."

"Hamilton Jaminson?"

"Falk's ambush went sideways. Dulles learned of it and brought you in to clean up the mess."

"If not here, where?"

"Argentina. These bodies are mere guinea pigs."

Gustain studied Strughold. His posture and walk became uneasy and labored—attempting to hide a slight limp?

"Nothing changed my mind," Gustain said.

"I need time."

"I have orders."

"Bear with me." Strughold paused and touched Gustain's arm. "Have you failed to recall significant moments in your life?"

Gustain grabbed Strughold's jacket lapels, shoving him against a cylinder.

"What have you made me into?"

Strughold held his arms above his head as Gustain pressed Strughold against the steel vat.

"You survived. I would not have harmed you."

"What was done?"

"Release me. We can talk."

Relaxing his grip, Gustain lowered the old doctor he believed a mentor. Never again would he trust anyone. To the CIA, he was an outcast, a hired gun manipulated by Dulles's absolute authority.

Gustain took another look at the well-lit chamber and questioned how many bodies hung in storage or reposed, like frozen lab specimens. With the laboratory hidden several floors below the packing house, were more rooms keeping secrets?

For the moment, he had seen enough.

His mind reeled. Thoughts of past, horrific dreams, rocketed from repressed memories, fought to surface from deep in his subconscious. Had Falk and Strughold formed him as an outlying version of Victor Frankenstein's monster? Cast not from plundered body parts, instead, molded by a modern-day Prometheus. Similar to the cunning beast, Gustain shared the same wants—his quest to vanish in South America and seek happiness swelled.

Strughold led Gustain to an autopsy table and swung out two stools. "Sit, this will take a moment."

"You were not part of this." Strughold waved his arms around the room in a complete circle. "Drugs and electro-shock worked with you. You reacted well. We brought you to Washington after a stay in our California safe house."

"Are there others?"

"It's not necessary to know that."

Gustain pulled his knife, snapping the jagged blade open, resting it against Strughold's larynx. "I'm not asking again!"

"Others have not responded as you."

"Last chance," Gustain whispered, pushing his face inches from the doctor.

Doctor Strughold raised a hand to his neck. Trickles of blood dripped onto the tiled floor.

"Identical twins. One received the same conditioning as you. The other a control subject."

"Twins?"

"They fascinated Hitler. He wanted their unique genetics to improve his Aryan super race."

"... and they are in the safe house?"

Strughold nodded as he wiped away the blood with his fingers.

"What else?"

"I prefer to show what we have done with our two."

"You are running out of time, Doctor."

"We have gone a step further."

"Go on."

"First, meet Pello and Fabian."

Strughold appeared to stall. Gustain's patience waned. Nothing he'd seen gave evidence to create a new Nazi Germany. Tanks of dead bodies and a room full of laboratory equipment only proved Falk and Strughold built a chemistry lab, not anything more than what he would find in a superior German school. For all he knew, the elaborate workshop could have been another diversion. Despite skepticism, he owed it to the man he once considered an ally and family.

"Paint me a picture," Gustain said.

"The two subjects, Pello and Fabian, became patients in these containers."

Gustain allowed the knife blade to slice deeper, bringing more blood. He saw fear in the frail doctor's eyes. Gustain recognized the former Nazi would not display weakness. He'd die with honor rather than disgrace the dignity of a German officer.

"They contracted a virus, poliomyelitis," Strughold said. "We kept them suspended for years until Salk's vaccine."

"You and Falk restored them?"

"They live in Los Angeles, fully normal."

"Show me."

"There is more," Strughold said. "We enhanced one with endurance, strength and intelligence as we did to you."

"That is not natural."

"You are essential. I watched over you."

"No!" Gustain shouted. "I was nothing more than a specimen...an experiment."

"You are the prototype. They filled our homeland with pacifists broken by defeat. Our Fuehrer detested weakness."

"What are you not telling me?" Gustain looked into the doctor's eyes, believing there was more than Strughold showed him.

"You are not ready."

"My family?" Gustain asked.

Despite the workroom's chill, beads of sweat dotted Strughold's face. Gustain listened and surveyed the cylinders and tables, expecting the crafty doctor lured him into a trap.

"What was the question?"

"Answer me," Gustain shouted. "What happened to my family?"

"Only Dulles knows."

"Where are Falk and the man he kidnapped?"

Gustain recognized Strughold's slight weight transfer, favoring one leg. His feet slid apart to balance his stocky frame on the stool.

Strughold shook his head and dropped to the floor, landing on a knee, awkwardly attempting to draw a pistol from under wide-cuffed, wrinkled slacks.

Gustain cursed for neglecting to check for a concealed ankle holster.

The aged doctor's sluggish efforts offered Gustain justification to make a quick kill with no sympathy.

The doctor fumbled, pulling his cuff away, and failed to draw his revolver from the hidden holster. Gustain pressed the knife's point snug against Strughold's throat, drawing a line of darkened blood.

"Want to live?" Gustain yelled. "Tell me what I want to know."

Strughold pointed to his desk. "My calendar. Jaminson is in the water tower."

"Why protect Falk?"

"He will reproduce a new genetically identical Fuhrer."

The knife blade sliced through the larynx, ripping deep into the carotid artery. Gustain grabbed Strughold's head, forcing his chin down, pressing raw cartilage against the knot of his bow tie, keeping blood contained, and splattering to the tile floor. Gustain held his once ally tight against him, feeling rapid convulsions lessen as the German doctor gasped for air, dying in his arms. Despite rage, sadness came for his former friend.

* * * *

Gustain removed the wrapped body from the trunk of his car, hoisting it to his broad shoulder. At the late hour, the lone witness, a hazy moon, watched over the remote sorting and packing house. How long would he have the place to himself? Two corpses, which he didn't plan on, needed discarding.

Returning to the lab, Gustain dumped the unknown body alongside Strughold, filling a concrete exam table. The killing in

Jaminson's hotel—unfortunate timing. The intruder had barged in, disrupting his work. He could no longer trust his long-time friend. Strughold and Falk worked for their interests. It was done and could not be undone. His temper bested him. He'd reacted in haste, a product of enhanced reflexes. Spotting the doctor's concealed gun confirmed he intended to kill anyone interfering with his clandestine operation.

His task waited, disposing of the bodies and clothes, leaving no trace—like dozens of previous killings. Strughold's slaying harmed the American space effort. For that, they would hold Gustain responsible.

The serrated blade worked efficiently, cutting away the victim's clothes, preparing the corpses for their last resting place. Gustain preferred hot-burning aviation fuel and a deep vertical grave for undetectable cremation. Instead, a large stainless steel tank provided a burial chamber until a cure for fatal knife wounds arrived.

Elimination of the sole person Gustain confided in had been troublesome. His void complete, he'd conclude the mission, hunt down the four targets Dulles hired him to eliminate, report by coded message, and disappear. Dulles valued Strughold's contribution to America's evolving space medicine program. Under no circumstance could he return to Washington, DC. Offshore banked cash and investments would have to last a lifetime.

Stepping from the fruit packing building, Gustain looked between metal Quonset huts and rickety sheds, keeping an eye open for slight tells, betraying a trap. Had he missed something Strughold and Falk hid from Dulles? Although his friend boasted of storing humans in a state of suspension—there was more beyond what he viewed.

He smelled a greater plan.

Rebuilding Germany to its former status called for a great leader, not restoring puppet generals. Its proud people demanded a dynamic Fuhrer.

Gustain saw a piece of the chessboard. His dead friend acted as a minor piece. Sacrificial pawns and knights in armor fighting 'til death. Where did the King and Queen hide?

Falk embodied not the missing part of Germany's re-birth, but their creator—a modern Prometheus.

Strughold required his partner to live. He gave his life in vain, attempting to murder a professional assassin. Falk was essential, not to the ongoing experiments in the Brea lab.

Something more.

The idea appeared absurd, but after what Gustain had seen, he'd accept anything.

CHAPTER THIRTY-TWO

Hidden in shadows and darkness, Birdie spotted a hand reaching. The lake's chilling water slowed reactions and drained energy as she fought to stay afloat. How long could she kick and flail? The muddy slope offered nothing to grab. Not a swimmer, she struggled to keep her head above water—the story of her hapless existence. YMCA swim lessons joined a crowded list of resolutions for the New Year.

Growing waves blurred visibility above the bank's jutting ledge. She had no choice but to grasp it—whoever it was.

Fingertips touched and grazed, slipping apart. She lunged, her face dipped below the whitecaps, as a large hand wrapped her wrist. Birdie grabbed, digging fingers into the firm arm, dragging her through the rough breakers.

"I'm afraid of water," the voice said.

He rose to his feet, pulling her to the bank, lifting her to the top of the grassy ledge. She tumbled to the overgrown lawn the instant she reached dry ground.

At least she hoped so.

Birdie didn't recognize the face of her Good Samaritan, kneeling alongside her. For a moment, neither spoke. Birdie coughed up water and fought urges to heave. Mud coated her knees and arms. Her best shoes, from Osgoods of Manhattan, were a loss. Exhausted, running made no sense. Legs and arms cramped, and for an instant, she wished her wealthy client and airplane had not entered her dismal life.

Hazy-dim light from the boathouse lamp gave Birdie a look at her knight in shining armor. He lacked the size and physique of Fabian, but appeared familiar.

"You're the cab driver," she said, retrieving her purse from the edge of the slope, thankful it eluded the water.

"I got worried," he said.

Birdie regained enough strength to pull to her knees, then to her feet. Her legs wobbled, and she let herself slump against a tree, refusing to allow him to see her weakened. The wind continued to howl, and the giant oak's trunk supporting her shuddered against her spine.

"Devil Winds are kicking up for sure."

She nodded, not understanding why the cabby had returned. Her concern remained with the home's resident. The last she saw Fabian, he appeared in his cell-like room, reminding her of New York's Rikers Island holding disturbed patients.

"Your car?" she asked.

"Up the street. I walked, afraid to be spotted." He stepped close, offering his hand.

Birdie, shocking herself, slung her arm away, halting his approach. The reaction startled her. Rejection became a product of her iron will to remain self-reliant. She had a job to do and trudged the small grade to the house, adding to the discomfort in her hip and shoulder, reminding her of an encounter with overhead stage rigging. She marched ahead, holding the cab driver for support. Wet clothes clung and pulled against her skin, making each step a struggle. She had a job and no time for self-pity.

Unsure of who occupied the home, Birdie walked, avoiding twigs and branches covering the lawn. She moved nearer the window, pushing aside long, thorny bushes she'd battled earlier. Fabian remained in the bedroom. The sedation appeared to have taken effect, placing him in a deep sleep. His bare chest rose and fell in a smooth rhythm. Birdie gambled and would enter, chancing no one returned, and Fabian continued unconscious.

Their intent for Fabian and Pello evaded her. A hunch told her there had been a connection, a strong one, to Jaminson.

Was Fabian human?

She withdrew her question the moment it pushed into her head, bearing empathy for the giant of a man—yet fearing him. With reluctance, she admitted, imagining Fabian's handsome face and muscled chest moving toward her in the chilly water.

Break-ins were not in her bag of tricks and chances were slim for a home tour invite from Shelley. The search for Hamilton Jaminson led to the isolated canyon. It added up. Jaminson and Shelley were seen together in South America and Los Angeles by her client. With no substantial evidence, by default, Shelley became the prime suspect and the house a crime scene. The white lab-coated man intrigued her, only as far as leading her to her payday locating Jaminson. A working girl with mounting bills couldn't afford to run off chasing imagined, sinister possibilities.

A felony led to jail time and losing her hard-earned New York PI license once her recent arrest record trickled through both state bureaucracies. Those reasons pointed to walking away—returning fresh with a different strategy. The reasoning solid and Birdie was confident Shelley would carry out her threat.

Lenora had hired her to do a job. She was on the doorstep of discovering the location of Lenora's former husband. She chose to not turn back from the trail.

Her concern, Lenora faced danger with Fabian's twin, Pello. She couldn't protect her tag-along client, who thought of herself as a partner.

Celtic Irish pride guided her. The Kelly clan fought land wars and survived lethal famines and no lesser a real Kelly than her treasured ancestors. She'd finish the current battle. Caught or arrested, she had faith in her centuries-old heritage to best what came at her.

Spending Lenora's cash became painless and second nature. She unrolled two hundred-dollar bills, handing both to the cab driver.

"What for?" he asked.

"For coming back and doing something else."

"You didn't rip old Ben in half," the cabbie said, inspecting the cash.

Birdie glanced at the large home and back to the driver. "I don't know your name."

"Cleon."

Not offering hers or a gracious handshake, Birdie continued. "If you're willing, there's two more.

"Name it."

"I'm cold. I'll make it fast," Birdie said.

Cleon removed his gray sweater, handing it to her.

Pulling it over her shoulders, Birdie managed a smile.

"A lady named Lenora Jaminson is at the Beverly Hilton. Find her in the bar. Tell her the PI located Shelley and to stay in her room. Got that?"

He nodded. "The second?"

"Come back for me."

"Why should she believe me?"

Birdie thought a moment. "Say she needs flying lessons."

"Slow night. I'll be back." The cab driver disappeared in the shadow of the thrashing giant oak limbs. Birdie sensed she dealt with a trustworthy man. He'd returned for her and saved her life, then gallantly offered his sweater. Cleon was a safe bet. He owned an honest face, looking her in the eye each time they spoke. She counted on him. What else could she do?

The warm winds continued dry and robust, and she remained wet and muddy. Not the way she wished to search a house, leaving a trail. Clothing needed removed and dried.

Birdie had little choice but to revive her Lady Godiva stage performance. Not as an English noble, but a scarred and mud-covered former Broadway actress.

The boathouse, raised and dropped on the choppy lake, provided a shield from blasting wind. Modesty being overrated, she had no time to waste. Birdie hung Cleon's damp sweater on a railing and removed her dripping clothes and undergarments. Holding tight to the rail, she permitted warm winds to caress her bare skin, leaving her refreshed. She scrubbed away thin layers of grime coating her dress and shoes, using wood shingles yanked from the boathouse. After a few twists and shakes to her skirt, bra, and panties, the howling gale dried them within minutes.

Remaining au natural to search the home tempted her. No loose threads or remnants of lake mud would give away her presence. Pinkerton's had taught her criminals left behind trace evidence and carried telltale signs from each crime.

Was it imagination? The wind storm, Cleon dubbed Devil Winds, warmed like those rising between New York's skyscrapers during sultry summers. Birdie remained undressed, enjoying the exhilarating passage of soothing gusts over her long, slender torso. With a tight grip on the rail, she turned to allow the drying, warm air to blow through her hair. For the first time since her stage accident, she felt no lingering ache.

With reluctance, she pulled her dried clothes on. The remarkable and blissful pain-free moment ended. Whatever triggered the brief relief had been worth it.

Her personal needs were not a concern. She was responsible for several lives.

How long had Shelley and her friend in the lab coat been gone? Time escaped Birdie. The distress of drowning muddled her perception. Minutes and hours blurred.

A complete search of the large two-story home would take too long. More than she guessed she had. Feeling the chronic dull pain in her shoulder and hip ebb back, she stepped from the swaying boathouse ramp. Waves splashed, banging and rocking the dock, reminding her of the drowning she'd escaped.

Birdie fought against the wind, fearing the mounting swells would drag her to the depths of the massive lake. This time Cleon would not be there. Her last step from the wood ramp caught her by surprise. A powerful gust carried a thick oak limb brushing past, crashing against the home's brick walls. If the abrupt cracking sound woke Fabian, bringing him to the window, she'd scrap her risky break-in plan and race from the house, hoping to catch the cab and escape. Moving from one oak tree to the other, Birdie reached Fabian's room.

He remained in the same condition, on his back, motionless.

With the home tucked away, deep in the dead-end street, she felt she'd remain unseen by neighborhood security or a rare passing car. Howling wind masked her missteps on scattered limbs and debris as she searched for an easy entrance, knowing homeowners to be careless. She found few options with ground-floor windows and doors.

Defeating a window lock became her choice of entry. She chose a bay window far from Fabian. Double-hung windows presented a minor challenge—a skill learned as a Pinky.

Shielded from the wind, she reached over her head and placed both palms flat and firm against the top pane, shaking the glass near the secured latch, vibrating the aluminum frame. The slow process took patience and a few stops to rest aching arms and shoulders. Success came, and the locking lever edged gradually to an open position. Birdie watched the room and the road, hoping she remained unseen. Barring a surprise house alarm, she'd enter. No security posters or window stickers warned prospective robbers, nor did telltale wires and sensors. If a dog threatened, she felt confident her calming manner would subdue an attack. She gave one final hard shake and freed the latch.

Birdie threw her leg up over the sill, climbed in, closed the window, and slid the curtains into place, leaving no sign of entry. A table lamp, its torn shade wrapped in a cellophane dust cover, lit the room. With luck, she was alone, and Fabian continued to count sheep.

An oval, rustic rock and copper fireplace dominated an open living area. Nearby, an antique roll-top desk pushed snug against a library table cluttered with file folders fastened with a stout cord—each bundled inside clear plastic pouches. She put off searching the desk, needing explore the house, hoping Jaminson was in one of the many rooms.

White walls, void of pictures and photographs, smelled of fresh paint. National Geographic's jammed floor-to-ceiling shelves. A collection of taxidermy mounts: corpses of raccoons, squirrels and birds perched inside a display shelf. Miniature spotlights glinted off pairs of frozen brown plastic eyes stared at her. At the foot of the glassed-in case, molted gold and green feathers lay scattered. Birdie flinched at the thought of Pello's envious parrot.

The house groaned as if alive. Windows rattled, absorbing barrages of loose debris battering its exterior. Birdie questioned if she'd detect anyone entering.

Undaunted, she searched the home, risking being shot and buried at the bottom of the lake.

Irish luck saved her once tonight. Could she count on it to persist?

She walked across polished wood floors, looking and listening. Hollow footfalls echoed in her wake. A dim hallway led to a gray steel door that stood out like an out-of-place bank vault, fortified with padlocks and sliding bolts. She tapped the compact pistol inside her purse for reassurance. Her ear against the metal, she heard silence in Fabian's room. To her relief—no sign of life.

She'd continue.

A spiral staircase, hidden in a laundry area, led upstairs. Birdie climbed the narrow stairs, aggravating her throbbing hip.

She couldn't shake the feeling of being watched. Had she walked into a trap? Had Shelley lured her inside as she had to the jazz club? Were there more like Fabian and Pello locked away?

Birdie found only empty, unfurnished rooms and cobwebs clinging to ceilings and walls.

Air blasts continued to intensify. Brush and heavy limbs battered the house, threatening to burst windows and doors. Under the foyer's large domed rotunda, a brass chandelier swayed. An ill-timed LA earthquake could disrupt her resolve and send her running from the sprawling house.

Birdie admitted being shaken and unnerved by the continuous winds. She'd seen enough. How long could her luck hold? She'd push it and return to the roll-top desk, her last hope to find hard evidence connecting Hamilton Jaminson to Shelley.

The closed desk slid open after a firm pull. Scribbled notes, in a foreign hand, and reams of hand-written chemical formulas crammed slots and narrow cubbyholes. Outlines of brown coffee cup rings covered a small desk blotter. The surprise came inside a deep drawer near her feet. A handgun rested in a black leather holster—not the standard American variety, a German Luger.

After a second glance, she realized what she almost overlooked. Judging it a prank or depraved gag, she flipped open several pages. It appeared genuine, although decades old—the prestigious cover of the 1938 Time Magazine named Adolph Hitler Man of the Year. The image rekindled youthful memories of newsreels depicting The Third Reich's relentless bombing of London. Distracted by those horrid remembrances, Birdie examined a pair of Argentine passports. Photographs identified Shelley and her lab-coated accomplice, Horst Falk. Shelley's travel stamps showed entries and exits to Argentina, Germany and The United States. Falk's—nothing. Each page remained unstamped.

Near the desk and library table stood a tall metal cabinet, out of place against the room's wood panels and white walls. The double doors didn't budge. Its lock refused her knife's prying, and every trick she knew with a twisted, bent paper clip.

She plopped herself into a chair and slid next to the roll-top desk, hopefully, the cabinet's keys were hid in easy reach. Detective work boiled down to drudgery and observation. She'd allow her eyes and mind to take over.

It helped to think of the key as not hidden but unseen, as stage magic was not real but an illusion, distracting the observer's attention. She visualized the key resting in a location, quick and easy to reach from her seat.

Birdie needed a touch of Irish luck. She'd leave logic to the snobbish and pretentious British mastermind, Sherlock Holmes.

On the other hand, the key may dangle on Shelley's keyring.

Reason and common sense screamed for Birdie to escape and run from the house. Live for tomorrow. Return to stake out the home and wait for the occupants to lead her to Jaminson. The gamble she took unnecessarily, with no thought, she'd placed an innocent cab driver at risk here and searching for Lenora.

Looking through the rows of cubbyholes and slots of the upright desk yielded an assortment of stamps, papers and envelopes, nothing gave her a clue to find Jaminson. About to leave, she tried again, dragging her palm inside the thin center-pull drawer. A slight rise along the smooth oak finish stopped her fingertips. She slid her hand from under the desk, satisfied.

The shallow drawer prevented Birdie from grasping her find. She slipped the narrow drawer from its runners, exposing the desk's bottom. Metal hypodermic needles rolled and fell to the floor. Birdie dropped to the carpet and placed the awkward drawer next to her. White medical tape held what she expected to be a key. Yanking the tape, the key fell and bounced on the floor.

The lock clicked. Tall doors of the cabinet swung open. Nothing extraordinary grabbed her attention. Loose papers and leather-bound laboratory notebooks—none interested Birdie. Chemistry was not the reason she'd broken into the house.

A handheld Kodak 8 movie camera and stacks of boxed tape reels filled a shelf. Birdie doubted the film contained remembrances of birthdays and christenings. She grabbed two red and yellow boxes.

Reel # 7, Brea lab- Post-mortem preservation of body fluids.

Reel # 8, Brea lab- body cool down and prepare for deep freeze.

She shoved the packets into her shoulder purse, vowing she'd force herself to view the expected morbid images on the slim chance they'd provide a lead to Jaminson.

On the bottommost shelf, matched brown leather satchels rested side by side, hidden by a small box safe. Birdie slid the cases from the cabinets and stopped. A thunderous crash, followed by tree boughs collapsing near a large bay window, startled her as a pair of tree limbs entered the room. Caution told her to leave. She'd be no use to Lenora locked away with Fabian.

Sliding the bulky bags back in place, Birdie tipped one bag, exposing a vanity monogram burned into the leather. It read—HJ.

Hamilton Jaminson? A coincidence?

They had forced the small locks, likely a hammer and screwdriver, judging by scarred brass and leather. Los Angeles Police would implicate Jaminson, and the found money, linking him to what occurred in the canyon home. She would not allow herself to think the coal and steel baron was part of what went on.

Birdie yanked the satchel's flaps to the side—hundred-dollar bills, wrapped in Federal Reserve currency straps, filled both bags. She sat on the floor, staring. Why had Jaminson traveled with so much cash? She ran her hands over the stacks and shoved them behind the safe, leaving the desk and cabinet as she'd found them.

She couldn't ignore her belief. Order existed in chaos. Disorder experienced in the past twenty-four hours positioned her for the discoveries: Moncy, Hitler, German firearms, and towering, handsome look-a-likes. None of it connected. She'd play it out—pushing her chips into the middle of the table.

Outside, Birdie walked from the home, relieved to avoid a confrontation with Fabian, ducking behind a bricked wall. Alert for approaching cars, crossed the long driveway, running, favoring her throbbing hip. Birdie took a last glance at the home's front door, hoping Fabian would continue sedated and locked in his room.

Stranded with no sign of human life on the canyon road, she became less protected. Fierce winds offered no mercy, showing no letup, lashed her, pushing her to stumble and fall to rough asphalt. Birdie inhaled to calm herself. Dry, blowing desert air carried the unmistakable smell of smoke.

Cleon had plenty of time and cash to find Lenora and return. How long had it been? She'd adapted to LA life as she had to New York; loyalty came with a price tag. Had she misjudged him?

Returning to the hotel, assuring her client was secure and safe, became the night's task. They had thrust her into something bizarre and a personal battle to survive. Exhaustion would not turn her into a coward. Waving a white flag is not an option for a New York City Irish girl.

Headlights approached Birdie winding through the canyon road.

CHAPTER THIRTY-THREE

Gustain sped through the narrow black-topped road, winding his way from the Brea Fruit Company and Falk's monstrous handiwork. Dulles had not mentioned Strughold and Falk preserving bodies or creating modern-day Frankenstein.

Winter moonlight illuminated remote homes tucked far off the street inside immense citrus groves. Fearing being noticed, he navigated without headlights. His car would attract attention and people would remember it because of the late hour.

Gut feelings told him to turn Strughold's lab into a burning inferno. Restoring Germany's Third Reich to what it had been under Hitler's Nazi government was an illusion, imagined by loyal high-ranking officers leading new lives in Argentina. Falk's greed led to Strughold's death. Gustain rejected Germany's old guard. Nazi dictatorship had robbed him of his final year of university lessons and a life of promise at Oxford or Cambridge.

How different his days might have been. Forced to enlist, he trained as a combat soldier, advancing in rank, competing for favor in Hitler's grandiose visions.

It became clear Strughold, and Falk operated the workshop near San Diego as a ruse, misdirecting Dulles and the CIA away from their ghoulish experiments deep freezing corpses for future restoration. Experienced with Strughold's cautious nature taught him the old German doctor remained tight-lipped until results proved successful.

What discovery could be worth the immense risk taken by the two men? Dulles kept his German doctors and agents on short leashes. Transgression punishments stretched from deportation to silent executions.

Strughold and Falk had achieved high military ranks, winning favor with the Fuehrer and honored with his rare award, The German National Prize—Hitler's version of the treasured Nobel Prize. Their heralded distinction became public, but their creation remained secret.

There continued another deeper layer. Strughold had gambled his life for something more than what he exposed in the packing house's basement. What Gustain couldn't guess—its significance grew to be worth more than their lives.

Gustain banged the steering wheel with both fists. A burst of anger had pushed him to kill Strughold without learning what they covered up. His onetime friend will take his secret to the grave, sharing it with Hitler in hell.

His mission so far was a failure; he'd killed a second non-target. He questioned the individual's motives for breaking into Jaminson's suite. Hamilton Jaminson's capture by Falk and Strughold smelled of CIA involvement gone wrong. Dulles accused Jaminson and the two women of conspiring to buy a classified CIA project from Falk—leading to the kidnapping of Jaminson. Strughold's role, white-washed, protected him as a valued asset to the Americans. Whatever had gone sideways—eliminating the remaining participants fell in Gustain's lap.

Gustain drove from the citrus groves and turned north, using a near-empty 57 Highway, returning to Hollywood to complete his assignment. Rest and a night's sleep remained a delayed luxury, as did a fresh change of clothes. Reaching into the jacket pocket, he removed the torn page taken from Strughold's desk calendar—the location of Jaminson's and Falk's whereabouts—Sunset Boulevard / Foothill Road / Water Tower.

Gustain tossed the scrap of paper inside the pages of a new Thomas Street Guide. He'd pursue the fresh lead to uncover Falk, like the well-trained soldier from his youth.

The conspiracy hatched by Nazi extremists, aspiring to return to their homeland, would end tonight. He'd locate and kill the shadowy Dr. Falk, the man Strughold credited as holding the key to the project they conceived. Birdie Kelly and Lenora, minor players in the developing mystery, would be his curtain call performance.

Gustain drove the streets of Hollywood, passing the Beverly Hilton Hotel and its bright lights illuminating rows of palms surrounding its grounds.

On impulse, he swerved, cutting across lanes, steering into the hotel's parking garage. His hunt for Jaminson and Falk had to be delayed. He'd detour and examine Birdies and Lenora's room for anything left behind. His troubles couldn't continue; they never had. Not a believer in good or bad luck, breaks had not gone his way since arriving in Los Angeles. His targets had a suite here, and in time, he'd uncover the ladies.

Gustain slammed the car door and entered the lobby through the garage entrance. Could he be losing his edge? He should have been more aware. Someone watched him approach the night clerk. Judging by their dingy garb, the man was far from being a guest or employee. He guessed the long-haired man in the lounge, sporting a stained flannel shirt and broad in the beam, was a cab driver.

At the elevator, Gustain chose a lower floor. He'd exit and, as before, use the emergency stairway. Whoever watched him was no pro.

Birdie and Lenora didn't answer their door at the late hour despite continued knocking.

He used the staircase and returned to his rental car. He hunted for larger game.

Exhausted, he allowed his head to relax against the steering wheel before pulling from the hotel. A check of his mirrors told him no one followed.

Military training blocked him from thinking of rest or the pleasures of a hot shower and a warm meal. His mission had suffered a breakdown, nothing he could not salvage.

The search continued. Priorities demanded uncovering Jaminson. Falk and his captive wouldn't expect a late-arriving guest, armed and eager to shoot first, bypassing introductions.

At the curb, near a lighted bus stop, Gustain checked his map confirming LA's confusing cross streets. After locating his current position, he circled the intersection of Sunset and Foothill Road, marking an X over the spot. He promised to stay patient, not rushing into an error; a deserved night's rest not far off.

Approaching Foothill Road, a red beacon flashed. The tall, well-lit structure appeared suspended in the darkening sky, materialized several blocks ahead, stealing his attention. The massive tower, unlike anything he'd remembered in Germany or America, may have been a mirage or hallucination brought by fatigue. Dense green hedging wrapped a chain-link fence overgrown with ivy, crowned itself with spirals of barbed wire. An exposed elevator centered within immense steel girders rose to its peak.

Closer, the odd structure at the top looked like a massive water tower found along a railroad line. Windows and a balcony circled the top of its three floors. Gustain left his car and craned his neck, taking in the bizarre structure perched on stilts hovering over a neighborhood of homes and businesses.

Overhead, a small plane's buzzing engine interrupted early morning stillness. Gustain, aided by clear skies and moonlight, spotted the craft banking and circling the out-of-place tower. In a moment, the twin-engine plane, towing a long streaming banner, turned north and faded behind a ridge of hillside homes.

This would not be a simple kick in the door, assault and barge-in. Reaching Jaminson and Falk required a better plan.

Gustain returned to the car after discovering the tower gate locked but lacked parameter security. Chances were good the elevator would not be operating and scaling the well-lit steel legs made him an easy target. His best choice—sit and wait for someone to exit or enter the lofty fortress.

Finding parking with a vantage point, regardless of the late hour, had been difficult. He squeezed into a slot near a curb, nudging close to a crosswalk. The road appeared free of pedestrians—no eyewitnesses. He remained at a distance to view the surroundings, allowing him to spot arrivals. Gustine gambled Strughold had scribbled Falk's and Jaminson's location on the desk calendar after a phone call, avoiding his formal work journal.

Chances needed to be taken. If Falk ran, he'd soon he'd be out of the country and hiding in South America.

Across the street, a Los Angeles black and white patrol car pulled from an all-night Texaco gas station. The patrolman must have needed a nature break and noticed Gustain surveying the tower. He'd committed the error because of sloppiness, something he could not tolerate. Not remaining aware of his surroundings cost him unwanted attention. How did he overlook the police cruiser in a well-lit lot? The cop had spotted him. He'd stuck out from the norm, making himself visible. Any decent patrol officer would question those suspicious actions.

He'd hemmed himself in with no backup plan.

Gustain held a legal Virginia driver's license, a clean driving record, and rental paperwork secure, tucked above the sun visor. There was little to fear. Nothing could be flagged in the state or local police history.

An inspection of the car's trunk would force him to shoot the innocent cop. Dried blood covered the spare tire, and a duffle bag stowed military-grade explosives. He read the situation as high risk. A cop working the graveyard shift had time to kill in the affluent beachside area. There was an excellent chance the bored, low-ranking officer may conduct a thorough check of the car and driver. The cruiser rolled from the gas station, easing into the flow of traffic, appearing to turn away from him toward a taco stand lit in yellow neon.

The overhead red and white lights lit up as the black and white cruiser made an abrupt U-turn and approached.

No point running. Gustain had placed himself in a jam. He sat upright and looked at the car as it pulled beside him. His handgun sat under the seat in easy reach. His heart beat faster.

The patrol car's spotlight flashed, lighting Gustain's face.

Remaining calm, he'd offer an uncomplicated response if questioned. The patrol officer, Gustain guessed, was judging him, assessing the situation.

Gustain heard the sudden banging and rattling of cans. A vagrant popped into Gustain's rearview mirror. Hunched and limping, the figure exited from the shadows of a neighboring alley. The unexpected visitor pushed a battered grocery cart overflowing with a collection of tin cans and glass bottles. The next moment, the tramp broke into a slow jog, building speed, accelerating to a sprint, bowing his head, ramming his cart into the passenger side of the stopped and idling police car. The overloaded pushcart nose-dived. Metal cans flew, and glass bottles shattered, spilling, covering the asphalt and the black and white.

In the next instant, two helicopters trailing the planes appeared and hovered over the giant water tower. Not long after, black figures fastened to ropes exited a copter, dropping to the round, sloping roof. The larger, trailing copter aimed spotlights at the brightly lit tower. In moments, both helicopters circled and fired automatic weapons, shattering glass and splintering wood. As quick as the onslaught occurred, it halted, followed by a barrage of small blasts shredding the tower's metal roof. Both copters continued to hover above the attacaked building.

A monstrous bright flash lit the sky, followed by an explosion from inside the tower, ripping the entire structure apart, engulfing the pair of copters. In less than a minute, orange and yellow flames slashed into the dark sky and blackened smoke billowed, escaping the remains of the wooden fortress, roaring into the early morning sky. Skeleton wreckages of the two attack copters burned after dropping ten stories, collapsing on a low-rise parking garage.

Gustain stood beside the vagrant, among cans and broken glass as the police car sped away. There was something familiar about the bearded, bleeding man gripping the Safeway pushcart Gustain couldn't place.

CHAPTER THIRTY-FOUR

The car's headlights appeared, through blowing dust and debris, illuminating Birdie. The yellow cab pulled from the road to the dirt shoulder and waited.

"It's Cleon," he shouted through a half-open window.

Birdie had retreated to the dry, dense brush, ducking below rocks and boulders.

The taxi rolled closer, inching toward her, crunching fast-moving tumbleweed under its wheels. Fearing being swept away by the hurricane-force wind, Birdie crawled, dragging her purse through rock and hard-baked ground to its open door.

"You hurt?" Cleon shouted.

Birdie pulled herself into the car and slumped in the passenger seat, sharing it with scattered newspapers and a brown crumbled lunch sack. For a moment, neither spoke nor made eye contact. Gusts from the canyon's dry foothills continued rocking the taxi. Jagged tumbleweed rolled and bounced, clawed at the car, trying to peel away the cab's roof, exposing her and Cleon to the devil winds.

"Get these often?" she asked, pulling knotted hair from her face.

"Not this bad."

Cleon eased the yellow and black cab back to the street, stopping close to a turtle struggling from the dirt and gravel shoulder to the asphalt road.

The encounters at the lake house reminded Birdie of the wind's damaging power, recalling the destructive ability in Steinbeck's *The Grapes of Wrath*.

In a short time, the devil winds had affected her physically and emotionally. Enduring the constant forces and continuous howling had drained energy and weakened resistance to continue. A turtle crossing in the cab's headlights encouraged her. She thought again of Steinbeck's good-natured character, Tom Joad and his discovery of the struggling desert reptile, both enduring a hostile environment.

"The city's calm, but these canyons are hell this time of year."

"Lenora?" Birdie asked.

"No sign."

"Check her room?"

"I asked the desk clerk to knock. Nothing."

Birdie noticed her watch—after two in the morning. Where had Lenora gone?

"I tried to get back sooner," Cleon said. "A couple helicopters crashed and slowed traffic."

The entire night had become a bust. She'd lost Lenora. Her free-spirited client enjoyed adventure and may have looked for a diversion, relieving her mind from the unpleasant realities. Hollywood entertainment came in many forms and costs at their hotel bar.

Birdie admitted she kidded herself into believing her client safe, tucked away, and relaxing. There was no escaping the truth. A high likelihood existed, Lenora fell into danger with Shelley and Pello responsible. A visit to the police would force her to explain breaking into the canyon home, possessing stolen items, and involving Jaminson's uncertain venture.

She wanted time. Her shoulder and hip stiffened, bringing mild agony every step, forcing her to slow. Getting off her feet and a long soaking hot bath in her suite's giant tub nearly trumped laboring detective work, questioning desk clerks and late shift housemaids. Birdie speculated new leads would return her to Shelley's home and a face-to-face with the cunning South American beauty.

"Beverly Hilton?" Cleon asked.

"No place else. Why not?"

"Someone asked the hotel clerk about you."

Puzzled, Birdie recalled the men posing as Western Union staff visiting Lenora's New Jersey airport hangar. Outside Lenora, her location in Los Angeles remained undisclosed.

"He wear a tux?" Birdie asked.

"Sports coat, but it didn't go with his pants."

Despite discomfort, Birdie sat up, resting her trembling arms on the car's dashboard.

"Anything else?"

"My head came to his shoulders. He sounded German."

Birdie's mind spun. Distracted by the news, she turned and watched the road's yellow lines pass beneath the cab. She envisioned an Alfred Hitchcock thriller and Gregory Peck stepping onto the roadway, directing them back to the house she fled.

"What did the clerk say?"

"The big German had your picture. Said you were a friend and knew you were a guest."

"He did?" Birdie asked. She forced a nervous swallow.

"The guy asked several times and finally let it go."

"What did my so-called friend do?"

"Don't think he believed the clerk—caught the elevator."

"He connect you with me?"

"I've been driving a cab for twenty years. I would have known."

Birdie had stepped into something bigger than a missing person case. Someone hunted her.

Correction, they had found her.

Did Cleon's discovery of the German connect to Jaminson?

The super affluent, like ordinary citizens, had problems. Difficulties occurred with equal measure to their wealth. None of that mattered. Whatever went on forced her to look over her shoulder, distracting her hunt for Hamilton Jaminson and Lenora.

Her hotel appeared against the backdrop of distant moonlit mountains. It had been a long day, and she'd not slept since leaving Manhattan. Thanks to Lenora, she had plenty of cash in her purse—thousands according to her count. She'd trade it for a warm bed and a good night's sleep.

Birdie tapped Cleon's shoulder. "Stop the car."

They pulled into a vacant parking lot near Hollywood jewelry and fur salons fronted by brightly lit palms.

"I need time to think."

"The meter's running."

She worked in a city as a stranger—lacking friends or favors to pull in. In addition, someone stalked her. Hotels were obvious places to search, and the tall German asking for her used a photograph. Did he already know she was a guest, or had he moved from hotel to hotel making inquiries? Should she consider going to another part of town, far from Shelley and the Congo Jazz Club?

Birdie admitted she ran from confrontation and suspected her hotel room was no longer a secret. If the German mystery man planned to harm her, he'd enter her suite and wait, not attack in a public lobby surrounded by witnesses. Could he have information on Lenora and Jaminson?

She deliberated while the taxi meter ticked off minutes.

Had her scrappy Irish blood lost fight? There was now a personal risk. Her client went missing, and she couldn't do her job on the run and in a panic.

Lenora, Hamilton Jaminson and the strange occupants of the lake house needed to stay her principal concern. No second-guessing; she could not abandon her watch.

She'd remembered the two film cases stuffed inside her shoulder purse and hoped they'd clarify tonight's happenings.

Was her mind thinking clear? What options were there?

A notion popped into her head, not ideal, and for certain, risky.

CHAPTER THIRTY-FIVE

"Turn around," Birdie said.

The cabby braked and pulled to the curb.

"My shifts over... the day's over, and I have family," Cleon said, not bothering to face Birdie. "Which is it going to be?"

"Back to my hotel," Birdie said. "I'm not hiding."

"I'm dropping you off, and don't expect me to come back."

For the next several miles, Cleon hummed and whistled. Not a word exchanged between the two.

She recognized the new show tune he entertained her with, *Bridge on The River Kwai*, appreciating the driver's savvy, recalling the film's British colonel's refusal to back down while a prisoner of war. Had her driver offered an off-handed morale boost as she was about to march into her hotel and confront the unknown pursuer? What other adversity could rival what she had faced the past twenty-four hours? None of the day's events in New York or Los Angeles proved to be as criminal as her minor break-in—if her mystery caller turned out to be a cop.

What she saw done to Fabian had been circumstantial, no actual crimes committed. Although Shelley's actions were strange and could be explained as medical treatment. She had only guesswork and the film boxes removed from Shelley's and Falk's locked cabinet. It was a stretch to think the two reels would shed light on what went on.

Lights of the Beverly Hilton appeared. Birdie kept her eyes on the entry portico. Few cars remained parked outdoors while a doorman, sporting a red-zippered jacket several sizes short of a proper fit, stood sentry near glass double doors.

The cab slowed and crept along Wilshire Boulevard, approaching a manicured row of hedges and lighted palms. Birdie needed to settle on a strategy. If the man asking for her wasn't police—who was he and what did he want?

She could walk into the hotel cold turkey, flying by the seat of her pants, placing a target on her back, as she was prone to. Who was her hunter with her photograph? LA was an unfamiliar game. The West Coast played by different rules. Curiosity drew her to scrutinize her new pursuer while fighting off growing intentions to back away. Exhaustion should have taken her to a warm bath and bed, instead, it took her to danger.

Birdie preferred to battle a single adversary. She, up to this moment, considered it Shelley. Recent events led her to believe something larger brewed below the surface. The beautiful young jazz singer concealed a great deal more than her client's former husband.

A second surprise opponent had stepped on her stage—into her hotel. How he fit puzzled her. A confrontation, she hoped on her terms, appeared unavoidable. Doubting coincidence, she sensed a trap.

Wars fought on two fronts were seldom won and left her vulnerable.

"I changed my mind," Birdie said.

"Where to?"

"I have an idea."

"I'd walk in and go nose to nose with the flatfoot. That's what I'd do for sure," Cleon said, breaking from his continual whistling.

"You think he's a cop?" Birdie asked.

"Not local. Maybe sheriff's department."

She'd never hesitated in the past. Fatigue, along with a heavy dose of caution, was blamed. Admitting the canyon's relentless howling squalls triggered uneasiness she had yet to shake off.

Whoever the pursuer was, he gave her a slight edge. She knew he hunted her.

"Is there a back entrance?" she asked.

"Where the trash goes out."

"Take me."

"Sanitation trucks pick up at night not to offend snooty guests," Cleon said, steering the cab to the rear of the hotel.

"Drop me here."

Birdie slipped from the passenger seat, slamming the door.

Cleon shouted, "I got the fare. Don't worry."

She watched the car drive off, this time certain for good. No encores for Cleon, he'd done enough. He had bailed her out of the chilly water where she faced drowning. He'd appeared helpful, although she couldn't help suspecting he'd been too opportune. Could she trust him?

Thinking of his clash with the long-haired street preacher for a moment, she sensed an inkling of familiarity between the two. Then again, her imagination read too much into an innocent encounter.

No guilt, but a little pride came from breaking into the remote lake home. Discovering Jaminson's luggage filled with money proved her instincts and concerned her. She'd left the cash. Her assignment was to find Hamilton Jaminson, and the satchels would have slowed her down.

At the late hour, it remained quiet behind the Beverly Hilton's less showy area. She hoped not to be spotted by security. Coaxing her throbbing hip to cooperate, she jogged, using the hotel's trimmed bushes and trees as screens to reach the tall, roll-up metal doors.

The canyon's wind squalls had spared Hollywood, although birdie continued to suffer from the relentless Santa Anna's, which had affected her balance and rattled her mental state. Feeling jumpy and drained of energy, Birdie wasn't thinking clear. If these were the first signs of exhaustion, they had picked the wrong time. She shrugged it off as superstition and a wives-tale related to the so-called devil winds.

Nearing the heavy doors, she spotted several smoke-blackened, rusted incinerators enclosed by a high cinder block wall.

She pressed her spine against the cement blocks, relieving growing stress. What she needed was a soothing hot oil massage, not the misery she placed on her unstable body. Would she reach the hotel, and how did she plan to confront the man hunting her?

The distant service doors remained closed, preventing easy access to the basement.

An abrupt sound startled her. Instead of raging, disturbing winds rolling through canyons, a bulky City of Los Angeles sanitation truck crept from behind nearby shops and restaurants, turning the corner of a well-lit street, climbing a slight grade, exhausting black plumes of smoke, and a sour stench.

She slipped between rows of corroded incinerators and the block wall, deciding to stay put and wait for an opportunity. Out of character, she couldn't recall a recent time she'd used a cautious approach, something she should make a habit.

Did she seek unnecessary risks as arousal to compensate for her gender in a male-dominated profession filled with former cops? Until Lenora's arrival, she'd packed and unpacked moving boxes out of boredom and lack of work. None of that made a difference today. Someone waited in the hotel, and it could connect to Lenora not being found.

The hulking flatbed sanitation truck eased into the hidden alleyway, stopped, and backed toward a roll-up metal door lit by a pair of hooded spotlights. A door flung open, and a passenger hopped to the ground, ran to the entrance, and pressed the buttons of a keypad. Soon, the overhead door clanked and inched open.

Birdie watched two men unroll a long steel cable from the rear bed. Her opportunity arrived as a winch dragged the large, trash-filled container up and onto the truck's skids. She approached the open door, slipping inside, entering the hotel's lower basement. The rotting odor hit her faster and harder than expected. An overpowering stench from the crypt-like chamber's rubbish would take weeks to scrub away.

The coast was clear, unguarded at the late hour.

Two flights of concrete stairs carried her to the lobby. Birdie avoided the oversized freight elevator, not willing to risk being trapped alone with her pursuer.

Near the front desk, Birdie glanced in her shoulder bag. The Super 8 reels remained in place next to the cash belonging to her missing client. She reminded herself the film may hold answers to what went on in the house on Stone Canyon Road.

Her hand slid to her small revolver. The compartment in her purse allowed gripping and firing the hidden, hammerless .38.

The hotel lounge stayed dark and vacant. Few lights illuminated the bar where earlier she encountered Shelley. The attractive singer appeared to be part of a conspiracy involving Jaminson. For Lenore's sake, Birdie wanted to believe he was an innocent victim.

Birdie placed herself in a vulnerable position entering the exposed lobby. Giant columns and lush tropical foliage provided her stalker unlimited cover. Knowing her pursuer was tall with a German accent gave her a slight advantage. She also relied on a few hotel guests lounging near a large open fireplace to act as a deterrent.

She ran out of options. The hotel dining room, thanks to the detective work of Cleon, was the last place they had seen her client. A remote chance existed, and Lenora returned to their suite. Birdie feared a trap, deciding to call the room from the safety of the public lobby.

Birdie chose a phone tucked away near the bellman's luggage area. Her hands shook, dialing the four-digit number. She admitted sensing fear, blaming a lack of food and rest, not her ability to cope.

Entering the hotel and pursuing her hunter confirmed her commitment to herself. She would not allow exhaustion to turn her into a coward. She owed it to Lenora.

As the telephone rang, she took a quick sighting of the expansive lobby. No one appeared to glance her way or show interest. The fireplace group remained engaged in quiet conservation and coffee.

Not expecting an answer, she let it ring. As it did, she scolded herself for sending Lenora back to the hotel. Birdie realized she'd underestimated her client's pride. Lenora would not retreat and accept being sent to her room. Unlike her stubborn client, Birdie let her mysterious man intimidate her. Hanging up, she'd changed her mind and would return to the suite.

Birdie hesitated and dialed the numbers a last time before confronting her dread—discovering Lenora sprawled on the floor, murdered. Again, Lenora's telephone rang. Phones existed throughout the lavish suite, including the three bathrooms. If Lenora heard the ringing, she'd be close to a phone.

Birdie gave her time.

The ringing stopped. Birdie paused—no voice responded. Someone listened, waiting. Breaths came in spurts. Nothing else. Birdie broke the silence, asking the deep breather for Lenora, not expecting an answer. Her client could have fallen into an alcohol-driven sleep. She remained willing to accept any explanation. Could her client be with someone? Birdie expected the worst and hung up.

Before returning to the suite, she deliberated.

The hotel night assistant straightened his tie and brushed the lapels of his blazer when Birdie approached. She swung her room key in front of her, requesting security. Not questioning a guest, the clerk picked up a phone, dialing four numbers. She waited, not turning her back to the lobby. Within minutes, a sweating, rotund man in a wrinkled sports coat, attempting to hide a handgun on his belt, entered through the glass door. Birdie hoped looks were deceiving, preferring a guard more physically imposing, but settled, given the late hour, and requested a walk-through of Lenora's suite.

Birdie waved off accompanying him; instead, she took a seat in a lobby chair with a broad view of each entrance. After many glances at her watch, twenty minutes dragged by with no sign of the stocky guard. Ten more passed and no one. She attempted to distract herself and imagined her plump watchman snacking from the suite's stocked refrigerator. There was the possibility someone entered the room—the same person asking for her earlier. She couldn't sit and wait much longer and convinced herself to join the security officer. He took his time—too long, if no problems existed.

Waiting, she assured herself, the respected Beverly Hilton, according to her wealthy client, catered to high rollers and employed the best-trained staff. On second thought, giving the square-jawed Dick Tracy five more minutes seemed reasonable.

The elevator door slid open, and the hotel guard walked to Birdie.

"The suites vacant."

"You're sure?"

"Checked every room and closet. Got on my knees and looked under the beds."

"Anything unusual?"

"Nothing."

"Should we have someone else look?" Birdie asked. Considering the events of the previous twenty-four hours, she cared less about offending the man's pride.

"I've been an LA sheriff for thirty years. The room's empty."

Birdie took the rebuff sitting in the armchair, too exhausted to stand and face the officer. She had choices, the first and obvious one; Birdie questioned the security man about Lenora. He knew her by sight, but had not seen her in the hotel.

As he walked away, he paused and added. "I noticed the desk phone off the hook."

Birdie concealed her reaction, knowing Lenora may have knocked it free, or she had encountered the man searching for her. After a hesitation, she limped, following the guard, and reached into her purse, pulling a hundred-dollar bill and palmed it into the security man's hands.

"Would you check on me every few hours?"

With a quick nod, he walked away, shoving the cash into his pocket. Birdie took the precaution, with no intention of sleeping. She'd stay awake with coffee and food.

Having another idea, Birdie walked to the front desk.

CHAPTER THIRTY-SIX

Birdie stepped to the registration desk, armed with a crisp hundred-dollar bill.

"I need a favor."

She didn't wait for a response. "Give me another room and a movie projector."

"Eight or sixteen?" the clerk asked.

Birdie paused as she fumbled in her purse, reading the boxes shoved deep into her handbag.

"Eight millimeters and anything but a suite."

As Birdie spoke, she dropped the new bill over the counter's ledge.

"No one gets the number. Got that?"

The deskman tapped the marble counter and smiled. The cash vanished into his pocket.

"I'll deliver it."

Her wardrobe and makeup could wait. High on her list of priorities, a hot cleansing bath. How many tiny creatures crawled unseen beneath her clothes from tonight's adventures? Next in line, a juicy room service steak and a viewing of the stolen home movie reels.

The Beverly Hilton boasted full security day and night. Birdie asked herself if the management knew of her basement entry into the swanky Hollywood hotel.

On arrival at the second floor, the desk clerk materialized from the far end of the hallway, pushing a wheeled cart carrying a black-cased Bell and Howell projector.

Exhausted and jittery, sleep had become a fond memory. Judging the late night and early morning activity, she questioned if Angelenos slept.

Birdie unlocked and pushed open the door to her new room. Without hesitating, she phoned the kitchen for the hot steak she promised herself.

"Where do you want it?" the clerk asked, walking behind her.

She pointed to an end table.

He removed the case and stood over the projector, glancing at Birdie.

His help was needed. Still, Birdie regretted his hovering presence. She lacked experience with home movies and complicated projectors. The machine might as well have dropped to earth from an H. G. Wells invading spaceship. Turning it on challenged her, much less weaving the film through the machine.

"Would you mind?" She walked to him and forced a practiced smile, ignoring an extended open palm.

The sooner he left, the better she'd rest. Two notions came from nowhere and pried themselves into her head. The clerk may have sold her out to the stranger looking for her earlier—and yet, the smug attendant stood in her room, willing to accept another gratuity. The other, was it crazy to believe the sudden interest in her occurred after Lenora vanished?

Then again, exhaustion made her jumpy and distrustful.

In minutes, the projector stood ready and loaded. Birdie crossed her fingers, it was a long shot the reels gave answers. Regardless of what she uncovered, it became the fruit of the poisonous tree and worthless to police. She'd violated evidence laws, voiding anything she'd seen in the house, including Jaminson's suitcases of cash.

"What wall?" he asked, breaking the stupor she'd fallen into.

Birdie answered with a blank stare.

"To watch your movie?" he said.

She dropped onto the nearby sofa, pointing straight ahead.

The comfort of the warm room and the soft couch relaxed her. Falling off to sleep would come quickly if she allowed it. She resisted teary, heavy eyes, to stay awake. Lenora was missing and in danger. The film was all she had from her adventure in the house Shelley and Falk kept Fabian captive.

Her night's efforts yielded little more than a cold swim, one she survived, thanks to her cab driver. Bug bites, plus aches and bruises, required weeks of recovery for someone who seldom ventured into the wilderness.

"Hit this to turn it on and off."

The clerk smiled and pointed to a silver toggle switch.

"Turn off the projector's lamp before stopping the film or you'll burn it." The clerk snapped his fingers. "Just like that."

Alone, she considered a steaming hot bath, and a few Irish whiskeys to go with her medium-rare steak and make amends for the miserable day. The sun would come up in a few hours. A little over thirty hours ago, she sat at her kitchen table, contemplating a walk in Central Park and a Broadway play. She counted on *The Music Man* to continue its long run. Manhattan offered ice, snow, and freezing temperatures, and sounded like paradise.

The movie projector was assembled, tilted against an ashtray, aimed at a pale yellow wall, ready to reveal what she'd risked her life for and endangered her client's. In the darkened room, Birdie limped to the machine, and snapped the toggle, fearing the film likely showed birthdays and family picnics.

Speeding, broken lines, and numbers rolled, bringing to life a pair of lab-coated men hovering over a nude male grabbed her attention. No sound, only grainy black-and-white images, slightly out of focus.

She guessed the two tended to a corpse but remained unsure. She recognized Falk in the laboratory. Dozens of hoses and wires ran from a motionless body connecting to equipment shelved next to the steel table. Falk injected fluids into the prone, unmoving form using dozens of hypodermic needles arranged on an adjacent countertop. The victim's face, unseen from the camera angle, prevented Birdie from guessing if they lived. No autopsy incisions showed across the chest and appeared free from external damage.

Birdie remained spellbound by what she viewed. The film's images ensured she'd stay awake. Her gut impression—the two prepared the body for future use, intending to keep it whole, not dissecting it as first suspected. The film continued to run, clicking through the noisy projector as the men stepped away, pulled off elbow-length black rubber gloves, and walked from view. The camera kept recording the tube-covered corpse. She looked for signs, not sure if the man was dead or vegetative—kept alive for a ghoulish experiment.

The pale, immobile figure prompted her to recall Boris Karloff's role as a grotesque creature, rising and stiffly walking, pulling away tubes and bandages, crashing instruments to the floor. Something else surprised her. A new participant arrived.

Her shadow blocked part of the macabre scene playing on her room's wall. Birdie stepped to the side, exposing the visitor.

She recognized the face.

Birdie stepped close to the flickering picture, plastered like a circus sideshow poster alive in her hotel room. Stringy long hair hid the caller, but the distinctive cane and limp left no question. She had a near-flawless memory for names and faces. It registered despite having seen the grim expression for a short time as he stood over her cab confronting Cleon. There had been no doubt she viewed the youthful cult leader, Elger Stepp, organizer of The Children of God.

A sharp knock on the door caused her to jump.

"Room service."

CHAPTER THIRTY-SEVEN

Pello cradled Lenora, tied and gagged, in his arms, carrying her from Shelley's car. Once inside the secluded canyon home, he pulled the pillowcase from her head.

"Put her in the bedroom," Shelley said.

"With Fabian?"

"They'll get to know each other."

Shelley released the parrot into the house. Its green and yellow wings spread and circled the oval copper-covered fireplace, perching on a worn armchair opposite a bookcase filled with mounted small animals and birds.

"We're leaving in a few days," she said, touching her stomach.

Falk looked at Shelley. "Is it true about Elger?"

Shelley rolled up a sleeve of her dress and pointed to her arm. "I need a booster if I am to continue."

"Answer me," Falk said.

"It came down to them or us," she answered.

"You knew they would do it."

"I wasn't certain."

"Of their convictions?" Falk asked. "Or Jaminson's mercenaries finding him?"

"It no longer matters. We'll begin again in Argentina."

"Using Jaminson's money?"

"To carry on your work."

"... and Strughold?"

"We don't need him."

"Same for Elger Stepp and his new martyrs for The Children of God."

"Only In his eyes," Shelley said. "He phoned me during the attack. I gave him approval."

"You provided him the explosives."

"I'll miss him and his passion."

"His disciples were excellent test subjects."

"Fabian and Pello disappointed me," Shelley said. "The parrot functioned better."

"They did not need to kill everyone."

"We removed Jaminson before Elger made the sacrifice."

"A small army landed on the roof? No one knew Jaminson was there."

The door banged against the wall, and Pello entered again, pushing Hamilton Jaminson, gagged and sleeping, tied to a wheelchair. "They will watch the airports. I am certain," Falk said.

"Same for commercial ship lines," she said.

"You have another way?"

"We'll be home in a few weeks."

Falk touched Shelley's stomach. "You will bring us glory for your sacrifice."

"I want to have the child in Argentina."

"Hitler's loyal officers will surround both of you."

"Not unless you give me whatever crap you have been pumping in me," Shelly shouted.

"Amino acid and hormones," Falk answered. "My life's work."

"With help from William Patrick," Shelley said.

Shelley dropped onto a sofa near the roll-top desk. Something about the room looked odd. Small items appeared out of place, but nothing seemed missing or broken. Yet, a peculiar feeling overtook her, which was shaken off—blaming a stressful long day and her nosey parrot. A night's rest would restore her for the journey. The life carried would lead Germany for the second time. She had permitted herself to become a breeding oven, growing harvested cells. They stood at the threshold of success after years of trial and error and enduring daily electroshock treatment.

She'd sacrificed her career for a wealthy German stepfather's dream. The return home would reawaken the dormant Arian race with a newborn Nazi leader. The cause belonged to hundreds of displaced German soldiers hiding as refugees in Argentina. If not for Juan Peron's generous nature, many would have not escaped and faced war crime trials.

Shelley's life changed following her mother's attraction to a wealthy, exiled Nazi general. As a child, she experienced his generosity, enjoying acting and singing lessons. Her stage career launched with success, and she soon learned everything in life has a price.

Falk's and Strughold's plan to lure Jaminson into believing he'd bought his private fountain of youth failed. They took his cash, but the miscarried strategy led to forcing her to scrap the operations. The Noah Institute near San Diego functioned as a decoy, screening their actual work. Falk's Brea lab, concealed from Dulles, succeeded beyond expectations, reproducing life from human cells, and remained known to a select group.

In private moments, Shelley, a once devout Roman Catholic, compared her purpose to the sainted Mother Mary. Not for a moment did she consider herself a heavenly woman, but performed her duty not as the will of God, but instead as the will of a new German nation.

Implanted in her womb and kept alive with electroshock were growing and replicating cells taken from Adolph Hitler's American nephew, William Patrick Hitler.

CHAPTER THIRTY-EIGHT

Discovering the occupants of the destroyed tower became his only choice to resurrect Jaminson's and Falk's ice-cold trail. Knocking on neighbors' doors, making inquiries, calling attention to himself, and would draw law enforcement questions.

Had the tower been a decoy, vacant, and bombs detonated by remote, intended to slow or stop his hunt?

His assignment, from the beginning, ran into obstructions. No mission went according to the blueprint, especially those drawn by men in starched white shirts and ties, contented and safe inside the walls of a military think tank. The moment he received instructions from Dulles, Doctor Strughold, his only friend, attempted to steer him off track, sparing Falk's life. He faced a conspiracy from multiple directions. What he saw tonight was well-conceived, but lacked execution, pushing him to believe someone outside of Washington had been the cause. The CIA's involvement remained in the back of his mind, and Gustain wouldn't rule out Dulles' strong-arm tactics.

He had played a role in the CIA ouster of the elected ruler of Iran, replacing him with a brutal dictator, saving British oil reserves. Over the years, he'd watched the CIA flourish, flexing its muscles, playing bully, and imposing America's recent status as the world's unquestioned leader.

Military senses told him he'd stepped between factions waging a clandestine cold war battle. Their methods indicated money and power, resembling his experience with the Shaw of Iran. Possibly the warring parties clashed over what he had seen in the basement of the Brea fruit packing plant. Bodies floating in steel artificial wombs prepared to populate a new Germany repulsed him.

The unexpected copter's strike came back at him. Commando's landing on the roof pointed to a rescue, like his war experiences. At least two, maybe more, explosions occurred at once within the tall structure, telling him an explosives professional handled the exact timing and direction of the blast.

Someone sacrificed lives and expected an attack. Gustain feared he'd witnessed a new third party interfere with his search. He wanted no part of the three-way relationship, particularly with an unknown combatant.

His thoughts turned to the Beverly Hilton. A visit to Birdie and Lenora may yield clues to tonight's disaster, regardless, entertaining himself with the two brought hope of pleasure.

Pulling from the parking lot, Gustain caught a glimpse of white light flash from beneath the doomed water tower. Thin at first, becoming broad and vanishing as if a signal. If another explosion came, he would not be in the area.

CHAPTER THIRTY-NINE

Birdie looked at the door and hesitated. The knock came again, followed by muffled shouts. Squinting through the door's peephole, she watched a thin uniformed hotel employee adjusting the cart's silver food trays.

A shiny brass name tag read Albert.

She reprimanded herself for her timid reaction and stepped back.

"Give me a second," Birdie shouted through the door.

She returned, carrying her handbag. Her finger wrapped around the trigger of her concealed pistol. With a free hand, she removed the chain and deadbolt and backed away, swinging open the door. The waiter guided the pushcart over the threshold, rattling glasses and plates, stepping into the room.

"You're Birdie Kelley?" He asked as he reached into the side pocket of his white jacket.

Her eyes froze on his hand, watching… anything resembling a gun would bring a hollow-point .38 caliber flaming through her leather purse.

The waiter fumbled to pull the object from his coat.

"Lenora Jaminson left this in the restaurant."

Birdie took the table linen and released her hold on the revolver. "What is this?"

"She had dinner with the piano player. I found it under her plate."

"You saw her with Pello?" Birdie asked, taking the white napkin.

"That's right."

Birdie turned over the folded cloth. Reading the message confirmed her fear.

**Birdie Kelley—with Pello. Shelley walked in.
They're talking. I will.**

She'd known from the start Lenora was far from a shrinking violet. Her client would not sit idle. Chances were strong, Lenora gambled, hoping Shelley and Pello took her to her former husband.

"She leave alone?" Birdie asked, knowing it was a long shot.

Albert shook his head. "With Pello and the woman."

She reread the scribbled and smudged note, making sure Lenora left no other clues.

"I cleared the table and almost missed it."

"You hear what they talked about?"

"Mrs. Jaminson asked about Pello's parrot. They didn't stay to order."

"Anything else, Albert?" Birdie asked.

"Walking out, Mrs. Jaminson said something about liking her house in the canyon."

"That's all?"

"The lady gave her a shove."

"Was the girl angry?"

He nodded. "Very!"

Birdie looked at the white-jacketed waiter and reached into her purse. It had taken a moment to see where the discussion headed. Los Angeles did not differ from New York City. Every Tom, Dick, and Harry had their hand out. Cold, hard cash greased the path for unearthing information. She'd recalled the New York theater usher—

bending his thumb, forcing him to his toes, dancing and spewing answers. The temptation passed. She had no intention of getting crossways with the spindly hotel employee. Another simple request would follow.

She laid a twenty on the food tray.

"I'm not sure I heard anything else."

She placed one more next to it and snapped her purse shut. "Try harder."

"The lady said she'd give her a private tour and laughed."

Ravenous and needing rest, the steak remained on the cart, and the already pulled-down pillows and crisp sheets would go to waste. Birdie opened her shoulder bag and slapped two more crispy twenties on the plate cover.

"This is simple. Can you do something else?"

She watched Albert shift from leg to leg, tapping the cart's handle. Birdie needed help and would pay for favors and hoped the waiter acted on his own from greed.

"My car's the red MG in valet. Bring it to the hotel's front door."

She considered the secluded incinerators behind the hotel as a drop-off. Birdie abandoned the idea, preferring to stay in sight of security and the doorman.

Albert remained silent.

"Can you do that?" She asked.

Birdie recognized her Irish temper geared up, about to make an unwelcome appearance, and resisted grabbing the waiter, pinning his Ichabod Crane physique against the room's wall. A firm twist of the young man's arm would teach him a lesson, but she passed.

"I work in the restaurant."

"Its my car. You won't get in trouble."

Birdie dropped three more of her client's twenties on top of the plate warmer. Birdie stood toe to toe with the smiling waiter. "Yes or no?"

It was a stare-down. One Birdie knew she'd win.

Albert backed away. "Give me ten minutes."

She used restraint, folding her hands around her waist to keep from shoving the room service attendant and cart from the suite. Birdie hoped she'd recall the route to the house in the canyon.

She had more to learn about the strange residents. Falk stood out as the central figure in the Super 8 film. The corpse toiled over in the unknown lab appeared dead. What had occurred in the laboratory pointed to the core of the mystery. The movie that played on her wall showed nothing, which led to Jaminson. The surprise appearance of the cult leader joining Doctor Falk had added to the confusion she needed to unravel.

Making matters worse, someone had an interest in her.

Birdie teetered at the edge, nerves raw from fear. How much chaos could she handle in one day? She carried old memories of fighting off a life-and-death attack by a trusted transit cop. The thought of her laying on Falk's exam table unnerved her.

The stakes grew. She could fold or stay. Her adversary's objectives remained cloudy, yet it became clear holding Jaminson was not their end game. The wealthy industrialist had been a pawn, needed for the cash discovered in Shelley's and Doctor Falk's home. Birdie guessed a passionate cause bound the two. Experience taught her those the most dangerous.

The second movie reel could yield answers or raise more questions. Time was not on her side. Could she risk hiding in the hotel? Would the police take her seriously with no direct evidence, only weak hunches?

Suspicions against Pello and Fabian were unconvincing. The law would see a caring doctor tending to patients. To most, the unnerving bird was an ordinary parrot, not the vengeful and defensive combatant she'd viewed. Her break-in exposed the hidden suitcases of money and reels of tape. Homes in the affluent neighborhood likely employed security cameras. The sound alarm may have failed, but she stood a strong chance of being captured on film, discredited, and arrested.

Her chief reason to avoid the Los Angeles police—the possibility of incriminating Hamilton Jaminson in the bizarre events risked the financial well-being of Jaminson's worldwide investments. That concern had been made clear to her. No confidentiality agreement existed, though violating Lenora's trust would damage her reputation as a New York City PI among elite clients she hoped to attract.

Her throbbing hip produced fear of a permanent limp and losing her flirty natural bounce, which brought looks of approval and admirers. Birdie admitted selfish reasons, hunger, and being stalked could keep her on the bench, out of harm's way. She couldn't suppress her desire to return to the Broadway stage and its glamor. Vanity and pride surfaced from time to time. Maybe one day?

She had three good, immediate motives to press on a missing client, the search for Hamilton Jaminson, and she needed money.

Birdie closed the room's door after checking the hallway; she'd tipped the first domino, fearing where the last would tumble and stop. Had she been drawn into a rigged croquet game, destined to lose, against the cruel Queen of Hearts?

Lenora's red MG arrived at the front doors, twenty minutes late.

Navigating the puzzling canyons of New York City's congestion, imparted patience. Birdie stayed confident she'd find her way along Southern California's foothills and maze of streets to the house hidden deep in Bel-Air Canyon.

The sun remained a few hours from rising over palm trees and the skyline of The City of Angels. Birdie needed darkness to locate and approach Shelley's home for a rescue. She did not know how to pull off the risky mission. Unlike her earlier visit, she'd remain alone. Cleon, her guardian angel cabby, would not protect her if she once again fell into the choppy lake. The roar of the winds would cover her movements. She dreaded the return and admitted the occupants frightened her.

Hidden in the lobby, she watched the MG. It idled, driver door open, under the covered entrance. Albert, in his white jacket, hopped from the compact car and jogged away.

The hotel appeared empty at the late hour. From the corner of Birdie's eye, she noticed a housekeeper vacuuming carpet near the lounge. Birdie felt secure. She'd taken the stairs, avoiding entering the lobby by elevator and attracting the desk clerk's attention. Once inside the car, she'd relax, and for a short time, feel protected. If followed, her pursuer would be easy to spot in the pre-dawn darkness.

She pulled her purse tight against her body, feeling the security and bulk of the revolver, allowing some control.

Birdie presumed the red-jacketed doorman was on an extended nature break. The path to her waiting MG looked clear and safe, sheltered from unknown spectators. No hotel employee or guests appeared near the lobby or entry. Birdie pushed open the glass door and stepped under the glaring bright lights of the entrance canopy.

A tapping and a soft voice came from behind.

"Please step into the car, Sister Birdie."

CHAPTER FORTY

Her mugger stood next to her. Birdie didn't turn to the voice, and instead, visualized a sharp kick to his kneecap. A surprise strike, her best gamble. Open space offered options against assailants. Once inside the car, she'd lose leverage and control, becoming a hostage.

The firm push in her back knocked her forward, stumbling, catching herself against the car's open door. Pain in her fragile hip and shoulder preventing a defensive counter. Memories of her accident—the agony of jagged bone and muscles tearing as she lay trapped under massive stage rigging, as she was now in no position to run or resist, hemmed against the MG.

Her purse slipped and fell, and, as it did, Birdie caught sight of the wooden Shepard's crook pressed against her.

"I don't wish harm to you." He prodded her with the rounded handle, not shoving but using it as a guide.

Birdie looked at the tall figure standing over her. The face shrouded in shadow, back-lit, appearing detached from their surroundings, illuminated by the hotel's bright parking and entry lights. She viewed a hazy rim of light, an orb, radiating, surrounding his head and shoulders, which, for a fleeting moment, seeming angelic.

"We meet again."

She forced back an outburst of screams, fearing her assailant's reaction. Exhaustion and hunger could be responsible for her sluggish reactions. Birdie remained stunned by the curious effects of the hotel's lighting on her mugger. Not sure of what had occurred, she sat passively, deciding her response.

The passenger door closed. Reflexes screamed for Birdie to yank open the unguarded car door and escape. She convinced herself she'd reach the lobby.

The aggressor slipped beside her, pushing against her in the cramped MG. The dreamlike glow vanished; she saw the face, framed by long, stringy blond hair.

"You were on the street yelling at my taxi," Birdie said.

He extended his open hand, not as an introduction, instead resting his palm on her shoulder.

"The Children of God have been taken home."

Birdie looked at the man next to her. He'd approached her cab on Sunset Boulevard, angered by her driver. The incident appeared minor, a slight skirmish with his flock of white-robed followers. No harm done. It had occurred as she followed Shelley and Fabian less than twelve hours ago. So much happened since she'd wiped it from her weary mind.

"Who are you?" she asked.

"Cleon didn't tell you?"

His hand remained on her injured shoulder. She noticed the big silver ring on his left index finger—a three-pronged Celtic spiral, an ancient symbol of her homeland, representing man's natural cycle: life, death and rebirth.

Despite growing anxiety, her chronic pain eased, little by little, leaving soothing warmth in her hip and shoulder. Birdie shook it off, crediting a blast of adrenalin brought by sudden fright.

"He said enough," she answered.

"Elger. Elger Stepp. Nice to meet finally."

Despite events, Birdie admired his alluring smile and deep blue eyes.

Her purse and handgun remained out of reach and not a concern. Instinct told her to blame weariness from the long day and cross-country trip. Calmness befell her the moment he placed his hand on her. His firm touch brought relief, and the aches continued to diminish. Not eliminated, but a level she'd endure, maybe accept.

"How do you know me?" She asked.

"Doctor Falk and Shelley. It concerned them you would become trouble."

"They're wrong." She lifted Elger Stepp's hand from her shoulder. "I am their problem."

"A minor one, Sister Kelley."

The time came to take control. She'd allowed the cult leader to manipulate her emotions.

"Then, get out of my car. I intend to fix that."

The words surged from her, yet lacked conviction, something she could not afford to lose or give the appearance of lacking at the moment.

Elger Stepp smiled. He held her purse by the shoulder strap and lowered it, placing it in her lap.

"You will need the small gun hidden inside, and much more. Be careful."

"You're letting me go?"

Elger looked straight ahead into the glaring hotel lights. "You'll make that decision after I show you how Falk and Shelley exploited The Children of God."

"What did you mean The Children of God were taken home?"

"My group of believers is dead, thanks to Shelley and Falk."

Birdie's curiosity took a detour. She'd allowed his charm and penetrating eyes to overtake her. She found it hard to break his gaze. He appeared polite and almost apologetic. Birdie formed a snap judgment, sensing Elger lost resolve for the moment. He lacked the demanding, grand sense of self displayed at their earlier confrontation. Birdie credited the shock of losing his young band of followers. In a small, puzzling way, she felt sad and sorry for the confused man sitting next to her.

She focused on his Celtic ring—three spirals grew from each pinnacle of the triangle representing human life, a cycle not controlled by humans. Elger recognized a higher power contrary to a cult leader's grandiose view and fantasies.

Birdie knew she could read too much into the simple Celtic icon, or he lured her with subtle manipulation. No longer a naïve girl, the encounter would not pull her away from her mission.

Elger Stepp's deep-set eyes showed no emotion, and Birdie felt a slight concern for the confused young man.

"Did you ask about me inside?"

"No. I waited here."

She deliberated, studying Elger. If he had been the stalker, her cabby mentioned spotting in the hotel, he lacked the German accent. She admitted chatting and spending an evening with Elger would have been a pleasure in a less stressful time. The attractive spiritual guru drew her into his divine spell. His slight hobble and Shepard's crook lent to his mystique.

Birdie pushed open the passenger door, expecting Elger to stop her exit—nothing happened, no threats. He remained seated and appeared relaxed. She hesitated. What did she miss? Standing alongside the car, she felt free of the chronic pain.

Could it have been a hypnotic ploy designed to manipulate her?

Two yellow cabs waited at the hotel's door. Birdie faced a decision.

Before stepping away, she heard him say.

"Gustain's inside. He will kill you."

"Who?"

Elger stepped from the car. "The CIA ordered him to assassinate you."

"You know this because…?"

"Killing you, your client, and Jaminson cleans up a government mess."

"Answer me! Why?"

"I'll show you what Shelley and Falk are planning—what this is about."

Birdie's thought was to walk away. She would not allow herself to trust Elger. For all she knew, he was obsessed with control, veiling it as love and tolerance like the charismatic James Jones. He almost drew her into his trap—a moment of weakness created by a lack of sleep and lighting tricks performed by her mind.

Elger extended both robed arms and walked closer. The brightness and glare teased her with a sleight of hand—street magic back-lit Elger's torso, creating a halo surrounding his shadowed form. She'd endured a great deal in the past twenty-four hours. Instincts failed her. Indecision tied her in knots. Lives rode on her judgment. She couldn't sidestep what she faced, a chance to see what Falk and Shelley concealed.

"I won't harm you," Elger said. "After you see, you decide."

Birdie spotted the stout security guard approach from the hotel. Elger carried no gun, or none she noticed in his slacks and loose-fitting robe and shirt. Perhaps a knife hid, tucked inside the Shepard's crook, or a concealed weapon worn near his ankle, accounting for his slight limp.

Her choice brought an enormous risk. Attacking Shelley's home and rescuing Lenora was a gamble born from anger and revenge. What she planned placed her and the hostages in jeopardy. Why she considered Elger's proposal baffled her. No longer fearing Elger, she experienced calmness, yet not allowing it to immerse her in total trust. Her revolver would stay close, along with common sense.

The encounter with Elger could explain the mystery of the canyon house. Whoever Elger Stepp was, she accepted him not as an ally but someone with information she needed.

"Tell me where you're taking me," she said.

"Falk's death lab," Elger spoke, this time in Irish Gaelic she understood.

Birdie looked at his Celtic spiral ring and entered the MG.

CHAPTER FORTY-ONE

Near morning, the vicious Santa Ana winds quieted. Shelley took a sip of strong black coffee. Her attempt to relax failed. Doctor Falk's daily amino acid injections left her stomach bruised. The life inside her belonged to The New Nazi Germany, an incubator carrying offspring formed from DNA extracted from William Patrick Hitler, Adolph Hitler's American nephew. She refused to think of the demonic seed as part of her, aware Europe and America would be repulsed by Falk's cloned creation.

Her purpose had succeeded, luring Hamilton Jaminson into a love affair, and believing he'd gained The Noah Institute, Falk's, and Strughold's life retention lab. Jamison's captured money remained locked away, prepared for its journey to Argentina. The German doctors had conducted reproduction research with funds siphoned from the cash-powerful CIA. Their secret breakthroughs were in jeopardy, needing additional money to go on. Falk and Strughold, fearing years of dedicated work at risk and without her knowledge, seized Jaminson. Because of the snafu and Falk's greed, the CIA and others hunted them.

Jaminson had turned into a burden, unneeded cargo. Killing the prominent financier risked creating more attention.

She, with no free choice, became the testing stage, carrying the bastard, cloned creation. Shelley considered Shakespeare's words she'd once brought to an admiring audience.

"For never-resting time leads summer on to hideous winter and confounds him there; Sap checked with frost and lusty leaves quite gone."

She didn't recall the sonnet's remaining lines voicing their ultimate purpose, youth, and prolonging Nazi existence in Hitler's rebirth.

Her hideous winter would find calm in Buenos Aires, easing the end of Germany's long winter frost—with the healthy birth of Falk's newly created Hitler.

Safely nested in Argentina, protected by a lack of extradition treaties and Juan Peron's power, hundreds of refugee Nazis, on the verge of death, made South America home. Falk's life extension gave hope to those dying officers. Fabian and Pello, once members of Elger Stepp's Children of God, had contracted an infectious spinal virus. Falk sustained the twins, preserving them in liquid nitrogen until Salk's discovery spared them from living a life with crippling paralysis.

Shelley touched her fertilized womb. She became the first to carry Hitler's superior DNA.

She looked at the grand piano centered in the room. Her sacrificed musical calling continued to entice her. Performing before admiring audiences, hailed as South America's queen of jazz, occupied her now imagined future.

Duty subverted her devotion to a stage career. She served by conscription, building a new and greater Nazi Germany—a cause embraced by defeated Aryan soldiers and imposed on her.

Her life could be different—free to pursue dreams and children....

"My documents are safe and packed," Falk said, walking into the room.

"It will be the two of us," she said.

"By ship?"

"Tramp steamer from Catalina Island."

"Our friend Pello?"

"The bird is more impressive."

"Should he have the same dose as Fabian?"

"Yes. They are no longer useful."

"Codeine will stop their breathing as they sleep."

"They served their purpose," Shelley said, and ran her fingers over the piano keys, banging random notes.

What had she become? Extinguishing and squandering lives to conceive a better race created her dilemma. Would the scheme work? Getting to the hired ship unharmed with Falk and reaching Argentina rested on her shoulders.

The large green and red parrot hopped and fluttered to the piano bench, perching next to Shelley. Gigi replayed the harsh notes, still louder, banging her beak, imitating the angry chorus again and again.

Shelley placed both hands on the keyboard to end the annoyance. Gigi continued hammering the ivory keys. Shelley understood the parrot possessed a jealous mood, protective of Pello and Fabian. Did the parrot comprehend Falk's intentions to kill the pair?

She slammed the cover shut. Gigi protested with high-pitched shrieks, flying off, landing near a tall cabinet, pecking at its glass doors. Did the bird connect, bonding with the stuffed, winged, and fur-covered creatures crowded inside? Shelley stared at the parrot, sensing Gigi took comfort in the assortment of lifeless animals.

How much intelligence did the parrot have? Did the bird try to share suspicions someone had been in the room? Shelley couldn't shake the same feeling. Earlier, she rushed from the house, failing to activate cameras and alarms. Shelley brushed off the thought, blaming uneasiness and concern for an absent Doctor Strughold and fears Dulles closed in.

She'd travel light, a single suitcase: gowns and sequined costumes left behind, abandoning her life's ambition. Sleep continued out of the question. Dozens of suspended living bodies, frozen in Brea, discarded. Tomorrow ended her American journey, while the temptation to run gnawed at her. She'd stay alert, expecting Birdie's return, realizing she'd underestimated the private detective. Her concern remained—the CIA hunted Falk, which led to her.

* * * *

Lenora pushed her back against the wall, struggling against taped wrists and ankles. Across the room, Hamilton Jaminson slumped, arms bound to a clumsy wooden wheelchair. Their cellmate's powerful and sculptured features provoked thoughts of Michelangelo's David sleeping nearby in a metal-framed bed clad in only white running shorts.

His presence puzzled her. The resemblance was uncanny. The familiar face belonged to the handsome piano player she admired, Pello. It couldn't be! He'd carried her into the room that held her captive. He remained unmoving. If he took in air, she didn't notice his chest swell the slightest. She needed time and hoped he'd remain asleep.

Lenora jerked at her constraints, working her tied wrists over her bent knees, pressed snug against her chest. From the awkward position, her fastened hands slid to her ankles. She undid the laces and kicked away her saddle Oxford shoe, revealing her prosthetic foot. Leaning forward and pushing her chest tight against her thighs, Lenora gained a grip on the wooden foot. After a slight push and twist, it popped free, falling from her ankle, exposing a wrapped ankle nub.

Pello or his look-a-like stayed motionless. Giving her footless leg an abrupt yank, her stump pulled loose, sliding through snug bindings.

Lenora remained curled on her side, and stretched her tied hands, replacing the artificial foot, snapping it snug into the metal slot. With the shoe in place, freedom came and a taste of confidence.

To escape, she needed Hamilton awake and walking. Lenora gripped the window sill and pulled to her feet. Her fatigued legs trembled, collapsing.

Laying there, face pressed against the wood floor, she questioned her judgment at the Beverly Hilton, allowing herself to be taken, becoming a hindrance to Birdie's plan.

Her efforts made it worse for Hamilton. The strategy placed her in a locked room with no escape. Her hope rested on the slim chance the scribbled message on the hotel napkin reached Birdie.

Hamilton moaned and rolled from one side to the other.

"No... don't know." His raspy breaths gave hope.

Lenora saw Hamilton relived the questioning and obvious beating.

His bruised chin and face drooped against his chest, unmoving.

Lenora crawled along the wood floor, she needed to be near him. Reaching Hamilton, she pulled at his limp arms.

"It's Lenora."

No added words came to his dry and cracked lips. She held his arm, feeling a weak but steady pulse. Her tied hands remained useless to comfort him.

Lenora feared Shelley and Falk would arrive, stopping her frantic try to break free. With a deep breath, gathering her little remaining endurance, she pulled her elbows apart, feeling the tape cutting her wrists. With a count of three, Lenora rammed both spread forearms against the side of her ribcage, hoping the sheer force tore her bindings.

The bands of tape didn't yield and, as revenge, appeared to strengthen their grip. She inhaled, determined to ignore discomfort, and put her remaining energy into a last effort to rip the stubborn tape from her swollen and bleeding wrists.

The first try may not have been her best. She had more in her. Slamming two sharp elbows into her rib cage brought extreme pain, possibly breaking a few. Nothing came from self-pity. Falls and injuries came from jumping horses, and she learned to live with aches and breaks—even the loss of a foot, courtesy of the sport.

This time, she expected the hurt to be worse. She'd heal. Victory came at a cost.

Lenora raised her arms higher, further from her tender side, and again rammed her arms around her rib cage.

A slight rip appeared. Lenora heard it over screams she failed to control.

She forced her palms apart, gritted her teeth, twisting and pulling until the tape split and tore away, freeing her hands. A sharp ache wrapped her sides, making each breath difficult. She collapsed, rolling to her back, taking deep painful breaths. Raw endurance won out.

Hamilton relied on her. She knew he had been beaten by the dried blood on his filthy suit and shirt and facial bruising. How much more could he endure? His safety rested in her hands.

Lenora examined Jaminson closer and found needle marks covering both forearms. She had located him alive and intended to keep them both safe until Birdie arrived.

What explained keeping him captive? A ransom was never asked. Questions would wait. She needed a way out.

She stood at the room's barred window. To the east, flickers of sunlight appeared.

Stillness.

Lenora became concerned. Something didn't feel right.

Broken and splintered branches covered the yard—the lake quiet and smooth. Nothing went as planned but, she expected Birdie to step from the boathouse.

Remaining calm, she resisted pounding on the metal door, avoiding attention. Steel bolts above and below the metal-clad handle secured it to an iron frame.

The body filling the bed stayed motionless. Standing over him, she hesitated to touch his arm, and gripped two fingers inside his wrist, below his thumb—no pulse. She poked a finger into his side, making sure. Lenora questioned if someone destined them for the same fate.

Lenora stopped herself from the urge to pound on the door. She leaned over Jaminson's slumped body. His chest continued to expand and fall. As she raised and stepped away, his head moved. She placed her hands near his face, touching pale, sunken cheeks through heavy gray stubble.

"Hamilton, it's me, Lenora."

His eyelids eased open but dropped and closed.

With her face close to his, she looked at him and cried.

She'd done a disservice to Birdie and Hamilton, placing them in vulnerable and dangerous positions. Birdie's instructions were simple. She was to return to the hotel lounge and observe Pello, then go back to her suite.

Lenora pressed an ear against the steel door. No voices or footfalls, only quiet. Blowing winds that unnerved her stopped, lending to an unnatural calm as if set adrift, floating isolated in the broad Pacific. The house and occupants provided no signs of life. Footsteps no longer slapped polished wood floors. How long had it been?

Loud and repeated squawks disrupted the peace. More followed, then nothing. Lenora recalled the parrot from the hotel bar. In a moment, the bird's name, Gigi, came to mind.

A shuffle of footsteps approached and stopped outside the door. A latch lifted.

"Who's there?" she shouted.

No answer.

The door swung inward, banging the wall.

Lenora remained beside Hamilton. She had only her fists for defense.

A shaking hand reached in, gripping the steel frame.

"Help... me." The voice gasped for air, forcing the words as he fell to his knees.

CHAPTER FORTY-TWO

Birdie drove into the darkness. Morning sunshine had yet to clear the Southern California foothills.

Elger Stepp made himself at home alongside Birdie, who slumped behind the MG's leather steering wheel. Her sleep-starved eyes teared and begged to close. A solid night's rest last came twenty-four hours ago, four time zones removed.

She assured herself that the imagined angelic halo wrapping Elger Stepp's head and shoulders had been nothing more than the glare of hotel spotlights playing tricks on her weary mind. They traveled with the hum of the car's tires as a distraction. If the charismatic leader of The Children of God possessed divine powers, he kept them hidden. There had been no gun, only a smooth, calming voice. No miraculous miracles forced her into the car. She came of her own free will, not understanding why, contrary to her intent to rush to Shelley's canyon home searching for her missing clients.

Birdie swerved the MG. The abrupt appearance of a pack of hunting coyotes burst from a cluster of dried brush near a rocky hillside. Inches spared her from driving into a guardrail as they exited the highway, toward the quiet streets of Brea.

"That came from nowhere," Elger said.

"I almost lost it," she answered.

Birdie drove, bouncing along the gravel shoulder. Her eyes refused to blink until they bumped back onto the blacktop road.

Elger reached to her arm, giving her a gentle touch.

It may have been her imagination or a clever parlor trick. The sudden fright diminished followed by warm calmness.

He leaned his lanky frame, reclining into the car's seat. Although a compact two-seater, he appeared relaxed. Whomever Elger Stepp professed to be, he had hijacked her without force.

In a few miles, the city street narrowed and climbed. They left Brea behind and converged into Carbon Canyon Road and rolling, endless fields of lemons and orange groves glowed in soft moonlight.

"Valencia's will be ready to pick in April," Elger said.

"This is what you wanted to show me?" Birdie questioned, shouting, but quieted as Elger guided his hand to the side of her face, caressing her.

Birdie realized she'd panicked, but calmed with his touch.

"Turn here and stop," he said.

Birdie did as told, steering off the twisting path. Elger exited and swung aside a pipe gate, signaling her to pass. Ahead, The Brea Packing Company sat at the base of a long, sloping, rocky hillside.

Elger touched her shoulder. This time with force. "Before we go inside, I want you to have this. This is an evil place."

He removed the large silver ring from his index finger, placing it on a small beaded chain. Reaching over Birdie's head, he hung it around her neck.

"Wear it for a long and prosperous life."

"I can't; it's yours."

"The Celtic spirals: life, death and rebirth will guard you as they did me for centuries. The emerald stone signifies your heritage. No harm shall visit if your heart is genuine."

Radiating warmth from his hand spread through her, soothing and lessening the chronic aches and stiffness of her shoulder and hip.

Her first reaction was to defy the cult leader's need for obedience and his outrageous spiritual fantasies. Instead, she'd tolerate him and resisted admitting to finding him superficially charming.

What other surprises would he reveal?

Elger held the MG's door open and pointed to a dimly lit scattered group of unpainted tin, rust-covered sheds, and Quonset huts.

"The large building houses tables and conveyors. It looks like an ordinary packing house, washing, and sorting fruit."

Birdie sat behind the wheel, remaining quiet, running her fingers against the silver ring dangling from her neck. Although she should have been troubled, Birdie felt at ease and comfortable.

Why didn't she resist?

Lenora stayed in danger while her hired private eye took a country joy ride. Her obligation called for her to speed away—leave Elger and his delusions. She had reality to face. Lives were at stake.

Confusion continued, her captor had not harmed nor threatened violence. To his credit, he remained tranquil. He'd, by some means, taken her captive without force. She'd accepted his invitation and traveled, not resisting, to the concealed Brea location. She could, with no struggle, bolt and drive away. He stood no chance of stopping her.

Birdie sensed honesty in her abductor, confident in his wish to do her no harm.

Elger turned, and with two fingers at his lips, delivered a sharp whistle.

"I'm not your dog," Birdie mumbled.

Why did she allow Elger Stepp to manipulate her? There was nothing distinct about the tall, youthful man—ordinary, by her standards. Long stringy hair gave the look of an Old Testament prophet misplaced into the Twentieth century. Had it been a coincidence she'd earlier encountered Elger waving his shepherd staff at her cab? Hours later, on film, he'd barged into the Brea laboratory as the silver-toothed Falk stepped away from a nude body covered with tubes and probes.

Birdie left the safety of the car. She had been misled in the past. Her handgun stayed in her purse, loaded and ready.

As she walked from the MG, a burst of light slashed across her path, reflecting in the fender mirror. Birdie turned to look—nothing appeared in the weed-infested lot or surrounding orchards. Daylight had been hours away. It may have been a flash of a passing car's headlights poking through the grove's dense leaves, catching her attention.

She paused, taking a deep breath, listening for out-of-place sounds from the nearby road.

Seldom did she trust others, yet permitted the offbeat cult leader to barge into her car. With little convincing, persuaded her to drive to an isolated orange grove in the wee hours of the morning.

The abrupt jolt under Birdie's feet lasted a few seconds, then stopped.

"What was that?" she asked.

"We get those, a tremor, that's all. Wait "til the big roller. They do damage," Elger said.

"...that was an earthquake?"

"Don't worry. It's not anything."

Birdie stayed motionless, fearful of taking a step. The gravel parking area remained intact, settled, and stable under her quivering legs, with no gapping cracks for her to stumble into.

Nothing made sense during this spur-of-the-moment detour. Had she, in her drowsy state, fallen into a fantasy rabbit hole and a strange land, following a bizarre path, searching for her client and Hamilton Jaminson? Lenora's hotel napkin note had asked for help, suspecting she'd be taken to Shelley's remote canyon home. Instead, her helpless PI failed, falling into the hands of a wannabe Messiah.

Birdie confessed, not understanding who or what Elger claimed to be. Had he manipulated her thoughts, or she'd undergone an emotional breakdown, enjoying his company?

She reached inside her purse, gripping the small but mighty .38 resting in its felt pocket. She'd not hesitate to pull the trigger at the first sign of danger.

Up to this moment, she had failed to notice the night's serenading chorus of katydids, and out-of-tune cicadas—omens to the winter night, coaxing its surrender, yielding to a new coming day.

High in the fading sky, shooting stars crossed paths.

Did the heavenly pair caution her?

Were they a fragment of her hallucinations?

Ahead, Elger held open a peeling, weather-beaten door, waving the flashlight beam, leading them inside. Whatever awaited, she refused to appear startled and reminded herself she was a street-savvy New York City private eye.

Birdie trailed behind, inhaling musty air, tramping along a dusty dirt floor, weaving in and out among worn conveyors, and empty, splintered wood crates. Another door led to a lower landing, and again Elger led the way, climbing down sets of metal stairs. After unlocking and disarming two matched steel doors, he pushed each of them open with his hefty shoulder.

Birdie followed into blackness, entering a room lit by voiceless faces of blinking gauges and dull, flashing red and green instruments. She couldn't help envisioning Alice in Wonderland's Cheshire cat, its luminous smirk perched above her. If a trap waited, she'd rely on the concealed gun gripped inside her purse.

Her pulse jumped several beats as long rows of fluorescent lights blinked in unison, lighting the spacious laboratory. Birdie relaxed after a surprise gust of fresh air pushed through the room, thanks to a rush of overhead fans.

"This is where Shelley and the Germans took the lives of my followers."

"Children of God?"

"They killed them, promising to bring them back to life."

"Shelley's responsible for that?"

Elger shook his head. "Doctor Falk. You noticed his silver front tooth?" Shelly gives the orders."

"I've seen him."

"A cross between Captain Nemo and Doctor Frankenstein. That's what he is."

"You would have fooled me."

"Hitler bordered on madness. Himmler, his top commander, embraced the occult and convinced his Fuhrer Falk was the reincarnation of a mythical god, Prometheus, giving life to humanity.

"And Falk built this?"

"Hitler believed Falk arose from Prometheus, carrying mysteries of man's creation."

"That means what?"

"Medical science can build the perfect super race," Elger answered. "Prometheus betrayed the god's secrets of life."

Birdie walked away, amazed and frightened by Hitler's beliefs in ancient mysticism.

Elger stopped her with a touch to her hand. "Hear what I say. This is the reason you came to California."

"Remind me what that is."

"The angry gods punished Prometheus, chaining him to a boulder. Eagles ate his flesh. Weary of the pain, he pressed himself into the rock, becoming one with it. A thousand years later, his wounds healed, and he escaped, arising as Falk. Hitler believed Falk's silver tooth was a sign he had emerged from minerals within the rock. He's Hitler's salvation, his Prometheus to rebuild Nazi Germany." Elger paused, resting his palms on her shoulders. "You're here to help me destroy this."

Birdie neared exhaustion and might have enjoyed outrageous tales of Nazi spiritualist beliefs if she cuddled with a soothing wine next to a warm Manhattan fireplace. Today was not the time for Nazi fables, although she couldn't resist and strolled the lab, running her fingers along chilled upright vats crowded against tall cinder block walls. The scene reminded her of massive chemical tanks lining the Jersey bank of the Hudson River. She guessed dozens more occupied adjoining rooms.

She walked from Elger, exploring what she judged to be a well-lit dungeon.

"Careful of ice crystals," Elger said, following behind.

"What's in them?"

"Bodies. Falk's experiments."

She yanked her hand away, wiping it against her slacks.

Birdie's question never came. She stopped dead still and held a finger to her lips.

Elger stumbled and stepped closer to her. She saw he would offer no tactical support.

"Night watchman?" she asked.

"No."

She felt foolish showing alarm and did her best to hide her occasional timid nature.

She failed.

On edge, rattled nerves brought her to near panic. She needed to take command and show backbone. In a room this size, anything could become dislodged and fall. A stray animal perhaps caused the bump in the night. Her ears searched for any slight disturbance. Clicks and rattles from gauges and pumps started and stopped, cycling fluids, while soft humming came from instruments stacked in shelves close to each vat. None matched the severe squeak that raised the small hairs on the back of her neck. If the Cheshire cat hovered on rows of pipes and bundled cables above, Birdie wanted the smirking feline revealed and advising her.

At least she convinced herself of that.

The noise repeated over the dull drone of pumps and compressors. This time she placed it, recalling it from gym class—rubber soles dragged, squeaking on a polished white tile floor.

Birdie remembered the unexpected light flash near the car, and now the squeal of shoes in the supposed vacant building. Someone followed.

Unwanted company waited.

Nothing hinted at the stalker's location. The intruder likely moved to a better position. She had no intention of allowing them to outflank her. Every enemy has a weakness. She needed time to assess the situation and uncover theirs.

Birdie questioned, had Elger brought an accomplice?

She liked her chances in darkness, although there were too many fixtures to shoot out, and the toggled light switches out of reach. In the vast and well-lit room, she stood no chance against a professional killer and needed to move to a position she could defend. Her revolver carried six shells. Birdie hoped she'd only need one.

Their pursuer remained hidden, hunting them, she guessed, choosing a clean shot. She shielded Elger, wanting to protect him, as they dashed toward a cluster of metal files and bookcases.

Birdie expected a flurry of shots. None came.

The noise may have been her imagination. She was well past exhausted, and her mind played tricks.

Separating gave them a better chance. The lab remained quiet, and Birdie took a quick look around. No windows existed on the lower levels, and she doubted she'd find a fire alarm.

There was no escape. She felt trapped and uncertain of Elger.

Birdie pointed to a line of heavy wood desks. "Move there when told. It's safer."

She planned to go on the attack and slip behind the long row of tall cylinders, becoming a moving target. From there, she'd have maneuverability, being alone, and spotting the intruder. The revolver was no longer in her purse: instead; she gripped it ready to aim and shoot.

On his own, Elger broke for the nearby desks. As he ran half-squatted, a silenced shot fired. He slumped to the ground, crawling, forcing his knees to push him to safety, leaving a smeared trail of blood on the white tile. A second shot exploded his skull. Blood oozed from his motionless body. Bone and brain fragments covered the floor. Elger laid flat on his face. Birdie resisted rushing to him. The last shot left no doubt he was dead. After the muffled round, the spent shell rattled against the hard floor, spinning and rolling.

The used casing bounced and flipped along the tile and stopped near a heavy granite exam table she'd viewed in the Super 8 movie. Birdie had an inkling of the shooter's position, although she expected the gunman to move after his shot finished Elger.

She gripped the Celtic spiral ring dangling from her neck. Birdie couldn't help questioning, was she to blame for Elger's death?

There was no time for doubt or second-guessing. Birdie shared the room with a cold-blooded killer hunting her.

CHAPTER FORTY-THREE

Shelley's canyon house remained still. Nothing stirred as if the world paused, deciding.

Pello, attired in his show tuxedo, pushed open the door, fell to his knees, gasped, and crashed on his face. Blood spotted his collar, then pooled, coating the tips of his long blond hair. Lenora limped from Jaminson's wheelchair, ignoring throbbing pain from her prosthetic foot.

Defying common sense and Birdie's instructions, she'd accepted the handsome piano player's appealing offer of a late dinner. Hours later, he lay at her feet near death. Could she overcome her icy indifference, blaming him for Hamilton's torture?

A man's life was at stake. She was in no position to judge.

Dropping to his side, Lenora placed an ear close to his face, hearing faint, irregular rasps. Her hands pried under his ribs and torso, grabbing his white shirt, lifting and pulling, hoping to gain leverage and roll him to his back.

Pello's limp body refused to cooperate. With little remaining strength, Lenora inhaled and gave a tug—succeeding. She wasted no time tilting his chin upward. Her mouth covered his as she pinched his nose, blowing air into his lungs. After a few minutes, Lenora paused and placed her ear next to his lips, expecting to hear light breathing.

She wanted to be mistaken, finding no pulse. Pello was gone. Could his death be an accident, or were Shelley and Falk responsible?

Their captors showed no mercy to their own. Lenora expected the same treatment, and escape became the only choice.

Lenora had the will but lacked strength to push Hamilton's bulky wheelchair, navigating steep, twisting canyon hills. She'd not abandon her former husband. How long had he endured torture? Would he pass away without regaining consciousness, never to speak to her again? Were they doomed to die alongside the identical twins? While Hamilton continued unconscious, escape was not possible. Birdie's arrival remained a slim hope.

It pained Lenora to concede age had caught up with her despite yoga and daily exercise. Exhausted, she doubted she could pull herself from the floor. Stress, exertion and lack of food took her captive as much as Shelley.

She made little sense of the day's bizarre and shifting events that once again flip-flopped. Instead of pampering her beat-down and aching body in a long, hot, soaking bubble bath, she found herself with Pello and his twin, Fabian, both dead. Hamilton slumped next to her, barefoot and beaten. She reminded herself, remorse went hand in hand with failure. Her mind must stay clear. Think first, don't make the situation worse.

Sharp screams came from the hall, growing louder. If this were one of her creepy nightmares, she hoped to awaken.

Adding to the day's oddities, a green and red bird poked his hooked beak and head around the door frame, peeking inside. With a swift flutter, the colorful bird launched across the room and landed beside her.

"Pello, Pello," the parrot cried, sounding almost human.

She recognized the aggressive bird, Gigi. The parrot continued to squawk, prancing over Pello's body, jabbing and pulling at the buttons of his ruffled shirt. Before brushing the bird away, Lenora heard a hoarse, and gravelly voice utter her name. Hamilton's haggard face lifted. He opened puffy, blood-shot eyes, staring in her direction. She feared he'd return to his comatose state after the sight of an overweight, screaming parrot pecking a corpse.

Lenora undid Hamilton's limp hands and feet. Free, he didn't rise from the wheelchair holding him captive. His arms rested on the chair's padded arms, unmoving. Pale yellowed skin stretched over bruised, hollow cheekbones.

Lenora's instincts told her to escape—now.

The parrot's persistent cries grew louder as she steered Hamilton past Pello's and Fabian's bodies. Leaving the room, she expected to be turned back, winding up dead, sprawled next to the muscular twins. To her shock, not a soul appeared. For no definite reason, Lenora gained slight confidence as she continued pushing the rickety, high-backed wheelchair down the hallway.

Loud, scratchy music paired with static came from ahead. "I only have..." played over and over.

Finding the library, she lifted the tonearm, removing the spinning 78 album. The familiar song by The Flamingos had been one of her favorites shared with Hamilton during intimate times. Had he done the same with Shelley?

For the moment, she had Hamilton to herself and safe. Following slow sips of water, his breathing and voice improved—far from his usual deep tone, but understandable. With a damp towel and soap found in the kitchen, Lenora removed crusted blood from his face. She couldn't prevent the cold shudder from running through her after touching his feeble body. He reeked of vomit and urine, a shell of the once robust man. She wrapped her arms around him. For the first time, she realized how frail he'd become.

Leaving him alone in the wheelchair, Lenora explored, hoping to find a gun, improving their odds. A small hallway led to the garage behind the kitchen. A dull light bulb exposed an open roll-up door. Wilted dry leaves and branches from the night's violent winds collected against the walls of the spacious garage. A black Dodge sedan sat alone at the far end, near a workbench. Keys dangling on a cup hook. She had not expected that kind of luck in her first try at auto theft.

The feel of the leather seat and steering wheel hinted at freedom. She and Hamilton could drive away, escaping. Hesitant, Lenora pushed the silver starter button. The Dodge sputtered and shook as if arisen from winter's hibernation and stopped. On the next try, she pumped the gas pedal and pressed the ignition switch hard and firm. A smooth, low rumble rewarded her, raising her hopes.

The engine ran. The dial arm of the red and black gauge sprang to half a tank, enough fuel to take them far from Shelley's home, completing her rescue mission.

Hamilton needed care. She hoped to keep him out of the news and away from police. She stood between him and probable death and wouldn't endanger his life further. Admitting Hamilton to a hospital invited unwanted attention and alerted the captors of his location. A thought struck her if he agreed. A return to The Beverly Hilton brought immediate access to hotel doctors until Hamilton's medical staff arrived in Los Angeles.

Leaving the garage, returning for Hamilton, she stopped and played a hunch, opening the car's trunk.

She'd left Hamilton alone too long and rushed to the library. In the spacious reading room, she discovered the empty wheelchair pushed against the circular stone fireplace. Hamilton propped a shaky hand against the wood-paneled wall. He smiled.

"Where have you been?" he asked.

"You need rest, you old Welshman."

"No hello? A friendly, how are you would have been nice?"

"We don't have time."

Lenora held her arms out, holding Hamilton, pressing him close. She couldn't fault him for being who he was—a world-class risk taker and adventure lover no one dared say no to. The globe moved at his command, at least until the last few weeks.

"How long have you been held?"

"What day is it?"

Lenora looked at her watch. "January six."

"I forget."

"You remember anyone?"

"Mudge. He had a silver tooth and muddy shoes."

"How about Shelley?"

"Does it matter?"

"Not for now," Lenora answered.

"I recall being in this house."

"Can you travel?"

"Not to a hospital."

"I didn't think so."

"I need a phone."

"We have to get out of here before Shelley returns."

Lenora saw the look on Hamilton's face. Despite his state, Lenora detected his tone turn defensive and backed away from her questions, knowing there would be a better time. She did a hasty exam. His heart, pulse and breathing appeared fine, the same for his pupils.

He'd inherited wealth and multiplied it a hundredfold while flaunting his highborn, aristocratic attitude—a clear-cut reason they were no longer married. Lenora had been foolish to expect appreciation after jeopardizing her life to rescue him.

What upset her was not his affection for the younger Shelley. Instead, his lack of acknowledgment for the risks she'd taken. Thank you did not exist in his vocabulary. He remained stubborn, attempting to regain control.

"My security team is hunting me. Conrad needs to know I'm safe."

"Conrad?" Lenora asked.

"My secret army. Planes and copters looking for me."

"That can wait."

"Argentina. I need to call Argentina and straighten this out."

"We should go. Shelley may come back. They killed two men in the next room."

"She set me up. I want to see her."

Lenora recognized Hamilton's severe distress. He'd avoid discussing his beatings and humiliation. With Hamilton Jaminson, wealth and privilege built a wall to hide behind. Despite the rundown state, he attempted to continue and rectify what had occurred. Trauma tangled his mind and mounted a silent war against him. The longer he hid guilt and shame, the more prolonged his healing.

The ordeal left him fragile. His clothes sagged on his shrunken frame. Lenora considered overpowering Hamilton, putting him in the Dodge—the trunk.

Before Hamilton located a phone, Gigi flew into the library, landing on the couch's scuffed arm. The bird jerked her head about the room, inspecting the two.

"We all die. We all die," Gigi screamed.

"Is she telling us something?" Lenora asked.

Hamilton took a seat on a leather sofa, twisting his head, mimicking the parrot.

"Annoying bird. Let's get out of here," Lenora said.

"I'll stay," Hamilton said. "When I get my cash, then...."

Gigi repeated, "We all die. We all die."

Lenora watched Hamilton teeter and stand after he pulled from the sofa. He continued, sluggish and awkward, showing no signs of cooperating and escaping the madness. Instead, he searched the room, yanking open drawers, pushing and tossing shelved books to the floor.

"I know, Shelley. My cash is here."

Lenora asked herself how familiar he was with the house. Is this where he spent time with Shelley on his frequent visits to Los Angeles?

She had no legal hold on him—powerful feelings, nothing more. He was free to live his life, and he ran true to form chasing dreams, following impulses, and throwing money at wild schemes. No obstacle stood in his stubborn way.

The morning sun poked into the home's windows, Lenora grew nervous, expecting they wouldn't be alone much longer, and made her mind up to remove Hamilton with or without his consent. His and her safety overrode irrational behavior in their relationship—he was about to become an unwilling passenger in the Dodge's spacious trunk.

Walking to him, she pictured using a fireman's carry despite the pain in her prosthetic foot. Once tossed on her shoulder, she wouldn't stop, for his own good, until Hamilton laid next to the spare tire.

The moment Lenora grabbed Hamilton's wrist, Gigi landed on his back, brushing her face, and pecked her neck, bringing a spot of blood.

"Boom, we die," Gigi squawked. "Boom, we die."

Lenora brushed the parrot away.

"Boom, we die," came again as the parrot settled on the wheelchair.

Hamilton pulled his wrist from Lenora's grip. "Hear that?"

"The bird's crazy," Lenora said.

"Shelley keeps dynamite in the house," Hamilton answered.

CHAPTER FORTY-FOUR

Elger Stepp, leader of the Children of God, lay dead in the laboratory. Birdie Kelley became the next target. A clue to the shooter's position came from the spent shell's ping against a metal drum and its roll across the tile floor.

The telling brass case proved why she favored a revolver—no casing to expel, revealing her location. Not a rival to the sharpshooter Annie Oakley, Birdie preferred close targets. In the past she'd fired her pistol twice, eighteen rounds inside a red-neck, upstate New York firing range, and a desperation shot striking her attacker's leather satchel.

Long rows of overhead fluorescent lights lit the cravenness lab. The odds turned even, neither participant could disappear in shadow. Expecting her foe to take cover opposite her on the far side of the room, Birdie crouched behind green metal file boxes and silver gas cylinders. No longer unprotected, her prospects improved, concealed in a position she could defend. The cost of a slip-up carried the risk of taking a lead bullet.

Waiting the attacker out became an option, allowing him to make the first error. A single shot in the killer's direction tempted her. She'd flush the sniper out, or possibly, in the room filled with chemicals, set off an inferno, trapping them both.

Birdie calmed herself, listening for the slightest telltale sound hidden within the low drone of fluorescent lights and instruments rhythmically clicking, marking time for her eventual showdown in the deadly chess match. Her task in the underground chamber remained, avoid the stalker, reach the door, and get away.

The day matched nothing she'd encountered as a Pinkerton or on the Broadway stage. She'd allowed Elger to ensnare her into the lethal contest.

Determined not to allow her dilemma to escalate—escape, not revenge, stayed her goal, although emotions proved unpredictable under stress. She hunted a missing steel tycoon, and without provocation, had become the target of an unknown killer. Her explanation—wealthy individuals played for high stakes. Winning and losing created enemies among combatants. How she fit remained a mystery.

On her knees, hiding behind an overturned table, Birdie viewed the exit and dark stairway leading out of the morgue. Like Eve's forbidden fruit, the doors invited her to try a foolish dash, exposing her to the killer's deadly aim, leaving her no better than Elger Stepp, lying face down, and a skull blasted open. Temptation faded, she'd stay cautious and protected, inching between the lab's tall vats, boxed files, and exam tables, staying quiet and out of sight.

She believed the killer had shifted positions, mimicking her, hiding in the many nooks ahead or behind. Birdie repeated to herself, patience was not a lack of action, instead, waiting for the right opportunity. That rationale, she hoped, would win out. Deep down, she admitted patience remained an unfamiliar caller in her life.

Coming face to face with the laboratories, shiny steel vats reminded her of Coney Island's funhouse and distorted mirrors reflecting her misshapen double. Choosing the correct or wrong path led to escape or entrapment. She wouldn't allow herself to weaken with fear or grow reckless. There would be only one winner in the face-off.

Birdie recognized reality. Walking out alive may not be in the cards. The lab became a maze. Eventually, she'd become exposed, forced to step into the open, becoming a target, confronting her hunter, a cold, professional killer.

Was it karma? Payback time, balancing life's scales against her slip-ups, misjudging criminal suspects, caused innocent people's deaths. She couldn't allow defeated thinking and dwelling on the past. Lenora remained her concern. She was no good to her client dead.

Cunning and skill, not Elger's Celtic ring, would free her. She was Irish born and bred and a long way from gullible—Elger's Irish lore of protection better-fit bedtime fairytales.

Birdie slipped from one giant vat to another, pressing her weary back against tall, cold cylinders, resting and checking her situation. The odds of a wrong turn and crossing paths grew. Judging the killer watched, she varied her pattern, running and ducking with frequent stops, listening for telling sounds.

Behind a row of steel and concrete tubs, Birdie dropped to a squatting stance. She heard nothing above the loud pounding of her heart. If her stalker followed, they did silently.

The new position offered cover and a panoramic view of the lab. Had the shooter remained? Could he have targeted Elger Stepp, escaping, leaving her alone in her foolish drama, hiding and dodging invented shadows, allowing pretend fears to rule? Her tired mind refused to stop and continued to conjure fantasies.

If it had not been the spiteful Cheshire cat looking down on her, it might have been the stalking half-bull and-man Minotaur pursuing her in the subterranean labyrinth of stainless steel tanks and flashing instruments.

Carelessness, mated with unfocused thinking, led to being shot and killed. How did she allow her conservative Irish roots to draw her to the remote citrus orchard and the bizarre Frankenstein show?

Blaming fatigue avoided the underlying truth—she had been negligent, allowing Lenora to return to the hotel alone.

At the first sign of movement, she considered launching rapid-fire rounds. No warning or questions, certain her antagonist intended the same. Elger lay dead, with a hole blasted in his head because of her.

Birdie glanced at the Celtic ring hanging at her neck. Its triple spirals, life, death, and rebirth symbolized strength overcoming adversity. Had that been the message Elger sent? She refused to buy his mystic lore and Falk's ability to create and restore life. She admitted she hoped for magical power from the ring.

Escape required abandoning the protection of the concrete tubs and clustered steel tanks and crossing the exposed lobby dividing the laboratory. At the distant double doors, she planned to hit the ground, tuck, and roll to safety. She'd leap up the stairs, flee the rundown building, and speed away in the MG, providing her stalker hadn't disabled it.

Birdie gripped Elger's bulky ring in her moist palm, squeezing it while raising her .38 revolver to her shoulder. With no thought of her battered hip, she sprang into a life-or-death dash.

"Halt!" the voice shouted.

Stunned, she staggered, stumbling, to stop. The pursuer leaped from behind a row of tanks, blocking her—his handgun leveled inches from her chest.

Birdie's injured hip collapsed, sending her crashing to the ground. Her revolver dropped from her hand and slid, spinning out of reach, bumping into the polished kick plate of the door.

The intruder stepped toward her.

"Stay there," he said.

"Who are you? What do you want?"

"I have a job. Nothing personal."

Birdie clutched the Celtic ring out of hope or desperation; she wasn't sure. She'd been outflanked and outsmarted. Her hunter waited at the only exit, not unlike a big game tracker staking out a watering hole. The match may have ended for her stalker.

Hers began.

There were always choices: stay calm, buy time, maneuver and counter-attack. The odds were not in her favor; she faced a long shot. Her slight advantage arose from the animal kingdom, knowing a female adversary to be the most dangerous when cornered.

"Why'd you shoot my friend?"

"He was with you."

"I'd like to know my killer's name," Birdie said.

"If it matters… Gustain."

Birdie shifted to a squatting position. Her hip and shoulder throbbed while she pulled her knees tight against her chest. She moved unhurried, remaining calm, not alarming her captor. The man in front of her showed no emotion and perhaps attempted to hide a satisfied smile. His clothes were modest, yet tailored to his tall stature. How had he gone unnoticed? She didn't spot his location inside the lab or his approach in the parking lot. The realization hit, Cleon, her cab driver, earlier discovered the same man asking for her.

"You were at my hotel."

"And we meet."

"What do you want? Money?"

"My job is to kill you."

Birdie shuttered and forced herself to lift her eyes from the black, deep barrel, resembling a cannon, about to blast a bowling ball at her chest. His bloodshot eyes told her he had gone without sleep. Deprived of rest, Gustain's edginess and fatigue might cause a quick trigger finger. In her favor, he could suffer from slow reaction times and balance—something she could benefit from.

"Would you like to pray or turn away?" he asked.

She glanced down at her new ring. What did Elger imply, no harm came to her by keeping a genuine heart. Was it foolish to think the cult leader died because he gave her a silver ring? Those ageless tales belonged with early Celtic legends she'd known since childhood. No ring or ancient magic would help her situation.

She'd faced death in her Brooklyn boatyard home, escaped, and wouldn't concede without a fight. Gustain stood a short distance away, near the tall tanks, and continued to hold his pistol on her. A deep breath calmed her, diminishing jittery nerves. Her plan, clear-cut, pop to her feet as if launched from a spring-loaded box and attack his gun hand, hoping to redirect his aim—prepared to accept the pain and damage of a glancing bullet into her shoulder or arm. She'd have ten seconds of adrenaline rush and expected to have the strength to disarm him.

Birdie scooted her feet and legs tight, close to her body, in position to launch upward and sprint toward Gustain's gun hand.

A sudden, low, and distant rumble advanced, sounding like an approaching train. The abrupt jolt lifted and dropped the concrete and tile floor several times, rolling like an ocean wave beneath the laboratory. Following the first strike, rapid, vibrating shakes jerked the building from side to side, pulling instruments and ceiling tiles from their places.

Birdie froze, paralyzed. Tall stainless steel tanks behind Gustain rocked, tipped, and tumbled from bases. More followed, crashing against others, one after another. Fighting shock, Birdie rolled and squeezed under a metal desk, escaping airborne debris and collapsing bookshelves. The lab's lighting flickered and went out. In seconds, emergency generators hummed, restoring light.

Liquid nitrogen hoses and pipes tore from vats and ruptured, raising a billowing fog, and filling the laboratory. Equipment not bolted or strapped to the wall smashed to the floor. A thin cloud of evaporating nitrogen continued to spread through the entire chamber.

Violent shaking and vibrating stopped. Birdie remained underneath the desk, safe and unharmed, unsure what waited in the destroyed lab. The surprise trembler spared her from Gustain's bullet. Her fresh fear: would she escape, or face meeting her maker after a slow and painful death, trapped in the catacombs of Falk's lab?

Her stage accident flashed, unwelcome in her mind—a collapsed overhead lighting structure cut short her young acting career. Today, she escaped death, spared by a natural catastrophe. Were these connected to Elger Stepp? Had he carried a message from her proud Nordic forefathers? Elger hinted she came to Los Angeles for something more.

After pushing away toppled pumps and small compressors, Birdie gambled and crawled from under the protective desk. She stepped over the massive "I" beam, lying inches from crushing her.

From reflex, she grabbed the ring hanging on her neck. Could it be her imagination? Releasing it, Birdie refused to consider the possibility.

The would-be assassin lay nearby, motionless, sprawled beneath collapsed tanks and ceiling tile. To her relief, no gruesome corpses escaped, floating free in the carnage.

Puzzled why a hitman targeted her, Birdie moved near his still body, unsure if he were dead. After watching the hired killer for a moment—it was more than possible he had a role in her search for Hamilton Jaminson. After what she'd witnessed, Birdie refused to discount any lead.

She rifled his pockets, pulling them inside out, finding them empty. In a rush, she'd overlooked his jacket. Birdie believed she'd developed an immunity to surprises. Tucked within his breast pocket, she removed a creased five-by-seven black-and-white photo—a mug shot. A close-up of her full face and another in profile. What startled her—Lenora's plane and hanger stood in the background, all taken as she walked to the bogus Western Union car in New Jersey.

Exhaust fans kicked in, drawing the nitrogen cloud from the room, while emergency shut-offs cut the supply. Birdie failed to locate his handgun and feared to search in the rubble, bringing down more unstable vats and submerged bodies. She spotted her .38 pinned under a tank. Its barrel had suffered damage, a small dent, maybe harming its bore.

Another jolt hit, tossing Birdie against a wall. Nothing fell from shelves or the ceiling. Instead, her trapped gun came free.

Birdie jammed her damaged handgun inside her purse and planned to retrieve Elger Stepp's remains.

Common sense directed her to escape to the outdoors and safety. The room above could crash, bringing conveyors on top of her, sealing her with the corpses. She owed nothing to Elger. He brought her to Falk's manmade purgatory.

Birdie glanced at the Celtic ring hanging on her neck. Guilt overcame her, assuming responsibility for Elger's unnecessary death. Retrieving his body, in a small way, would show gratitude.

Climbing over and through tumbled chairs, tables and crushed glass, she arrived at the shooting site—no sign of Elger or blood splatter.

The puzzling leader of The Children of God had vanished.

CHAPTER FORTY-FIVE

The bundle of keys hit with a dull splash and sunk.

Within Shelley's mind, they made a thunderous slap, reminding her of fruitless years indulging Falk and Strughold. Local San Pedro fishermen desiring the sleek sports car were welcome to it. Like her crushed dreams, the Corvette's keys rested in the slimy mud of the cold Pacific.

Her music career evaporated with nothing remaining but a memory and disgrace. Argentina became a far-off thought. A glance at her watch reminded her that in hours, Lenora and Hamilton Jaminson would disappear in the explosion and fire.

Falk's greed led to robbing and seizing Hamilton Jaminson, forcing Shelley to flee. She admitted a reluctance to defraud the American industrialist, leading him to believe he'd gained Falk's life suspension technology—the fountain of youth. The unexpected arrival of a persistent Birdie Kelley and her client added to the tangled web of chaos concealing Falk's cloning research from the CIA.

She walked from the wharf, guiding her hand on the dock's smooth, red-painted handrail, saying goodbye to her ambitions. Along the way to her dream, she'd stumbled, compelled to carry the seed of Hitler in her womb.

The last pushcart bumped, rolling down the narrow ramp of the canvas-covered truck, completing Doctor Falk's transfer of handwritten and microfilmed files sealed in waterproof, floating chests. Shelly trusted there would be room on the cramped rear deck for the collection of experimental data on *Saint Jude*, her hired fishing boat. Decades of irreplaceable, gruesome human experimentations were trusted to a patched-up craft she doubted seaworthy.

Shelley watched a sluggish Falk stumble as he guided a trembling hand, inspecting each container. She hid her relief. The unmarked package survived his scrutiny.

Strughold became a no-show. His private phone went unanswered, and since Brea's shutdown, the heralded space medicine doctor was no longer needed to shield Dulles and the CIA from Falk's breakthrough.

The captain was set to launch. Shelley expected to dock in Avalon in an hour. Calm seas, lit by a rising, warm California sun, promised a smooth voyage to Santa Catalina Island. Falk's research was aboard and secure, leaving little room on the rear deck, forcing Shelley and Falk to squeeze inside the wheelhouse, sharing space with the captain and stench of raw fish.

Diesel engines rumbled. Twin propellers churned San Pedro harbor's murky waters while the crew member hopped on board after releasing stern and bowlines. An observing colony of seagulls launched from neighboring ships, squawking bon voyage, circling the departing boat.

Shelley watched the bow's gentle rise and fall on the early morning sea. The first step of a long journey got underway with no backward glances, leaving behind bitter memories—her new life began.

Local law enforcement, cooperating with the CIA, covered commercial ships and airlines. Intuition, from years of hiding, told her Falk would forever stay hunted. Dulles took Falk's disloyalty personally and sought vengeance. His contract killer was not far behind and would eliminate all involved in the betrayal.

After shelling out an inflated fee, Shelley booked space for home on *The Black Swan*. The Argentine flagged tramp steamer carried a reputation for disregarding international shipping laws and had transported Nazis fleeing wartime Germany. She touched the cash-filled satchels at her feet and speculated the ship's captain would demand more money once he saw the number of boxes.

According to the London shipping broker, the delayed arrival from Mazatlan was expected at two to five days, maybe sooner or longer. Shelley discovered the Argentinian ship's late schedule hinged on the captain's financial arrangements with a Mexican customs agent.

Shelley ventured from the cramped wheelhouse escaping Falk's and the fishing captain's cigars, she presumed, rolled from Cuban truck tires. After an inspection of the cargo, her package remained tucked among Falk's records and appeared secure and dry during the smooth passage.

Inhaling fresh sea air while keeping a firm, white knuckle grip on the bow rail, she fought the urge to empty her nauseous stomach as she wedged against the ship's freight. Falk would not have the pleasure of seeing her sick.

Patting her growing belly, she regretted the implant of Hitler's genes. Falk and Strughold, in the guise of enhancing the Aryan people, robbed the lives of harmless war prisoners to expand the horrific knowledge held in the metal and wood trunks she leaned against.

Her cause had nothing to do with the rebuilding and return of a pure German race. Her relationship with the doctors was a destructive by-product of her duty to family and her mother's greed.

She couldn't continue the charade. Her mother and Nazi stepfather lured her into servitude with the promise of fame.

Escaping the CIA, while preventing Falk's papers from reaching Argentina, could ease her guilt-ridden conscience. The Catalina safe house provided short-term refuge. An educated guess explained Strughold's sudden vanishing and betrayal. He'd exposed Falk's hidden work, explaining the CIA's hunt for them. Their trail appeared covered, she hoped, anticipating *The Black Swan* setting anchor in the deep waters near Avalon.

The morning's gray, orange-colored sky shimmered on the flat water. Shading her eyes, Shelley spotted the island's notable landmark. Well-lit and twelve stories tall, the Catalina Casino provided a navigational marker into Avalon Bay. The dance hall and movie theater cheered her, restoring memories and ambitions of a stage career, absorbing life-giving energy from adoring audiences.

She escaped to the scenic island to resurrect her soul and protect Falk's horrid work from reaching the people she once swore allegiance. From this point forward, she'd look over her shoulder, suspicious of everyone. Since an abbreviated childhood, her mother warned of a hungry tiger lying in wait to eat the goat. It was the way of nature in the treacherous game she took part in. It took years to realize her mother had married a ravenous Nazi tiger living as a goat in the safety of her home country.

The fishing boat slid alongside the dock, bumping against tires of the Catalina pier. The lone crew member jumped from the ship and tied frayed ropes to front and rear dock cleats.

It took a moment for Shelley to pause from her daydream. Falk stood beside her, flashing his silver tooth, tapped her shoulder.

"Penny for your thoughts," he asked.

"The parrot?"

"I left the garage door open. Gigi will escape."

"We have work to do," Shelley said.

"My taxidermy mounts …"

"We had no room."

"Those lifelike creatures gave the illusion of immortality."

"They were dead and creepy."

"To you. For me, a reminder of the challenges faced in my work."

"Gigi's near-human intelligence will be missed, Doctor. Nothing else."

Shelley stepped aside as men walked to the marina carrying wood chests and boxes. She spotted her shoebox-sized package pass by, crammed among Falk's books and documents.

As always, she concealed private thoughts deep inside. It took more than a penny, although she feared they'd become transparent to the stoic Falk. There had been times she questioned her affection for Hamilton Jaminson. Never romantic, apart from arrogance, he exposed a caring tenderness.

She brushed aside unrequited feelings, grabbed both satchels of Jaminson's cash, and set her foot on the boat's gunwale's unfinished wood. Greeted by gasoline blended with decaying fish, she stepped to the dock.

Taking a seat behind the wheel of an oversized, flatbed golf cart, Shelley looked back to the bay's calm dark waters. Shelley bit her bottom lip, hoping her unsettled stomach calmed. Her plan required luck and coordination between many people.

Could she survive swimming in the cold water?

Next to the fishing boat, two more electric carts towing trolleys arrived. In moments, the workers tied and secured Falk's containers.

* * * *

While Falk napped, Shelley stood on the balcony of their isolated, cliff-side cottage, their home until the ship docked near the island. Boxes and trunks lined the single hallway and living room. The suitcases of cash remained with her. Waterproof bags protected bundled hundred-dollar bills.

Shelly stared over the panoramic view of boats and yachts anchored in the crescent-shaped Avalon Bay. Far to the north, past Long Beach and the City of Los Angeles, behind building clouds, Shelley spotted veiled jagged lightning flashes.

Could she survive the sinking of the fishing boat?

Shelley looked in on Falk. He continued sleeping, unmoving in the small bedroom.

Jamison's money remained safe and would stay close. She expected Falk to challenge her for control and confiscate the million American dollars.

Hidden amongst the boxes, her private insurance traveled unnoticed alongside the whorish archives of Falk's cruel wartime experiments. The shoebox-sized container remained unknown to Falk. Its contents, a direct means to the life she once dreamed.

CHAPTER FORTY-SIX

Shattered glass covering the lab's floor crunched under Birdie's shoes. She stumbled, gripping the back of a chair, preventing another fall. Collapsed metal cabinets filled with monitors and instruments laid at her feet. The chaos left her puzzled why she'd allowed Elger to bring her here.

Alarmed at not finding Elger, she stood at the spot of his murder, moving aside tables and ceiling tiles, questioning had the massive quake shifted his body or covered it. As she stepped back, a steel post slipped, smashing a metal file, but not before grazing her head.

Birdie touched the swollen and tender gash at the side of her forehead. Specks of blood stained her hair, and a blouse purchased on Gimbel's lay-a-way required mending. She had no clue how long she'd been unconscious following the second round of shakes.

Her aching hip and shoulder, added to her new wounds, reminded her she drew near to her allotted nine lives—a superstition from childhood. How often would she land on her feet? The assassin had her in his sights; she'd met her match and accepted death when the quake hit.

How long would she stay in the man-made Purgatory, surrounded by dozens of corpses trapped inside steel tombs? The next quake could yank the tall cylinders free from their braided metal umbilical cords, flooding the lab with lifeless bodies.

Birdie held up the unexpected gift from Elger and considered the ring's three spirals, rejecting ideas of mystical protection, despite the violent tremor that spared her life. Voodoo belonged to miss-fits carrying crucifixes in Greenwich Village.

During the mayhem, a fourth party may have entered, removing Elger. Birdie continued gripping the silver ring, wondering why the cult leader came prepared, expecting to give her his cherished Irish heirloom.

As a New Yorker, Birdie became accustomed to subway power failures stranding travelers beneath the city. Remaining calm was the answer. Panic was not. She hoped the shakers had ended, although they had saved her life. Focusing on what she controlled relieved a little of her fears.

She sought a sensible explanation for Elger's disappearance. Bodies don't vanish on their own after taking a severe wound and a finishing shot exploding the skull. Bone fragments and pooled blood remained near his shepherd's crook—no footprints or smeared body fluids showed signs of being dragged.

In the brief time since knowing Elger, she developed a fondness for the delusional, long-haired cult leader. The intrusion into the secret lab exposed Falk's horrific testing to her own eyes, something she would not have imagined. Beneath Elger's self-centered veneer, he hid a caring nature. Birdie gripped the Celtic ring tight in her palm. No words were found to pay tribute to Elger.

The kind act gnawed at her. She'd neglected to thank him for his genuine concern. Had she judged him harshly? Despite his confused state, he sought to protect her.

Birdie let the silver ring drop from her shaking fingers and fall, hanging from her neck. She'd never forget Elger's gentleness.

She needed to escape the morgue. The concealed underground bunker's thick concrete walls showed cracks and faults. The citrus packing plant, crowded with conveyors and tables, sat overhead. How long did she have before more support posts buckled, collapsing the entire building? She faced being crushed, dying in the rubble, before rescuers arrived. Chances were good that no search party would arrive at the hidden catacombs buried in the out-of-the-way canyon's orange grove.

Her missing person investigation turned personal. The complicated hunt for Lenora's former husband belonged in the hands of the FBI, not a green private investigator. Today, she witnessed an assassination meant for her and observed a lab violating the laws of mortality. The moment she boarded her wealthy client's helicopter, she should have stepped off and sprinted across the frozen East River. The hefty cash advancement sat in a bank in the middle of New York City and would revert to the state should she die.

Sketchy evidence surrounded her, implicating many in Hamilton Jaminson's disappearance. She could not place his reputation at risk and parade into a Los Angeles police station. Each encounter involving Shelley, Falk, and the grisly laboratory implicated her client's former husband.

The thought would stay private—Jaminson possibly took part in the elaborate scheme. His part possibility a charade to create and regenerate life. Birdie had no intention of sharing her speculation with Lenora. Fate played a part, keeping her alive in the masquerade. She intended to go on and follow the only trail she had—the one leading to Shelley's remote home.

Her frustration floated dangerously close to death. The adventure in the rabbit hole drove her to near madness, as the Cheshire cat warned Alice. How long could she go on? Death stood at her doorstep, seconds away, intending to escort her to eternity. Was the money Lenora paid her that important? She'd stared down the gun barrel and said farewell prayers. At the moment, she didn't recall her rapid and silent pleas and promises. Had she believed, on some adolescent level,

Elger's assurance of the ring's guarding her, hitching her faith to a remorseful cult leader who sold out his followers to a Nazi's effort to recreate Lazarus escaping his tomb?

Nothing in her Wonderland journey came as chance. Oddball, as the events appeared, something connected them. She missed several puzzle pieces linking the little she knew. All Birdie could do was dig and scrape until they had. As a former Pinkerton, she'd accepted perspiration as ninety-five percent of working a case—the other luck. She speculated the remaining five were a gigantic myth. The other Pinkerton tenet, "We never sleep," rang true.

Her integrity showed signs of slipping. Operating inside the law had turned into a challenge. Finding the leather bags of cash in Shelley's house tested her ethics. No longer a Pinky, she strived to work within the agency's honor code and principles but strayed enough to think of herself as near the edge of becoming a rogue PI.

Mild aftershocks continued, shifting and rolling storage tanks across the lab. Birdie's luck held. No bodies emerged. Long rows of fluorescent light tubes flickered, threatening darkness. The next tremor could bring down the entire structure. If that possibility didn't frighten her, the nightmare thought of dozens of escaping, defrosting cadavers flooding the basement would.

After viewing Super 8 movie reels taken from Falk, Birdie accepted Elger's morbid explanation of Doctor Falk's search to prolong and create human life. It connected to Jaminson's trip to Los Angeles and the satchels of cash. In either case, it made no difference how she'd go ahead. The goal remained clear, locate Hamilton Jaminson. It appeared her best chance was to hustle to Shelley's home and rescue Lenora.

She'd wasted precious time searching for Elger's body, justifying it as repayment to the cult leader's effort to safeguard her, offering his Gaelic silver ring for divine protection. Birdie owed him the decency to remove his corpse from the rubble.

Her search produced nothing, and despite the overpowering urge to continue, fatigue and fear stopped her, defeating her.

Conceding, Birdie pushed her way past fallen tables, bookcases, and hoses, dodging water spewing from overhead pipes.

She spotted Gustain's body near the double doors leading to escape. The mystery man, intending to kill her, met his death. Birdie wished to confirm that and found no pulse. Whoever he was no longer posed a threat. There was no doubt he planned to put a bullet into her head. Birdie kept her damaged .38 in her hand. Worthless, but she gained a sense of security.

She reached the double doors. No one appeared. Birdie followed her training and cleared every open room and hallway, hurrying, not rushing, not allowing herself to become a stationary target.

Once she climbed the final staircase and pushed out the door, she escaped the dungeon and limped away into shadows shaped by early sunshine. Her lungs welcomed fresh air scented by new, sweet-smelling oranges. The aroma and view of the surrounding citrus grove became paradise.

Birdie reminded herself Gustain may have an accomplice, possibly two, and she remained in danger. It also explains Elger's body vanishing. She used the cover of tin buildings and woodsheds to approach her car. Now was not the time to let her guard down. A rifle shooter could send a bullet her way from countless locations.

Her hands trembled and held tight to her spiral ring. She stepped along the gravel path and turned the corner of a shed filled with packing crates, following a weed-infested trail to the parking area and dusty MG. She swore several days had passed, and she'd aged years, adding more white hairs. Her confusion was likely caused by extreme exhaustion or delayed trauma—something her therapist warned of. The horror of dead bodies, her death, and viewing Elger Stepp's brains blown out in cold blood replayed in blurred fast action. After enduring The City of Angels, she needed a long sabbatical from people. A retreat to an ocean island appeared ideal. She'd settle for New York City, to her dismal apartment, and a new occupation as a paid dog walker.

The MG waited, and she hoped the killer had not tampered with it. The tiny car had few places to hide anything dangerous, and she'd give it a once over.

Startled, Birdie came to a sudden stop behind a broken-down shed. A man, she thought familiar, leaned against the yellow idling taxi.

It seemed an eternity since Cleon drove her to the Congo Jazz Club, leading to the clash with Shelley. Bits and pieces of the elaborate puzzle fell into place and formed a rough picture. The cabby didn't fit. Was it possible he tailed her, or did he connect to the dead men inside the destroyed lab?

Positive the driver spotted her, Birdie stepped back, bracing her spine against the steel of a rusted shed. The third, unknown car baffled her. She ran through possibilities: Her shooter, Gustain, may have arrived in the suspicious cab; if so, there was a third player to account for.

Unarmed, her pistol damaged, she stood little chance against three.

"Birdie. It's Cleon, your taxicab driver. I pulled you from the lake."

She knew the raspy voice. Was it too much of a coincidence? He'd appeared each time she'd gotten into a jam. She couldn't allow herself to walk into another trap. Birdie reached inside her purse, grabbing her pistol.

CHAPTER FORTY-SEVEN

Like gunslingers, they faced off at close range, eye to eye, in silence. Over the flat hum of fluorescent lights, both heard the hollow, steady ticking, growing until it consumed the vacant garage.

"Hear that?" Hamilton asked.

Both turned toward the unexpected sound.

Lenora waited before speaking. "It's under you."

Hamilton stepped from the car. As he did, Lenora took a knee on the dusty concrete floor, running her hand under the seat.

"It's definitely ticking," she said in a whisper.

Hamilton grabbed Lenora's wrist, attempting to pull her to her feet. She waved him off and stood, holding a scuffed brown leather briefcase.

"This is crazy. This isn't happening," Hamilton said.

"Should I?" she asked, pointing to its brass lock.

"No." Hamilton Jaminson stumbled and backed away.

"I'm gonna set it down," Lenora said.

Her impulse was to drop the case and run. Hamilton struggled to walk. His reactions turned numb, and Lenora recognized he'd cramped, unable to move.

Using the extreme care of placing a sleeping infant into a crib, she crouched to lower the case. Her quivering fingers slipped, jarring the briefcase against the concrete floor.

The single brass latch snapped open. Lenora frowned, cringing at Hamilton.

"Boom, we die," the parrot squawked, flying out the open overhead door.

She kneeled over a red and gold Eveready six-volt battery, an alarm clock connected to black and white coiled wires poked into a small cube of what looked to be gray modeling clay.

"Military plastic explosives," Hamilton said.

"Look at the timer," Lenora said.

"Leave the damn thing. Let's go!"

"We won't make it."

"You drive," Hamilton shouted.

The ticking bomb remained on the garage floor, counting down. Lenora pointed Hamilton to the passenger seat.

The Dodge bounced over the low gravel berm. Hamilton looked back at the canyon home while Lenora sped, spinning the car's tires on the dirt and loose rock, veering, and fish-tailing onto the asphalt.

Moments later, a shock wave hit the car.

The explosion destroyed the home's garage doors, brick walls, and tile roof in a bright flash. Red and yellow flames, ignited by ruptured gas lines, shot from the demolished home. As Lenora and Hamilton turned and watched, shingles and fragments of wood joists collapsed into the blazing house. Blast debris, carried in the wind, pelted their car. A few glowing ambers landed on the rocky terrain, burned and extinguished. Others didn't.

Hamilton touched her shoulder. "Of the roads less traveled," he whispered. "I made a poor choice."

"Robert Frost?" Lenora asked.

Hamilton nodded. "Our paths, I regret, diverged once upon a time."

"I picked this road because I wanted to find you," Lenora answered.

"I made the wrong decision back then."

Lenora heard the unexpected words and humble tone of Hamilton's curious means of saying sorry. She silently accepted—this was the best she would get. She turned to him, and as she did, the winding road caught her by surprise. The car veered into grassy undergrowth. Lenora slammed the brakes, sliding, stopping at the edge of an unguarded rocky cliff.

"That was close," Hamilton said. "You're exhausted. The road tricked your eyes."

In a few seconds, Lenora spoke. "I almost did what Shelley couldn't."

"We're fine now."

"I should have seen it coming. It was a setup, both times. She planted the car bomb and put the keys in plain sight just as she did the fountain of youth."

"You found the briefcase," Hamilton said. "All's well that ends well. Take us home."

"I'm missing something," Lenora spoke. "Shelley killed those decent men we shared a room with. She wanted us dead. She would have made sure."

They sat for a moment with the running car. Neither spoke, yet she sensed they knew what needed doing. Lenora argued with herself, knowing the safe path—retreat and consider her search a success. Hamilton was safe, her original aim. Birdie Kelley likely was tucked in, safe at the hotel. Lenora could, with no guilt, call her rescue mission finished. Why did she have second thoughts about her private investigator and the events of the past two days?

"What's next?" Hamilton asked.

"Tell me how to get to Van Nuys."

After returning to the road, Lenora jammed on the Dodge's breaks.

"Shelley may have outsmarted us," she said.

"What?" Hamilton asked.

"We found it too easy," she answered, slamming both palms against the steering wheel. "She knew we'd be suspicious."

"The parrot warned we would die," Hamilton said. "It's a game."

"Shelley put a second bomb in the car," Lenora said. "She played us."

CHAPTER FORTY-EIGHT

Lenora wrapped her arms around Hamilton's waist and rushed from the black Dodge. Behind them, on the canyon road, flames grew, consuming Shelley's isolated home.

"Fires in these hills and canyons spread fast," Hamilton said, breaking free and stopping.

"We're not going near that car," Lenora said. "She could have hidden the bomb anywhere."

"The fire needs reporting," Hamilton said.

"I can't leave you here, and you're in no condition to hike out."

"There's a flashlight in the glove box. We can search the car," Hamilton said.

"Too risky. It could go off anytime."

She was in charge. Hamilton remained in no shape to decide. Lenora draped his arm over her shoulder and gripped Hamilton's waist, leading him from the idling Dodge. Lenora held him tight against her, supporting him in a three-legged race for their lives. Her prosthetic foot twisted and wobbled, threatening collapse. She kept her balance navigating through rough brush and rock, unsure of a safe distance against the expected blast and sharp metal and glass. The climb was slow, each step removed them farther from the car and a raging house fire that endangered the valley.

Hamilton continued to struggle and weaken, stumbling over loose gravel and stone. Lenora steadied him, keeping him on his feet. Hamilton's long ordeal left his slacks and jacket hanging from his frame, making it easier to control the once bulky man. After enduring their scramble up the slight grade, Lenora coaxed Hamilton to sit on a small outcropping of boulders. He did without complaint, surprising her, worrying her more.

Lenora guessed they'd reached a safe location, distant from the car and the home's raging flames. The wildfire posed the greater danger— mild wind carried smoke and red embers threatening spot fires.

"We'll wait for a car to pass," Lenora said.

Hamilton appeared to regain a slight amount of strength. Lenora freed him from her grip, leaning him to the side, allowing his head to rest against the rock wall.

"Stand out there," he whispered, straining, forcing a finger toward the mountain road.

She dreaded leaving him unattended. Hamilton needed a hospital, and fire threatened the canyon's dry brush with them sitting downwind in the middle of its path.

Lenora stood in the center of the narrow road, determined to flag down the next passing car. She'd experienced Southern California traffic. Seldom was there a break from highway congestion. Cars filled highways and surface streets seven days a week non-stop. Traffic reporters packed the sky with helicopters and planes, updating commuting conditions. Then again, here she stood in a Los Angeles canyon—no cars in sight. She hoped one of the many airborne radio and television journalists spotted the explosion and spreading fire.

The sound of thrashing blades caught her attention, bringing relief. In the hazy, smoky sky above narrow canyon walls, four helicopters lumbered toward the burning house. In seconds, the wail of approaching sirens boomed off sheer cliffs, challenging Lenora to locate their position. She didn't have long. A caravan of three Los

Angeles County firefighting trucks, alarms blaring and lights flashing, drove past, never slowing, forcing Lenora to hobble from the center of the bending, single-lane road.

Following them, an ambulance arrived, veering off the road, skidding into a dusty turnout. Lenora staggered toward Hamilton, expecting her prosthetic foot to fail, making her useless to him. She could only watch her former husband struggle, resisting and fighting off safety constraints as they placed him into a metal rescue stretcher and lifted him into the first aid truck.

As Lenora climbed in alongside Hamilton, the blast raised the distant black Dodge off the ground. The car that aided their getaway, saving their lives, burned inside the fury of hot, dancing red and yellow flames.

Her copter trip to Catalina waited. Obligations leaned to Hamilton, and she wouldn't leave his side. Admitting him to a hospital became a priority. Her prideful Hamilton Jaminson needed her, and she needed him. He offered a second chance on the road she'd not taken.

CHAPTER FORTY-NINE

"Elger Stepp is my son," Cleon shouted across the grass and rock field.

Morning daylight gave Birdie a clear view of the unexpected visitor. Startled, she hesitated, allowing her weary mind to catch up with the past thirty-six hours. A day's sleep and a long, hot bath would cure her fatigue. She lacked time for luxuries or feeling sorry for herself. People had died in front of her, and there was a job to do. Birdie admitted she played in the major leagues with sandlot skills. A change was necessary for her to survive.

"Came to help," Cleon said, stepping closer.

It took a moment for Birdie's clouded mind to repeat the name, hoping it registered. Instead, it was Cleon's taste in fashion. The familiar tattered and food-stained vest exposed him. How could she have forgotten? The cab driver possessed an uncanny knack for appearing during her moments of need. Her waterlogged body would lie at the bottom of a reservoir without his return to Shelley's house.

What role did he play—savior or persecutor?

After surviving Falk's laboratory, she remained hesitant of offers help, regardless of who. She guessed two assassins had tracked her and Elger into the secret basement lab. The cabby's arrival presented a fresh suspect for Elger Stepp's killing. Cleon might have acted with Gustain to shoot Elger. Instincts, gained on the streets of New York, told her he had been an innocent cab driver who'd lost his son. Yet, she'd not take chances.

She's viewed the two deaths, Elger by a bullet and Gustain crushed by steel tanks stuffed with preserved bodies. Second-guessing her examination of Gustain's corpse—she had feared for her life and hurried to escape the collapsing building. She might have missed a faint pulse. The body rested under massive beams and steel drums. If there had been one, she was in no position to remove the mangled remains. She had no obligation to rescue the man who stalked her and killed Elger.

Birdie couldn't stay and debate Cleon. She lived on borrowed time, needing information fast. Birdie pulled her damaged revolver from her purse, aiming at the cab driver, gambling he carried no weapon.

"Where's your son?" she shouted.

"His spirits in a better place," Cleon answered. "What remains will perish by flames." He pointed to the fire in a large metal stock tank.

"You did that?"

"What he wanted."

"How did you get inside?"

"We're wasting time. You need my help."

Birdie lowered her pistol, trusting the cabbie's story. "Who killed him?"

"Don't know. I tried to stop him. It was too late. After the quake, I couldn't leave Elger."

"His killer's dead."

Cleon nodded.

She limped toward the cab driver. "How was Elger involved?"

"He provided his dying followers hope. After they passed, Falk preserved their bodies waiting for cures."

"Children of God believers?" Birdie asked.

"They were dead. It's not a crime. Elger promised a second life."

"They were all Elger's disciples?" she asked.

"Some. Others were homeless. He hated the Nazis. Just wanted to help his children."

"Shelley, have another place?" she asked.

"Kept a house on Catalina Island."

"Catalina?"

"Off the coast. Take the San Pedro ferry."

"Any chance of an address?"

"Never been there. My son talked about Wrigley's scuba shop. Shelley did some diving."

Birdie looked to the fire and stepped toward the raging flames, recalling Elger's kindness and concern. She held the ancient ring in her palm, not mentioning it to Cleon. It belonged to Elger, and she intended to leave it with his cremated remains.

Cleon caught her by one arm, stopping her. "Let him go. There's nothing left. He wanted you to have his ring. It will guard you if your heart is pure."

Birdie recognized the words Elger once used.

* * * *

The ceiling and fruit conveyors high above the lab collapsed, narrowly missing Gustain. He opened his eyes. Through a layer of dust and tangled iron, he took pleasure from the last morning sky he'd seen. A metal beam trapped his leg. The initial collapse didn't kill him, but a heavy support post ensnared his leg.

He'd failed. Birdie had been in his sights.

She was more attractive than Dulles' grainy surveillance photos. As usual, he'd remained unaware of the reason the CIA targeted her. The agency assigned his orders to protect national security. That and the money had been good enough for him.

He'd waited for Birdie at the lab's entry, knowing she'd deliver herself to him. The foolish delay cost his life. A question haunted him, why did he pause pulling the trigger? Earlier, with no hesitation, he'd eliminated her companion. The price paid for his sin was dear. He lay trapped, injured—snared, enduring pain burning in his shoulder and leg. Unlike an ensnared wolf, he was in no position to chew away the entangled limb.

Jaminson, Lenora and Falk were no longer his worry. Ending his existence offered an honorable solution. He faced that decision but waited. German military training taught him his body had abilities to restrict pain signals to his brain. Earlier, he'd slowed his heart and pulse, convincing Birdie of his demise.

California intended to be his last assignment, and it would. The job targeted helpless civilians. He may have been too casual and overconfident. Six rounds remained in the clip, with one needed. Arrest risked CIA embracement. His shadow tailed him since arriving in Los Angeles—they were near. Death no longer disturbed him. Instead, it became an escape.

Gustain struggled, fading in and out of consciousness, fighting pain and loss of blood. Thankful, he'd breathed his last breath seeing the blue sky and shining sun. His German homeland remained a memory. Walking on the grounds of his ancestors would endure in his spirit. He passed on no children to farm the motherland he loved and fought for. Nomadic life was not the existence intended. He'd become an efficient assassin—too valuable. Dulles would not allow him to be captured or retire.

Footsteps, crunching on gravel, pushed through rubble and waste, approached from the exposed parking area. His pistol lay under him, tucked close to his side, hidden by his jacket. From behind a cluster of steel cylinders and packing crates stepped a man. Gustain recognized the caller and reached for his gun. The visitor nodded and raised his right arm, pointing to Gustain. The gun fired once and then again. Gustain didn't pull his handgun.

His chest burned. Death followed the second gun flash.

* * * *

The Catalina Duchess moored alone at the end of the dock, taking on passengers hauling surfboards and bicycles when Birdie arrived. Aided by several stops for directions, the tiny MG convertible delivered her to San Pedro after enduring Southern California's congested morning roads.

Birdie held a one-way ticket and a scrap of paper with a scribbled name. She had little choice but to follow Cleon's tip. With a purse full of Lenora's cash, she boarded the ferry to locate her missing client and Jaminson.

Ahead of San Pedro, she'd returned to Shelley's canyon home, finding a burned wreckage. Questions got her referred to a fire captain and escorted to a wet, narrow street crowded with hoses and firefighters.

While they walked, the captain leaned close to be heard over spraying water.

"We got here early and found no one. When the fire's knocked down, we'll look again."

Birdie hoped for positive news, recognizing the officer displayed sensitivity, not revealing his men's last search would be for charred bodies. His cautious response gave her a spark of confidence Lenora remained alive.

She had an hour of sailing time and planned to find a quiet seat, and prop up her aching legs—her next rest uncertain. Birdie had a name, Bill Wrigley, given to her by a cab driver she didn't trust one hundred percent. If Cleon were part of what went on, he deserved an Oscar.

The mid-week ferry carried dozens of passengers and crew, filling less than a quarter of the seating space. Birdie located a padded bench near the main deck and closed her eyes, attempting to nap despite a white-uniformed crew member shouting safety instructions. She didn't reach a deep sleep amid roaring engines and chattering children, but rested, wedging an orange life vest under her head and neck.

To her surprise, her forehead gash, courtesy of the timely earthquake, remained stable. The slight amount of bleeding stopped almost at once. Her head appeared mended. Earlier in the MG's rearview mirror, the wound seemed worse. Until she saw herself in the ferryboat's window, she realized she'd suffered a less severe injury and blamed her dazed state of mind for misplaced distress. She feared more scars to her patched body, adding years to her fading appearance. Birdie ran a hand across her tender forehead, trusting she wasn't yet a circus sideshow attraction.

Vanity and a tendency to become involved in cases played more of a role in her life than she'd believed. Doubts crept into her mind. Was being a PI that important?

How long had it been since she'd faced Gustain's gun barrel pointed inches from her face? Birdie clutched the ring hanging at her chest. She'd escaped, dodged instant death, given another chance, not by Elger's mystical ring, but by an unpredictable force of nature—nothing else.

Celtic, old-country lore belonged tucked away in her youth with Santa and the Easter Bunny. Should she consider accepting the outlandish notion, she'd commit herself to New York's Bellevue looney ward. She appreciated Elger Stepp's intentions, despite his misguided affiliation with Shelley and Falk.

The impressive silver ring had unique charm and beauty. Its history, according to Elger, was unquestionable. Unfortunately, it reminded her of the grizzly scene in the tomb-like Brea lab. Melting it offered a rich set of earrings. The idea was discarded. She preferred nothing to remind her of the California fiasco. If she survived, Birdie promised she'd show up at her shrink's office.

Ducking through the narrow cabin's door, she stood alone at the stern, watching twin propellers churn the Pacific waters frothy. In the background, San Pedro and Long Beach faded in the morning mist. Birdie looked forward to leaving the mainland. A change of scenery might break her run of terrible luck.

Removing the ring and chain from her neck, she held last night's brief, tender moment in her mind. Elger had slid the bulky ring from his forefinger, and inserted it on the chain, believing he provided her divine protection passed down by generations of Celtics. His sincerity and concern unexpectedly touched her heart.

Not what she imagined, but it had been the closest she'd come to getting a ring from a man. Somewhere in Manhattan, Hollis wore Owen Roe's ring—one that should have been hers.

Birdie looked over the stern to the boat's beating spray. The simplest and quickest way to remove the irrational myth Elger Stepp placed in her head sat in front of her. Letting it slip into the cold Pacific removed the tale of mystical power and her foolish thoughts of Elger.

She squeezed the ring in her hand, reaching toward the water. Muscles in her forearms and hands stiffened. Fingers drew in, driving broken and chipped fingernails into her skin, trapping the ring inside the clenched fist. The next second, the ferry swerved, tossing Birdie sideways, landing her on a wraparound, cushioned seat. In the blue stretch of waters, a lone kayaker drifted. Fatigue took its toll on her reasoning, leaving her unprepared for the shock.

Glaring, shimmering light of the Pacific deceived her weary eyes beyond her imagination's acceptance. Elger Stepp stood atop a long kayak, shaking his shepherd's crook, shouting words that should have been drowned out by the ferry boats powerful twin engines. Instead, Birded understood as if he spoke them in private.

"The ring will guide and protect you."

In seconds, the image disappeared. She looked again into the glittering water.

Where he'd appeared, a group of pelicans floated.

"I need rest. I can't trust my eyes. Someone murdered Elger," she mumbled to no one.

"Pelicans make a pod. Crows are a murder."

Embarrassed, Birdie turned away from the crew member to avoid further attention. She returned to her seat, staring at her shut hand, as the ferry slowed approaching Santa Catalina's resort town of Avalon.

Her fingers relaxed, letting the bulky ring drag long loops of chain from her palm, allowing it to serpentine and slither into her lap as if it lived. The urge to dispose of it no longer existed. It dropped into her purse's velvet pocket alongside the damaged pistol.

CHAPTER FIFTY

Birdie pulled the note from her purse, reading the name. Her last clue to uncover Shelley rested in the hands of a Santa Catalina dive shop owner, Bill Wrigley. Thoughts of parochial school and prayer to Saint Jude, patron of desperate situations, passed as quickly as they arrived. Her future was in her control, not a first-century martyr or mystical Celtic ring.

The visit left her in awe of Catalina's unspoiled natural beauty. The small island near Los Angeles offered an excellent refuge. She, too, ran from a trail of dead bodies, needing to avoid the police.

Ornate and colorfully painted wood homes mixed with cozy storefronts scattered the hillside overlooking the crescent bay. Lacking traffic lights, golf carts, and motor scooters easily moved along narrow, uncluttered streets.

It took a few wobbly steps down the ferry's ramp for Birdie's bloodshot eyes to catch sight of a quaint dress shop. Her clothes, wrinkled and scuffed with blood and chemicals, would do for the moment. Hair, nails, and face a total loss required hours of Broadway makeup magic. After a glance in a store window, the gash on her head appeared healed, to her surprise.

She wanted Bill Wrigley. More accurately, his cooperation to examine his shop's sales records and dive logs with the hope they gave Shelley's full name and island address. Bursting into Wrigley's shop as an outsider, with no legal right, risked him becoming defensive. She first needed to calm herself and take a moment.

The bizarre case pushed her to move fast and recklessly since hired by Lenora. Hurry, don't rush, Birdie repeated. She wanted time to gain her bearings and professional poise if she hoped to convince Wrigley to cooperate. Haste forced errors, and she promised not to make the situation worse. She'd seen enough killing to keep her in therapy for years.

Birdie placed even odds Shelley and Falk traveled to Santa Catalina. She reminded herself she gambled with her client's money and her own life, recalling threats Shelley made at the Rio Jazz Club.

Experience showed fugitives fled to familiar areas. The island offered restricted space to hide, with limited escape routes. Shelley would not pin herself into a corner without options. As far as Birdie could figure, boats and a small airport dominated travel choices. 'She couldn't stake out both.

After taking a room at a bed-and-breakfast, aromas of freshly ground coffee enticed her. Seduced, she continued looking Avalon over, getting comfortable, and hoping to spot the offending coffee shop.

Did she believe she'd see Shelley casually strolling through town?

Slight and occasional steep grades of Avalon left her exhausted and her hip throbbing. A peek into the dress shop found earlier would wait. Birdie spotted her craving, something more suitable, a few storefronts from her bed-and-breakfast.

The Book Café displayed a barrel-sized coffee cup hung over a mullioned window featuring stacks of new and older books. Not up to par with New York's Caffe Reggio, but any port in a storm.

After arranging a mug of coffee and buttered toast on a small doily-covered table, she took a seat offering a bay view. The sparkling water allowed a daydream to wander into her weary mind. She could only imagine what life would be like on the idyllic island.

She'd own a boutique dress and jewelry shop appealing to tourists and locals. And without question, star in community theater while keeping a hand in the local PTA. There would be time for scuba lessons with Bill Wrigley, making her a genuine island native.

What drew Shelley and Falk to the tranquil location? This was no vacation get-a-way for the odd pair. On the small island, visitors would not go unnoticed, unlike Los Angeles. Shelley lured her to the jazz club, trapping and threatening her. Could she have again? Birdie took a sip of coffee and stopped the passing gum-chewing server.

"Can I ask about Catalina?"

"Ask. No secrets here, honey."

"Is there more to Avalon? Less public?"

"You want privacy? Visit Two Harbors; they'll give you all the space you need."

"That's on Catalina?"

"Up the coast. Real secluded."

Birdie let the name Two Harbors sink in, adding it to her list to search, and continued, recognizing she'd stumbled onto the island's busy body.

"Know Bill Wrigley's dive shop?"

The server, Birdie guessed the owner, pointed a red fingernail to a long row of palm trees several hundred yards to the north and east.

"Behind the palms across from the docks, that's his place."

"What's he like?"

"Quiet. Keeps himself to himself, and he's related to this." The waitress removed the gum from her mouth, held it out to Birdie, and placed it in an empty ashtray.

Puzzled by the gesture, Birdie looked at the well-chewed gum. "That means what?"

"Like the Chicago chewing gum family."

"He has money and owns most of this island," the waitress said.

Suckers and desperate PIs played long shots. Knowing Shelley and Falk kept a house on the island, and the dive shop existed, brought Birdie hope her slim odds improved. Unless she convinced Wrigley to help, her convoluted case was no better off than the day Lenora barged through her apartment door.

Birdie persuaded herself to stay optimistic Lenora, and Jaminson remained alive, possibly as human shields. A call to the Beverly Hilton, from the shop's payphone, had not located her client. Lenora continued absent, with no word since her dinner napkin note stating Shelley had taken her.

Could Birdie struggle past the sad memory of Elger Stepp? His senseless death gnawed at her. Had remorse sparked her to imagine his aura floating in the Pacific?

The encounter with Gustain inside the lab confused and stunned her. Well-dressed and confident, the tall man possessed no emotion, a killer taking orders, pulling the trigger for money, not personal passion. She had stared down his gun barrel, prepared to face her maker. The unexpected occurred. At the moment he was about to take her life, he offered her a chance to turn away and pray.

She'd wager her best pair of shoes and purse Washington, DC steered this affair. America changed following the war. Long shadows of the Cold War crept across Europe onto American soil, igniting Russian and Nazi fears. Government agencies could covertly be at work. From what she'd seen the past few days, Shelley and Falk played a part.

Birdie had no real clue of Jaminson's involvement beyond his disappearance or the reason. As an ex-showgirl and former Pinkerton who shielded Broadway starlets from the press, she lacked experience in hush-hush foreign affairs. Spying on cheating spouses seldom placed your life at risk. The best she could do—counterpunch—so far swinging at air and shadows, not understanding why or who wanted her dead.

She'd leaped into the rabbit hole the moment they boarded Lenora's copter and continued to tumble deeper into darkness, tangled in the middle of Hamilton Jaminson's abduction and happenings inside Falk's lab. Her assignment had not been to uncover the bizarre events of the past few days—only to find a missing person. No matter how she dissected the chaos, she faced separate adversaries with no way to step away from the target plastered on her forehead. Deep within her, a suppressed thought grew—how long would Irish luck hold?

Reporting suspicions and what she'd seen to the Los Angeles Police would label her irrational, and her wealthy client eccentric. There was nothing substantial, only wild tales of twin giants and an aggressive, jealous parrot—no photographs, letters, or anyone alive to give credence to the bizarre lab in Brea. The unique silver ring in her purse is all she had. What conclusion would law enforcement draw?

Shelley and Falk fleeing to Catalina was a first step intended to lead to an ultimate destination. Their morbid work required a supply of humans near death, test equipment, and privacy. The island fits none of the criteria, judging by what she'd seen.

Travel by foot, scooter, or golf cart was the sole mode of transportation. A fifteen-minute walk brought Birdie to a row of tall swaying palms casting long shadows over the dive shop. A metal sign swung over a weathered brick and cinder block building near a vacant dock guarded by a posting:

Private. Reserved for Pay Day.

Beside it, another advised.

Park here to meet Smith & Wesson.

The printed notices signed, Wrigley Dive Shop. As a Manhattan native, she appreciated the value of curbside parking and skirmishes. The idyllic community of Avalon had related problems.

Birdie knew her as Shelley, nothing more, complicating finding the South American beauty. If Shelley dove often, Birdie crossed her fingers, Wrigley, with little prompting, would recall the stunning young woman. Birdie had carried a second plan, cupping a hundred-dollar bill in her palm, prepared to buy information. Worst case, she'd raise the ante until allowed to dig through sales recipes and dive logs.

Wet suits hung next to aluminum air tanks on heavy pipe racks fronting the store's casement windows. The polished wood door resembled historic eighteenth-century clipper ships. Brass hardware highlighted a copper porthole centered on the front door.

Birdie stopped before gripping the black metal handle. A message, scribbled in longhand, hung to the side, tacked to the door's frame.

Closed. Gone diving. Back in a few.

No date or expected arrival.

Birdie felt the thud in her stomach, her longshot had hit a roadblock. The taunting note dared her to break in. For good measure, she shook the handle, rattling the door hinges and lock. Nothing changed. The slight temper outburst waned. She retreated before nearby shops noticed the disturbance.

Climbing steep hills, marching door to door, like a Fuller Brush man, would bring unwanted attention, attracting local police. There was no choice except to wait. Near the docks, she claimed a bench unused by seagulls. The delay forced her to consider—with no authority, what did she plan to do with Shelley and Falk? She had no power to stop the two. She wavered, questioning her stamina to continue a misdirected crusade to avenge what? The atrocity in Brea was not her business. How often did she remind herself Lenora paid her to retrieve her former husband? Another voice questioned. Who was behind Gustain's hunting her?

Shelley and Falk were on the run, not from a struggling private investigator, but someone powerful. She and Lenora were nothing more than a nuisance, an irritant to brush off. Letting Shelley and Falk escape looked to be a quick solution. She'd bluff, boasting backup forces, demanding the return of her client and Jaminson. To catch one, she may have to let go of the other. Falk and Shelley were not her concerns.

In a small way, she took credit for destroying Falk's sinister plans and the blame for Elger Stepp's slaying. Down deep, she wanted to stop Shelley.

The trip to California brought her close to the hated Nazis. Hitler was dead in a cave, yet the war felt as if it continued. Americans resumed building bomb shelters after celebrating victory on the front pages of newspapers and confetti-covered streets. Yet Shelley and Falk worked in America to keep Nazi dreams alive. Birdie attempted to shake off the beaten attitude creeping into her. Fatigue tried to conquer her mind and body, making a coward of her.

A few nights on Catalina, at her client's expense, would refresh her and boost her morale. Where else did she have to go? Eventually, the unconventional, free spirit, Wrigley, had to return. Birdie formed a second backup plan, just in case. She prepared a list of tools for a break-in.

Walking along wood-planked and concrete docks, passing large and small boats moored inside numbered slips lining Avalon's curving shore, Birdie admired the island's mountainous surroundings. Under pleasant circumstances, she'd stroll barefoot in the soft, warm sand. New York City in January offered a steady diet of sleet, snow, and bitter cold. This may be as close to utopia as she deserved.

In the distance, near the southern edge of a rocky cliff, jutting into the Catalina channel, she saw something she believed an illusion. The object appeared as a smudge against the blue sky, not breaking speed records, but moving.

The intruder's rusted hull poked around the rocky ledge. Curious, Birdie watched the ship approach. Its sharp bow churned foamy white water, plowing through the tropical Pacific. The vessel sailed beyond rows of yachts and boats moored inside the crescent harbor. Far from a lavish ocean cruise liner, it was more of a drifting shipwreck alien to the tranquil seascape of Catalina. The beach and docks were vacant with her the sole witness. Would she watch a rush of landing boats spilling from the ship's belly, attacking the small island? A week ago, the thought would have been dismissed as a childish fantasy. Today, Birdie expected unconventional.

The arrival may be routine, and commonplace to island inhabitants. What experience did she have to make judgments? Ocean cruises arrived and departed New York Harbor daily. Birdie turned, forcing herself to walk away, planning a lazy hot bath before revisiting the dive shop.

As she did, she spotted an answer to her curiosity.

Bolted to a narrow platform waited a pair of silver coin-operated binoculars, the same she'd used atop the Empire State Building. She climbed the short stairs to the observation deck, gaining a better view of the ship. After digging nickels from her purse, she dropped one into the slot.

Adjusting the bulky viewer, Birdie found the freighter—the flag flown was unknown.

Three horizontal bands, light blue and white, surrounded a yellow sun centered on the single white band. Panning to the bow, Birdie made out the name. Block lettering against rust-streaked riveted steel plates read *Black Swan*.

The vessel remained at a distance and appeared it intended to sail past, perhaps to San Francisco or Alaska. Her time elapsed, and the binoculars clanked shut, demanding payment. Intrigued, she slid in a second nickel. The freighter's wake lessened and slowed.

Birdie reached into her purse, grasping her banished Celtic ring.

The chill came from a north breeze, far from matching New York's arctic blasts, yet penetrated the marrow of her bones, setting off a hunch. She'd made the correct decision, abandoning Lenora. The derelict's anchor dropped.

CHAPTER FIFTY-ONE

Building dark clouds in the north continued to creep toward Catalina. At their edge, a pastel moon rose awaiting sunset.

The approaching storm didn't detract Birdie. She dumped her change purse, emptying it on the concrete platform, collecting nickels to keep the binoculars alive, and aimed at the ship. She had no explanation for her reaction to the anchored freighter. If the island natives noticed the strange boat, they neglected to react.

More viewing time added no new information on the *Black Swan*. The viewer's shutter clanked shut. Out of nickels, Birdie's Irish stubbornness kicked in. She'd stay put, watching the ship float silent, alone in deep water, and miles offshore.

The mysterious craft arrived and dropped anchor. She could do nothing about the out-of-place arrival. Birdie kept watch, guessing boats that size don't stop without reason.

No harbor patrol approached, and local police appeared not interested. All was well and on the up and up, she supposed. Bus and subway schedules fit her city-dweller lifestyle, not the comings and goings of ocean-going ships.

After hours of no activity, Birdie ended the long, violent day. Starved and drained of energy, doubt crept in. Could the spree to Catalina be a colossal gamble—a hunch based on words of the assumed father of a former house painter turned self-proclaimed religious leader? The clever ploy had gotten her out of the way.

For what reason?

Could another assassin track her?

Instead of climbing the short ramp and stairs, retreating to the quaint B&B, Birdie spotted the old-fashioned, English-style phone booth. The call to her client's hotel suite went unanswered after a dozen rings. She declined to leave a message, not sure who she'd trust.

Lenora carried her cash in her purse alongside a useless pistol. The money provided confidence she'd buy answers if they existed on the small island.

Despite skepticism of spiritual power and mystical force, Birdie acknowledged remarkable occurrences after accepting the ring from Elger Stepp. Her life had been spared inside the Brea lab. Had the young cult leader used mild hypnosis, trapping her in his fantasies, drawing her into blind obedience? She resisted the foolish idea, yet circumstances beyond human control argued against her.

Could Gustain's death be imagined?

The ancient tale of the powerful spirals had been repeated often as daily catechism lessons. Until experiencing Elger, the old Celtic legend had been pushed away and lost. There was no room for storybook fables in New York and making it on the big stage. Birdie admitted being blinded in her quest for a star on her dressing door. Celebrity became the elusive gold at the end of her Fifth Avenue rainbow.

Yet, here she sat alone, a failed actress turned PI, staking out a ship that could merely haul the island's trash. Was she delusional, imagining a group of pelicans in the Pacific Ocean as the resurrected Elger Stepp?

She chased something, not knowing what.

Like the youthful Alice in her upside-down Wonderland, the Cheshire cat transformed into a curious, broad smile. The wicked Queen of Hearts and her court to a pack of cards. Was she, too, lost in madness? What did Birdie expect the shadowy freighter to become?

She welcomed the thought of awakening on a warm sandy beach floating in gentle ocean waves, escaping the dream's strangeness.

Chilling raindrops bounced off the pavement, and she settled in, determined to keep watch on the *Black Swan*.

Yielding to Celtic superstition and nothing else, Birdie placed the large ring and chain around her neck. The words of her grandmother rang with the clarity of someone beside her.

"The three spirals: life, death and rebirth, give strength to move forward and overcome adversity."

Could she discover the ancient symbol's promise?

Her mission to find Lenora and Hamilton Jaminson came first. Shelley existed only as a stepping stone. What occurred in Brea and the capture of Jaminson was no doubt connected. Falk and Shelley's intentions were not her concern. Why had she obsessed with them?

For the moment, she needed food and rest. A melting Hershey bar, found in her purse, did its best to satisfy. Her attention focused on the mysterious ship anchored in the distance. No explanation for its presence came to mind. Several passenger ferries arrived and departed while walkers and their pets passed, showing no interest in the moored ship. Soon, she'd abandon the watch, favoring a medium rare steak and a snug warm bed.

First thing in the morning, she'd show up at Wrigley's and uncover Shelley's address, if the irresponsible owner Wrigley showed up. Her mood needed improving, and that meant a good night's sleep, followed by plenty of coffee and a hot breakfast of waffles. Birdie took a last glance at the dark ship hulking in the distant waters. Few crew members roamed the open decks. She persisted in asking why it had arrived.

A passing look over her shoulder showed a flicker of light reaching from the sullen ship, appearing as a small searchlight across the grayish sky. It continued for a few minutes and stopped quickly as it began. Birdie, not expecting anything, glanced toward homes surrounding the bay. To her surprise, a matching flash flicked high on the hillside. It could be a flashlight, a struck match, or a window lamp turned on and off.

Possibly a response to the sullen, waiting ship.

CHAPTER FIFTY-TWO

The derelict ship floated off the Santa Catalina coast. No boats arrived, nor departed the nesting *Black Swan*. An approaching thunderstorm's dark clouds had stalled to the north, flexing their power, releasing muted flashes within its core.

Birdie's stubbornness and curiosity forced her to stay at the elevated observation platform. Breaking the monotony, she placed another call to the Beverly Hilton. No answer came. Disturbed, she took a chance, promising a generous tip, and persuaded the desk clerk to send security to Lenora's suite.

The image of the frumpy hotel cop making himself at home at the suite's well-stocked bar ran through her tired mind. After what felt like an eternity, the counterman confirmed her fears. Birdie conceded she didn't expect her determined client to sit in her room. Disappointed, she left a message and would call back.

The ship's signal flashed a second time. As before, a weak light in the hillside responded. Birdie guessed Morse code, and it might as well have been ancient Greek.

She lacked clear-cut facts to base her notions on. As a PI, she seldom had precise information. What she often had were snapshots pieced together, a grainy view from a high elevation. Her interpretation solved cases and sometimes caused the loss of lives. PIs who prospered made correct calls. To join their ranks, decisions in critical situations needed to be firm and accurate. Plans and tactics often went sideways. It was up to her to adjust on the fly. Birdie recalled Dwight Eisenhower's observation. "No plan survives first contact with the enemy."

Instinct persuaded her the ship connected to Shelley. She'd wager its unknown flag belonged in South America and Shelley's ticket to escape. What Birdie had was her belief. Nothing more.

Birdie snapped her fingers.

The nearby coffee and bookshop brought an idea. Their lights remained on, and from there, she could watch the suspicious ship.

The store's disappointing assortment f books lacked an encyclopedia or World Atlas. Crime fiction and heavy romance filled shelves surrounding busy dining tables.

Before giving up, she noticed, stuck in a tiny corner, a rotating metal rack offering travel guides and maps. She located what she had been looking for. Near the base, a glossy plastic bag enclosed a bright, colorful book. Pulling it from the stack, she discovered the title, *Children's Flag Adventure*. Birdie tore open the seal, placing the thin paperback on a glass case, thinking what decent parent forced this on a child.

Flipping pages, not bothering with the index, a map of South America appeared. The opposite page displayed a bright radiating sun, centered on the Argentine flag.

Her hunch paid off, bolstering her confidence. The two bolted for South America and immunity to finish their inhumane work. If Lenora and Jaminson accompanied them, it was certain Falk had drugged them, as he had Fabian and Pello.

The ship and destination made sense. Newsreels reported Juan Peron's Argentina harbored German war criminals. Birdie recalled Lenora told of a Buenos Aires visit accompanying Hamilton. During the stay, Hamilton met with former Nazi officers and Shelley, the jazz club's featured act. Birdie saw a ray of sunshine on her case that appeared about to close on opening night.

She left The Book Café unsure of a plan, admitting the evidence flimsy for the police, but it stacked up against her notion, Shelley and Falk took temporary cover on the island to escape.

The hillside answering light beam had to have come from Shelley. In the darkness, she'd been unable to pinpoint a location. A home or one of many hotels could have sent it. Something was about to happen. She'd march back to the boat docks, hunker down in the wet sand, behind drying nets and wait. Birdie needed very little—two cups of hot coffee, and a table cover removed from below the service bar would do.

A hundred-dollar bill replaced the tablecloth.

Fleets of commercial fishing boats docked near the ferry's slip, close to Birdie's original arrival. Heavy nylon nets hung over wooden poles allowed a view of the ship and hillside homes. Satisfied with the privacy, she hoped to avoid police enforcing no beach use after sundown.

Birdie wrapped herself tight in the tablecloth, protecting herself against the cold Pacific wind. In minutes, she realized the cotton sheet failed miserably against the night's chill. Stakeouts and stale coffee were the dread of PI's and cops. Sitting on subjects came with her job, as did kidney infections.

A trio of rapid flashes appeared on the hillside, followed by a series of short and long bursts. The ship countered, returning a sequence of light flickers. The quick exchange, Birdie guessed, contained instructions for Shelley and Falk. Could she hold out positioned between the two? Shelley and Falk were due to make a move.

Had the convenience come at the cost of being ensnared in the Mad Hatter's time-stopping tea party? Was she doomed to endure an uncaring, bitter chill, seemingly suspended in time? Somewhere, had she had a falling out with time, losing its perspective? Her riddle's solution lay in the message she'd failed to solve. Had she misjudged the ship's intent? If sleep came, she knew, unlike Alice's peaceful awakening, she'd become a victim of the island's misplaced time, dragged to sea by a vengeful, unsympathetic, chilly tide.

No added signals appeared from the hills or distant ship. The thin tablecloth wrapping her shoulders and chest did little to cut the night chill of a north breeze off the cold Pacific. A warm fire was the answer. She mulled retreating to the comfort of the coffee shop when she recalled the Beverly Hilton's bar matches. With plenty of driftwood surrounding the beach, she considered risking it, using the tablecloth as kindling.

Pinkerton training came to mind. Her instructor often reminded fatigue created cowards and affected judgment. Any size fire gave her position to local police and her suspects. She didn't seek a welcoming committee from either.

Shaking off bumps and bruises went with the job. Impatience or discomfort could not force her from the watch. She hoped ships like trains and airplanes disliked delays, sitting idle cost the ship owners' money. Too cold and hungry to sleep, Birdie forced herself to move and walk between the long lines of hanging nets.

Faint moonlight exposed swift, frothy white swells pushing toward her, climbing the coarse, sandy, narrow beach. Near shore, ship bells played an off-beat chorus.

The freighter remained at anchor. Nothing changed since she'd begun the watch. Could Shelley or the ship's lookouts know she watched? Birdie gave herself an F for surveillance skills and failing to disguise herself. Someone might have spotted her the moment she walked off the ferry. Her time on the Broadway stage and former makeup artist, Jerome Merrick, taught cosmetic tricks, enough that she'd be less visible to Shelley.

If tailed, she'd made it easy, becoming lax.

Recalling her last meal, besides toast and coffee, escaped her. Lacking food left her sluggish. Hunger mixed with the cold could defeat her. Once home, she'd visit the garment district and Keens Steakhouse—sit at the small bar devouring a King's cut prime rib, taking pleasure in gaining a dress size. She'd never leave Manhattan. California taught her the sprawling state held too many surprises.

A bright flash grabbed Birdie's attention. A steady light stream moved, bouncing across the faraway hillside. Soon, a second followed, possibly a motor scooter or casual walker needing an after-dinner stroll. The break in the monotony over the past few hours brought excitement. Avalon, from where Birdie hid, appeared to have rolled up its few sidewalks.

The two lights continued, vanishing and reappearing between homes, traveling across and then down the hillside. Birdie guessed the pair moved too fast for walkers, deciding on golf carts or scooters. Whatever they were, it was a sign of life, and she'd watch, expecting the travelers to connect with the waiting vessel.

Thanks to the half-moon lighting the bay, she'd spot any craft leaving the steamer.

Birdie glanced away for a moment. Her hope died. The traveling lights vanished as fast as they appeared. She dismissed it as a false alarm, going back to her failing efforts to keep warm and avoid food thoughts.

Twin beams reappeared, popping from an alley in the compact business district, and moved under faint street lighting leading to the docks. Birdie stepped behind the nets, watching two golf carts slow and bump from a curb, crossing the single lane. Each bore cargo boxes knotted to the passenger seat and rear platform. They approached the ramp to gated slips. The lead cart stopped under a lamppost.

Birdie didn't need a second look, but took a long, hard one. Patience, aided by Irish luck, had paid off. She uncovered Shelley but feared a showdown, recalling the Rio Jazz Club encounter. The moment came near. Alice was about to come face to face with her mad Queen of Hearts.

Did she expect the mismatched pair to arrive in German military uniforms complete with swastikas? The two appeared as ordinary tourists, not someone conspiring with Nazis and experimenting on human bodies.

Shelley unlocked a tall wrought-iron gate and waved Falk inside. Under the dock's long row of lights, she caught a view of Falk and a twinkle of his silver tooth.

Each rolled past rows of moored catamarans and small yachts. Reaching the end of the brightly lit dock, they stopped behind a cabin cruiser.

They formed a chain of two and began off-loading boxes, placing wrapped cartons on the boat's main deck.

Birdie weighed possibilities. There was no certainty of Lenora's and Jamison's location—unguarded inside the speed boat or the hillside home. Birdie traded the release of her client and Jaminson, allowing the two to sail away on the waiting freighter, deliberately freeing criminals dangerous to America and the world.

Lacking leverage and a working handgun, Birdie dreaded split-second decisions. Could she match Shelley's experience and street smarts? The likelihood existed. If forced, could she save only one?

The other consideration gambled with her client's life—allowing the speed boat to leave, betting Lenora and Jaminson not on board.

Unwilling to concede, Birdie shed the tablecloth and moved closer, hiding behind the Catalina Express ticket booth. On her knees, she watched the two unloading cartons. Not admitting to the superstition of her homeland's ancient lore, she pulled the Gallic ring and chain from her neck, wrapping it around her chilled fingers, not praying, nor worshiping, but meditating.

In a moment, she heard Shelley.

"One more trip."

Birdie caught a break as Shelley and Falk drove away, allowing time to inspect the boat's cabin.

The dock's gate slammed and rebounded, banging hard against the deadbolt lock to stay open. She escaped climbing the fence, avoiding the risks of a fall and injury. Fresh in her mind, the near-drowning and dodging death reinforced her fear of water. Relieved, she walked in, playing the role of a haughty yacht club member. She regretted not buying the sundress seen on her arrival.

Locating the boat, Birdie studied the docks and beach before stepping over the gunwale. She stopped, knowing she sacrificed precious time, staring at the distant hills, hoping to discover Shelley's destination. Patience rewarded her. She spotted the familiar lights traveling among hillside residences.

Shelley and Falk traveled at a steady rate, vanishing in and out, passing behind homes placed like contemporary cave dwellers along the steep slope. Birdie's eyes became navigation tools, approximating the two's location. Watching the moving lights, she waited until they stopped and gauged landmarks. A spotlight lit an American flag, and tacky out-of-season Christmas decorations gave an estimated elevation. Not dead reckoning, but enough. Barging into the wrong home became a worry.

Her first hope to find Lenora and Jaminson rested in the boat. Heavy canvas wrapped the stacked crates on board, which were secured in waterproof bags. All of it, she guessed, was vital to Falk's work. Birdie checked her watch, realizing she'd become distracted. Time ran short. A consideration struck. She'd overlooked the prospect of a third person watching.

Stepping through the tight galley and cramped sleeping quarters, she found no sign of Lenora or Jaminson. Four bunks looked fresh and not slept in. Everything appeared in order, clean and neat. She supposed the boat rented, intended to be abandoned after reaching the waiting freighter.

The second trip may carry Lenora and Jaminson, or she guessed, allowed Falk to inject a dose of poison into their hostages. Could she reach the distant house in time for a rescue?

Returning to the boat's helm, Birdie spotted the matching lights moving and confirmed her hillside locations, checking each marker, measuring with her fingers: A lighted American flag, and red and white Christmas lights. The landmarks would get her close. If Lenora and Jaminson were not with Shelley, the house in the hills became her next target. Would she find Lenora and Jaminson dead?

Climbing to the dock, Birdie caught glimpses of a new unexpected flash far out into the channel beyond the bay. A clang of a ship's bell carried from the waters between Bill Wrigley's dive shop and the freighter.

CHAPTER FIFTY-THREE

Aiming the golf cart's spotlight, dodging the cocktail club's crowded street parking, Shelley slowed and waited for Falk. Vespas and bicycles jutted in and out along the narrow brick road.

She didn't want an accident.

From the vantage point, she viewed the bay and distant freighter. Farther north, she hoped the storm veered from the island.

Forty minutes remained before the *Black Swan* raised anchor for Buenos Aires. She rechecked the Morse code message, confident the captain would stick to his word. Her plans stayed on schedule, and Falk's documents were in hand, soon to join her package of M-3 explosives.

Escaping the cluttered tavern traffic, Shelley reached beside her, tapping Jaminson's wrapped satchels. His cash belonged to her, representing a new life far away from Nazis and Argentina's dictator, Juan Peron. From the nightclub's wide-open doors and windows came Doris Day's, *Que, Sere, Sere, Whatever Will Be Will Be* and, for the moment, echoed her outlook since the decision.

She regretted allowing the rented boat to go unguarded, trusting Catalina's claims of a crime-free island. The small yacht carried much more than Falk's horrific research gained at the expense of brutalized Polish and Jewish captives—it represented her new freedom.

Fresh starts in her world came with high-stake risks and odds-addicted gamblers avoided. Her homeland, she'd regretted, welcomed Nazi war criminals—for a price. Today, she planned to invite herself to her home, courtesy of Hamilton Jaminson's unintended gift—a small piece of the wealth he'd amassed on the backs of desperate immigrants.

Somewhere in Los Angeles's remote hills and canyons, Lenora and Hamilton Jaminson became victims to the car bombs she'd planted. Her other obstacle, Birdie, had become a non-factor with the death of her clients.

Thirty minutes remained. She would make sure her farewell package stayed hidden among Falk's papers, as planned.

Shelley eased the golf cart to the curb, keeping an eye on the front tire, watching it drop to the wood dock. Next to her, the carefully wrapped putty-like M3 explosives stayed secure.

Safe on the pavement, Shelley stared back to check on Falk, waving him toward the dock. To her surprise, the metal entrance stood open. Not how she recalled leaving it. Racing against time, she couldn't afford slip-ups. Overlooking closing the gate risked her mission's months of preparation—exposing her escape cruiser. With no choice, she assured herself again of Catalina's security and lack of crime, according to Chamber of Commerce travel brochures.

Falk arrived, steering past her and through the wide-open gate, signaling her to follow. At the boat, Shelley stepped away, not assisting Falk. Instead, she inspected the boat, forcing him to complete the transfer of sealed, waterproof files. The calculated maneuver pushed Falk to do heavy moving and lifting, freeing Shelley to arrange the cargo and explosive near the twin inboard motors. As hoped, the doctor wore down and admitted exhaustion, excusing himself to the galley.

Minutes later, Shelley checked her watch and looked in on Falk, finding him asleep. His age deceived most. Not her. From years of experience, she knew the cagy German doctor would detect anything suspicious. His mind and body remained nimble and alert.

Two bright flashes arrived from the immediate north, on the dot from where she expected. The time came to ease the boat and its cargo from the slip. Shelley expected another signal a few hundred yards from the waiting freighter.

Motors cranked over, one at a time, alarming a flock of nesting seagulls. Twin inboard Evinrudes ran smoothly as she pulled back the duel controls, revving the powerful engines, hoping to relieve anxieties.

Shelley needed a last check and climbed below, finding Falk continued sound asleep, propped against a cabinet door. He gripped a handgun.

Locating a blanket inside a storage chest, she wrapped her colleague and slid a soft cushion behind his head. He'd softened over the years, becoming less harsh, yet he kept his dominant German presence, willing to kill those hampering his cruel, inhuman experiments. She dismissed an urge to kiss his balding skull, knowing they soon separated forever.

Free of mooring lines, at low throttle, Shelley eased from the slip and headed away from the quiet harbor. Not open sea, yet she felt liberated from Nazis and the daunting presence of the American CIA. Her conspiracy, misusing CIA funds under the guise of developing a fail-safe truth drug, ended tonight.

She turned her head to shore, glancing at long lines of drying fishnets, sensing a stalker. Shelley wrote it off, as she had so many times, blaming overcharged nerves. Looking over her shoulder—a way of life she'd become resigned to. She doomed herself with the CIA's vengeful leader, Dulles and South American Nazis demanding the Hitler infant she'd birth.

Dulles's displeasure led to silent assassinations, especially of those he'd recruited before Germany's surrender. She carried in her womb a product of Falk's research and Hitler's DNA. Shelley tapped her stomach. She'd allow the seed to grow and nurture, becoming her child, withholding it from loyal German soldiers in Argentina who intended to resurrect Nazi dominance.

The boat trimmed out and rode smoothly, nearing the *Black Swan*. Few lights lit the waiting ship. Shelley watched to the northeast, expecting a signal. She considered it a potential trap. Could an army of CIA agents wait on board the freighter?

Distractions compromised the scheme. Her mind required focus. Events would occur in rapid order, putting her life at risk.

Two lights flashed from the dark water.

The moment had arrived to grow strong and carry out the rehearsed plan.

Shelley slowed and swung the boat parallel to the large waiting ship, slipped the twin motors to neutral and put out the running lights, drifting in the current away from the freighter. She continued, shielded in darkness several hundred yards distant.

A glance at her Rolex dive watch showed two minutes to zero hour. She stepped from her dress, left the bridge, grabbed the watertight satchel of cash from the stern, and sat, balancing on the gunwale facing choppy black seawater, inhaling and exhaling, clenching the package at her chest.

Cold air became uncomfortable. She feared what came next.

Shelley held tight to the container and slid from the rail into the chilly Pacific. The weighted case dragged her straight down, becoming invisible in the dark water until she spotted the light below her feet. She'd practiced remaining calm, holding her breath while suspended in shocking, frigid, deep ocean water. Under the pressure of the moment, she stressed, bringing worries of her reflexes gulping for air. How long could she endure surrounded by cold blackness? She'd gone two minutes in the past. Could she trust her lungs?

The light flashed once more. Shelley relaxed and released the satchel, letting it fall away, freeing her from the rapid descent.

Through the dark water, she spotted the wet-suited diver grab the free-falling bag and then her while placing a scuba mouthpiece near her face. Life-giving air touched her starved lungs at the right moment.

Swimming below the surface, she heard the muffled explosion. Seconds later, shock waves jolted them.

CHAPTER FIFTY-FOUR

Birdie stepped from behind rows of fishing nets moments before the blast lit the sky, shredding Shelley's boat as if it were a child's wooden toy sailing a Central Park pond. In seconds, reverberations carried to shore, thundering through the harbor's natural bowl, leaving a smell of motor oil.

Spotlights from the waiting freighter flashed in unison, bringing life to the dormant ship, each focused on the demolished power boat. Birdie made out shadows of Shelley's burned-out boat. Remains of its smoldering skeleton listed, struggling to stay afloat. Flecks of splintered mahogany and shredded paper encircled the dying craft and floated airborne as fiery confetti.

Lifeboats, suspended over the Argentine freighter's deck, remained in place.

Avalon's emergency sirens sounded. A fireboat, flashing red and blue lights, sped from behind the Opera House.

The blast had consumed the wood hull and cabin, dooming the vessel to a grave on the ocean floor. Birdie saw no chance of the two passengers and cargo surviving the inferno. During a weak moment of hunger and frustration, earlier emotions had pushed her to consider boarding the boat and confronting Shelley. Fortunately, she reconsidered and conceded, allowing Shelley and Falk to escape unhindered.

She found it harder to fulfill her only purpose, which was to rescue Lenora and Hamilton Jaminson, for which she had been hired.

Sabotage was possible and not ruled out, although no fires or gunshots preceded the unexpected explosion. Reservations about the *Black Swan's* involvement and why Shelley had stopped her cabin cruiser short of the waiting freighter picked at Birdie.

Her beef with Shelley finished, conceding envy, coveting her youthful beauty and talent. Birdie saw no cause to celebrate. The case remained open, no nearer to finding Hamilton Jaminson than the day she arrived in The City of Angels.

Threats to her and gruesome experiments prolonging human life became routine. Staying on the job drove her to doubt her wisdom and sanity. Had the murdered leader of the Children of God, Elger Stepp, and the archaic Celtic ring he'd given her encouraged reckless confidence?

For the moment, Birdie's spirits lifted. Her clients had not been aboard the destroyed craft, keeping their rescue hopes alive. The downside is Shelley's and Falk's shattered remains rested on the Pacific floor, carrying with them Lenora's and Jamison's whereabouts.

Once completing the job, she'd collect her fee and, with a first-class airline ticket, race home from the madness. Like the confused and lost Alice, Birdie didn't understand the nonsense of her hectic world. Senseless encounters led to deaths reminiscent of Wonderland's Mad Queen of Hearts, condemning croquet players to nonsensical beheadings.

Blending among the forming crowd, Birdie strolled past onlookers. She intended to flee before police gathered eyewitnesses. Knowing the dead victims placed her at the top of a short suspect list. She had no time for questioning, reciting half-truths countless times, while stuck in cramped interview rooms choking on stale cigarette smoke. Lacking an alibi, the police might detain her for questioning.

She eyed the pair of abandoned golf carts near the empty slip and counted on the disaster to hold the gathering crowd's attention. The dock's gate remained open, allowing her to take Shelley's three-wheel cart and flee before police closed the marina.

Driving from the beachfront, Birdie again heard half-muffled clangs of a ship's bell. She hesitated, waiting for the muted ring to repeat. She guessed it originated in open seas. Glancing in the waters outside the bay, she spotted a vague silhouette of a large yacht. Looking closer, thanks to a sudden touch of moonlight, Birdie noticed a distant lone figure on its upper deck. No sails fluttered, drifting lethargically in the shadows of dark clouds, beyond the moored boats, moving north, absent of running lights.

Birdie relied on a fatigued memory to recount the fix she'd taken on Shelley's location in the hills above Avalon. With dawn approaching, she worried about losing her well-lit reference points. Without them, locating Shelley's home turned into a guessing game.

Quaint Victorian Spanish stucco and ranch-style homes lined the roads, perched together, overlooking the distant Southern California mainland. The golf cart struggled as Birdie climbed hills and weaved along streets, unable to spot the lighted flag and backyard lights. She's lost perspective on the hillside. Homes sat higher in elevation than they appeared from the waterline.

Uncertainty she could not afford crept into her brain, attempting to defeat her. She battled time, realizing Jaminson and Lenore may already be victims of Falk and Shelley. Despite the early hour, Birdie considered searching house to house, knocking on doors. Two lives were at risk, and she was desperate. She'd put on a friendly face at each door, willing to do anything.

Birdie drove the golf cart, examining the tightly spaced addresses, and looking into backyards. The hunt was critical. Her clients may have been left to die.

Her second time circling the block located her landmarks hidden behind thick bougainvillea and overgrown wild grasses.

Birdie approached an open front door. Entering, she noticed the house empty with a dusty carpeted floor. Scattered on it were red and gold feathers. Birdie recalled Gigi, the assertive parrot and the bird's scrappy defiance, jealous of her chatting with Pello.

A trap crossed her mind. She'd watch for trip lines at her ankles and grenades attached to closed doors. Birdie feared the South American beauty as a threat from her watery grave as much as in life.

The single-story wood house furnished with bare mattresses and folding chairs gave Birdie the feeling of a Bowery Street flophouse. It was clear the residence went unused—its likely purpose was a safe house for their escape. Stepping into the tiny kitchen, coffee and bacon reminded her she had no memory of her last hot meal.

Birdie repeated her Pinkerton training to herself—enter each room, expecting it occupied.

A wood-handled carving knife lay in the sink. Being cautious, she grabbed it and held it at her side with the intention of not allowing a second ambush. A search of the small house took minutes to discover it empty—no sign of Lenora or Hamilton Jaminson.

The possibility lingered, Shelley had hidden Lenora and Hamilton, dead or alive, at a third location. Keeping Jaminson's disappearance from the media was no longer critical. Her best choice was to file a missing person's report.

Birdie recalled Lenora's rushed note on the Beverly Hilton napkin. If her client had been in the house, she was savvy enough to leave a sign. Birdie repeated her search, this time looking in small places. An hour of rummaging discovered nothing, possibly confirming Lenora had not been brought to Catalina.

Before meeting the local police, she'd pay another visit to Bill Wrigley's dive shop with or without permission.

CHAPTER FIFTY-FIVE

Birdie had endured the sagging bed and threadbare sheets of the Sea View B&B. Despite worry and discomfort, she'd slept like a hibernating bear, regaining energy, and bringing back the grit and determination she needed to survive. After showering and dressing, a check in the bathroom mirror confirmed she could no longer tolerate her two-day-old, tattered, and stained clothes.

That was the least of her troubles. Her search got tougher. The unexpected blast took away her few leads. Birdie ran short of ideas after Shelley and Falk perished in the violent boat explosion. Visiting Wrigley became unimportant. With Shelly's death, she'd follow up with the scuba shop owner as a formality and write a report, hoping her client turned up.

Breakfast at The Book Café looked promising, lifting her sober mood. A sidewalk chalkboard boasted a breakfast special—Island Morning Delights: waffles, eggs, and pineapples, hitting a home run. Anything topped last night's stale vending machine Hershey bar. The Argentine freighter no longer hulked in the channel, disappearing after Shelley's boat exploded. She guessed the captain pulled anchor and steamed to international waters, avoiding local police and Coast Guard.

Birdie added the Argentine freighter to a list of question marks she had no intention of resolving. If the curious ship were responsible for Shelley's death, she considered writing the crew a thank-you note.

Her client and Jaminson remained missing. Birdie blamed herself for abandoning Lenora, returning her to the Beverly Hilton for safety. At the same time, she admired how cagy Lenora had been to allow Shelley to take her, leading her to Hamilton Jaminson.

The next question, if not the freighter, who was to blame for last night's chaos? The possibility of a revengeful follower crossed her mind. She considered her cab driver, Cleon, who oddly arrived in her times of need and claimed Elger Stepp, leader of the Children of God, his son.

After visiting the elusive Bill Wrigley, she'd locate Cleon through his taxi company. She could not ignore remaining a target—looking over her shoulder became second nature.

Would there be others in Gustain Hilger's footsteps?

Bill Wrigley may surprise her and give a reliable clue to last night's explosion. Then again, she wouldn't bet on it. She'd allow one more day to track him down and scratch him off her list of Shelley's contacts.

Remembering last night's horrible scene after a night's sleep and with a fresh, logical mind, she couldn't avoid recalling the sound of a ship's bell soon after spotting a light flash in the blast area. Not a fan of coincidence, Birdie questioned what brought a gentleman boater out at the late hour and why the yacht lacked running lights in the dark, open water. She found it hard to believe the captain of the unknown boat didn't slow or help the damaged craft. Morbid curiosity, at least by New Yorker's cold standards, would have fueled a glimpse.

What prevented the passing yacht from assisting became the $64,000 question.

Birdie waved to the server, strolling table to table, refilling coffee while forcing small talk.

"I asked about Bill Wrigley yesterday."

"Ever find him?"

"You know where he lives?"

The waitress hesitated and poured coffee into Birdie's mug.

"I'm not stocking him, nothing like that. Just looking for a friend."

Another pause.

Birdie placed three twenty-dollar bills next to her napkin and watched them vanish into the server's apron pocket.

"Don't know the address. Find the biggest house and boat in Two Harbors, and you got him."

Her purse was full of Lenora's cash, ready to spend on a trip to Two Harbors.

Birdie planned to return to the marina. For a start, Birdie needed a fresh wardrobe, something lighter that suited the island mode. Passing several storefronts, she found the answer and slipped into the boutique clothing shop. She could not bear another minute in the foul-smelling clothes.

The V-neck sheer, polka-dot dress hid her scarred shoulder and drew attention to her athletic figure. It was a welcome break from the blood and dirt-stained knock-off Dior skirt and blouse she abandoned with the store clerk.

The change did her good, lifting morale. Working in a perm and salvaging wrecked nails could wait. Real detective work remained. She gave herself until tomorrow before returning to the mainland, resurrecting her search for Lenora and Jaminson.

Finding Wrigley's Dive shop locked and his boat missing strengthened her hunch, pointing to Wrigley's involvement. In what way, she wasn't sure.

On an island dominated by ocean craft, Birdie needed a hired runabout, one she could run. By noon, she'd play her gut feeling and see for herself what secrets Two Harbors kept.

CHAPTER FIFTY-SIX

In his customary faded blue Yale sweatshirt and favorite beach khakis, Bill Wrigley lounged on the top deck aboard his custom Hatteras yacht, enjoying the morning. Sunshine and an ice pack soothed red and black bruises absorbed from the blast's shock. Below, Shelley slept in her cabin, wrapped in a blanket. He gave her time to relax and revive from her escape.

They had risked injury and death swimming from the explosion. As expected, the freighter vanished, and Shelley's rented boat and contents lay demolished on the channel's bottom. C3 plastic explosives killed Falk and destroyed his journals—every trace of his gruesome experiments.

Wrigley had dropped anchor near his home, far from the excitement, keeping out of sight from harbor police. He'd escaped unnoticed. A bottle of Charles Krug red, chilled in a sterling silver top hat, waited to celebrate Shelley's new independence.

"Regrets?" Shelley asked, walking next to Wrigley.

"That was an enormous risk."

"You too," Shelley said, running her hands along his shoulder, massaging his bruises. "You shielded me."

"You could have used fewer explosives. If we'd been closer…"

"We may not have survived," Shelley finished.

"But we're fine. You destroyed everything and Falk."

Sitting next to Wrigley, Shelley pulled her blanket snug over her shoulders. "I wanted to be sure."

"You checked the cash?"

"All there," she answered, "I demolished your boat."

"Your mind's made up?"

Shelley tapped the slight bump of her stomach. "I'm raising my baby."

"Are you positive? I know doctors."

"I've seen enough killing,"

"Two Harbors keeps secrets."

"My house ready?"

CHAPTER FIFTY-SEVEN

A new dress, food and a night's sleep had brought optimism and a bounce to Birdie Kelley. Feeling lucky, she walked to the waterfront and checked Wrigley's shop.

No signs of life showed. The doors were locked, and his boat slip remained empty. Finding Wrigley would have been a shock, disturbing her latest idea.

Birdie spotted the marina's payphone near the Avalon Bay observation deck and decided to again, as she had done many times, attempt to find her lost client. With newfound confidence, she dropped a dime and dialed the Beverly Hilton from memory.

The hotel switchboard answered in her familiar tone and connected the call.

Birdie glanced at her island map, distracting herself, controlling anxiety expecting her client's continued absence. For a moment, she imagined hearing Lenora and pressed the handset tight to her ear—the voice was not the operator.

"Lenora, is that you? You OK?" Birdie asked.

"It's a long story. I have Hamilton, and we're safe."

Birdie recognized her client's calm, conservative tone. Reassured, it wasn't a dream or an imposter.

"I'm in Catalina."

"Leave it. Case closed. We got what we came for. Your job is finished."

"You're satisfied?" Birdie asked.

"Why shouldn't I be?"

"Shelley and Falk are dead."

"Were you involved?"

"It was an accident," Birdie answered. "I need to check a few loose ends."

"Good! We're done, and so are you. Hamilton wants to put this behind him. The money, Shelley, the whole thing. He's been through enough."

"I'm sure he has." Birdie took a breath and dropped in more coins. "Someone tried to kill me and…."

"Tomorrow, noon. Clover Field, Santa Monica. We'll talk."

"You two go home," Birdie said. "There's something I want to do on my own."

"We'll wait. When can you be here?" Lenora asked.

"Can't say."

Before hanging up, they paused, each waiting for the other. Birdie knew her client well enough; she liked to get in the last word.

"I owe you a big thanks," Lenora said. "And a check."

Birdie held her breath and waited.

"Fifty-thousand. You're worth every penny," Lenora said. "Now, the case is closed."

More than expected, Birdie bowed her head and held back tears, resisting performing an ecstatic jig inside the AT&T phone booth.

"Sounds good," Birdie finally answered.

The money would give her a new start. Could she walk away from what bothered her on the island's far side? The chance to return to snow and ice-covered Manhattan with a comfortable bank account tempted. She had nothing to prove, the mystery of Jaminson's disappearance was solved. Her client declared it over. What else did she have to do?

Lenora's indifference to Falk's and Shelley's deaths was understood. Birdie had an itch, and it needed scratching.

"Your check will be on the plane," Lenora said.

"Leave it at our hotel. I have to do this."

"Better yet, in their vault with your name on it."

Birdie lowered the phone to the cradle and questioned her wisdom. Quitting now was sensible. How many times did she need to remind herself Irish luck would not last?

Stepping out of the booth, Birdie understood her client's immediate concern for her former husband's needs and nothing else—not even her PI.

Could Birdie admit her client solved this case without her? She wanted no more excitement after averting her death, kneeling at the feet of a gunman.

The question nagged.

Who piloted the third mystery boat at the scene of the explosion?

Bill Wrigley remained on her list, and she intended to visit his home at the far end of the island. The village of Two Harbors held secrets interesting to Birdie.

Her hired Chris-Craft inboard waited at the wharf, fueled and ready to drive off. A day trip north grew from speculation, not fact. She'd asked the charter manager how a boat exploded on its own. He offered no answer, assuring Shelley's rental was in excellent condition, inspected, and filled with fuel. He emphasized Wrigley's Boat Rentals took pride in offering the safest and fastest boats in California.

Stepping into the mahogany-hulled runabout, Birdie gave it a search before taking a seat at the wheel.

She hid the surprise behind her broad smile, learning Shelley also rented her boat from Bill Wrigley's fleet. Birdie looked toward the scuba shop. His boat slip remained empty—no sign of *Pay Day*. Could it have been the same craft spotted moments after the explosion?

It was a weak theory by a desperate PI with little to go on. The case was closed by the client. Lenora offered a generous fee and bonus, expecting nothing more. Birdie understood Lenora's fear. Digging into Shelley's motives risked implicating Jaminson in the secret Brea lab.

Birdie had seen the violent blast tear apart the powerful boat. The unknown yacht seen remained a witness or played a role. Why did a small part of her not accept Shelley's accidental death?

It was over. The sensible step was to return to Santa Monica and catch the offered flight home. In eight hours, she'd be lounging in her apartment as a well-to-do woman.

The adage, don't trouble trouble 'til trouble troubles you, came and went from her mind as she steered the polished wood boat from the dock. Continuing the closed investigation on her own time, she blamed an overactive intuition. She couldn't shake the idea Shelley's explosion had been planned, and possibly the yacht in the vicinity contributed.

With a few pointers, Birdie felt secure managing the small craft in the coastal waters. Thankful, the surrounding storm bypassed the island; she continued, navigating the brief journey. Twenty miles of smooth water appeared harmless and safe, requiring slight boating skills—not much beyond handling a car. She motored close to the shoreline's rocky cliffs and sparse cover of eucalyptus trees, aiming for Long Point, jutting into the calm, coastal waters ahead in front of her. The Pacific remained calm with light wind on the island's protected, leeward side. Rays of bright January sun soothed her and warmed her shoulders and arms. It wasn't too late for a New Year's promise to relax, work out, and find time to appreciate the outdoors.

Who was she kidding? She'd joined the YWCA time after time and had yet to attend a single exercise class. The last occasion she'd jogged the trails of Central Park—she couldn't recall.

She'd enjoy the short day trip unhurried. Expectations of finding anything new were low, yet she needed to quiet her keen imagination and examine Two Harbors. Irish good fortune may smile on her, or she acted recklessly and sailed into a setup chasing Wrigley and his boat.

Spotting Long Point, the landmark of massive rocks and boulders, Birdie steered farther into the deep channel, safely passing her navigation mark. In the calm waters, she throttled back, allowing the boat to drift. During her trip, she admitted to enjoying the pleasure of maneuvering the rented runabout. Fear of drowning remained, and she would never forget her close call and rescue in the lake near Shelley's house.

Birdie opened her island map, spotting her destination, circled in red, on the plastic-covered chart, ten miles to the north.

"What next?" she asked. Confidence grew in her boating skills. Her mission, she admitted, lacked a firm strategy beyond finding Bill Wrigley. She had no legal right to question him about last night's accident.

The undisciplined style had become her method of operation. Well-paying clients expected investigators to control reactions, methodically solve problems, and not carry reckless emotions into each case. She was nowhere near *Dragnet*'s Sargent Joe Friday's demeanor.

She lacked an address. According to the coffee shop owner, it was the largest home on the island. The voice in her head shouted—first-rate PI's get a description.

With growing confidence, Birdie pushed the floor throttle full-speed forward with no time for regrets. Two Harbors grew close, and Birdie slowed to a stop. From where she floated, she was minutes from motoring into the thinly populated harbor and village.

Birdie looked over the washed-out beach and overgrown landscape. Nothing rivaled its prosperous neighbor Avalon to the south and wouldn't appear on a Santa Catalina travel poster.

Clustered fishing boats moored near an abandoned skeleton of a weed and bamboo-infested Quonset hut. Squawks of seagulls, rotting plants, and decaying fish greeted her. More ships appeared—none identified as the illusive *Pay Day*. The journey had proved a waste, leaving plenty of time to return to Avalon and catch a ferry to Long Beach.

What made her think she could sail into Two Harbors and the missing pieces of her case would fall into place? The search had been a grind from day one. Why prolong the closed case? All ended well for her client. There was no more to do. Money and freedom waited at Clover Airfield and Lenora's plane.

She hunted a ghost. Bill Wrigley's ship was not in the harbor. As a precaution, she'd gas up, topping off the twin tanks for the ride back to Avalon. The rented Chris-Craft handled like a car except at reduced speed and didn't respond as she slowed, maneuvering to an open spot near a row of unpainted buildings and a pair of dated fuel pumps. Birdie aimed the bow at a large red Texaco sign and dock space. She guessed the boat would fit.

"Reverse the motor. Slow it down!" an unseen voice shouted.

Disappointed, her mission failed. Birdie resented interference. She'd gotten the boat here and would park it how she pleased.

"Throw me a line." A lady stepped from the shadows, sporting a straw hat and baggy bib overalls.

Birdie lifted a tight coil of nylon rope from near her feet, tossing it to the woman's outstretched arms. In seconds, she'd pulled the twenty-foot motorboat against a row of tire bumpers, wrapping lines to the wharf's front and rear cleats.

The dark-tanned attendant went to work and reached above her head, pulling a metal nozzle and hose from a tall Texaco pump and snapping it on with a bump of the long spout.

"Fill it?" came the question.

Stunned, Birdie looked at the lady leaning on the craft's stern. For a moment, Birdie didn't believe her eyes, hoping the sun's glare and shadow conceived another delusion. A bright red and gold parrot sat on the attendant's shoulder, glaring at Birdie.

"Meet Gigi. Want gas or not?"

"Fill it," Birdie said.

"First timer?"

"What?" Birdie asked.

"Here in Two Harbors we don't get many visitors in January."

The parrot bobbed side to side, as it had in the hotel bar.

"Gigi have a twin?" Birdie asked.

The attendant continued to kneel over the stern, filling the fuel tanks. "Sure does. They're social and need a companion."

The surprising tropical bird rocked, swaying like a prizefighter, as he had during her first encounter with Pello. However bizarre, she saw the bird recognize her, recalling their meeting, and spat, vying for the handsome piano player's attention. Birdie added the event to the list of odd twists and did her best to stay unphased, hiding her surprise.

"Your name?" Birdie asked.

"I'm Gigi's sitter and friend, Ning Po."

Birdie recalled Pello mentioning the parrot was a twin, yet this was too much of a chance occurrence. She stumbled into something unexpected. Birdie went slow, Ning Po would be helpful or dangerous.

"Two Harbors?" Birdie asked. "I only found one."

"Other side," Ning Po pointed. "Go west. Hike it in twenty minutes easy. An hour by boat. I sell gas there too."

"Shelley, home. Shelley, home," Gigi screamed, flapping her long wings.

"Shelley? She say Shelley?" Birdie asked.

Before Ning Po answered, the parrot hopped from her shoulder to the dock's rusted tin roof and flew west, disappearing among tall palms.

"Twenty-eight dollars," Ning Po said, hanging the gas nozzle on the pump's hook with a loud clank.

"Who's Shelley?" Birdie asked.

Ning Po shook her head and held out her hand. "Twenty-eight dollars, please."

Birdie noticed the once pleasant lady wilt and become mute, letting the conversation fade to a nod and strained smiles. She'd look for herself and take the short walk, guessing her welcome committee finished.

Sidestepping Ning Po, Birdie undid her lines, paid, and moved, steering ahead to a vacant pier, away from the filling station. Feeling like an experienced sailor, she tied off to a worn and split piling post, hopped to shore, and began the hike between bays, venturing into the village of Two Harbors.

Few buildings and homes populated the area, giving her the sense she'd landed on a remote South Pacific island. She coupled that with the shock of Gigi, knowing the pugilistic parrot recognized her and continued a jealous hostility. If she allowed good judgment to decide, she'd hop into the Chris-Craft, speed away to her life in New York, and spend her days in Macy's designer dress department.

After a final look back at her rented boat and the gas attendant, the lure of adventure won out. Rejecting notions of returning to Avalon, she slipped Elger's Celtic ring over her head. Sensible or not, the blessing of her Gallic ancestors created a sense of safety. She'd ignore her earlier misgivings and ventured into the village, trekking along the dirt path, testing the Celtic myth to protect, as Elgin assured.

She scolded herself. How did she overlook the obvious? Two Harbors, two bays. Why did she not see it? Birdie waved off the question, knowing the frank answer validated her private doubts. Where else was there to find Wrigley? She'd traveled this far, and prying a little more may satisfy her curiosity.

Alone, with no defense, her damaged pistol in her purse did no good. Few homes sat scattered along the path and on opposite hillsides of the horseshoe bay, reminding her of derelict New Jersey trailer parks. The residents she'd come across avoided eye contact, ignoring her. Two Harbors kept secrets ran through her head, recalling the coffee and book shop owner's words.

A handful of cars parked near a two-story hotel and western bar. Fenced by wagon wheels, it appeared to have been built as a movie set, old and unattractive, providing a setting for an Alfred Hitchcock grisly murder. She laughed at herself. Once again, she'd created nonexistent trouble. No one lurked intending to shanghai her.

Sudden gusts carried gritty sand, stinging her face as she approached the remote second bay. Ning Po's estimate had been correct. Birdie stumbled, passing rows of oaks and patches of wild grasses jutting from dunes scattered among prickly cacti. Not picturesque as Central Park in spring, but less crowded and quiet. Birdie admitted she enjoyed private moments, allowing herself to lighten up. Her shoulders loosened, and tenseness in her lower spine vanished, as did her chronically tender hip.

She suspected being watched, not followed. Someone had an eye on her, according to the hairs on the back of her neck.

A rusted and toppled signpost signaled she'd arrived at Cat Harbor, the town's second marina. Like her landing spot on the east shore of Two Harbors, the neighboring windward region also lacked prosperity. One significant difference sat across the choppy cove.

The immense steel dock extended far into the bay. At the end, floated what she hunted. *Pay Day* reposed in her regal, private slip dominating the harbor.

CHAPTER FIFTY-EIGHT

The empty stretch of beach, void of humans, was rich with scurrying sandpipers and wildflowers, while bashful crabs burrowed into small dunes kept Birdie company as she hiked along the shoreline.

She squinted, shading her eyes against gusty, blowing sand. Looking across the bay's choppy water, past Wrigley's yacht, she almost missed the solitary home sculpted into a forest of tall oaks high on the hillsides.

The three-story granite and limestone fortress clashed with the remote village's modest brick and wood cottages. The hillside chateau, complete with drawbridge, better fit a Scottish seaside castle set to combat seventeen-century invaders.

She arrived to chat with Bill Wrigley, nothing more than a conversation with no intent to accuse him of playing a part in last night's disaster.

Twenty-four hours ago, she'd been abducted and threatened with death—they had held a gun to her head. Birdie needed answers, not caring where they came from. Wrigley remained, besides Hamilton Jaminson, her only link to Shelley.

Climbing the steep, rocky path to the massive wood door, second thoughts of bursting in uninvited on the wealthy Bill Wrigley entered her mind. Birdie looked up at the watchtower walls, half expecting to be greeted by tubs of boiling oil poured through the castle's battlements.

Nothing remained but to knock on Wrigley's door and get to the point, catching him off guard—learning what he knew about his SCUBA student, Shelley. Birdie intended to bulldoze Wrigley, giving him no chance to stonewall her. There was no need for polite talk, allowing time to create a story explaining why he sailed near last night's accident, failing to stop.

Birdie's cagey side caught up to her as she approached the arched stoned entrance.

PayDay waited, floating in front of her.

Uncertainty and hesitation made their appearance. Birdie paused.

She'd had a poor view of the explosion and admitted doubt.

A vague image came to mind as she studied the craft in Wrigley's dock. Could she be mistaken? Catalina was a rich man's place to play, showing off expensive toys. She'd better be certain before approaching Wrigley and his hoard of lawyers.

Birdie recalled two brief impressions from last night—a muted ship bell's aborted ring and a blemished recall of the boat's expansive open decks. The sighting had come as a surprise. The distant ship appeared from the dead of darkness, appearing under a patch of sad, waning moonlight. Birdie conceded she functioned in a daze and mild shock following the unexpected explosion and chaos.

She'd operated on adrenaline and a dose of panic, a cocktail all too familiar. She admitted fleeing the scene with good reason. Yet, she ran. If Wrigley had done the same, she would not condemn him—unless he had been complicit.

Lenora and Jaminson were safe, and Shelley and Falk were dead—her mission completed. What she did wasn't necessary, nothing more than satisfying curiosity. Wrigley's name was coupled to Shelley and drew Birdie to learn if the connection was much more than diving lessons.

In a rush, needing to tie up the loose end, she brought zilch to defend herself. Her damaged pistol remained in her purse. The Celtic ring carried around her neck served as a memory of Elger Stepp's death, nothing else.

Birdie chuckled. She'd become attached to a simple trinket but disallowed its promised magical Irish powers. Luck and coincidence played a role in escaping death and injury, nothing more. She earned her reward. The check and a private plane waited in Los Angeles.

How could she face herself? She needed an answer to what had occurred last night.

Unsure of giving away her surprise arrival, she opted for a last-second change of strategy. It was doubtful she'd gain permission to examine his boat after blunt questioning. Instead, a desperate urge to look at the ship overrode logic and common sense.

She retreated, walking away from the confrontation planned. The moored ship played the least threatening and a simpler target. Wrigley would be saved for last. The odds were even, in her mind, the boat in front of her had been the one she'd seen near the explosion.

The warm January afternoon winds calmed as Birdie stepped to the beach, walking past the yacht. The ship appeared docile, rocking with a steady rhythm.

She approached the vessel, intending to draw out anyone inside. Spotting no one, she moved towards the dock's gate and several no-trespass warnings. Confidence grew with each step. Since arriving, she'd seen little signs of life, understanding why the chatty café owner considered Two Harbors a place for secrets. Birdie paused, looking back at the hillside house deciding. She had the feeling the large home watched.

Reaching the wood dock, she challenged her throbbing hip, climbing the waist-high gate.

Eyes looked at her. She wasn't alone.

Shameless brown pelicans and seagulls loitered along the dock's railing. Unfazed, feathered heads twisted as Birdie hobbled, sandwiched between roosting flocks, refusing to surrender their squatter's station.

Startled by the lone bird's bright red and green plumage, she stumbled, nearly falling. The parrot's sudden presence surprised her. Was she once more in Alice's dream? Had the precocious bird replaced the white rabbit as her guide in the strange world?

Birdie refused intimidation by the aggressive parrot. Gigi mingled among the cluster of colorless gray and brown birds and offered no reaction, remaining quiet while Birdie passed.

She underestimated the size of the burgundy and beige yacht. It appeared larger than expected, over eighty feet, and guessed it seaworthy to journey the world's oceans. She couldn't be sure. Various reasons could explain the boat's presence late last night—something innocent as a romantic cruise admiring the scenic harbor or a delayed return from the mainland.

Birdie side-stepped a heavy coiled rubber hose and swung open the ship's rail, walking onto the yacht's smooth, buffed teak deck. She trespassed. It bothered her less on each occasion. Was she becoming too reckless, a danger to herself and her clients?

Her attentive audience persisted, turning their sharp beaks in harmony, keeping pace as she crossed from one side to the other, inspecting the ship. What she searched for, she did not know—counting on her skills of observation, looking for what belonged as much as what did not. Criminals carried away telling evidence and left behind signs of their presence.

Nothing she saw on the washed-off upper deck aided her recall. She was far out of bounds and shouldn't be on the ship, sticking her nose into Wrigley's life. There was no case to solve, and she admitted prying into others' lives had become a compulsion well enjoyed.

If she were to continue, she needed to hurry. Wrigley, or worse, the police could arrive. Stubbornness kept her on the yacht. Her hip throbbed, and pain grew as she stepped into the ship's salon that carried her back to her time spent in New York's plush Ritz Carlton.

Birdie stood on polished marble accented with inlaid mahogany. Pale gray leather sofas and chairs grouped with tables surrounded a grand piano and wet bar. It made no sense leaving the opulent boat unlocked and exposed, aside from a distraction. She expected someone to return and secure the lavish craft.

Time ran scarce. How long had she snooped?

Birdie pushed open a sliding wood-framed glass door and walked to the ship's rear. She let herself drop into a cushioned seat near the stern. Looking at the extended swim platform, she recalled her days climbing from the shallow, chilling waters of Long Island Sound into a rented rowboat, heaving a leg over its side and flopping, throwing her chest and arms into the cramped boat.

Birdie saw a green, crumbled canvas shoved against the luxury cruiser's gunwale, out of character for the neat and organized ship. Every item on the craft appeared stowed and secured in well-designed compartments.

Struggling against her defiant hip and throbbing shoulder, Birdie rose to her feet and yanked the tarp aside, uncovering a pair of SCUBA tanks, masks and fins. Not surprisingly, Wrigley ran a dive shop using *Pay Day* as his dive boat. From her time reading and dreaming of exotic travels, she'd learned the yacht was not excessive. Well-heeled customers expected pampering on exclusive diving adventures. Her clients, Lenora and Jaminson, set the pace for extreme indulgence.

She spotted a mounted ship's brass bell at the stern, a common adornment, and offered nothing to show it as the muffled ringing she'd heard. Next to the main deck's door frame, as she re-entered the ship, Birdie noticed a small dead insect. Picking it up, she discovered more. A close look told her she held a charred black sliver of wood,

The burned residue may have come from Shelley's shattered boat, now resting at the bottom of the Pacific. If so, she found a connection and dropped the evidence into her dress pocket.

She had something tangible.

Embers from the blast, carried by the prevailing wind, floated over the entire harbor and island. What she uncovered may have drifted to Wrigley's nearby moored boat. Burned remains travel miles, covering homes and boats sailing near Catalina. It was not evidence for a courtroom, but Birdie believed she had moved past square one. She had good reason to suspect Wrigley's yacht had been in the explosion area and escaped the scene, going dark, turning off running lights, blind to boaters and witnesses.

Wrigley hid something, and Birdie intended to discover his secret.

Birdie stopped. An over-grown vine-covered pergola shielded the path from the house to the dock. An unseen army may well have passed, converging on her.

Hearing a door latch click in a distant part of the ship, Birdie's heartbeat raised, and a cool sweat broke across her face and shoulders. She reached inside her purse, grabbed the handgun, and remembered it useless. There was no mistake. She had company besides the roosting pelicans and seagulls.

Would her good luck charm work?

CHAPTER FIFTY-NINE

Soft jazz music played in the yacht's lounge as Birdie walked in. She paused, recognizing *My Foolish Heart*, and eased the sliding glass door shut behind her.

Bill Wrigley smiled and stood, stepping from the grand piano. Curley puffs of white hair poked from under a Sun faded red ball cap.

"You make it a habit to trespass?" he asked, pointing to a sofa.

"Why didn't you help last night?" Birdie asked.

"Why are you here?"

"Answer the question," Birdie said, walking toward Wrigley while she examined the bar and dining area, hoping they were alone.

"My ship, my rules. Sit down."

Wrigley stepped to Birdie, grabbing her shoulders, lifting her, dropping her into a deep leather chair.

Stunned, Birdie hid her agitation at his unwelcome arrogance and show of dominance. Did the aggressive gesture aim to intimidate or flatter himself, proving command of the moment? Years of rejection struggling to make it on the New York stage and later, as a female PI, produced thick skin. Wrigley's theatrics would not interfere.

Establishing a dialog to clarify what Wrigley knew of Shelley remained the goal.

She couldn't guess his age. His physical strength and smooth facial appearance contradicted his white hair. Pello came to mind, and from reflex, she expected Gigi to arrive and continue the combat. For a moment, Birdie had the sensation she'd returned to where the chaos began days ago, in the Hilton lounge while Pello entertained at the piano.

Birdie suspected her host awaited her, alerted by Gigi or the meek gas attendant. It no longer mattered. She'd walked into his snare as she had into Shelley's. He hid something. She was positive. The burned fragment of wood in her dress pocket, coupled with the eccentric parrot, convinced her of a connection between Shelley and the explosion.

A hidden second door slid open, catching Birdie's attention. Shelley walked in carrying a coiled nylon rope and SCUBA gear, dropping it at Birdie's feet. Drawing from on-stage experience, Birdie held back, hiding amazement to find Shelley alive. Birdie's fairytale of bizarre surprises continued. She'd played a chancy game and had been backed into a corner by the South American beauty. She feared Shelley's clever games, as Alice had endured the unscrupulous Queen of Hearts improvised croquet match dooming the loser to a beheading.

"Who did you expect to convince you and Falk were killed?" Birdie asked.

No reply came, although Birdie guessed the answer. She needed to stall, delaying their plans.

"You have Jaminson's money. Let me go."

Birdie looked at Shelley and Wrigley. He pointed a gun at her.

"That notch above your chest, where the collar bones meet—try something cute, I'm putting this hollow point there."

Shelley tapped the air tanks with her toe. "Put this on."

Birdie had no intent to let Shelley know Lenora and Hamilton survived. She looked at the diving gear and considered charging

Wrigley, catching him off guard. While gathering her legs under her, Wrigley stepped close, forcing the handgun to her temple.

"Don't think about it. This Ruger's hair-trigger could fire on its own."

Once the air tanks were on Birdie's back, Shelley fastened the shoulder straps with a snug yank and attached two weighted belts around Birdie's waist. Her hands tied, crossed in front of her, allowed her to reach the mouthpiece dangling at her chest.

Shelley pushed Birdie toward the yacht's expansive rear deck. The belt's lead weights and bulky air tanks caused her to stagger and struggle for balance, removing chances of a swift counter-attack.

Wrigley lowered the Zodiac runabout from the yacht's second level. He powered the twin engines and, with a burst, floated it to the luxury ship's swim platform. After another hard nudge from Shelley, Birdie struggled to stay upright and stumbled to the rear deck to the waiting Zodiac. The temptation to turn and leg kick Shelley popped into Birdie's mind, grew, and vanished in seconds. Her hip could not execute what her brain envisioned, besides Wrigley held the gun leveled at her chest. Opportunities dwindled as time passed. She needed to find a weakness to attack.

Birdie guessed they planned a one-way trip, allowing her precious minutes for a countermove. An attempt, successful or not, needed to occur soon. There was little chance of a rescue in the empty harbor, with no witnesses outside of pelicans and Gigi.

She blamed herself, not appreciating Shelley's skill in orchestrating the day's events. The boat Shelley rented and its destruction masked her get-a-way from Falk and the morbid lab in Brea. She never intended to board the South American bound ship. It served as a prop in a clever sleight of hand, distracting witnesses near the staged explosion. And, of course, the freighter's crew would carry the tragic story to those expecting the two runaways.

Many had died in the past days, and Birdie couldn't speculate on the number before her arrival. Birdie walked into a trap, one she could have avoided. Thanks to her unneeded meddling, she'd soon be as dead as the corpses suspended in Falk's destroyed lab.

Nothing discovered on Catalina mattered to her client. This morning, Lenora made it clear. Unless a miracle occurred, she'd die for no reason, never again seeing the bright lights of Broadway. She'd gone a long way to find trouble—the kind not needed to be found. Yet, here she stood in a new yellow polka dot dress, hands tied, face wrapped inside an uncomfortable dive mask, bound in SCUBA gear, about to become a human anchor.

Who would feed her cat?

Only Lenora and Wrigley's boat leasing manager knew her location. Lenora planned to fly to New York City while the boat manager had most likely blown the whistle on her.

Birdie wiggled her wrists against the snug rope, creating enough play to hold the mouthpiece and air hose in her palm and fingers. Shelley trailed while Wrigley waited inside the Zodiac inflatable. Twin tanks on Birdie's back and diving weights added bulk, turning her into a weapon. A lunge, spearing her head and face into Wrigley, forcing the pistol from his hand, became a desperate choice. With luck, she'd gain control of his Ruger.

This was her life, with seconds to decide. Destiny laid in her hands, and it was not to be dropped into the Pacific.

Wrigley leaned forward, grabbing Birdie, guiding her into the small boat. His firm grip controlled her as if she were a child's hand puppet.

"In the hole, ya go. In the hole, ya go," Gigi screamed, landing on Birdie's shoulder, causing her to stumble. Her chance vanished, and she cursed herself for not trusting her gut. What did she wait for?

"I warned you to stay away," Shelley said.

Wrigley smiled and shoved Birdie into the small boat's center seat.

"Sometimes Gigi's almost human," Birdie said.

"Gigi and Roxy act like it," Shelley answered.

"Hold on," Wrigley shouted, pushing the hand throttle forward.

The Zodiac banked. Its rounded, blunt bow raised from the flat water and sped from the harbor, heading north along the western coastline of the barren and rocky isthmus that fashioned the northern shore of Catalina Island. Birdie sat on the bench beside the parrot, flanked front and back by Wrigley and Shelley. Gigi shrieked in German. The words resembled a firm, human voice, sounding more like advice than a trained pet's ramblings.

Birdie once considered Gigi a nuisance and nothing else. How had she overlooked the obvious? The parrot was a twin. Roxy and Gigi connected with Falk's work, although she no longer cared.

The Pacific waters turned choppy the farther north they traveled. No sign of boats or settlements came as they sped beneath steep, rocky hillsides and sharp ledges, giving Birdie no hope of rescue. No one spoke over the loud, racing twin outboards until Wrigley slowed, turning sharply, entering a cove hidden by jagged rocks. In moments, he ran the flat-bottomed boat to an abrupt stop onto a smooth sandy shore.

"I don't care what happens to you, Shelley," Birdie said. "My clients, dead or alive, don't want the money. The cash is yours. No one is coming after it. I'm off the case."

"And yet you are here," Shelley said.

"Want more money? I can do that," Birdie said.

Birdie twisted in her seat and watched the eyes of her captors. Neither answered. The isolated cove pushed deep into thick sheets of limestone cliffs, sheltering smooth blue, unspoiled water ideal for a relaxing swim—far from what Birdie guessed Shelley and Wrigley intended.

Wrigley pointed his gun at Birdie, motioning toward the narrow flat shoreline. She stepped over the Zodiac's low-inflated sides, tripping, nearly falling into a washed-up cluster of dead trees.

"I'm expected at the airport. Don't do this. Nobody's hurt," Birdie said.

Wrigley waved his handgun. "To the rocks."

In a few steps, Birdie stood over a small, circular pit, worn deep into a broad, flat rock near the water's edge. Its walls shaped smooth by centuries of storms and relentless waves battering the rugged western shoreline. She couldn't guess its depth, only seeing darkness.

"High tide comes in later. The base has holes the size of fingers. It'll drain after a while," Wrigley said.

"Someone will search for me. People in Avalon know I'm here looking for you."

"We're civilized, you have a chance to survive," Shelley said.

Wrigley tossed the remaining rope around Birdie and tied it snug to her waist.

"You could get hurt if you fell," Wrigley said, grabbing and shoving Birdie into the pit and began to lower her.

Birdie wedged her elbows, attempting to keep a grip on the flat rim, struggling to avoid a free-fall. Her feet and legs dangled inside the hole, pushing, forcing her feet and toes to grip smooth vertical walls.

"You have air in the tanks—for how long, I don't know," Wrigley said, turning a valve. Finished, he grabbed the nylon rope. As he did, Shelley stood over Birdie.

"Take this personally," Shelley said and kicked the side of Birdie's head.

Dazed, Birdie's legs flailed. Her bound hands scraped, grabbing at the wall's slick sides, hoping to slow her fall. Uninjured odds for an escape were terrible. A crippling injury doomed her inside the deep chimney-like hole.

In seconds, she jerked to a sudden stop, hanging suspended from the rope gripped about her waist. Birdie clung to the line as she sunk deeper into the pit. Her bare feet settled into a sandy bottom.

She clutched the Celtic ring at her neck, questioning Elger Stepp's sanity and his belief in the ring's Irish spiritual power.

Framed in the hole above, Wrigley stood, joined by Gigi.

"Pirates called this The Dragon Den. They tied rocks to prisoners, drowning them."

CHAPTER SIXTY

Birdie wrestled against her bound hands, gnawing at the rope holding her captive. She heard the powerful Zodiac pull away, stranding her inside the deep pit. Screams went nowhere against crashing waves and the roar of twin engines.

No situation improved with panic. Remaining calm gave Birdie a chance to survive the eventual incoming tide. She maneuvered the breathing mouthpiece into her lips, discovering the tank's compressed air flowed only when she inhaled. How long would precious oxygen last once seawater submerged her inside the ocean dungeon?

Chances of discovery were remote. Lacking much of a beach, the rocky location would not appeal to locals or tourists. Wrigley's snug knot remained firm, although she continued to push and pull, gaining little slack, struggling until the flesh on her wrists rubbed raw and bled. Sheer walls tapered, narrowing, prevented sitting. Her legs were tired, working against the heavy dive belts and tanks strapped to her waist and back. Relief came from bracing her feet and leaning against the chimney-like wall.

The arriving tide would flood the hole, and slow drowning became her fate. Focusing on action, not self-pity, mattered. Each minute alive offered a remote possibility of escape.

Through the overhead portal, Birdie watched the sunny day give way to evening. Incoming waves crept nearer, beating against rocks and boulders, splashing into the opening taunting, warning of more. The little strength she'd had vanished, attempting to rip away the weighted belts anchoring her to the bottom.

Elger Stepp's Celtic ring hung from her neck, reminding her of its promised protection.

She'd skirted death often. How many more lives did she have?

How long could she deceive herself? She would not live to see the night's stars.

Another tug and twist to the rope brought more blood to already raw and bleeding wrists. Wrigley's seaman knots held firm. It may have been her imagination; the air tanks strapped on her throbbing back lightened.

A leak shortened her life expectancy. Did it matter?

Eventually, the tide would roll in, washing in streaming cold ocean water on top of her. She'd stay weighted to the sandy bottom, taking in oxygen, unknowing when her final breath would come. She hoped for a miracle. Her ancestors passed down tails of winged creatures sent to rescue troubled Irish warriors.

For days Birdie had defied pain, and risked her life in an insane Nazi world, lacking laws and logic, to find her client's missing ex-husband. She never understood the events that surrounded her or the connection to Hamilton Jaminson.

In her weary state, she envisioned the empty aluminum air tanks floating her to the top in the same manner Alice escaped to the surface, fleeing the evil Queen of Hearts, and returning to the safety of her sister. Freeing her bound hands would allow her to unstrap the two heavy diving belts imprisoning her.

Loud squawking came, which she ignored.

Birdie guessed the island's native birds settled in for the evening. Her neck and shoulder ached from the kick Shelley delivered, which kept her from looking overhead. She found little comfort, pressing the air tanks against the wall, expecting the rush of cold Pacific seawater to fill her grave.

"Hello. Hello," screamed a high-pitched voice.

In the daze, she'd drifted in and out. Birdie imagined a hazy image of Elger Stepp hovering above, like the illusion viewed days ago from the deck of the Catalina Duchess.

Birdie became conscious, realizing she had actual company, fearing the aggressive parrot, Gigi returned with Wrigley and Shelley.

"Help me," Birdie's raspy voice answered as waves of cold water rushed in, splashing on top of her, knocking her off balance.

"Roxy can. Roxy can," the parrot squawked in a clear tone, circling close above the pit.

Birdie twisted to see the clear sky and viewed her Celtic miracle. A star dropped from the heavens and plunged into the hole.

Downward the mighty bird came, claws extended.

Was it a dream, a hoax—a cruel trick her psyche played, taunting her with the folk story of her ancient Irish forefathers?

Cold water, coming with more force, splashed Birdie's face and covered her legs, reaching her calves. Roxy perched on Birdie's bruised arms—talons piercing her bare skin. The parrot's large, curved beak hooked above the wrapped nylon cord, ripping and tearing the bands gripping Birdie's wrists. With every new surge, Roxy jumped, dodging, finding safety from the falling water, perching on the air tanks. Each time the parrot returned to tear at frayed scraps of rope.

Seawater rose to Birdie's thighs, gaining force and filling the pit.

Birdie watched the shredded bindings wearing thin and, with a burst of eroding strength, gave a sudden twist—no luck. Roxy clawed near Birdie's bare arm, bringing thin lines of blood. The parrot cocked her head, snapping her large hooked bill against the remaining cords binding Birdie.

Obvious to Birdie, on the finishing strike, the brave bird injured its beak.

The frayed rope fell from Birdie's wrist and arms. Rushing seawater pounded the beaches' rocks. With each surge, growing water filled the pit. Birdie unbelted the leather shoulder straps, removing the bulky air tanks. She rotated the canvas and metal weight belts and peeled away electrical tape layers, gripping the brass buckles closed, letting both belts drop next to her feet.

The incoming tide became a savior. Chilling Pacific waters continued to splash, covering the beach, and immersing Birdie. Buoyant saltwater lifted her from the sandy base her feet had buried into. Roxy hopped from Birdie, flailing to gain lift, bounced off tight circular walls, flapping furiously to escape the narrow pit and fast-rushing water. Struggling, the parrot beat its wings harder, scraping walls with claws and outstretched feathers. She fell back several times, never quitting. Finally, her wings grabbed air, breaking free—leaving a trail of green and red plumages floating in the rising water.

Birdie guided her hands and feet in a waving motion, brushing against the limestone sides as she lifted, afloat in the fast-filling hole. Continuous torrents of seawater beat against her face and shoulders, slowing the journey to freedom. Overhead, the edge appeared. For a moment, she feared Shelley would arrive.

Rescued from drowning twice, she admitted it was time to improve her swimming skills beyond dog paddling. The frothy water felt cold and soothing to her aching body. Approaching the top, she found Roxy perched on a stone ledge frazzled, shaking, and flapping her broad wings. Puffs of down stuck outward from damaged and missing feathers.

Birdie recognized the pugnacious Gigi had an opposite twin, Roxy, who'd become her lifesaver. Falk came to mind. His experimenting fingerprints covered the extraordinary parrots—he'd altered the two with opposed personalities.

Were other secrets kept on the small island?

Reaching civilization and returning to New York became her goal. She thought of Roxy's injuries; they needed to be cared for if the scrappy parrot allowed her.

Sitting at the top of the flooded pit, Birdie pushed her bruised palms on the submerged beach, lifting herself out, fighting against the strong inflowing current. Her legs felt detached, no longer a part of her as she wobbled through rising knee-high seawater, stumbling, arms flailing, beating against a rushing tide.

Panic was not about to overtake her. Water continued rolling in with growing force. Weakened, she risked being knocked over and smashed, like seaweed, into the boulders and ledges surrounding the cove.

Chest-high water pushed Birdie close to a jagged rock shelf. Diving, she grabbed the thin ledge and held on as a massive wave roared in, pushing her against the stone wall. The upsurge lifted her, allowing her to climb to an outcropping covered with dried brush and bird droppings. Barefooted and trapped with no food, she watched the large sun melt into the far-off horizon. Hiking the rocky and treacherous ground appeared as her only way out. She survived because of the scrappy parrot and questioned her stamina to make the hike.

Did Birdie imagine Roxy stayed, at a distance, to escort her to the village of Two Harbors?

Could she trust its inhabitants? Would her Irish luck guide her back to the rented boat?

She grabbed the Celtic ring hanging on her neck, refusing to admit what her heart knew. Magic omens did not belong in this century, much less parrots showing up on desolate beaches once occupied by pirates and abandoned treasures.

What she was positive of, Shelley and Wrigley were off her radar. As of now, she signed off on the case. Her personal interests almost cost her a burial at sea.

The tide continued to roll in, crashing with force, covering the small rocky landing she'd climbed from. She wasn't alone. Roxy, nursing a chipped and broken beak, flew in and perched near her. They would spend the coming chilly night alert for passing boats and aggressive hunting coyotes.

At first, she believed her ears played tricks, hearing the beating sounds of a helicopter. She had no matches or mirrors for a signal, only a soaked sundress. Removing it, Birdie flailed it like a flag over her head as the low-flying copter became bouncer fading daylight. Surprising her, Roxy responded, leaping and flapping wings, mimicking Birdie. The parrot flew to the slow-moving helicopter and made a sudden dive toward the landing skids and perched, grasping its claws to the steel pipes.

Birdie continued waving her dress until the copter pulled up like a halting stallion. Hovering, it tilted forward, rocked, and moved from the water and approached, flying over Birdie.

"We'll put down on a mesa above you." Lenora's muffled voice of salvation carried over the engine and rotating blades thanks to the copter's loudspeaker.

Birdie began her hike, feeling each rock and pebble cut and stab her tender, bare feet. A missed step forced her to a knee, looking at the vanishing beach. She didn't believe seeing it. Her rented Chris-Craft floated in a pool created by the rising surge. Occupying the boat's front seat, she recognized Ning Po, her gas attendant. Next to her—her duplicate, complete with matching faded bib overalls and blank expression. Perched on the speedboat's wooden stern sat a healthy red and green Gigi.

Had they arrived to confirm the incoming tide finished her, or to rescue her?

Roxy returned and landed, digging into Birdie's injured shoulder. She stroked the ruffled feathers of the battered parrot, knowing the debt owed.

She watched for a moment, realizing more of the bizarre results of Doctor Falk's work. From movie newsreels, she'd learned of Nazi Germany and Hitler's obsession with twins. Hitler judged they held secrets to human genetics and heredity to improve his Arian race.

It took Birdie a second to connect what she experienced the past few days. Had it been an elaborate charade? She'd faced the possibility Doctor Falk had created a duplicate Shelley as he had Fabian and Pello—a magical sleight of hand distracting her. Had the Shelley double and Doctor Falk boarded the waiting South American steamship carrying the actual cloning research transferred from the Wrigley yacht.

THE END

ABOUT THE AUTHOR

Robert Joswick's life has twisted and turned, swiftly moving from being an abandoned child, window washer, college then professional football player with the Miami Dolphins to a successful career in the business world. These unique challenges, along with riding his Harley Davidson up and down the coast of California, give him insight into a wide range of personalities and behaviors, coloring his novel's characters with a mix of flaws and endearing frailties. He earned a BA and an MBA and, after retiring from the business world, studied fiction writing, English literature, and political science. He has published a number of articles for a regional Southern California magazine, Urban Living and writes for a national publication, Referee Magazine.

MASS TRANSIT
A Birdie Kelley
MYSTERY
ROBERT L. JOSWICK

NOTE FROM ROBERT L. JOSWICK

Word-of-mouth is crucial for any author to succeed. If you enjoyed *Blood and Iron Rules*, please leave a review online—anywhere you are able. Even if it's just a sentence or two. It would make all the difference and would be very much appreciated.

Thanks!
Robert L. Joswick

We hope you enjoyed reading this title from:

www.blackrosewriting.com

Subscribe to our mailing list – *The Rosevine* – and receive **FREE** books, daily deals, and stay current with news about upcoming releases and our hottest authors.
Scan the QR code below to sign up.

Already a subscriber? Please accept a sincere thank you for being a fan of Black Rose Writing authors.

View other Black Rose Writing titles at www.blackrosewriting.com/books and use promo code **PRINT** to receive a **20% discount** when purchasing.